BRUTE

AUDREY OSBORNE

This book would not have happened without the never-ending support of my husband, Nicholas. I love you so insanely much.

Mekenzie, you told me my story was good enough. Brute wouldn't have seen the light of day without you.

To my real-life Roralei. Grace, I love you more than I'll ever be able to tell you. Thank you for being my sister.

And to anyone who feels unfinished.
You have time.

Contents

DRENNICA
BAETON
ALUNIA
WINTER REGION
•PEAKS OF DESPAIR
•RANGE OF UNREST
AUTUMN REGION
•TARRIN
•COSIMA MOUNTAINS
VERITAS SEA
SPRING REGION
•BLACKWOOD VILLAGE
•TUNSTEAD
•BLACKWOOD FOREST
•BERKTON
•SUNCREST HEIGHTS
•NAPORIA RIVER
•PIXIE MARSH
SUMMER REGION
•THE SWAMPS

This book contains themes that may be disturbing to some readers, including attempted drowning, adult language, sexually explicit content, parental death, mass tragedy, and weird men.

1

RAELENTHIA

DISTRESSED-LOOKING HAY BALES MOCK me from 30 feet away; poorly painted targets, half-faded from time and the elements. A sharp wind rustles the trees surrounding the clearing. I take a deep breath to calm my nerves and steady my trembling hands. The more frustrated I am, the sloppier I become. It's been years since I attempted archery.

As a child, I would sneak out to this field behind the castle and practice with the bow I managed to sneak from the armory. I wasn't half bad back then, I managed to hit the target straight on from 70 feet away. But as my schooling became more rigorous, I couldn't practice as often and my skills waned.

One of the only people who knew was my closest friend and fellow hell-raiser, Dessielle. She was a smidge taller than me, regardless of being a year younger. Her dark coiled hair only reached her shoulders, but it framed her round face perfectly and showed off her violet-colored eyes. Eyes that have watched me try and fail to find something I excel at.

Drawing the arrow back toward my face, I exhale and release, missing my target for the fourth time. The ground, now filled with scattered holes from my many attempts, begs me to stop. I let out a frustrated sigh and collect my belongings before pulling the burlap sheet back over the hay and walking toward the castle. For weeks, I've been trying to relearn my former hobby. For weeks, I've failed miserably.

Dessielle tells me I'll find my niche eventually, which is easy for her to say. She's been a talented pianist since we were children, and once she mastered *that,* she picked up the violin. The woman could pluck a harp just by looking at it.

The halls are ghostly empty as I travel up the stairs to my room to clean up before breakfast. My mother values having any meal as a family, regardless of conflicting schedules. "It's the one moment we have to sit down all together," she says.

I bathe quickly and begin to make my hair look presentable when a soft knock sounds on my door, and it opens. A round face peeks through the crack and steps in.

"You're up early this morning," Willow says.

I look at her through the mirror as I try to smooth back my long reddish hair into a braid. "Couldn't sleep," I call out. It's not a complete lie, I *wasn't* able to get sleep. Never mind that it was my own fault since I stayed up all night reading...again.

She looks around the room and sees my clothes laid out on my bed, and a draining bath beside me. "You did everything yourself, already?"

Her hand lands on her hip with a huff, and she shakes her head. "What do you keep me around for?"

I turn around quickly, forgetting about the strands of hair tangled around my fingers. "For your company, of course." She rolls her eyes before approaching me and swatting my hands out of the way to finish the braid herself.

"You can leave the braids to your sister, Raelenthia. You have different talents." She's right. Roralei can create the most intricate patterns in her hair. It started with small plaits on her head, and sometimes on mine, and now she comes up with styles I've never seen before. I'd envy her creativity if I wasn't so proud of her. She's like that in every aspect of her life.

I used to joke that her skin was so pale because all her color went into her art. At only eleven, she's an incredibly talented artist.

I nod slowly with a strained smile. Willow finishes the rest of my braid in silence and ushers me out of the room after picking out a different dress than the one I had laid out. Apparently, peach isn't my color. Instead, she puts me in a bronzy shade of orange. I make my way through the hall and down the stairs until I reach the parlor where the rest of my family is already waiting.

Mother and Father sit next to each other like they always do, instead of at the heads of the table. When they're not working, they're practically inseparable. "There she is!" my father's cheerful voice booms.

My mouth forms a straight-line smile as I take my seat next to Roralei without trying to draw further attention to myself for being late.

"We were starting to wonder if you tried to sneak off again," my mother complains as she raises her eyebrows dramatically.

"I haven't done that since I was a child, Mother. That's a bit dramatic, don't you think?"

"Weren't you the one back then who said that being 15 made you no longer a child?" She replied with a cocked brow.

Roralei chuckles next to me and I jab her in the arm with my elbow. She looks at me with her mouth agape before turning to our father who simply shrugs and looks back at his food. He's never been one to get in between our bickering.

"Don't forget you have your lessons this morning, Rae." As if I could forget about having to see Miss Woodstock.

I assure my mother that I'm aware of my schedule today, which earns me a look that tells me to *watch it*. She isn't a fan of "*I know*" as a response. My eyes grow wide as I stick out the tip of my tongue at her. She chuckles under her breath and shakes her head before starting a conversation with Father.

Roralei is fidgeting under the table, picking at the skin around her nails. Leaning over I whisper, "What are you working on next?"

Her eyes light up as she tells me about the massive piece she started two days ago, filled with autumnal colors and intricate leaf patterns. She's painting the fountain in the center of the courtyard, and I have no doubt it'll be beautiful. Everything she makes is.

Once the remnants of our family meal are cleared from the table, we're dismissed by our parents to head to our teachers.

Miss Woodstock has her back to me and is writing on a board when I enter. The space smells of still paper and old room musk. I'm in the middle of trying to purge the scent from my nose when she notices my arrival. "What is going on with your face?"

Hello to you too, Miss Woodstock.

Our lessons are always the same. Kingdom history, map work, reading old texts. The reading is the only part I really enjoy, we rarely touch on something I don't already know. I've known the layout of Alunia since I was a girl, and yet we always come back to it, as if anything has changed. It's been the same since the Great War, Alunia and Baeton are still intolerant neighbors.

"Go to the shelves and grab the book we started last time, and open to page 61." The back wall has shelves filled with brown pages and torn edges, including the book we started last lesson. I've read almost every book in the fiction case, give or take a few. Non-fiction, unfortunately, is what most of our lessons require.

My seat squeaks when I return to it, and I flinch at the shrill sound. Miss Woodstock's head snaps toward me and she clears her throat, reminding me to open page 61.

Hours pass by uneventfully before I'm finally released. She remains sitting at her desk as if I'm not in the room while I walk to the shelf and put the book back where I found it. Before I leave, I trail my eyes over the fiction titles in search of something I haven't already read.

The shelf above it seizes my attention. A small placard reads, "Private Collection." Miss Woodstock's reserved titles. A midnight blue spine of ample size stands out to me. It's not any title I recognize: *Plenteous Kermera*. The name pulls at a loose thread at the back of my mind, but I can't trace the source. I look up to see Miss Woodstock still engulfed in her work.

I'll put it back before she even notices it's missing. I grab the book and place it under my arm before leaving her at her desk and going to my room.

2

M Y BED SITS IN a nook cut out in the wall, decorated with a
grand white arch. It's as if my bed has a room all to itself. The
soft greens and blues that decorate the room help pull together the
calming space. The fireplace seems like it is powered by magic because
it's always lit. Willow swears she doesn't tend to it *that* often, but I'm
thankful for the constant warmth, nonetheless.

My bathing room may be my favorite place in the castle, its deca-
dence unmatched. The marble tub sits on its gold claws in the center
of the room with tall candelabras near the head of it.

After staring at the objects around me as if they'll speak to me for
some time, a knock sounds at my door, making me jolt where I sit on
my bed. Louder than Willow's usual force, Dessielle wouldn't knock,
she would let herself in. That only leaves—

"Knock, knock, princess!" He calls from the other side. Reynard has been in my life for as long as I've had memories; he was around the castle a lot growing up.

The handle turns on the massive wooden door and his lean frame enters the room. Half a head taller than me with bright red hair and eyes that are so pure green, they remind me of Peridot.

"Where've you been, huh?" He says as he strolls in like it's his own room.

The edge of my bed caves in as he sits next to me, causing me to sink into the middle. "I've been a little busy being a princess, I'm *so* sorry," I reply with the same amount of sass he presented.

He nods enthusiastically and purses his lips. "Right, I forgot you don't have time to deal with commoners." I glare at him while I take off my shoes and walk to my armoire, placing them with the others.

"Oh please, you know that's not true. I see you as often as I can, Reynard."

"Would you have more time for me if I was…a royal guard?" He nods excitedly and offers a boyish grin.

I whip my head back toward him, my eyebrows shooting to my hairline. "You got it?!"

He nods excitedly and flashes a devilish grin. "I got it, Rae! Did you doubt me?" He comes to me with outstretched arms and spins me when I return his embrace. Reynard has dreamed of being in the Royal Guard since he was old enough to hold a wooden sword.

"Not for a second," I say as I grip the side of his arm. "You've been working so hard for it."

He rakes his freckled fingers through his fiery hair. "Thanks, Rae. You were one of the people I was most excited to tell."

"That's incredible! I'm so proud of you, I know how badly you wanted this." Ever since his father passed away five years ago, he's been training with a new motivation.

He nudges me playfully with his elbow. "Who knows? Maybe I'll get placed as a close and personal guard for a certain princess," he says with a wink.

My eyes turn to slits as I tease, "Not if I have anything to say about it."

Reynard places his fist against his chest and groans. "You wound me, Rae."

"I'm sure you'll recover," I laugh.

I usher him from the room, otherwise I'll never get anything done today.

Once again in comfortable quiet, I set about finding a hiding place for the book I borrowed from Miss Woodstock. I put it underneath my mattress, which may not be the stealthiest place for it, but good enough for now. I decide to meander over to Roralei's room; it's been too long since I ruffled her swan-white feathers.

The halls of the castle are covered in ornate wallpaper with wood paneling. Paintings are sparsely placed along the wall; some of our family, others of the royal families before us.

One time, Roralei painted portraits of everyone in the family. Mother *insisted* she deserved another one. She said it didn't capture her likeness and made her look old. Father joked that she *was* old. I don't think I've ever seen her face turn red so quickly, a stark contrast against her pale skin and bright white hair.

I received many of my father's physical qualities, the pink hue to my skin and my red hair. King Aidmar has a strong jaw and nose, with bright auburn hair. His facial hair is often in a full yet well-maintained beard he keeps only about two inches in length. His eyes are a swirl of warm yellow and brown. My hair is much lighter than my father's due to my mother's coloring. Some strands almost look pink, like the two shades combined into one fine piece of hair.

I lightly wrap my knuckles against my sister's door. I hear her soft voice call, "Come in" and I find her sitting in front of her vanity near the window practicing what looks like a new braid style. She has many of our mother's features; her white hair and brows, but her eyes are a darker green than our mother's. More of an olive instead of Queen Calliope's bright chartreuse. She was born three months after my 12th birthday. I remember waiting right outside the birth chamber for *hours* until Father finally told me I could come in. He insisted that 12 was too young to be inside. She had white hair then, too. Just a dusting, but it was as bright as ever.

Her picked-at fingers move slowly as she crosses one group of hair over the next. I watch silently, entranced, as she finishes. She smiles at me in her mirror before getting up and running toward me. I pull her into a big hug, careful not to mess up her latest feat. When we peel apart, I gawk at her talent. "Now where did you learn this one?"

She shrugs her shoulders and says, "Myself, I guess. I took two kinds of braids I know how to do and tried to combine them." She runs her hand over the plait. "How does it look?"

I look it over, making sure to take my time before looking back at her round, delicate face. "It looks perfect. You did so well!"

Roralei smiles and walks back to her vanity to put away her things. She's insufferably neat for her age. I suppose she lets her mess come out when she paints. Mother requires her to put a protective lining under any area she chooses to place her canvas. She paints mostly landscapes, anything she can see around the castle. She selects different windows and sets her things up in front of them so she can have a front-row seat to capture her latest interest.

I sit on the edge of her bed, content with watching her move through her daily activities. "How are your paints doing, Ro? Running low on any?"

"My paints are very happy thank you, I'll let them know you asked," she says with a giggle. When I roll my eyes, she concedes. "I have plenty of paint. Thank you, Rae."

We sit together for a while, and she tells me about her lesson with her much friendlier teacher, Ms. Bramstone. They spent the morning ensuring she knew Alunia's four regions and their leaders. She doesn't say it, but I can tell she wants to get back to painting. I don't miss the fact that she's slowly putting together her art supplies, so I dismiss myself and tell her I'll see her for supper.

After wandering through the halls, I find myself in the library. Two rows of great cathedral windows sit on top of each other to the ceiling, where there's a sparkling chandelier. The large desk in the center is covered in left-open books and forgotten pieces of parchment. A small oil lamp sits near the edge, a true fire hazard.

My mother sits on a small couch in front of the dark blue shelves. I've read probably hundreds of titles in this room. I make no noise when I enter, but she looks up anyway, sensing my presence. Mother's intuition, or something. "Where has Ro run off to now?" she asks before looking back down at her book.

"She went to paint. I'm sure she's found an ideal place by now." I start to sit beside her on the couch, and she moves her feet to the floor to make room for me. "Such a talented young girl."

"She's getting really good, you know. We should put some of her paintings in the halls. She'd be so excited, she wouldn't stop talking about it until the winter solstice, and maybe even past that," I joke.

"Perhaps we will. It would provide some encouragement, and I want her to continue. The Gods know how hard it's been for you to find your passion, she's lucky to have found hers so young."

She's not wrong. I bounced from hobby to hobby when I was Ro's age. Nothing felt like *me*, so I stopped trying when I lost interest. Which was often. "Just be grateful my hobbies didn't include things like live animals or cooking. The castle could've been a lot messier if I hadn't found a much quieter way to spend my time."

She smiles, not taking her eyes off the page. Deciding to leave her to her reading, I start toward the door. Before I make it through, she tells me about a dinner she's hosting next week to welcome the new soldiers to the guard. She wants to boost morale and decided the best way to do that is with good food and wine. "Don't forget to invite Reynard," she calls on my way out.

I make sure to close the door behind me to give my mother her privacy, something she rarely gets these days. I'm not sure she ever wanted to be queen. After the late Odin and Freya no longer held the crown, the townspeople and council voted for who should take the position. Due to my parents' heavy involvement in the war efforts and their popularity among the people, they were eagerly chosen to step up. Whether or not they *wanted* the position, I'm unsure.

I spy Reynard a little way down the hall leaning near a lit sconce. As I approach, he lifts his head and flashes a cheesy grin. He's such a fool, I can't help but smile back.

"Just the man I was looking for."

His eyes widen as he cocks his head.

"Don't get your hopes up. You get a night off this week. My mother wants me to inform you that you'll be attending a Royal Guard dinner as a guest, not on duty."

He brings his fist down in a swift movement at his side. "*Yes!* I'm ready to celebrate. I spent so much time training for the Guard, I was worried I'd forget how to have a good time."

I chuckle, jealous. "I'm glad *one* of us will have a good time."

His brow furrows. "What do you mean? You'll be my dance partner for the night, so you'll have a *fantastic* time."

"Dance partner? It's just dinner. I plan on remaining seated."

He swats his hand, dismissing me. "Oh, come on, you know how dinners get. Enough faerie wine and the General will take his clothes off. Hell, we could join him," he says before playfully punching me in the arm.

"There isn't enough wine in the world for that."

Unphased, he continues. "You wouldn't make me dance alone, would you?"

"I most certainly would," I insist and cross my arms against my chest. Reynard clasps his hands, pleading.

"Fine," I sigh. "*If* there is dancing, I'll give you *one*."

"Aha! I knew you wouldn't let me down." He gives me a curt nod and a cheeky two-finger salute before walking away. "See you around, Rae."

3

I ARRIVE BACK TO my room to find a body sitting in my reading chair. My heart stalls in my chest before I realize it's Dessielle. "Dessi! You scared me," I confess, as my hand flies to my mouth. "How'd you even get in here?"

"A lady never tells."

"Yeah, well a lady also doesn't sneak up on people in their bedrooms."

"Oh, you're fine. You would've just let me in anyways, no big deal."

I incline my head with slitted eyes and respond, "The big deal is invading my private space, you deviant." She doesn't take well to that and grabs the small pillow in the chair at her side, chucking it at me.

I swiftly duck and grab one from my bed, ready for a battle of stuffed room décor. She holds out a long round pillow like a sparring sword before advancing me and jabbing me on my side. "You'd be dead right now if this was real."

I plunge my pillowed weapon in her direction only for her to jump away at the last moment. She attempts to roll forward onto the ground.

In a dress.

She gets tangled in the fabric, and I seize the opportunity to thrust the cushion into her back. "That was a feat for the history books," I say breathlessly.

Dessielle rights her clothing and returns to the chair with a huff. "Right, just because your opponent made a fool of themselves. You'd do *wonderfully* in battle."

I settle in on my bed with crossed legs and hold the winning artillery to my chest.

"Anything new to report?"

"Reynard got the job," I cheer.

"I didn't doubt he would. He's had his eye on it for years."

I chuckle softly in agreement. He's a persistent person; more tenacious than half the people I've met.

"He asked me to dance with him at this dinner my mother is hosting for the new guards," I mention.

She quirks a brow. "Dancing, huh?"

I shrug. "Yeah, if the evening picks up. Maybe someone will see he's a decent dancer and want to sweep him off his feet."

"Sounds like you'll be one sweeping," she mumbles.

A snort leaves me. "Oh, please. He's too clean-cut for me. He's got his whole life planned out down to the year. His job in the guard, when he wants to be married—"

"And what, you don't want those things?"

"No, I do. He's just too—"

"Boring?"

I groan. "I need passion. Someone with grit. Someone rough around the edges, who isn't afraid to get dirty. Reynard eyes everything with a pulse."

Dessi chuckles. "He *is* quite the flirt." She raises one brow at me. "You want someone dirty?" My eyes roll back, and my shoulders fall.

"Hey, don't let me stop you. I wouldn't mind a handsome stranger getting a little rough with me," she says and repeatedly raises her brows.

"That's not what I'm talking about, and you know it. But, if said roguish stranger *did* come along, I wouldn't complain." I smile and drop my face in my hands, blushing as I remember my last romantic encounter.

I'm not sure romantic is the right word. It was a few nights with a woman I met at a market stall. She smelled enticing and made good conversation which, after a dry spell, was apparently all I needed. She was there to sell bread starters, I think.

Or maybe it was rugs. The relations, like her trade, are hazy. Damn wine.

Dessielle is suddenly in front of me, snapping her fingers in my face. "Um, hello? Where did you go just now?"

I gently shake my head and bite my lip. "Nowhere in particular," I reply. "I've told you before, we've been friends for years; it's never going to happen. Besides, I don't think I'm looking right now anyway."

I fall backward onto the bed, my hair spilling around me. Dessielle moves to the footboard. "If you ever get desperate, I bet he'd climb the height of the castle for a crack at you." Before I have the chance to argue, she's out the door.

4

WHEN I WAKE UP the next morning, it's to Willow opening my curtains. She's not very tall, the top of her head reaches my ear when she stands next to me. She almost resembles a teapot with her round figure and short stature.

She wears similar clothing most days, always a long-sleeved, lightweight gown with a white apron around her waist. Her light brown hair is peppered with white and grey strands and is often in a braided bun. I remember when she introduced me to her son Fredrick all those years ago. He wasn't much older than Roralei and was *still* taller than his mother.

"These blasted curtains, they really mustn't be so tall," she says with a huff. She must be able to get them open because the room fills with harsh light. "Your sister has already requested you in the sunroom."

I sit up and stretch my arms wide, letting out a substantial yawn. "The sunroom this early?"

"I believe she wants to show you the progress on her newest piece. It's coming along quite nicely," she explains. She then disappears behind the bathing room door, and the sound of falling water echoes off the stone floor inside. I perform my daily morning tasks and let Willow braid some hair back from my face, leaving half of it down. "I told her she has to wait until after breakfast, your parents are waiting for you both."

I smile warmly and stand from the vanity to pick out a simple dress from the armoire. "Thank you for your help, as always." She nods and pats my shoulder before leaving me to dress for the day.

Roralei's hair this morning has a small braid wrapped around her head, and the rest of it pulled back into one larger braid. A few pieces have fallen out from her vigorous morning activities. She bolts from the dining table as quickly as she can after breakfast. I didn't want to tattle on her attempt to skip the meal, so I decided not to tease her in front of our parents. "Well good morning, early riser," I say when I follow her into the sunroom.

She whips her head in my direction and smiles. "You're always so sleepy. Every morning, I walk past your room, and I hear you snoring."

My mouth falls open. "I do *not* snore."

Ro turns from her canvas to raise an eyebrow at me. "Tell that to your mouth."

Hearty laughs fill the glass room, and Ro turns to face her newest painting of the courtyard. It has a large circular pool at the bottom filled with crystal clear water and two smaller pools above it in the center. It almost resembles a thinly layered cake in her painting since she isn't finished yet. Leaves in various shades of fiery orange and red lay around the ground and in the water.

I walk behind her to get a closer view of her canvas. She has a gift; her hands are without age and yet manipulate a brush with skill far beyond her years. Our mother repeatedly insisted that I learn to play piano or violin or become a seamstress as she did. I pushed back and told her I wanted to learn to use a bow. I think she thought I was joking.

I wasn't.

The sunroom is made almost entirely of glass, with thin iron rods connecting each giant window to the other. It's as if we're under the magnifying glass of a giant, except giants are few and far between nowadays. The few of them that were left contributed to the Fae effort in the Great War that further divided the kingdoms of Drennica, and many lost their lives. The handful, if that, that remain are tucked away on their own space of land in in the hottest region in the country, Summer. Their skin is so rough and textured, it sometimes looks as if they are made of porous stone.

Other creatures exist on Drennica, though I haven't seen them all. There is a junglescape in Summer that is full of lush flora and diverse wildlife. Sirens inhabit the large bodies of water surrounding the continent. The pixies in Spring are wonderful creatures, despite them always trying to take my jewelry off my body when I'm around one. I understand they love their treasures, so I never make a scene, but I let them know I intend to keep everything I arrive with.

Ro doesn't talk while she works, content with my presence as she pours herself onto the canvas. She usually invites me here for easy company, or for artistic feedback, even though I couldn't even draw a cloud. It's easy to lose yourself in books. I think that's why I love them so much; I can be somewhere else even just for a little while. I plunge into reading a previously started book while she finds her rhythm.

5

D AYS OF ME WAKING up before the rest of the castle for target practice seem to bleed into one another. Occasionally I hit somewhere on the target, but when I try to mimic my previous position, I miss it again. Then, every time I sit in Ms. Woodstock's class, we dip more and more into the book we've been trudging through for ages. It isn't until she asks me if I've seen one of her novels that I'm reminded that I haven't gotten around to reading it.

I don't tell her that I took it; I still plan on reading it. It will reappear soon... When I finally get around to it.

After fidgeting with myself in the mirror for too long, I decide to go find Dessielle since she lives in the castle with her mother Salma. Salma helps tend to the gardens for the kitchen since she has a keen eye for plants and spices.

When Dessielle's mother Eliya died, Salma spent years trying to make enough money to start her own shop. She wanted a storefront to set her apart from other gardeners as she thought it would attract more business. She and Dessi ran the shop together for years until my mother asked her to take on the title of the Royal Garden Keeper, a role I'm pretty sure she made up. She moved into the castle with Dessielle right before my 16th birthday.

I was immediately enchanted by Dessi. Her deep skin was a shade I didn't see much in the castle, given my family's fairness. Her hair was much shorter then, coiled and half pulled back with a ribbon to show her face. I could tell she was fuller than I was, and that wasn't from age. I thought at first that I was younger than she was, and maybe *that* was why my figure didn't look like hers.

I was sorely mistaken.

She never made me feel less than her, always insisting I was the true beauty in our friendship while I said the same to her. We have since learned to agree to disagree.

Her door is slightly cracked, something she does when she's playing music and doesn't want to have to answer the door. The closer I get, the clearer the soft notes of the piano sing. I can always tell what mood she's in by the type of music she plays, and today she seems calm. Happy.

After pushing in the door, my ears are immediately filled with sweet music. I used to be jealous of her musical talents; now I'm simply in awe of them. I take a seat next to her on the bench. I could watch her play for hours.

"Come to watch the master at work?" she asks without taking her eyes off the keys.

"Why, are they around?"

Her fingers come to an immediate halt, a sour note ringing through the room.

I can't help but laugh, which fuels her false outrage. "Kidding, of course. Did you come up with that yourself?"

She rights her posture, her chin shifting forward proudly. "I did. What do you think?"

"I think you honor me with your friendship," I say earnestly.

Dessielle's brows pull together, and she places an arm around my shoulders. "Ugh, I love you."

My pale pink skin looks almost pearlescent, the tulip color Willow puts on my lips and cheeks is the perfect touch. She pulls two small sections of hair from my temples and brings them to the back of my head to fasten them in a braid. She then wraps it around itself to create a delicate braided bun at the back of my head, then leaves the rest of the hair down my back with a soft curl.

Willow moves around me, pulling small sections near my temples apart from the pulled-back hair. Her freckled arm reaches over to my vanity, retrieves the sun orb lying there, and brings it close to the strands. After holding it there for a few moments, she puts it back with the mess.

"The pixies outdid themselves with this birthday gift. I can't imagine trying to style all this hair without their magic."

My father visited Spring when I was Roralei's age, and he told some local pixies all about me and my "curious" nature. The two young lords in Spring are a few years younger than me, and we traded letters for years about what it was like growing up in our respective kingdoms. Five years ago, on my 18th birthday, I received a gift from the eldest prince, Wilder: a glass orb filled with light magic. The light that shines from it emits a heat that doesn't harm the skin. It's been used on my hair for almost every event since he gave it to me.

"Have you heard from Wilder much lately, Raelenthia?"

"Not recently. Last I heard, he was traveling with his partner Sorain through the jungle since neither of them had been. I think they plan on seeing the entire continent during their honeymoon." I smile down at my hands, happy for my old friend. Wilder is one of the warmest souls I've ever known, he and Sorain are perfect for each other.

"That's nice, dear. He was so pleased you and your family could attend their wedding last year, I'm sure he's awaiting his turn to attend yours," she hints, poorly.

We finish arranging my hair, and then it's time to slip into my dress. It hugs my waist favorably, while graciously allowing me to breathe. I look over myself in the full-length mirror outside my bathing room door. I twirl my hips back and forth, watching the deep purple shades of the skirt shift in the dim lighting. "You look beautiful, Rae. You look so much like your father." And she's right, I do look like him.

I step closer to the mirror to get a better look at my face; the face that has half-human blood. I forget that sometimes, having never stepped foot into Baeton. My father has repeatedly turned down my requests to visit. He says it's too dangerous, and I know it shouldn't bother me, but it *does*. I'm the first half-human princess in Alunia's history. Before my sister came along, I was the only one in existence.

I take one last look in the mirror before I walk down the hall and retrieve Ro, who opens the door before I can even knock.

"Are you that hungry?" I ask.

"How'd you know?" She asks with a laugh.

We head down the stairs to the main dining room, much grander than the parlor where we have family meals, as the dinner draws nearer.

Our mother and father are waiting just outside the room where we can hear lots of booming voices. A soft clinking comes from inside the room, and the voices quiet. Our parents walk in first, and we trail behind them and find our seats near the far end of the table.

With a nod, everyone but my parents take their seats. Their King addresses them first. "Welcome everyone, and congratulations on being chosen for the Royal Guard." Applause sounds throughout the room. "Alunia has had countless soldiers. Some of whom gave their lives for their kingdom, and their fellow Alunians. We thank you for your sacrifice and dedication to your kingdom."

Mother clears her throat. "While tonight is meant to welcome and appreciate the newest additions to the select group of the Royal Army, we also need to address some rumors we're certain you've heard by now," she says.

The room quiets once more. "We want to always be truthful with you and to do that we must keep you informed. There has been no direct statement from Baeton that they are planning an attack. And while that obviously isn't required, nor common for their kind, we want to let you all know that we have been investigating and will continue to keep a close eye on the situation.

If we hear anything of concern, we will immediately alert the bell-towers and gazettes to ensure you remain aware and prepared. As of right now, there is no threat. And we wish to celebrate that fact with you tonight." Cheers erupt from the table.

Father raises his glass. "Please, enjoy yourselves. There is plenty of wine and food," he finishes. The entire party follows suit, followed by cheerful music while conversation levels increase.

An assortment of food is scattered on the table including sausage and peppers, chicken with citrus flavors, and a lamb stew. When I finally get my hands on the serving utensils, I fill my plate with a little of everything. The cooks are some of my favorite creatures in the castle. And I'm *their* favorite, too, because I never have any notes.

As people become more comfortable, the noise level drops. Guests start to isolate into smaller groups instead of shouting across the table, lessening the tension in the room. Now that they're calmer, shoulders drop from the release of stress. A copper tray covered with cups of wine makes its way around the table, and I happily take one and start sipping.

Maybe sipping is the wrong word, because too soon, my cup is empty. Dessielle walks by the room and does a double-take when she sees me inside. I didn't stop by her room earlier so she could see my outfit, something I'm sure I'll hear about later. She gives me a smile and a hand gesture that conveys her approval. She walks in and gives polite congratulations to the guests as she makes her way toward me.

Dessi is a welcome guest anywhere in this castle, so her being here isn't abnormal.

She stands behind me and leans down to whisper in my ear. "How long before one of these buffoons drinks themself to sleep?" she says. I have to stifle a laugh, and wine almost comes out of my nose. I feel her hand pat my shoulder twice, and then she's off to mingle once more. When I look up, my parents give me a concerned look due to the redness in my cheeks from choking on my drink, and I assure them I'm fine.

A set of eyes lands on me, and I can't stop myself from glancing over to see it's Reynard. He doesn't look away when I catch him. His brows pull in and he nods his approval as well, giving me a hand symbol that says *nice*. I mouth a silent *thanks, you too*. My cup is cool between my fingers, so I grab another glass once I finish mine and hold onto it for a while, making sure to take smaller sips this time.

A quicker song begins to play, and several soldiers get out of their seats and move through the archway to an empty, larger portion of the room meant for bigger parties. In an instant, Reynard looks back at me in question. More and more people join the revelry, urging Reynard from his seat. I don't watch, but I feel him move around the room until his presence sits heavy at my back.

He holds out his hand in question. I place my cup on the table and follow him as a waltz starts to play. He places his hand rather firmly on my hip and pulls us nearly chest to chest. We step and stride as we float around the room. We move around the entirety of the floor twice before the swell in music signifies a partner change.

I remove my hand from Reynard's and place it into the palm of my next partner. He gives me a slight dip of his head and a small smile before placing his empty hand delicately on the side of my waist. He initiates a beautiful spin turn, allowing the skirt of my gown to flutter around me, and I catch it shimmer in the light.

When I am righted once again, I look to see my new partner.

No, not new. I'm somehow back with Reynard, his palm quickly finding the small of my back. When another partner change arises, he pulls us back without breaking our step and then seamlessly blends us back into the group after the partners have been exchanged again. He looks down at me through his copper-colored lashes and winks before spinning me out of turn, taking his hand off my back, and letting me turn one too many times. When he pulls me back, the music comes to an end.

He lifts my hand to his lips and plants a kiss on my knuckles before taking a step back. "If you'll excuse me for a moment, Rae. I'll find you in a bit," he says before turning away and walking back to the table.

I look around to find Dessi, who decided to linger at the party due to its informality, and fill her in immediately. When she sees me coming, she excuses herself from the conversation and meets me along the wall. "It looked like you were having fun," she says.

"He's not half bad. It was a touch awkward, he forgot to trade partners a few times," I explain.

She gives me a look that says "We'll talk about it later" and goes to dance with someone I haven't been properly introduced to.

When the music for the Volta starts to play, I feel a tap on my shoulder while in conversation with a burly man who used to run a bakery on the outskirts of his village before he was chosen for the Guard. I look over my shoulder to see Reynard, once again with his hand extended. When I start to shake my head, he uses those same pleading eyes from before, and I give in. What's one more dance? Almost everyone is dancing now, so I would be the odd one out.

We start our foot tapping and glide through the first few jumps.

"You look great tonight, Raelenthia," he declares as I descend from a lift.

"Thank you! You cleaned up nicely," I reply honestly.

"Ah, you know me. I have to keep up my looks for the ladies."

"Of course, you can't disappoint the ladies."

"There's only one girl I need to impress tonight." He gazes down at me with a charmed smirk.

A playful rumble of protest leaves me. "Always such a flirt."

The other soldiers seem to be finished for the night, and I'm grateful for it. I don't think I'm capable of more socializing tonight, properly drained.

I find Roralei lying in the fetal position on a chair, head nearly hanging off the side. She's dead asleep and no one seems to notice, so I scoop her into my arms and head toward the stairs. She's much harder to lift now that she isn't five. As I walk, I pass by Reynard chatting with some other guards. His brows pinch together as he looks at the limp princess in my arms. I mouth, "She fell asleep." He nods and leaves his conversation to come over to me.

"Do you need any help? That's a lot of stairs." He's right, going up these with no additional weight than my own is a challenge. But I'm committed at this point. And stubborn.

"That's alright, I think I've got her. Thank you." I want to go to my room, shut the door, and sleep through tomorrow.

He doesn't move though, so I spit out, "You could keep me company though if you'd like. It's a bit of a walk back to her room."

He gives a faint smile before replying, "You know, I'm getting rather sleepy myself. I think I'll head out, too."

Neither of us says much for a minute or two. When I break the silence by asking him if he enjoyed the dinner he says, "It was one of the best nights I've had in a while."

When we finally reach Roralei's room, he opens the door so I can squeeze her through the frame. Reynard peels back the covers so I can place her into bed. She's far too exhausted to have me wake her up to change clothes, and we've all woken up in clothes from the night before at some point, no matter our age.

Reynard and I exit the room, softly shutting the door behind us. We take the 30 steps down the hall to my door before I say, "Thank you for the dancing, I ended up having a good time."

"I'm not surprised. It is *me*, after all."

"Forgive me for doubting your abilities," I bow slightly at the waist. "Won't happen again."

His hand comes up to briefly rub the outside of my arm. "Goodnight, Raelenthia."

6

W HEN I SAW WILLOW last night dancing with her son, I made
sure to tell her not to show up today. I wanted her to be able
to have a good time and not worry about being up early this morning,
so she's at home with her family.

Tangled in sheets and drool on my cheek, I'm grateful. I don't
remember how much faerie wine I had last night, but it was enough
to give me the deepest sleep I've had in months. I didn't wake up once,
which is rare for me.

My feet dangle off the side of my bed before I slowly rise, trudge to
my window, and open the curtains. My eyes are assaulted by piercing
bright light, so I yank one of them closed again before going to my
bathing room. I scrub my face with my hands and sit on the stool
before my vanity for a few moments, letting the events of last night
file back into my memory as I take care of my morning needs.

Dessi and I didn't get the chance to catch up last night after dinner, I was so exhausted. Aside from the few dances we managed to get together, we didn't speak much, too caught up in other conversations. After I get dressed for the day, I wander down to her room so we can talk about everything that happened last night.

Without knocking I waltz into her room, but I don't see her. She isn't in her bed or pinning up her hair, so I go to her bathing room door. As my hand reaches for the knob I hear giggling, and my hand freezes. My slightly pointed ear seals with the door and that's when I hear a deeper voice with hers. A male one.

My hand launches to my mouth as I turn and move out of the room as quickly as I can without making any noise.

You know what? Good for her. We can talk later.

I return to my room and dress hastily before going down to eat with my family. Father leaves on a hunting trip today, so he won't be at the table for long. He was supposed to leave a few hours ago, but it seems he and the other party members *also* had a bit of fun last night. My father hardly ever lets himself go. He feels that since he's the king, he can't have the smallest lapse in judgment or vulnerability. He holds himself to a much higher standard than other members of the court because of his background.

Being born a human has made him a devout ruler; always trying to prove that he's worthy of his position. My mother does her best to assure him that he is, but that doesn't stop the fear from latching itself into his brain. It's the deadliest monster there is, fear.

The table in this room is always set, regardless of the time of day. Two candelabras sit outside of two marigold bouquets, kept fresh and blooming all year round due to Salma's affinity for plant life. She isn't particularly powerful, not like those blessed with more intense gifts from Spring, but she has a paramount green thumb due to her knowledge of proper gardening techniques.

Roralei sits one seat away from me, hastily feasting from her breakfast plate as if it will vanish from sight if she isn't quick enough. I imagine dancing so vigorously that you fall asleep in a chair *would* cause such ravenousness.

"Did you have fun last night, my dears?"

"My feet hurt, Mother. I danced so much, I'm afraid I'll have holes in my shoes. I've already found a blister this morning," complains Roralei.

Mother smiles sweetly at her. "I saw that. I was wondering how long you would last before sleep took you. I'm glad you had such a wonderful time." She looks at me, then. "And what about you, Rae? Did you have a good time with your dance partner?"

My spoon stops its ascent halfway to my mouth, and I look up to see her eyeing me from across the table. "It was fun. The food was good, and I had lots of pleasant conversations."

"That's very nice dear. Who else did you speak with? Anyone catch your eye?" My mother is never one for subtlety.

"Reynard and I shared a few dances. I also danced with Dessi and Father, and even Ro a few times before she dozed off."

"I'm glad you enjoyed yourself."

Father finishes his meal first, stands from the table, and plants a kiss on Mother's head. "I need to be heading out now, my loves. I'll be back in a few days. While I'm away, Roralei, you're in charge here."

She laughs and runs to hug his side. "I'll be a great ruler, Father. Be careful." I stand and follow suit, hugging him tightly.

Roralei is next to finish her meal and excuses herself to go paint in the sunroom. Mother and I finish ours in silence, desperate for quiet after the night we had.

Housekeepers slowly start to clear the table, and I wipe my mouth with my napkin before surrendering my plate. With a goodbye to my mother, I start the ascension back to Dessielle's room. Surely, she's had enough time to dismiss her late-night tryst.

I knock on her door this time, unwilling to barge into something I may never be able to scrub from my eyes. When the door opens, it isn't my best friend, but a tall dark-skinned man with a shortly kept beard. And he isn't fully clothed. His eyes widen at the sight of me, and he quickly shuts the door in my face.

I hear Dessielle's voice from inside call, "Just a second!" and I bring both my lips into my mouth to stifle a laugh. The door reopens and the same man appears, this time wearing clothes. "My deepest apologies, princess, I didn't mean to slam the door on you. Or appear indecent," he says while he rubs the back of his neck. Dessi opens the door wider and pops her head out from behind him. "Don't mind him, Rae. He was just leaving." Her eyes shoot to his face. "Weren't you?" He nods his head before reaching down to grab his shoes from inside the room and stepping out of the door frame.

Before he walks away, he turns to Dessi and asks, "Can we get together sometime? Maybe tomorrow?"

She bites her bottom lip and offers a seductive smile. "That sounds fine, I'll see you then." I wait until he's out of earshot before I say "Nicely done, Dessi. Was he at the dinner?"

She scratches her head with her pointer finger and ponders the question. "I believe so? I'm not entirely sure," she confesses with a shrug before falling back onto her bed. "What are you doing here, anyway? It's early for you."

I throw my hands up at my sides. "Why does everyone think I sleep like the dead? I sleep a perfectly normal amount of time." She rolls over onto her stomach and crawls to sit at the foot of her bed.

Flopping down next to her, I recount the night. We discuss everyone in attendance, from their attitudes to their dancing. We seem to have the same consensus on most of those in attendance, aside from a few people we didn't have much time with.

"Ro had so much fun, she was passed out on a chair by the end. I had to scoop her up and walk her back to her room with Reynard."

Her brows pull together. "He walked back with you?"

"He offered to carry her back for me, but I had already committed. So, he tagged along."

She nods. "Strange. I thought he had already left for the night."

I shrug. "I thought I saw him leave with some other guards, but he was back before I thought much about it."

"Maybe he forgot something?"

"Probably. Or he came to pick up any drunk creatures before the night was over," I tease. "Speaking of which, the man who left your room this morning?!" I shove her arm in jest.

She blushes, kicking her feet like a young girl. "We'll see if he's still interesting during the day. I don't remember much of our conversation last night, so hopefully it wasn't some fluke." She rolls onto her back to stretch her arms. "I feel like I need a nap," she yawns. "*Someone* kept me up all night." She winks, and I leave her to get some rest.

7

FATHER'S BEEN GONE FOR a few days now, and the castle feels strange without him. After my lesson with Ms. Woodstock this morning, I decide to wander through the halls for a bit to clear my mind. I hear voices coming from behind the door of the war room, which is unexpected. My parents have hardly used that room since the end of the Great War, which was before I was born. On light feet, I stride to the door and place my ear against it. My mother always said it wasn't polite to eavesdrop, but that didn't stop me as a child. I would frequently listen to the briefings that soldiers would receive before going on a mission. I even tried to sneak into a mission, or several, too confident in my skills with a bow. I was always thwarted before they ever left the castle gates.

With my ear to the door, I quickly recognize one of the voices as my mother. One of them is the General, and another voice I can't place. They sound distressed, so I slow my breathing and pay attention.

"What do you mean he's injured?

My eyes widen, awaiting the assurance they're not talking about my father.

"There was a hunting accident, your Highness. He'll live, but he won't be able to go on the mission."

Mission?

I hear my mother sigh, and then there's a pause. "I'm glad he'll be alright. Did my husband tell you who to put in the man's place?"

A soundless breath leaves me. It's not him.

"He didn't. He said he would leave it up to the team's leader if he wanted the extra body or not, and that he can fill it if he wishes."

My heart aches in my chest. Before I gave up archery, I wanted to be a soldier. I was convinced that I was good enough to be one, maybe even in the Royal Guard. *I* wanted to be the person going on missions and protecting the kingdom. But I was born a princess, and that wasn't my fate. Hell, I'm still unsure of what it is. The men and women at the Royal Guard dinner have all found theirs, and I can't help but feel jealous of them.

Feet shuffle behind the door, causing me to scurry back down the hall. I make it far enough that when the door opens, I'm just coming around the corner. The two men leave and walk opposite of me, and I see my mother's stressed face even in the dim hall lighting.

"Are you doing alright?"

She smiles, but it doesn't reach her eyes. "Yes, dear, I'm fine. Just dealing with some chain of command things, don't worry." She places a kiss on my forehead and leaves the hall.

As if I could forget what I just heard.

Why is there a mission, and why isn't anyone talking about it? I haven't spoken with Reynard since that dinner; I've done well at avoiding him.

Alone in the hall, and so close to answers, I duck into the war room and shut the door behind me. I can't remember ever being here. Father always told me it was for adults, and that I didn't need to worry myself with matters of war.

I'm all grown up now.

As I look down at the map on the table, the speech my parents gave at dinner comes to mind. I've heard some of the rumors they mentioned, about Baetonian forces stirring across the Range of Unrest. They told everyone that they weren't true; that we were safe.

They wouldn't have lied.

Papers are scattered across the desks, filled with notes I don't understand about the regions and their defenses. Summer is safest in an attack on the continent since they're the furthest from the icy grasp of Baetonian Winter. On the map, I see figures placed all over Drennica. The Alunian regions are labeled, as well as Baeton behind the mountains. There are small figures near the mountains on the Baetonian side that I'm wary of.

As my eyes trail along the various maps, I wonder if maybe that's what the mission is for. A group going to scope out more details; it would make sense. Meanwhile, I'm stuck here. As usual.

A door closes from down the hall, and my bones rattle under my skin from the flinch that rocks me. I sneak back out of the room with more questions than I arrived with.

I toy with the thought of speaking with Reynard about possible self-defense training. Whether the rumors are true or not, I want to be able to hold my own. He's a skilled fighter. I know that much is true, or he wouldn't have gotten his position in the first place. If anyone can teach me how to protect myself from a threat, it's him.

Perhaps tomorrow I'll have another teacher.

8

Knowing he's most likely to be in the armory, I head there first thing after breakfast. Clashing metal is a sign I'm on the right track. The stone hall allows the sword swinging to echo through the lowest level of the castle. When I pop my head through the open archway, he halts.

"I need your help," is the first thing I say.

"Is everything alright?" Reynard places his training sword on the empty spot on the wall and pushes his sleeves up to his elbows.

"How would you feel about teaching me to use a sword?"

His eyes practically jump out of his head. "*You* want to use a sword? Raelenthia Norrel, princess of Alunia?"

"If you're going to joke about it, then never mind." Before I can storm out of the room, his hand locks around my bicep and he pulls me back.

He looks less joking now. "I didn't say I wouldn't do it."

I shake off his arm and walk to the back wall filled with weapons. The stone bench against it isn't comfortable, but it's grounding, so I sit. "I don't want to feel useless anymore," I confess. He doesn't reply right away. He sits next to me on the bench and lets me finish. "Everyone here has their purpose. Their calling, fate, whatever it may be. I have nothing. No talents." When he starts to interject, I hold up a hand.

"I can't use a bow anymore. I can't paint. I can't play any instruments. I need this... Please."

He nods slowly, contemplating. "You got it. I'll help you, Rae."

I exhale a deep breath. "Thank you. When can we start?"

Reynard looks around and replies, "What are you doing right now?"

We both smile, and I feel more at peace.

The training room is an entirely stone space. The walls and the floor are made of the same hard grey rock, it almost hurts my eyes. It's fairly large, about the size of the courtyard in the center of the castle, but with much less outside light. The windows here are much smaller than any other room and have no glass in them, just an iron pane about the size of a kitchen cupboard.

A wooden table stretches along the entire right wall. It's covered completely with various swords and daggers, knives and axes, even a mace or two. Over the table are hooks holding even more weapons ranging from crossbows to lances and spears. I leave Reynard's side to stand in the middle of the space.

Reynard grabs two daggers off the table and places one in my right hand. "You know how to use one of these?"

I give a closed-lip smile and nod. "I think so. I used to chase you around outside the castle with one when we were children, remember?"

He laughs at my child-like smirk. "You really did, huh? I almost thought I dreamt that. I want to start with these to see what you already know and practice different movements before handing you a sword, which will be much harder for you to hold. Once we're confident with your footwork and reflexes, we'll get to the big stuff."

The blade becomes slippery . Here we go.

We move to the center of the room again and stand opposite of one another. I lunge first, aiming for his gut. He quickly lunges out of the way and aims his right at my neck. We reset, and he chuckles, the sound circling me in an echo off the stone floor. "You went for the easiest shot there was. Anybody would expect that."

This time, we circle each other for a minute trying to read the other person's movements. He lunges at my left shoulder, and I dodge just in time to move my dagger toward his left side. But he anticipates my move, and he blocks me before we reset.

The next time Reynard charges me, I evade his weapon and lash with my full effort at the top of his thigh. His clothing would prevent any real damage if it had struck the way I wanted, but he's too quick.

I attempt to disarm him, swiping my dagger underneath his during his next slice so I'd be the only one left with a weapon. He instead disengages for a quick moment and then points the blade directly at my face.

We continue like this, taking jabs at each other and moving around the room. Grunts and shuffling fill the space for what feels like hours.

When we're both sweaty and tired, I turn to place my dagger back on the table.

Reynard takes this opportunity to come up behind me noiselessly and aim his dagger at my neck. "Who said we were finished?"

He spins me around to face him and lowers the dagger from my breathing space. "You really need to watch your back, Rae. In a split second, I could've ended you."

Our heavy breathing is deafening.

"I think that's enough for tonight. I want to try with the sword tomorrow."

Reynard eyes me hesitantly, unsure of whether he should grant me my wish. "No way, you're not ready. We just started, Rae."

Embarrassed that I haven't somehow mastered this new skill in record time, my mouth turns down in a pout.

He doesn't budge.

"Ugh, fine. I'll see you tomorrow."

"I'm finished!"

I jolt awake, having dozed off in a winged armchair, my book lying open on my stomach. In front of me is a giddy Roralei holding a paintbrush.

After I rub the exhaustion from my eyes, I place the book on the table beside me and stand to look at her finished piece. My eyes rake over the painting, the vibrant oranges and yellows, the clouds as real as the ones scattered over Alunia this afternoon.

"Ro, this is incredible. You're talented beyond your years, I mean it."

Roralei puts her paintbrush into the cup that holds the rest of them and comes to stand beside me. "Thanks." A proud smile spreads on her youthful, pale cheeks. "I think this may be one of my favorites."

She grabs the sheet from the ground in front of her easel and runs it over to the bin to be laundered. Mother would have a heart attack if the flooring here got ruined; it's the original hardwood placed centuries ago. I start to grab her other supplies: her palette coated in layers of past projects, her jars of paints left scattered around the table.

"What did you learn in your lessons today, little sister?"

She takes the containers from my hands to be emptied. "Miss Bramstone told me all about the terrain manipulators!"

My brow furrows. "Is that the first time you heard of them?" I knew about them when I was much younger than she is.

Ro shakes her head. "No, I knew about them. But rumors are different than facts," she states. "I can't believe they made the Range of Unrest all by themselves."

I nod, my thoughts drifting to the massive mountain range. "It's impressive, isn't it? No other structures stretch that wide on the continent. And to think they were made by other Fae... I'm forever in awe of them."

She tells me all about the other kinds of magic she's learned about in her lessons. Light magic is common, especially in those with long family trees from Spring. Miss Bramstone didn't touch on fire magic too much since it hasn't been around for over a century.

I don't think it truly went away. My theory is that those with fire magic were forced into hiding because they were dangerous. Roralei agrees with me, and a harmless question about her studies turns into an hour-long discussion about our theories about the continent. Drennica is massive, and while I've left Autumn to visit the lords and ladies of the other regions, there's still much to be explored. It's also incredibly old. The Great War was roughly 300 years ago, and only *then* was Drennica separated by the Range of Unrest. However, the actual age of the continent is unknown to me.

"Let's let these theories stay between us, Ro. I don't need you getting into any trouble."

"Like the last time I went to play knucklebones in the village square outside the castle?"

My mouth falls open. "You played knucklebones without me? That is the very kind of trouble I am talking about. Unacceptable," I complain and rub my hand on her crown of fine white hair.

We finish cleaning the room in silence, and she takes all her supplies to the closet they reside in. The armchair I found comfort in before welcomes me again as I reach for the book I fell asleep with, the same one that hasn't left my thoughts in days. I had almost forgotten about it until Willow was taking apart my bed to be cleaned and she found it underneath my mattress. My face turned beet red. Hiding things like a child from their parents...

This strange blue book continuously pops into my head now. The more I read about this civilization that depends fully on one another, the more I dream about a place like it existing on our continent.

Afternoon shifts to evening, and a housekeeper comes to the sunroom to call me to dinner. When I enter the dining room, Ro and our mother are already in their seats. Ro is telling her all about her new painting and insisting she can't see it until she adds the finishing touches.

"I'm sure it looks perfect now, why can't I see it yet?"

"Because Mother, it will be *more* perfect after I add leaves from outside. I'm going to find some in the courtyard tomorrow and stick them to the canvas with tree sap so the painting comes *alive*," Roralei explains enthusiastically.

"Have you seen Ro's new painting, Raelenthia?"

I take my seat. "I have, but only a peek." I look over and wink at Ro. "I was reading in the sunroom while she was painting it so I saw the process, but even I can't wait to see it with the finishing touches. I'm sure it'll be worth the wait."

Several castle workers come in with our meals and place them on the table. Since Father isn't here, his seat has an empty plate in front of it. Mother requested long ago that his seat never be left empty during meals because "he's always with us in spirit."

Tonight's dinner is a stew with beef, carrots, and potatoes. Stew isn't an uncommon meal here, given the cooler weather. The gardens are kept lush with all sorts of autumnal vegetables to use in casseroles and stews.

"Roralei told us what she did today, now it's your turn Raelenthia. How did you spend your afternoon?"

I wipe my mouth with a nearby cloth. "I did some light reading and accidentally fell asleep in the sunroom. The warmth on my skin combined with the cushioned chair made for a very cozy sleeping spot."

Roralei spends the rest of dinner telling me about the next spot she found to paint.

"It's massive! I'm not sure how I'll get it to all fit on one canvas; maybe I can shrink it down. Or maybe I'll get an enormous canvas. It can be hung in the grand hall when I'm finished, which will likely be *weeks* from now. I'll need more paints as well. This is going to be a *very* big project. Could I stop my lessons for a while to spend more time painting?"

Our mother makes a sound like a chuckle and a scoff before blurting out, "Absolutely not, Roralei. Any giant paintings need to be completed on your own time. Your lessons are full of information you'll need as you get older, as well as the history of this kingdom. You must not miss them unless necessary."

"But Mother, this *is* necessary. I'm not going to be a queen; I'm going to be an artist. World famous artists don't sit in class for hours a day."

"That might be true, but right now you are a princess, and princesses attend their lessons. Isn't that right, Raelenthia?"

I look between the two of them, debating whose wrath is more manageable. Since I do not wish to face my mother's fury *or* hurt Roralei's feelings, I choose both. "I'm sure famous artists were once in school themselves, Ro. You can learn more about art history and colors and things. It doesn't all have to be boring."

Mother smiles at me and mouths "thank you" before returning her attention to her meal. Roralei seems to consider my rebuttal and shrugs her shoulders. She lifts her dish to her lips and sips as quietly as she can before Mother catches her not using her utensils. Luckily for her, she finishes her slurping before Mother lifts her eyes again, and we look at each other and laugh.

Mother looks between us both, convinced she must have missed a joke. "You girls…"

We're both overcome with laughter, earning us another concerned look from our mother.

"I'm glad you two think you're funny." She places her cutlery on the table. "You know what else is funny? Cleaning up dinner as a thank you to our cooks and cleaners for putting together such a wonderful dinner the other night."

We both protest silently, mouths agape. Pleading eyes do us no favors, and Mother shoos us into the kitchen to help clean up.

Roralei is hardly tall enough to reach inside the large sink so I assume my position as the dishwasher while she finds a cloth to dry them. I fill the basin with water and begin scrubbing. When I scrub a bit too vigorously, water splashes out onto Ro's arm.

She looks at me, dumbfounded. "Hey! You got water on my arm!"

I scoff. "Hardly; it was the smallest bit. This water is reserved for the dishes, not little princesses. Although it might help you, I think you have some paint dried on your skin."

She drops the rag and turns over her arm to see that I was lying. She squints at me, grabs her rag again, and winds it around in her hands. I realize what she's doing a second too late and she whips me with the tail of the cloth, leaving what I'm sure will be a welt on my thigh.

"You did not just do that." I scoop my hand into the suds and splash a small tidal wave in her direction, soaking the front of her dress. She squeals and runs to the other side of me to abuse my other leg, but this time I'm prepared with a rag of my own.

We circle, facing each other with our sopping wet weapons until I finally lunge at her, earning another squeal as she makes a run for the other side of the kitchen. I chase her until she's near the sink, and place my hand in the basin to splash her again. I wind up my arm and send more of the bubbly foam in her direction just for her to jump out of the way at the last second, revealing none other than our mother.

Dear Gods.

Her eyes are closed, her mouth open, standing in utter disbelief. As am I. She wipes her eyes with her fingers and looks around the room. She says nothing, walks over to the basket of freshly folded linens and reaches inside. She pulls out an identical rag to the one in my hand and looks at me with more fire in her gaze than the sun itself. The next second, she is running at me as fast as her heeled slippers will carry her and winding her rag. It connects with my skin before I fully comprehend what's happening.

Roralei gasps from her spot on the other side of the kitchen and makes a run for the dining room. This battle requires more space and she's decided the entire castle is fair game. Mother and I look at each other and nod before running after Ro. The empty halls echo with laughter and the sound of towels hitting fabric, all of us hitting just hard enough to scare but not enough to bruise.

Mother sneaks around a banister and Roralei runs right into her, underestimating her stealth. They both scream and fall to the ground in a mess of fabric and hysteria.

9

T HE THREE OF US sit in the hall for a while, talking about everything and nothing at all. We eventually go back to the kitchen
and clean the mess we made while cleaning up dinner.

Dressed in a loose lilac silk gown that reaches my knees, I settle into
bed after lighting the candle by my head. The smell of stale paper hits
my nose as I open my borrowed book again. *Plenteous Kermera* cracks
open the cage around my heart as I read about imaginary children
separated from their families after tragedy, and how many of them
ended up being placed into a home they didn't recognize.

We have several orphanages in Alunia, one in each region. The
crown funds the homes and leaves their direction to nobles in the area.
I used to visit them when I was a child; I would play with the other
children and read with them, or *to* them if they couldn't. I haven't been
in quite some time. I make a mental note to stop by again soon.

After a few hours, Reynard knocks on my door with clothing in his hands. "If we're going to train with swords tonight, you're going to dress properly."

A vest of chainmail lays in his arms, as well as thicker breeches than I care to own in this climate. "Go ahead, put them on. I'll wait out here."

It takes a moment for his words to sink in. "You mean it?!" I take the clothing from him before he can change his mind, leaving my bedroom door open for him to enter.

"I can't deny you anything, you know that."

After the quickest outfit change of my life, I come around the divider to see Reynard stand from the ottoman and look me once over. "Impossible. How do you make training clothes look good?"

"Very funny," I say as I attempt to swat his arm. This chainmail is heavier than I expected.

He trails his hand out in front of him, telling me to lead the way.

Back in the training room, the moths in my gut take flight. A dagger is one thing, it's smaller and easier to manage. A sword is a counterweight; I'll have to move differently and anticipate my body's movements to wield it accurately.

I lift one from the wall, deciding to go with a smaller piece. It sits heavy and cool in my palm, dipping my shoulder down.

"I'll let you get a feel for it on your own, find your rhythm."

I move to the center of the training area and lift the sword as if about to strike. The weight of it pulls on my wrist and lower back, areas I'll need to strengthen if I want to be of any use. When I have a handle on how the weight feels against my body, Reynard meets me in the center.

"This is called the fuller, it's the strongest part of the sword," he says pointing to the lower half, near the hilt. "When defending against a blow, don't use the flat or the tip," and points to the higher part of the blade, "that's the weakest."

"Got it."

We both assume a fighting stance and I step in to deliver an overhead attack. He easily parries the attack and resets us. "You left your entire midsection open, which might not have been so bad if I wasn't directly facing you."

This time, he starts with the same movement and moves his sword down toward me. He maintains eye contact with me as I raise mine to block when he suddenly lowers his sword to my leg, using his previous momentum to make contact.

My weight almost shifts from underneath me, and I'm barely able to right myself instead of toppling over. "What the hell? You're supposed to teach me, not throw me on the ground." My tone comes out more defeated than I intend, and I shake off my disappointment as I find my footing.

"I'm teaching you by not taking it easy on you. People don't always fight fairly, you know. It's best that you learn by doing."

We go through a few rounds of clashing and quick footwork before needing to take a rest. I untwist my flask of water and take a few sips, the cool water shocking my system as it moves down my throat. Reynard sits down next to me and holds out his hand for the flask.

"Didn't bring your own? Seems like a *trainee* move to me."

He takes the flask from my grip without me offering it to him. "I was a little preoccupied with making sure you had proper attire. Or would you prefer I slice your delicate princess clothing and provide your skin no thicker protection?"

Fair point.

After what feels like a much too short rest, we move back to the weaponry table. Reynard insists that I pick a heavier sword for some reason, and we settle on one that's just a few stones heavier than my first choice. Back in the center of the training ring, he teaches me more functional ways to block and defend against attacks, and we practice those until my bones feel like they're vibrating.

Finally, after being thrown on my backside more times than I'm proud to admit, we put our weapons away for the night. I reach around myself to remove the outer layer of chainmail on my torso, but my arms are too tight and tired to remove it.

"Here, I can help."

"No that's okay, I can do it."

"Stop being so proud for a second and let me help you," he laughs.

Reynard's hands make quick work of what I struggled with, his fingertips grazing my heated skin.

He stays there for a moment, metal in his grasp, and I can feel his breath on the base of my neck, tickling the hairs there. He finally moves the piece forward until I can slip my arms through the holes, and I step away, desperate for air after the weight of the vest. When he holds up the cover for me to take, I place it with the other outerwear at the end of the weapons table.

I walk back to him, hopeful. "Can we do this again tomorrow? I want to keep working at it."

Reynard shrugs. "Sure, I don't see why not. If it makes you feel better, we can do this every day."

Relieved, I lean into his side. "I'd like that."

Willow wakes me up with far too much enthusiasm for the day ahead. I have a lesson with Ms. Woodstock and I'm pleading with the Gods I never pray to that she doesn't notice I haven't returned her book.

My dress this morning is pale green with cap sleeves and a small flower in the center of my sternum. I run a brush through my hair and let Willow braid it all back, and then I pull out a few pieces near my temples.

Miss Woodstock seems chipper this morning; she must have run into Lieutenant Aidman before class. The two of them have a strange friendship and I'm unsure if it's beneficial for either party. She clears her throat and announces, "We'll be reading poetry today, and then doing a bit of map reading."

Surprise colors my features. "That's a diverse lesson."

"If you'd rather go over the same five things as the last few years, be my guest. My apologies for trying to give you something a bit different this morning."

"No, no! Poetry sounds amazing, which title should I find?"

We start by reading and analyzing a few smaller poems, some about the seasons, others about death and life. Many of them go by in a blur, Miss Woodstock analyzing them herself and me blindly agreeing, until we come upon my favorite poem. It's dated around 100 years ago, and it tells of a love so deep, the loss would feel how the sky does when a star falls; a light it once knew, no longer being in reach.

A soul searches for its partner.

In every life, whether friend or lover.

A soul deserves it's equal,

does it not?

When mine finds its match,

torrential storms,

blistering winds

would hold no power

in keeping me away.

I dream of finding a love that intense. So strong, it keeps me awake at night. Something so passionate, it feels like lightning in my veins. A love I never have to question or worry about. I want to be an *everything.*

I've met many Fae, both male and female, that I've felt for. Some more strongly than others, but none so much that my waking moments were consumed by them. It was more often infatuation, and it went away as suddenly as it came on.

Miss Woodstock pulls out the map of Drennica and points to the region colored in white.

"What region is this, and who resides there?"

I know the answer without having to think about it. "That's Winter, humans live there."

"And the name of the kingdom?"

"Baeton. I've known these answers since I was a girl, Miss Wood-stock. Give me something a bit more complicated," I tease.

She moves around the table and points to the lightest green area on the map.

"And what about here?"

Another easy one. "That's Spring, pixies live there, as well as other small faerie species. There are no other kings or queens in Alunia, but there is a castle where noble Ladies Nymeria and Indigo live. They oversee the lighter season."

The stone woman cracks a small smile. "Very good, princess. I've taught you well."

"You have. I can name them all, I'm sure of it."

"All of them, huh?" Her pointer finger lands on the darker green portion of the map.

"Summer. Fae live there, as well as giants and orcs, and other rough-skinned individuals." I pause, trying to remember the nobles there. Summer is, probably, the one I am least familiar with.

"Losing momentum, are we?" she says as pokes my shoulder with her index finger.

I swat her hand away. "No, I am not losing momentum," I say through my teeth. "I just need a moment to collect my thoughts." A few moments pass of me wracking my brain for this stored informa-tion. "Aha! Lord Evrin and Lady Caira." A wry grin forms on my face.

She points her hand to the darkest region on the map, not joining the celebration of my small victory. "Last one, princess."

The autumn region.

"Queen Calliope and King Aidmar live in Autumn, and rule over the entirety of Fae domain on Drennica."

"Well done, Raelenthia. I think that's enough of the map for today." She rolls up the aged, thin paper and places it with the others in a bin beside the bookshelf.

Before she finishes, my conversation with Ro manifests in my thoughts. "What kinds of magic are there, Miss Woodstock? I know of terrain manipulators and light magic. But how is it *possible* to create entire mountains out of nothing? Doesn't all magic come from nature?"

Her face looks intrigued. "It does, but nature moves in different ways. It's not strictly earth or water magic; nature seeks to protect itself. We see it with insects, and how their skin camouflages in their environment to provide safety. Earth does the same thing; it will grow around things in its way like unearthly objects. That power is usable, able to be called on by someone with enough heart to deserve protection."

"And what about fire magic?"

"What about it?"

"Well, where did it go? I've seen it mentioned before in texts, but it never goes as in-depth as I hope."

"That's because fire magic was dangerous. It was only ever gifted to Fae with wild tempers and grievances. It's unpredictable, and it's where it should be. In the past."

"Surely it couldn't have been that bad," I pry.

Facing the board, she takes a deep, calming breath. "I'll see you back here for our next lesson. You're dismissed."

Touchy.

Unhappy with her answer but certain she isn't open to more conversation, I leave the room with my things.

With an empty afternoon to fill, I decide it's been too long since I did any target practice. I've been busy with my combat training. I retrieve my bow from the back of my armoire and head down to my range. It isn't the range the Royal Guard uses for their target practice, mine is smaller and more private. I was told archery wasn't for young princesses so I would practice in secret with a bow I stole from the armory.

The length was a bit too large for me back then, I wasn't tall or strong enough to hold the bow by the grip or use the sight. Now, it's like slipping into a well-worn pair of shoes. I reach for one of the arrows I had hidden away with the bow and nock it. Putting my eye on the sight, I align it with the target and draw my hand back toward my face. I take a deep breath, and...barely hit the hay at all. The arrow lands almost on the edge.

I reset, grabbing another arrow from the quiver. Deep breaths clear my mind as I find my footing again, tilting my arrow slightly upward. This time when I release, I make better contact. The arrow lands to the right of the hay-filled sack. With a few arrows left at my back, I repeat the process until I reach back, and find the quiver empty.

Collecting the arrows takes a moment, as the last few I managed to sink into my makeshift target were lodged aggressively deep. I have to put my foot up on the sack to get leverage. I don't plant my foot properly, and fall back onto my butt. A frustrated huff goes out into the clearing "Fantastic..."

"I thought you might be here."

My skin jumps from my body. No one else knows about this place—would know where to find me. Except maybe...

Dessielle rounds the corner, her dark yellow cape flowing behind her as she walks. "Old habits, Rae?" She holds her hand out toward me and helps me stand.

I brush the grass and leaves off my legs, collected during my fall. "I guess you could say that. I was decent back then."

She nods, reminiscing on the day we built the range.

"You kept telling me to add more hay. I said it was too full, and I think I *may* have just been proved right."

I scoff. "I would never say such a thing." We chuckle, the memories flooding back.

"I think that's enough, Rae. They're getting too full," Dessielle claims.

"They need more, Dessi! Targets need to be solid; I don't want them falling over when I shoot at them."

She raises one brow at me. "You think you're so strong you'll knock over a target? I doubt it. If you want more hay, you have to go get it. My legs are tired." She sits on the ground next to our too-soft targets and wipes the back of her hand across her forehead.

"Fine, I'll finish these all by myself." I stroll around the corner to the stables, taking several bundles of hay into my hands that aren't assigned

to be horse feed, and carry the awkwardly shaped stuffing back to our spot. Halfway there, I put down the bails and readjust my grip on them.

"Your father is right; you really are stubborn."

My mouth falls open. "Am not!" I say, as I grab a fistful of hay and throw it at her. Her hair is a wild mane around her head, the curls particularly prominent today. And the hay gets caught everywhere in them.

"I'm going to get you for that", she says as she scrambles off the ground and runs at me, full force. Luckily for me, her full force is slower than normal due to the cape at her back. We chase each other around the stables until the groom from the stable calls out "You two, stop! You can't keep stealing hay!"

We squeal with terror, laughter ringing in our ears, and head back into the castle where I help Dessi clean up her hair that I made a mess of.

"We were reckless back then, weren't we?" she ponders.

"Were?" That coaxes a laugh from us both. "We did a great job though. They're still here after all this time, ready to be used again." I nock another arrow, finding the angle again and landing the slightest bit closer to the center than my previous attempts.

Dessielle claps cheerfully from behind me. "With a little practice, you could be really good," she says.

10

WITH LESSONS IN THE mornings, afternoons filled with reading, being dragged around by Roralei, *and* getting humiliated with weapons late into the evening, my sleep schedule has been greatly disturbed these past few days.

Walking toward the parlor for breakfast, I hear my mother's concerned voice. I stop outside the doorway, staying hidden from those inside the room. I put my head as close to the entrance as I'm willing and listen to the conversation. I'm getting quite good at eavesdropping; a fact my mother would *love* to hear about her eldest daughter.

"When will they be leaving?"

A soft, feminine voice answers her. "Two days from now, Your Majesty. They're readying their supplies as we speak and are still looking for another soldier to take Esra's place after his accident."

"And how is he doing? Esra?" My mother asks.

"He's doing much better now, thank the Gods. He hadn't lost as much blood as they thought; it looked messier than it was," she explains.

"I'm glad to hear that, he's a good man. Will he make a full recovery?"

"The healer seems to think so, Your Majesty."

"Tell Davian that he can have anything he needs. He's doing the kingdom a great favor, we are at his service."

Faunia, employed by my parents to deliver messages, exits the room abruptly. We barely avoid running into each other.

"Oh goodness, my apologies Faunia. I really must look where I'm going."

She waves her hand to disregard my words and responds, "No, please, I've gotten so clumsy these days," and walks around me to go wherever she had set off for.

When I walk into the room, Mother is pinching the bridge of her nose with her eyes closed.

"Is everything okay?" I ask quietly, not wanting to startle her.

She looks up at me and says "Oh, yes dear, almost everything is alright. One of the guards that went on the hunt, Esra, was injured a few days ago. They sent a party member back with him to ensure he made it safely, and he filled us in on the situation."

"Oh Gods, will they be alright?" I ask, truly concerned despite the lack of surprise.

"There was a hunting accident, that's all they could tell me right now. Esra wasn't up for much chatting when he arrived, and the man who brought him wasn't around to see the incident happen. He's with a healer now, he needs to take care of himself and get some rest so he can recover."

Not wanting to push her more on the subject, I sit for breakfast as we wait for Roralei to come in and join us.

After enjoying a full meal of pork strips, goose eggs, and rye bread, I find myself roaming around the castle before my lesson. One wall in particular is scattered with paintings of previous rulers. The late Queen Freya and King Odin have one outside the dining hall.

Other paintings in the hall are various landscapes from around the kingdom: the marshes in Spring, the swamp in Summer, and even Autumn's lush forests.

When I arrive in the classroom, there is a book open and lying on my desk. Miss Woodstock sits behind her desk with her fingers interlocked on her lap.

I take my seat and look at the open text before me.

Queen Freya and King Odin – A Complete Biography

"We'll be examining the history of our late rulers this week, starting with your parents' predecessors," she states. "What do you know of how they died?"

Having heard the stories many years ago, I reply, "They fought in the Great War alongside their soldiers. They believed a ruler should fight with their armies to show strength and encourage morale."

She nods, looking at what I assume is another copy of the same book. "And how did they die in that war?"

"They made a great sacrifice and saved hundreds of lives."

"Yes, but what *exactly* did they do? What was their grand sacrifice, Raelenthia?"

I don't believe I ever learned that. It wasn't something I ever questioned as a child, I was simply taught that they sacrificed their lives to secure a path for Alunia to win the war. No larger explanation was ever required.

"I...don't know."

A long sigh pours from her. "The book in front of you will explain some things that many might not be aware of."

The book tells of the lives of Freya and Odin before they sat on the throne, and how they grew up in Summer. It explains how they met, Odin got caught in a riptide and Freya jumped in to help. He swore to repay her and insisted on seeing her again after that day.

We study until the words before me bleed together and I'm afraid I have forgotten how to read when we come upon the most recent information written on the former royals.

I shake my head to try and clear my vision, sure that what I'm seeing is due to visual exhaustion.

"It says here that their bodies were never confirmed found after the fighting stopped. Is that true?"

She keeps her expression unreadable. "It is. Some reports from that time said that their bodies were found and collected to be burned and put to rest with the others, but some questioned the integrity of that information."

"Why would there be conflicting reports of something like that?" Royal corpses aren't something easily overlooked.

Miss Woodstock shakes her head and responds simply, "We don't know," and walks from her desk to stand by mine. "Rumors at the time said that Freya and Odin simply ran away; they abandoned the fight due to an unknown motive. Cowardice, emergency, injury. No one has ever been able to confirm the truth."

"So, no one knows if they actually died, but if they're *alive*...where would they be?"

Her eyes are distant. "That is an excellent question."

My lesson today leaves me with a multitude of questions that have answers lost to time. Ms. Woodstock said that books about their suspected disappearance are uncommon, only a few exist on the entire continent.

How is there not more discourse about this?

Being raised in the castle, I assumed I had a thorough knowledge of Alunia's history. But I was born after my parents' rule began, so all I truly know is what I've been alive to confirm.

Which, in a history spanning centuries, I'm learning is absolutely nothing.

11

I GET NERVOUS BEFORE every training session with Reynard. If the humans *do* decide to initiate another war with Alunia, there's no telling if someone skilled enough to fight will be able to remain by my side for every moment of the day. I'd have to fend for myself. I feel a bit more comfortable now after holding a weapon and familiarizing myself with something previously so daunting. I only hope it'll be enough to keep me alive.

Before I realize the time, a knock at my door interrupts my train of thought. I huff an amused breath through my nose and chuckle to myself at the timing of Reynard's appearance.

We quickly make the descent to the training room, the halls a bit more crowded than the normal flow at this hour because of Father's close return. No one pays us much attention besides a couple of passing glances.

Once we have the door latched behind us, I turn to Reynard.

"I want to truly spar tonight. An even fight. I need to see where my skill level is without you coddling me."

His eyes twinkle with the prospect of a challenge. "Okay, Rae. You got it."

When I choose my weapon for tonight, it takes a bit longer than normal. This will be the sword I use to demonstrate how much I've learned, if anything at all.

I finally choose one with a black handle and a silver guard. It's about half the length of my entire body and weighs on my arm with the same severity. We gather in the center and slightly dip our chins in recognition.

He advances with more speed than he's previously used with me, causing me to hesitate. I'm not quick enough to counter his actions. I barely lift my sword to block his chop in time, and the strength of his swing forces my arms to lower.

I regain my composure, push him forward with all the strength I can muster, and resume my close stance just in time to respond to a horizontal cut toward my left shoulder.

Reynard spins away from me and uses that momentum to bring his blade to my right shoulder with the same movement. He almost makes contact, but I duck underneath his blade and propel my weapon into his side upon straightening. He dodges by jumping backward and then starts at me feigning a low attack, quickly switching to an overhead swing that connects with my shoulder.

If this tunic wasn't so thick, my skin would have broken on impact. The force knocks me to my knees, allowing Reynard to aim his sword at my throat.

"Yield," I groan as I drop my head.

Breathing heavily, he holds out his hand and pulls me back up.

"You're going to want to take care of that later, it'll most likely bruise," he advises.

"What am I going to tell the healer? I fell down the stairs, shoulder first?"

Reynard rolls his eyes. "Obviously not, you can say you ran into a doorframe or something."

I incline my head. "At full force?"

He laughs and assumes a short fighting stance. "Ready for round two?"

Hours of this back and forth have my body covered in already darkening welts.

"I'm going to look like a bruised fruit. Could you ease up a little?"

With a chuckle, he says, "You think your opponent is going to use less force, Rae? I'm coming at you as an enemy. The number of bruises should show you that you still have much more practice to do. In different clothing, you'd be bleeding out right now."

A shiver rattles my bones at the idea.

"Besides, it's not like this is a skill you need to have."

"I guess not, no. But all this talk of Baeton and war is making me nervous. Can you blame me for wanting to be prepared?"

"You're a princess, Rae. You have guards for that exact reason."

"Yes, but other people can't fight my battles forever. I thought learning how to fight would make me feel better." I take a seat on the stone bench, a little defeated.

"I get it. It's not like you're training to be a knight, you wanted to think you could protect yourself."

"And what if I *did* want to be a knight?" I don't mean for my tone to sour, yet I will my fists to unclench.

He scoffs. "Being a princess isn't enough for you?"

Mouth agape, I stare at him.

"Be realistic here, Rae. You're going to be queen one day. Take the throne, settle down," he puts his hand on my shoulder in an attempt to be comforting. "You can't be a knight. You know that right? Tell me that you know that."

This chainmail suddenly feels like it weighs a million pounds.

"I think I need to go."

"Raelenthia, you can't be serious. Let's talk about this."

"Maybe later. Right now, I need some air."

I fumble with the chainmail, refusing his help this time, and sulk toward the exit.

"Rae, come on," he calls out.

I take the steps two by two and flee back to my room. In my bathing room, I see the tips of my ears have started to turn red. Splashing cool water on my face helps a bit, enough to clear my head.

Can't.

I am so tired of "can't."

I pound on Dessielle's door with the force of a battering ram, breaking the skin from my lips with my teeth as I wait for her to let me in.

Light from the hall illuminates her groggy face as she slowly peels the door from the frame. Confusion is carved on her features when she realizes it's me. "Rae? It's late, what are you doing here?" she asks with sleep in her voice.

That's all it takes for my walls to come down. The tears I had been forbidding suddenly resurface with waterfall strength, and my vision becomes blurry. I hate being a frustrated crier.

Dessielle pulls me by my shoulder into her room and guides me to sit on the side of her bed while she looks for something to wipe away my tears.

When I've finally caught my breath and sobs don't threaten to interrupt my words, I tell her everything. Am I being a bit dramatic? Perhaps. But if anyone is going to listen and understand me, it's Dessi. I've confided to her about my fears of the future, about the weight of the crown slowly fracturing my spirit. Sometimes it feels as if my worth depends solely on my position in the kingdom and I think tonight it all just...boiled over.

"Oh, Rae," she says as she strokes my hair, takes a seat next to me on the bed, and lets me have my moment.

My glossy eyes lift from the floor to meet her sympathetic violet ones.

"I'm tragic. I have no talents, no skills, no real dreams. I wake up and go to my lessons and meals and then I read. That's all I *ever* do. I *have* to be meant for more than this," I say, my voice thick with more unshed tears. "Sometimes I wish I could get away for a while."

She chuckles. "You and me both. What do you say we go on a trip or something? Somewhere calm, that we know we like. We could visit Spring, it's lovely there year-round. And then when you're ready, you can come back and start thinking about the future again."

I nod, contemplating. "That sounds refreshing. But time doesn't stop for me. The kingdom keeps moving forward, and I have to do the same. My father has enough to worry about after losing one of the men assigned to the mission he's sending out."

"What mission?"

How have I not told her this?

"Do you remember the speech my parents gave the night of the Royal Guard dinner? About the rumors of Baeton inciting another war?"

She nods. "They said they weren't true; that we didn't need to worry about them."

I nod. "That's what I thought too. I overheard my mother talking with a General a few days ago... They're sending a group of spies into Baeton."

Her eyes widen in disbelief. "They're doing what? I thought they said we were safe!"

"They did. But maybe they don't know what they don't know. They have suspicions, so they're sending a task force to verify their statements are correct."

Dessielle nods slowly. "That would make sense. Feeling jealous?"

"Jealous of what?"

"I just meant since they're leaving Alunia, that's all. Not the whole 'going on a mission' part, but I know you're itching to see the human kingdom."

I don't often forget where my father came from. He was human before he met my mother, and only became Fae during the ceremony of their wedding, when their lives were joined with their union. His ears may not resemble those of most of his citizens, but his lifespan and capabilities are certainly not human.

"My father has always insisted that he won't let me go. I've told him I'd bring guards and I'd stay well hidden, but he always refuses."

"He has good reasons to, Rae. They despise us simply for what we are. They're unkind. I don't blame him for wanting to keep you from it."

"*That's* what's unfair. Everyone else knows where they come from. And I can't even see the other side of who I am."

My eyes shoot to Dessi's.

"What?"

"That party is missing a member."

"Yeah, you said that already."

"I'm going with them tomorrow."

A laugh escapes her. "Right, Rae. Really, what?"

Silence.

"You're joking. What do you mean? Y—You want to sneak into a *mission*, with *trained* soldiers, to go to the human kingdom? That's insane!" Panic swells as she speaks.

"You just said so yourself, they're trained soldiers. It's the safest way I could go!"

She starts pacing, too filled with disbelief to stay still. "Except for the fact that you're the *princess*. You wouldn't make it to the stables, let alone through the castle gates," she points out.

"I'll wear a disguise. Whatever uniform they're wearing, I'll wear one too. I'll cover my hair, it'll be perfect!"

"Your parents are never going to allow this, you know."

I remain silent once more.

"Rae... You wouldn't."

"I think I might," I say as I tentatively bite my lip. Dessielle knows how badly I want to see Baeton. A few years ago, on my eighteenth birthday, is when I started spiraling about not knowing who I was. Dessi joked and said, "A princess, duh." While true, it did nothing to cure the gnawing in my soul.

"You can't be serious. A mission like that could take much longer than you think. To a kingdom that wants you dead! If word got back to your parents that you even *attempted* to escape? This sounds like a suicide mission."

"It's only suicide if I die, Dessi. I have no plans to die."

Those violet eyes show genuine concern, and I know this situation is bringing up memories of her mother. Eliya died in battle during the Great War when Dessielle was still a young girl.

"I'd be surrounded by soldiers the entire time. There's nothing to worry about."

Her face looks bleak as she replies, "And what about those guards? What if they discover that you're not a knight? What happens then?"

Trying to remain optimistic, I say "They won't find out. And if they do, well, I'll cross that bridge then."

Her shoulders rise and fall heavily. She isn't happy with this idea at all.

"I know you want to see Baeton, and I know you want to get away and clear your head, but don't let that cloud your judgment here, Rae. I'm all for self-discovery but this isn't a good idea."

Growing dejected, I plead with her. "I need time. Time to figure out myself, my purpose, and what I want. This mission can grant that for me, even just for a little while. You can either help me pack a bag and send me off with warm regards, or wait until I return from the trip. I would love your support in this."

I hold out my hand for her to take.

She hesitates for a moment and then places her palm in mine. "Just...promise you'll be careful. Please."

A small smile breaks on my face. "I promise."

12

WHEN I HEAR THE giant wooden doors slam shut from down below, I know Father and his party are home.

I quickly run a comb through my hair and pull it back into a loose braid before pulling on a lightweight, flowy, amber-colored dress. I'm still trying to put my slippers on my feet as I move down the stairs and finish just in time when I turn the corner into the parlor and bump into my father's surprisingly broad chest.

"Well good morning to you too, sunshine," he says with a hearty laugh.

I hug him tightly around his midsection. He's taken aback by my enthusiasm, stumbling a bit before righting himself and putting his arms around me as well.

"Miss me that much, Rae?" He says looking down at me.

I nod into his chest. "Yeah, I guess you could say that."

When I pull away, I look at the towering King of Alunia. Born human, yet one of the most devoted people to this kingdom there has ever been. I can only hope that he'll forgive me for disobeying him.

He insisted that I never enter Baeton out of fear for my safety. He's told me stories about the evil that resides there and, regardless of my heritage, forbade me from ever taking a trip to see the human kingdom myself. A rule I plan on breaking today.

I finally let him go and find breakfast waiting for me at my seat; a luxury I'm sure I won't have while on the road. I scrape every bite of food into my mouth before taking my plate to the kitchen.

After looking around to make sure the room is otherwise empty, I grab a few things from around the space. Some cheese and bread, as well as a drinking horn to put into my bag. I also fill a few small pouches with assorted nuts from the cupboard. I seem to have forgotten that I can't get from this kitchen to my room without someone seeing the odd collection of food in my arms, so I set them in one of the empty cupboards to come back for later.

Roralei has now sat down for her breakfast, so I go back into the room to see her.

"Have you finished your latest project yet, little sister?" I ask hopefully.

With a mouth full of food she replies, "Almost. I need to add a few more things before it's truly finished, though."

My heart sinks. I was hoping to see the final piece before I leave. With sorrow in my gut, I reply, "That's alright. I'm sure it will be beautiful."

She smiles up at me, still thoroughly enjoying her breakfast.

I place my hand on her shoulder and squeeze lightly, prompting her to look up from under her icy-white lashes.

"Will you make one for me, next?" I ask. "I would love to have one in my room. You can paint whatever you'd like." I hope I don't appear so brooding that she'll take notice. Though, I doubt much could pull her from the meal in front of her at this moment.

"I can do that! I've wanted to paint what I remember of the pixie marshes, so maybe I'll do that next."

I smile sheepishly. "Thank you, little sister."

I exit the room before I change my mind about this trip entirely.

Unsurprisingly, I find my mother in the library. She is poring over a romance novel I've seen her read several times before. It's one of her favorites, she never grows tired of it.

I clear my throat upon entering the room.

"Oh, goodness Raelenthia, you startled me," she says with her hand on her chest to ease the spike in her heartrate.

"I'm sorry," I reply coyly.

She must sense my unease because she marks her page, places the book on the small oval table before her, and uncrosses her legs. "Is everything alright, dear?"

Her concern chips away at the confidence I've been clutching onto thus far. "Everything's fine." I rub my hand on the outside of my arm. "I think maybe I didn't sleep well last night," I lie.

Suspicion sits heavy on her features when she replies. "Alright, dear. You know you can tell me anything right?" My mother has always been very trusting. She trusts that I know what I want, and that I'll take care of myself. She has faith in me that I'll make choices that are in my best interest. It makes me feel confident.

"Yes, I know. Thank you." I move from where I've been standing behind the chair she's perched in, grab her book from the table, and hold it out for her. "Don't let me keep you from reading, I'm sure it's a good one."

The left side of her mouth pulls into a smile. "It is. It's plenty broken in, I always come back to it when I don't know what else to read."

She grabs my hand after taking the book and rubs her thumb across the top.

"I love you, Rae. I hope you feel better soon."

I hope so too.

I leave her in the library and return to my room to grab the bag Dessielle is letting me borrow. It's unassuming: worn dark brown leather with a lengthy strap, and a brass latch to seal it. It should be just enough room for what I'll need. Last minute, I throw in my borrowed book. It's a long trip, I could use some light reading.

I make my way back downstairs and double-check that the kitchen is empty before shoving my collection of snacks into the kit. I'm not yet confident in my bow skills to catch my food. So long as we make it far enough from the castle before anyone grows suspicious, there won't be enough reason to turn the entire party around and start over. They'll have to keep going, and I'll make myself as useful as I can.

Since I've never been allowed to visit, I'm not sure how long the trip will take. If all goes well, hopefully no more than a fortnight to get there and the same to get back. I haven't heard any mention in my prying of staying long in the icy kingdom; the longest part of the journey should be the traveling itself.

The last time I rode on horseback was just a week or so ago, I took Winnie out into the Blackwood Forest to stretch out her legs. The chocolate brown mare has been letting me ride her for over a decade. She has a mild temperament with me and has never gotten aggressive. The same cannot be said for any of the male stablemen. For some reason, she has never responded to male touch or affection well.

Dessielle is already in my room when I return. She's pacing the floor with a fingernail between her teeth. Her eyes find me immediately once I enter the room and she rushes up to me to brace either side of my arms.

"Are you sure you want to do this? I can find some kind of magic that will turn you into a frog or something, then you won't have to worry about anything ever again. I can carry you around in my pocket," she pleads.

"I'm positive," I chuckle. I've wanted to see Winter for as long as I can remember. Being half-human made for a tense childhood, I can't even understand or appreciate my history because I haven't been allowed to learn more about it. Father forbids it. There's too much that I don't know. "They can't keep me in the dark anymore." I let a breath out of my nose. "If I end up sitting on the throne one day, I'll need to have an understanding of the neighboring kingdoms, as well as the other continents. For now, I'll start with our neighbors in the Northeast. My self-loathing is simply the force of wind pushing me from the dock." I reach up to rub my thumb over the worry in her brows.

Dessielle lets out a long sigh. "Fine. For the record, I understand why you're going. I'm still going to be worried sick."

I chuckle. "That's fair." I pull her close, bury my head in her full hair, and inhale deeply, soaking in her jasmine scent.

"You need to come back to me in one piece, alright?" She says with the utmost intensity.

"Yes, ma'am." I salute her, tears stinging my eyes. "I'm going to find Roralei before I look for the rest of the party," I say more to myself than Dessi.

"You do that, Rae." She pats my arm and steps aside, clearing my path to my bedroom door. When my fingers graze the handle, I turn my head back to her.

"If Reynard comes looking for me, come up with some lie. I don't want him to come looking for me."

"I'll tell him that you're off galivanting with a beautiful stranger and will be back later," she says with a dry chuckle.

I laugh honestly. "Sure, let's go with that." I force the tension from my shoulders before stepping into the hall.

Roralei is down the hall in her room. I can hear her singing from behind the door, something she does mindlessly while practicing new braids and twists. I crack open the door and peek my head inside. "Ro?"

"Come in!" She calls. She resumes her song.

I stand behind her at her vanity and admire the work she cannot yet see. My hands smooth over the ends of her hair. "It's getting so long. Do you think you'll cut it?"

She purses her lips, her features unsure. "I don't think so, I like my hair long. Your hair is long," she explains.

I nod. "Yes, it is. Your hair will reach the length of mine in no time with how well you take care of it. I'm sure of it," I chime.

She turns to face me with her hands still crossed through paths of hair behind her head. "Will you sit with me in the sunroom later? I want to finish my painting."

Unsure of how to deflect without coming off disheveled, I respond "Perhaps. I'll see what my schedule looks like this afternoon." I stand and run my hand over the crown of her head.

"I love you, little sister."

"I love you too, Rae."

13

F EELING CONTENT ENOUGH IN my silent goodbyes, I go to the training room to see if the rest of the party might be gathering there.

My feet freeze to the stone floor when the voices inside reach my ears. I peek around the corner slightly, enough to see the clothing the soldiers inside are wearing, but not enough to be perceived. Behind one of the figures in the room, I make out a pile of grey clothing. The other bodies in the room wear the same.

Strange, since our army wears shades of black and brown. The ensemble covers the entire body, with gloves and boots covering the portions where fabric cannot reach. Militant symbols are sewn with silver thread onto the arms. On the chest are sewn-in pieces of protective metal that look like no Fae armor I've ever seen. This design is a strange choice.

Two of the men have face coverings over their mouths, the same silver thread from the suit lines the mask.

How convenient.

The other two men standing in the room have their face coverings down around their necks. I don't recognize them as guards of the royal gates, which means they're less likely to recognize me. The two with their faces concealed are nearly impossible to identify, but I'm confident I've never seen them before either.

When they finish speaking, the pack files out the door that leads to the stables. The moment I no longer hear the crunching of their weight on leaves, I rush into the room and rifle through the few uniforms on the table. One of these must be small enough to fit me, and to my surprise, I find one. I quickly change and hide my clothes behind a loose stone low in the wall near the door I entered through. As a child I would hide treats and letters in this hole, knowing that no one ever came in here without serious business.

My long fingers tuck my plaited hair into the neck of my inner layer of clothing before pulling the hood over my head until it fully shields my hairline. I pull the face covering up to my nose and look over the weapons available. A blade with an ivory hilt stands out to me. The guard is gold filigree with small stones up the grip that look like fire moves inside them.

She'll do wonderfully.

I lean against the door the group exited from and listen for any sign of life on the outside. Confident that no one is within range of seeing me, I crack open the door and slide my body through the opening, staying close to the wall. Voices travel from inside the stables, and I recognize one as the same voice I heard addressing the group in the training room. "I'll take the white one," he says. The group calls out various coat colors of horses kept in the stable, and I breathe a bit easier when I don't hear Winnie chosen by another. She'll ride with me.

That's when I hear another familiar voice – a stableman I know as Parker. He's helped me care for Winnie for years, preparing her for our early morning rides together. If I go in there now, he'll recognize me. Keeping close to the wall, I try not to lose sight of him. He disappears behind a corner for a moment, only to come out the other side of the stable. He doesn't look over at me, doesn't even walk in my direction. He goes to the back corner of the building. My eyes follow him until he reaches down to unbutton his breeches before he–

Gross. He's relieving himself outside.

I take the unsettling situation as an opportunity to rush over to the stable entrance. One last deep breath, and I turn the corner, walking straight to Winnie and grabbing her saddle from the stool next to her tail end. I need to act like I belong here. When I start attaching my bag to one of the buckles on the harness, the same voice as before pipes up from behind me.

"And who are you?"

My hands freeze. Here goes nothing. I turn to face him, his left eye catching my attention first with its icy blue color, and the other a warm green.

"Esra got roughed up during the hunting party. I was told to fill his place."

The man eyes me suspiciously but doesn't pull his sword or call for the stableman. "Great, more new people. I thought I told them we didn't need anybody taking his position. Why didn't anyone tell me this?"

"Beats me. I awoke this morning with directions to get dressed and go to the stables immediately. I guess they decided to fill the slot themselves at the last minute. Something about ensuring maximum work quality." I do my best to keep my voice from shaking at the intensity of his stare.

His mismatched eyes look back and forth between mine. I plead to dead Gods that he can't see the bead of sweat threatening to drip down my forehead. After contemplating for a moment, he takes a step back, accepting my answer. "They fill you in on what we're doing? It'll be a long trip."

I nod. "They briefed me on the basics. Said that you'd fill in the gaps." The less information I have to offer myself, the better.

The large blonde man sighs heavily. "They always leave this shit to me," and he pinches the bridge of his nose. His voice is low as he says, "Baeton has secrets. Some of those secrets threaten Alunia, and our job is to find out what they are. We're going to Baeton to gather intelligence on what their next move could be and bring it back here to alert the King and Queen of any ill intent. Got it?"

"Simple enough," I reply.

His head nods, glad I'm not one to ask questions. "What do I call you, kid?"

My heart sinks. How had I not thought I'd need a different name? My eyes dart around the stables, and I see a small, reddish horse. I clear my throat to stifle the smile attempting to overtake my face under the mask.

"Roan."

He extends his right hand to me and replies, "Davian." I shake it and then turn back to Winnie. My heart is pounding like hoofbeats on stone. The other men in the room look back to their horses, trying to hide their eavesdropping. Except for one.

"What happened to this being a small mission?" He says loudly, clearly annoyed that the plans have seemingly changed. His hood hides most of his face, but I can see the warm, tan skin underneath the covering.

The man goes up to Davian and whispers to him for a moment before coming up to me. Avoiding eye contact seems to only work on animals because he gets much closer than I anticipate.

"We don't need anyone else," he says, only loud enough for me to hear.

Startled by his bluntness, I hesitate to answer. "I'm just following orders," I tell him.

"Where are you from to have gotten here so fast? Live nearby, do you?"

I thought I was free from my questioning. "I do, actually. Not that it's any of your business. Got here in record time because I was personally requested." Too bold. That's too easy to check.

He looks me up and down and huffs before returning to his horse. Only when he's across the stable do I have barely enough room to take a breath.

When the horses are fed and ready, I mount Winnie. The men do the same with their mares. Parker, the stableman, comes back inside and the floor is suddenly very interesting because it keeps my head angled away from him. Davian seems to be the head of this mission, and he guides the group outside. I'm able to get a better look at the other men in the cool light of the morning.

The one behind Davian has both his hood and face covering down, his warm ivory skin and coffee-brown hair on full display. His short beard is the same color as his hair, though it looks messy.

Davian's hair is a white blonde that reaches past his shoulders. His beard is full, but unlike the other man, his is well-kept. He's a well-built man, about a head taller than me with broad shoulders. He wears the same uniform that I do, but it looks as if they're the same size. His is stretched out to maximum capacity, and mine sits loosely upon my skin.

The other two men are harder to take in, their hoods still up and their heads facing away from me. Davian points to the man who voiced his distaste for my being here and says, "You, to the back. You'll cover the rear." The remaining man looks over at him, seeming uncertain.

I see the fabric covering his head move, like a nod. He turns his buckskin horse around and trails behind the group. As he passes me, I sneak another look at his face. Though the hood and facial covering are still in place, his eyes slice to mine briefly. Goosebumps rise on my arms when his dark amber eyes seem to flick me over, presumably to figure me out. He looks even taller than Davian while on his horse, his torso almost to be the same length as my legs. Speaking of legs, his pants are filled—

"Roan, let's go."

I didn't realize the group had started moving. The man at my back didn't move around me, leaving both of us trailing behind now. Not the best first impression.

When I notice we aren't going to the front of the castle but to the gates to make our exit, I call out to Davian. "Is the king not doing a send-off? I thought that happened for all military expeditions."

He angles his head back towards the rest of the group and responds, "Not this one. This mission is mostly off the books. They don't want the public to worry about the threats until we know the severity of them. We'll be on our own out here." And he looks forward again.

We pass by the front of the castle, and I look back at the entrance. Guilt for leaving my family without explanation rises in my throat, but I can't turn back now. This may be my one chance to see the human kingdom without the pressure of my title. I'll come back safe and tell them all about my journey and what I've learned. They'll forgive me, then.

I look up to the windows above the first level of the castle when I notice quick movements through the glass. Dessielle is standing at one of them on the second level, waving frantically at me from above. A smile spreads underneath my mask and I dip my chin in response before looking back to the path before us. She'll keep an eye on Ro for me.

With one last look at my home, I harden my features and ready myself for the journey ahead.

As we cross under the pointed stone archway that separates the castle from surrounding villages, Davian waves his hand at the man standing guard atop the wall. His stare lingers on me for a second too long, making my palms sweat inside my gloves.

The accessory strikes me as odd, as it isn't that cold in this region. We'll be traveling for some time, and temperatures don't drop low enough in the evenings to warrant such insulated clothing. But any questions I deem unnecessary float aimlessly in my head instead of coming out of my mouth to limit any excess attention on me.

The two men up front make casual conversation about previous missions they've been on and what treasures they've found on them. The two other men don't interject, and neither do I.

The man in front of me lowered his hood after we passed through the stone arch. His mask remains in place, but I can see him a bit better now. His skin is a golden brown, and the dark chocolate curls on his head are cut short. One curl has broken free from the rest, laying over his right temple. I don't believe I heard him speak the entire time we were in the stables. I saw him chatting with the man behind me when we first mounted our horses, but they spoke in hushed voices, not willing to include the rest of us in their conversation.

When I see the Blackwood Forest up ahead, my face twists. I ride with Winnie here; this is in the direction of Summer. Why aren't we cutting through Autumn to get to Winter?

"We're moving toward Summer," I finally decide to say out loud.

"Wow, she's good. Where'd we find her?" The man behind Davian says.

"Shut it, Hart. She came on this morning; she wasn't filled in properly."

"I've got something that would fill her properly," he mutters, his voice sour.

I bite my lip, unsure if I should retaliate. Before I can decide against it, I say, "Is your wife that willing to share, Hart? Must not be a grand feature." The words are out before I can fully comprehend that I'm responding.

A dry chuckle sounds in front of me. The man turns to look at me, mask still in place, and nods approvingly. Davian barks out a laugh from the front of the line and chimes in. "I bet Layla would love to hear you're offering yourself to other knights, Hart, and I won't clarify which ones."

Hart's face pales, and his head swivels like an owl so he can glower at me directly. "Don't talk about my wife," he demands.

"Don't threaten me with your parts," I counter, holding his stare.

Irritated, he turns back around without another word.

No one speaks again for some time after that. The sun is high in the sky, and the horses are hungry. The Blackwood is full of greenery despite its name, so we pull off the trail and let the horses graze about while we all look around for harvestable snacks. I happen to know that there are bushes in these woods filled with budberries native to Autumn. They aren't hard to find, but the berries themselves can blend in because they look like leaf buds. They're small and round, tiny green things. I find a bush nearby and start pulling the tart fruit into my hands.

Footsteps sound behind me, and I look back to see the man who nodded at me standing not far away. "Spend a lot of time in these woods? How did you see those?" He asks. He sounds young, not much older than me, but I know better than to guess the age of Fae.

"A bit," I reply, standing with the berries cupped in my hands. I hold them out to him, and he plucks a few from the pile and holds them up to look at them closer. He's a bit taller than me, but not by much. "I ride here sometimes to clear my head. I've been a few times." An understatement.

He raises a few of the berries to his mouth and pops it onto his tongue. His eyes widen when he starts chewing, almost moaning at the flavor. Mouth still full of berries, he says, "This is incredible. I've never tried one before, I thought they were just growing leaves." I can barely make out the words because he's putting more and more of the berries from my hands into his mouth.

He shoots his hand out into the space between us. "The name's Jaali," he says with berries in his teeth. I return the gesture and grasp his hand firmly. "Roan."

Jaali nods. "Isn't that the name for a red horse?" He remarks. I blush heavily, my face growing warm. I clear my throat before replying, "It is, yes. My parents are farmers," I say; as if that would explain why I would have the same name as a foal. I admit it wasn't the savviest choice, but I hadn't thought about my name being recognized before I set out this morning.

He seems to take my word for it though, taking a seat next to the bush I'd been picking from. The berries he took from my hands are gone, leaving both of our palms empty. We each take turns picking from the bush, sitting in silence, and eating from the plant.

The man from the back of the party spots us sitting together, and an emotion flashes through his eyes so quickly that I'm unable to distinguish it. He prowls toward us, a deep crease between his brows. Jaali stiffens when he looks up, like he'd forgotten we weren't alone while grazing.

"What are you doing over here?" he says in a deep, gravelly voice. The goosebumps from earlier return on my arms and I'm suddenly grateful for the length of these sleeves. He isn't speaking to me, but his eyes are trailing along the edges of my hood as if he can see through the fabric *and* my false confidence.

Jaali shoots up from the ground, and I can now see how large this man truly is. Jaali is a few stones taller than I am, and this...thing, is at least a head above him. I think I may be right about my earlier estimate, he may even be larger than Davian.

"My bad, I was getting hungry." Jaali looks over at me, then. "Roan was just showing me some of the safe plants to eat, and we decided to sit."

"If she wanted to sit, she should've stayed home. Not like we need her here anyway." The man looks at me. His mask is still covering most of his face, but I can still see some smaller scars around his brows and temples. Fae heal rather quickly from small scrapes and things, so those had to have been fierce gashes.

I hold my hand out to him with a sickly sweet smile, offering the same berries as a greeting. He looks down at it, then back at me, and turns and walks away. What a little...

"What's wrong with him?" I ask once he seems out of earshot.

Jaali tosses a budberry into the air and catches it with his mouth. "Pearce is a little rough around the edges. He doesn't mean anything by it, he just gets riled up sometimes." Ordinarily, I would brush off a prickly attitude. Something about this man though seems more than stubbly, he's like a briar.

"It's only the middle of the day. What would have him so irate already?"

His brows raise as he chuckles. "You'd be surprised."

"Enlighten me."

Jaali considers me for a moment and then explains what I already figured. "He expected to have one less person on the mission. The unanticipated doesn't sit well with him."

I watch him continue scarfing down berries. This man will eradicate the strain if we stay here much longer. "You seem to know him pretty well," I gather.

He shrugs slightly. "We're from the same town. Moved up the ranks together, went out on missions and whatnot. I've known him a long time."

"Sounds like you guys are friends, then."

He's stopped picking fruit off the bush and is now taking a pine needle from the ground and tying it in knots. "Yeah, we go way back. Far back enough to know that he'll warm up. It's day one, he'll wear down eventually."

I nod, but as I look up to find the man I now know as Pearce, I'm not so sure. My sight lands on the scar by his left temple, and then those smoldering eyes cut to mine. He must've felt the pressure of my stare the same way I feel his now.

Davian calls out to the group, breaking the trance I was locked in. Jaali and I leave our bush behind, bellies full of tart produce. Hart mounts his horse as quiet as he was before our rest. Davian settles onto his as well and starts forward. Jaali swings his lean body onto his rich-colored Marwari with ease and pulls his mask back on, leaving his hood down. Pearce falls into step behind me, thick waves of some emotion rolling off him.

As we continue through the Blackwood Forest, I see other paths Winnie and I frequent. This trip so far has been nothing new for her, simply visiting old stomping grounds.

A little before nightfall, a break in the trees reveals the forest's caretaker, Blackwood Village. The village is a short ride from Tinted Creek and sits on the outskirts of the forest closest to the castle. The people who live there are charged with maintaining the Blackwood Forest, sourcing lumber to the kingdom, and introducing saplings to the area. Their proximity to the castle keeps them in close relation with the crown; it's where we get most of the firewood we use for warmth and cooking. Davian's head doesn't turn to look at the village, so any hopes I have of a visit are slim. As we ride past, I see smoke rising from many chimneys.

Up at the front of the pack, Davian and Hart are laughing much harder at their own jokes than I think necessary. Jaali turns his entire body around on his horse so he's facing the rear. What the hell is he doing? And how did he not fall? For a brief moment, I think he turned around to look at me, but his eyes move past me to Pearce.

"You doing okay back there, pal?" He asks.

"Incredible," I hear Pearce grumble. I don't know how Jaali is friends with someone so dry when he seems like such a jester.

Jaali stretches his arms out around him and feigns a yawn. "Yeah, it's nice up here, too. Sailing through the middle, completely unnoticed. It's cozy." His hands rest behind his head now as if he were lounging on a bed.

"Turn around, Jaali," Pearce demands.

"Why would I do that? I'm not on the lookout right now, you are. I've got a great view from here, man." His eyes slide to look at mine and he winks at me.

I stifle a chuckle to not draw attention to the mess back here. Pearce doesn't sound amused; a combative huff leaves him. He seems tired of his friend's antics. "If you don't turn around, I'll push you off."

Jaali's eyes fly open before he slowly turns back around on his horse with the same grace as before. I lean forward on Winnie to avoid being heard by Pearce. "He wouldn't really push you off, would he?"

He turns only his head this time, his body staying glued to the saddle. "I've seen him do worse over less. I'm not going to test it." A shiver runs over me. These damn goosebumps.

14

WHEN THE SUN'S DESCENT casts tree shadows on the ground, our pace slows. We've made it through maybe half of the Blackwood now, probably close to Tunstead; a town near the waterfront that leads to the Veritas Sea. Tunstead has one of the largest populations in Autumn due to its proximity to water and lush forest. It's also not too far from the borders of both Summer and Spring, making the vegetation and climate more diverse.

When chimney smoke from the town comes into view through the last light of the sun, Davian holds his hand up to slow us.

"We'll camp here for the night." He dismounts and brings his horse over to a tree, looping the reins around the base to keep her from running away in the night. The rest of us follow suit and pick out trees in the small clearing to secure our horses.

Hart is the first to wander off, going to look for firewood. This close to Summer, it won't get cold enough to need a fire at night. But if Hart wants to buzz off for a while, I won't be the one to stop him.

Jaali asks the same thing I'm wondering. "Tunstead isn't far from here, why aren't we staying in an inn?"

Davian answers, "Something wrong with being in the great outdoors?"

Jaali rolls his eyes.

"We just got started, here. We've been out less than 48 hours. Can you wait another day?" That seems good enough for Jaali because he gives a small nod with pursed lips.

Pearce is sitting by his horse still, whittling a branch from the forest floor. Whatever he's making doesn't look like much, only a pointed end right now. I move back to Winnie and clear the floor around her legs in case she needs to lie down in the middle of the night. The other side of the tree seems like a perfect place for me to settle down, so I clear the space and take a seat. There's more grass this close to Summer, which is helpful; Autumn floors can be a bit sparse.

I stretch my legs out on the grass with my arms perched behind me. Jaali looks around the floor by his horse. "Does anybody have a pillow?"

Pearce chuckles dryly from where he leans against a tree, hood pulled over his eyes. When he shakes his head, a dark lock of hair peaks out from underneath. It's longer than I expected. Davian laughs as well, arms crossed underneath his head while he lies on a thinner patch of grass. Leaves rustle from behind a bush near us and we all sit up, senses on high alert.

Hart comes through the shrubbery and laughs at us. "Just me, you wusses. Keep the knives away."

With that, we all settle down while Hart finishes lighting the purposeless fire. I attempt to find sleep but struggle without my usual comforts and lush bedding. I can almost hear my silk sheets calling for me.

After a few minutes of trying to decipher if I'm insane, I *do* hear my name being called. One eye cracks open and peers into the dim night. I roll onto my side and jolt when I see Jaali lying much closer than where I last remember seeing him. "What the hell are you doing?" I whisper.

He shrugs. Well, as much as he can with one arm pushed against the ground. "Can't sleep."

"Too bad, go find your own patch to lay on," I say through gritted teeth.

"If you both don't keep quiet, I'm going to throw you in the Veritas." Pearce's words cut through the dark.

My legs rub together, stupidly affected by the sleep in his voice. "We weren't speaking to you," I spit out.

"No but you've woken me up, so now I'm your problem," he bites back. I sit up, propping myself on my elbows to look at him.

"I thought weasels sleep straight through hibernation."

He lifts his still hooded head to look at me through the darkness. The flames in the fire are still burning bright, enough for the light to cast on his concealed face. In the orange glow, I can see his jaw clench beneath his mask.

"They don't. So shut it, both of you." He says and jerks his head toward Jaali for the latter.

"Alright, fine, I'll just go lay over here and stare at the trunk next to my head," Jaali grumbles. He rolls away from me on the ground, a tuck and roll movement. The man is unpredictable and thoroughly entertaining. Visions of flames flickering on a harsh face lull me to sleep.

We rise before the sun in the morning, each of us getting up and tying our things back onto the horses in the quiet of the early light.

"Our goal is to make it past Suncrest Heights by nightfall," Davian announces. That should be easy enough, that area is just past the Autumn line, over a half-day ride from our current position. The hills reach so wide, they occupy both Summer and Spring land. There are small villages on either side; maybe tonight we'll get a real meal.

I look over at Pearce petting his hand over his mare's mane, and it almost looks like he genuinely cares for the animal. I suppose he could, he is an animal himself anyway. Jaali is lying on the back of his horse, fully lounging with his legs out in front of him like he had been on the ground last night.

After I mount Winnie, I pull her in the direction of Jaali. Stopping before he opens his eyes and catches me, I reach out and swat the rear end of his horse. The creature rears onto his hind legs, causing Jaali to roll right off the side and onto the dirt ground.

"What was that for?!" He exclaims.

"Just paying you back for your little scare last night. Disturbing my sleep certainly earned you a roll in the dirt," I snicker. Content with my childish revenge, I set out to follow Davian and Hart as they make their way forward. They clearly aren't concerned for our safety, leaving us to meander in the back. Although if anyone tries to approach us from the rear, I'm sure Pearce will turn them to stone before they do any damage just for closing in on his personal space.

Jaali trots by me just mere seconds later, having righted his position on his horse much quicker than I expected. He throws a vulgar gesture in my direction, and I laugh loudly, uncaring of who looks.

"What's so funny back there?" Hart calls from further up.

"The back of your head," answers Jaali. This earns a boisterous laugh from deep in my chest, so rocking that I almost lose control of Winnie. Hart doesn't dignify our jokes with a response, but since his hood is down, I watch as his ears turn a bright shade of red. His head does have a rather strange shape, now that I'm examining it.

As we get closer to the Veritas Sea, we'll need to keep an eye on the shoreline. Kelpies and sirens frequent the areas nearby, both creatures are known for luring you to a watery grave.

The closer we get to the joining line, the higher the temperature rises. We'll run into both Summer and Spring on our quest, with warm climates all around. That is...until we eventually reach Baeton.

Suncrest comes into view out in the distance and the sun isn't at its highest point yet. We're making excellent time; maybe we can convince Davian to let us stay in a real bed tonight if we make it to Berkton before sundown. It's just past Suncrest Heights, across the Naporia River. The further we get on this trip, I question why we aren't taking a ship across the Veritas Sea. It would make for a much shorter journey; we could dock right on the edge of Baeton and travel up through Spring. When we come to a stop to quickly feed and water the horses, I ask Davian that exact question.

"It would be faster, yes, but it would also give away our position to the humans. They'd be able to see us coming once we got close to the tip of Spring if we arrived by ship. The smartest strategy is what we're doing now: laying low."

We set off again near midday. Suncrest Heights comes into clear view well before sunset. The giant rolling hills are the only feature like it in Alunia, the largest rounded peaks on this side of the Range of Unrest. The green of the mounds fades from a darker aged green to a bright fresh shade in the distance. The hills stretch between both Summer and Spring, affecting what grows in the soil surrounding them. When we come to the border between my home and the adjacent lands, the soil fades from the familiar brownish green to lighter, livelier shades. The shift is gradual, but I know the moment we cross officially into Spring because the temperature eases the slight chill that usually rests on my skin like a cool blanket.

A few more hours, and we are at the base of Suncrest Heights. The hills themselves are spaced fairly far apart when you're actually in them, though they look connected from a distance. We're able to travel in between them without issue, keeping up with our currently set pace. The closest town to our current position is Berkton, so I think now is a good time to ask about a real place to sleep.

"Davian, shall we ride for Berkton for shelter and food? The horses are tired, we need to pace them." I say while stroking Winnie's neck. I'll say anything for a decent night's sleep.

He doesn't stop moving, but he nods. "I think you may be right about the horses. We have a long way to travel tomorrow, and I want them to be well-fed. We'll head that way." I grin underneath my mask, grateful that no one can see my cheesy expression over a hot meal.

There isn't a bridge near that area of the river, but it shouldn't be too deep along the edge of Summer. The heat makes the water levels lower; it will be easier to pass through.

As the sun is beginning to set, we come to the edge of the Naporia River. I look down and see that the water is grazing the bottoms of my boots, so I know the feet of the men around me are soaked. Winnie's coat is wet up to the bottom of her stomach when we emerge.

I see light from inside an inn, confirming they have vacancies. We stride into the stables at the back of the building and arrange our horses for the night. Winnie is mostly dry and comfortable before I leave her at the stable.

We crowd inside the aged wooden building. A fire roars in a makeshift living area, the stone floors harsh after being on soil for so long. Hart marches up to a desk with a glassless window and places his balled fist on it—loudly. How well mannered.

"Five rooms, please. And meals for each of us."

The woman behind the barrier looks us over one by one before responding, likely trying to determine what kind of party we are. We do seem like a very diverse bunch.

"I only got three rooms. One's got two beds; the others have one." She looks down the line of us again. "Should be enough to fit the lot of you." And she wipes her hands down the front of the apron tied around her waist.

Davian and Hart look at each other. "I'll take one bed; you take the other?" Hart questions. Davian nods and then looks to the rest of us.

"You all can figure out your own arrangement. Don't kill each other. I'll come wake you in the morning." Hart snatches a key from the woman, and then the men disappear.

Jaali is next to grab a key. Both Pearce and I shoot daggers at him with our eyes as he calls out, "Good luck, you two!" and bolts up the stairs.

The aproned woman looks at Pearce and says, "If one of you kills the other, clean up after yourselves."

She hands me one small brass key with a single piece of navy ribbon tied to it. "Up the stairs, third door on the left. The dining hall is closed, but I'll have some plates sent up to the door. Listen for a knock," she offers.

"Thank you, miss." My feet stick to each step as I slowly trudge my way up the small, rickety staircase.

The bolt barely clicks open before Pearce tries to push past me to get into the room first. His arm grazes the fabric on my torso, and I gasp softly at the contact. The weasel hears me, his hand hesitating to turn the knob. His eyes slice to mine, the heated amber seeming far too warm to match his demeanor. He turns chest to chest with me, leans his shoulder into the door, and goes in.

He sits on the edge of the bed facing the left wall. The bed isn't quite as large as the one I have at home, but bigger than a child's bed.

Pearce sighs heavily. "If you snore, I'll smother you," and his gaze settles on me like a pile of bricks.

With the warning, I sit on the side of the bed closest to the door. In case he tries to kill me in the night, I have a better chance of escaping.

Facing the wall, Pearce removes his hooded cloak. He lets it fall behind him onto the bed, and I see the back of his head for the first time. His hair is dark like black licorice, with a soft wave pattern. It's not curly like Dessi's, but it has waves like the ocean that reach past his fully pointed ears. It's almost nice.

He goes to remove his face covering when there is a knock at the door. His hands halt, and he goes to open it. Two plates of food sit just outside the opening. Plates in hand, he walks over to me, still sitting on the edge of the bed fully clothed. He holds one out, and I glance up at him from underneath my hood and offer a simple, "Thanks."

"Yeah."

Another knock at the door has Pearce mumbling under his breath. This time when he rips it open, Jaali is standing outside with his plate and pleading eyes.

"I missed you guys. Can I eat in here?"

Pearce looks at him, annoyed, but moves to the side to let him in without a word.

I scarf down my food and pull my mask back on, hardly tasting it but grateful for the substance and full belly.

The men are sitting side by side still facing the wall, intent on giving me some privacy. Not that I'm ashamed of anything, I have on the same underclothes as they do. I remove my boots and cloak to rid the most annoying clothing items first. I start to unbutton the silver globes on the front of my top when Pearce turns his head to the side. His profile is sharp, his strong jaw working to break down his dinner. His lips are pulled to the side so far that there's a small crease forming. Is he smiling? The dim light in this room hollows out the contours of his cheekbones to the point of devastation. He looks haunting. He might be handsome if he wasn't so rude.

When his head starts to turn in my direction, I quickly snap my gaze back to the buttons on my front. I make light work of undoing them and shimmy the long sleeves down my arms, freeing them to the comfortable warmth of the room. Leaving the mask on until I get into bed may make me look foolish, but it's the best option I have right now. I'm not showing these guys what I look like, we're still too close to home.

I go to undo the button on my trousers when I feel a face turn to mine, and eyes scanning me from across the room. I refuse to look up at him and, eventually, I'm able to force my fingers to move again. I'm not sure how I get them undone without stumbling, but when I pull the pants down to my ankles and step out of them, I feel better. Lighter. That is until a flush runs over my entire body.

When I look up at the source of the heat, I see that Pearce hasn't looked away. He seems to snap back to reality and looks back at Jaali who hadn't had a break in speech this entire time.

He must've zoned out during their conversation. I shake off the thought and get under the covers, finally peeling off the mask and tucking it under the pillow for easy access. The bed isn't horrible, it's softer than the ground we were subject to last night. A shower would be lovely, but I know an inn like this would have basins with a dark history. I don't trust the integrity of any bathing room Willow hasn't cleaned. That woman could cleanse dirt from the earth.

After a while of pretending to sleep, I hear hushed whispers from the two men still sitting on the edge of the bed, facing the pathetic fireplace on the opposite wall. I roll over as quietly as I can and aim my ear in their direction.

If they wanted privacy so badly, they should've made sure I was actually sleeping or gone out in the hall.

Once I'm settled and the thin quilt doesn't make any more noise, their conversation resumes.

"You could lighten up, you know? We have to be with these people for a fortnight at the *least*. You might as well be civil."

A short grunt is Pearce's first response. "I've been plenty civil. They all still have their heads."

"And they'll still have them when we return. Except maybe Hart... He's a real ass. Roan though, she's nice. She's got the wit to keep up with me and that takes most people a vast amount of effort." I smile even though they can't see me.

"I don't like it."

"Like what, her?"

"We were told they weren't filling that spot. She's just one more set of eyes that will be looking at the two of us too closely when we get to Baeton. It was hard enough to get on this crew. I want to know how she got here. That story she gave Davian seemed too convenient."

The weasel...

"She could think the same thing about us, though, Pearce. Quit it with the attitude before you *give* them a reason to look into us."

What about him is so special that he thinks I'd waste my time paying attention to him?

"Alright, fine." He says with a huff.

I close my eyes again, afraid he'll be able to see them if he looks over. I didn't expect to make friends with any of these people, but Pearce has been questioning my place on this mission since before it even started. An agonizing thorn in my side, and a danger to my operation.

If he knew who I was, he could say the same thing about me.

I squeeze my eyes tighter like that will make me fall asleep faster and make me forget what I've heard.

Jaali finally goes to his room which stirs me again. I don't feel the bed move once the door closes. When I turn over, the other side of the bed is still empty.

"Pearce?" I whisper into the dark space.

Nothing.

"*Psst.*"

"What."

"Where the hell are you?"

"On the floor."

He can't be serious.

"It's probably filthy down there, what are you doing? Just get in the bed, you idiot."

"I'm good."

"Fine, have it your way. Get no sleep and smell awful come morning. More room for me."

A heavy sigh.

And then...wood creaking.

The bed shifts beneath me, and suddenly I'm sinking toward the middle.

My shoulder brushes against the outside of his arm, and the ice of his skin sends a tremor through my body.

"You're freezing."

"Are you not done talking? I'm off the floor. Take your win, and shut up."

I huff, frustrated, and readjust myself on the bed with his added weight. In doing so, I accidentally graze his thigh with my backside. There's no wondering if he felt it. His breathing halts and his muscles tense. No air moves in the room.

I choose to stay still, feigning ignorance instead of stirring up another meaningless tiff and causing us both to lose sleep. After a moment, his breathing resumes. We lay that way until I finally doze off.

15

KNUCKLES WRAPPING AT THE door is what wakes me. I look around the room to find Pearce already dressed and putting on his boots. I didn't even hear him get up. My hand quickly finds my mask and puts it in place before I face him.

"Grab food if you need it and meet us by the horses as soon as possible," Davian commands from outside the door.

Jaali comes into our room, chipper as ever, not sensing the palpable tension.

I place my foot on the side of the bed closest to the door and reach for my pile of clothes on the chest next to it. I pull on my trousers first, covering the cotton undershorts of the uniform. The buttons move much quicker this time and I shrug on my coat and cloak.

The three of us leave the room together and I take the key back to where the woman from last night sits with a tray of miscellaneous foods. "Glad to see you all made it," she says.

I smile back at her even though she can't see it, and hand her the room key. "Yes, it seems we all remained in one piece." I joke.

Jaali points to the food in front of her. "Where might we find some of that?"

She nods her head behind us to the right. "Back that way. Take what you need, the rest of your friends are waiting for you outside."

Dry pastries and nuts of various kinds are scattered on a long wooden table. Bitter oranges, grapes, and apricots are some of the only fruits that grow in Spring, and they fill the other spaces. I only grab what looks appetizing. While I recognize these foods from my travels, the kitchen at home always has something to my taste. I miss the dining room right now. Jaali grabs more than the rest of us, eating on our way out. I nod at the aproned woman one last time before exiting the building, and we catch up to Davian and Hart.

Winnie is excited to see me, proving her namesake to still be true. She was incredibly boisterous as a foal, and she remains that way to this day. We make quick work of our breakfast and I slip Winnie a few bites of mine, knowing she prefers something sweet.

Once we're back on the trail, we start heading toward the land bridge between the two sides of Spring territory. The pixies insisted on having a piece of land that touched both Summer and Autumn as payment for being so close to the human kingdom. Summer isn't greedy, they didn't mind. As long as the swamps remained in their territory, they were fine with the loss of land.

We should reach the Spring castle tomorrow if we keep our quickened pace. The temperature is even nicer in Spring than our current location; it's one of my favorite places in Alunia.

After hours of quiet and uneventful riding, we spot a lake not far ahead. It's in the middle of a land bridge, water from the Veritas and the outer coasts mix there making a pool of clear, cool water. When Hart realizes what's in front of us, he shouts, "Oh, thank the Gods. I need a rinse," and heads in that direction. Davian looks back at the rest of our hopeful faces and looks up at the clouds with a sigh.

"Fine, go. But be quick about it, we need to cover a lot of ground today to reach Caelfall at a reasonable hour tomorrow."

Jaali and I both book it toward the small lake that Hart is already waist-deep in. It's the most peaceful I've seen his face, yet. Pearce follows at a more reasonable pace and steps down from his horse. I find my own space on the edge of the water and peel my boots off my cramping feet. Stirrups are not the most comfortable thing to be in for long periods.

I throw my boots off to the side on the grass and peel off my jacket, tossing that to the side as well. I decide to rinse my hair in the water since everyone will be too caught up in themselves to take notice of me. After days of sweating from riding, and the pollen of being in different regions, my hair feels no smoother than straw. The grass is soft against my back as I scoot my head into the edge of the water until my head is hanging off the side, and my hair is fully submerged. There's a steep drop off, almost clifflike into the water. If I look back hard enough, I can see my hair floating out like reddish-blonde seaweed behind me. I might as well lay here for a minute, let it steep.

After a bit of peaceful soaking, I hear a plop in the water not far from me. I look over to Pearce sloppily throwing water on his face as he kneels on the edge. He cups his hands, lets water fill them, and throws the water at his face. Most of it hits his target, but a few droplets land on my forehead and mask.

"Could you do that somewhere else? I'm lying here."

The sound of moving water stops. I peek one eye open and see that he is once again cupping water, but he doesn't splash it on his face. He throws it directly at mine, soaking me from the chest up.

I gasp from the splash against my skin and sit up immediately, my wet hair coating my back. "Really? Now I'm thoroughly soaked, dammit."

"I can have that effect," he says from where he kneels.

Grunting angrily, I get to my knees with my hair dripping behind me. I look over at my top and boots, which didn't make it out un-scathed. "Those might not be dry by the time we leave," I groan.

"Maybe not. Guess you should go home since you're complaining about something as trivial as wet clothes."

Air huffs through my nose as I graze the front of my teeth with my tongue. And I have an idea...

I whip my head forward, flinging my soaking wet hair onto Pearce. The flinch on his face tells me my aim was good enough for petty payback. When I try to whip my head back over, he catches my hair in his fist, preventing me from straightening.

"You really shouldn't have done that," he growls. He pulls me forward by my hair until my face is over the river.

"What the hell are you doing?" I say as I try to squirm free of his hold. It doesn't work, and he pulls on the strands, tugging my roots.

Pearce lowers his head next to mine, his lips almost brushing my ear. "I told you we don't need you here. If you won't leave, I'll *make* you."

He starts to push my head toward the water, and I resist as much as I can against his grip.

"Pearce, stop, this isn't funny." It's more annoying than anything else. His hold on my hair is bruising, and I swat away the wish that this was happening under different circumstances.

"Is that how you ask for something? I think you're supposed to use a certain word." When he pushes down again, I give in. "Please!"

He halts, his grip still firm on my hair. "Please, what? I don't think I can hear you well enough, I'm unsure of what you want from me."

I squeeze my eyes shut to prevent my tears of frustration from slipping free. This is ridiculous. I'm not going to beg him for anything.

He realizes that too. With his bruising grip on my head, he shoves my face beneath the surface of the water. Not freaking out is paramount; I can't let him know how much he's affecting me. I start to panic, despite my wishes. My mask sticks to my cheeks and nose, suffocating me.

When he finally decides to grace me with clean air, I cough up more water than I expect to and catch my breath before pleading desperately. "Please, let me go," every word clipped and muffled by the dripping facial covering.

"That's better." He straightens me so I'm kneeling upright over dry land again before he lets go of my hair.

"What the hell is wrong with you?" I mumble, frustration flowing freely.

"The list of what *isn't* would be much shorter," he replies.

I stand and grab my shirt from where I threw it and start to walk away.

Who does he think he is?

Before I can stop myself, I'm turning around back toward the river. I drop my top on the ground again to at least keep *that* somewhat dry after what I'm doing. He turns around to face me, confusion pinching his brows together. I continue stomping right up to him. He holds up his hands in surrender, or to push me, before I use every ounce of strength I have to shove his body into the river. He's huge, so the splash is loud.

"What the hell is going on over here!?" Davian shouts as he runs over from wherever he was when I almost suffocated.

I shrug my shoulders and look right into his eyes. "He tripped," I lie.

"Quit this nonsense, boy, and stop playing in the water. We need to rest well tonight so we can close the gap between us and the border." He storms back off to his menial task while shaking his head.

Pearce is tall enough to reach the bottom of the lake. The water goes up to his chest, and his hair sticks to his face and neck. If only he weren't such a nuisance.

I check the area to see if anyone else has turned around to see the progression of our shenanigans, and a wet hand wraps around my ankle. I look down a moment too late and all of a sudden, I'm being yanked into the river. I topple onto him, and we crash into the cool water. Once my feet reach the floor, I flatten them and push myself up as hard as I can. When my head breaks the surface, I immediately start to cough up water. I'm a capable swimmer but being thrust into the water unprepared doesn't allow for breathing technique.

Strong hands clamp onto the sides of my waist and hold me steady, keeping my head above the water. Holding me is a disturbed Pearce. "Let me go," I seethe.

"Still haven't learned to say please, have you?" I clench my jaw under my mask, and his eyes flicker down. His gaze lingers there for a moment before tracing along the edge of my face as if he can see through the mask.

"Please," I seethe, looking into his scalding eyes.

"Please, what? Use your words." He finally looks from my covered lips to my eyes and holds my stare.

I'm suddenly all too aware of his hands still firmly on my hips. "I'd like to get out now."

Pearce's eyes flick down one more time before he hoists me up to sit on the ground. His grip lingers on my sides for a moment. He seems to remember himself and drops his hands, places them on the ground, and hops out of the water like it's a single step. He storms away, water pouring off him.

Once I've cooled off enough that my heart resumes its normal pace, I dry off and mount Winnie. She can sense the change in energy, her movements as skittish as my thoughts. I feel his stare on me as I tighten my few belongings to Winnie's harness. The man has hardly said a full paragraph to me, yet he inspects me as if I both infuriate and intrigue him.

The rest of the men finally exit the lake and don their clothing. Jaali rides his horse over to me and casually chirps, "Man, I feel better. Relaxed. You?"

"I feel incredibly frustrated," I bite back.

"How can you be frustrated after a bath in the great outdoors?" His cheery timbre implies he didn't see anything that occurred in the water, which eases some of the embarrassment. He shrugs and starts onward, falling in behind Hart and Davian.

I take my place in the line of movement and stiffen when I feel Pearce's presence behind me. A shiver runs through my entire being when I close my eyes and feel almost like I'm back under the water.

I tilt my head side to side, stretching my neck to ease the tension rebuilding there. He lets out a husky breath behind me, and the goosebumps return. The lake's cool water did nothing to soothe me.

Sometime after first light, Caelfall becomes the slightest bit visible. By the time the sun lowers behind the horizon, we're met at the small, unassuming gate that surrounds the Spring castle. The Ladies of Caelfall have sent out a receiving party, having recognized that we are no threat. I adjust my face covering to make sure I'm concealed and pull my hood slightly further down my forehead. I wasn't aware that we'd be stopping by the castle; I thought we'd merely been using it as a landmark.

The wind in my sails deflates. Lady Nymeria and Lady Indigo haven't seen me in years. Surely, they would recognize me, knowing my parents as long as they have. I'll have to avoid direct contact with them. Davian goes ahead of the group to greet the steward before us.

They converse for a while before the steward announces that we'll be following him to the stables before we are shown to our rooms.

When Davian turns back to us, his face hardens. "Our rooms? What's this, another delay?" Hart questions.

He exhales sharply. "Unfortunately, yes. The Ladies of Caelfall have insisted that we attend a small party tonight. I informed them of our instructions and that we will need to enter through their land connection to Baeton. They said their payment for such a thing is to drink with them. They *also* insist that we wait to leave until morning. A tedious but minuscule price to pay for accessing a less traveled side of the human kingdom." He mounts his horse and trails after the steward showing us the way.

Dinner and drinks? How am I supposed to avoid recognition if we're meant to stay overnight? I'll have to keep a low profile throughout the evening.

Once I ensure Winnie is comfortable, I join the rest of the group outside the stables with the steward. Hapley, he says his name is. Hapley has us follow him in a single file down the dimly lit hall and up the stone stairs. The Ladies must be occupied, sending a receiving party in their absence. Maybe they won't be able to make dinner after all.

16

ALL OF US ARE pointed towards our rooms, each of them with a private bathing room, Haply points out. *Finally*. Before he leaves us alone, he says, "There are clothes in the closets of each of your rooms. Please, after you get a chance to bathe, pick whatever you'd like to wear for the party tonight. We'll have your uniforms laundered before the morning." My heart sinks like an anvil. I won't be able to wear my hood?

My head tilts to the left and right, Jaali and Pearce's rooms on either side of mine. We open our doors in unison, and I'm greeted with the scent of sage and citrus. The room is elegant, yet simple. Nymeria and Indigo have always had exquisite taste, sticking to a Spring color palette of pinks, yellows, and soft greens for décor. This room is no different. I stroll over to the bed and decide to undress before sitting on clean linens in dirty clothes. The sleeves peel from my arms due to the warmer climate before I fold the rest of the clothing and leave it by the door with my boots like Hapley instructed.

The copper tub has several scented liquids on the side of it, and I drop them in the water generously as I would in my baths at home. Once the water is scalding enough to melt my tension, I lower myself to my shoulders. A few deep breaths allow the smells of jasmine and vanilla to fill my nose and seep into my sore muscles. It pulls at my heart, and I sit for a while, imagining what Dessielle might be doing right now. She's probably doing the same as me, actually. She would soak for hours if her skin wouldn't prune. "Pruned fingers can't play music", she tells me. Dessi is terrified of wrinkles, despite being centuries away from the formation of one.

When I'm satisfied with the cleanliness of my skin, I move on to my hair. I hadn't realized how much I miss Willow until my arms tire from scrubbing my roots. I submerge my head in the bath, and a memory flashes in my head of Pearce forcing the same upon me in the lake. I gasp underneath the surface and sit up to eject the water from my throat in a fit. After I finish hacking and can breathe somewhat regularly, I decide it's best to leave the bath and find something to wear to this party.

Hapley wasn't joking, the closet is *filled* with garments. There are pieces for both masculine and feminine frames in a range of sizes. I trail my hand along the edges of the racks and stop when I feel silk. The almost black dress is floor length with a slit far up the right side. There is only one side to the neckline, going over the left shoulder. I pull the dress to my torso and look down at the shape of it. It looks like it would fit, so I remove the dress from the hanger and slip it on.

The bodice practically molds to me. The neckline is perhaps a bit too low for a dinner party... Which means Dessi would vote *yes*. I look at my silhouette in the mirror. My chest is constrained in the unforgiving material at the neckline, making even my lacking breasts spill over the fabric a bit. My right leg is completely exposed, the slit ending right underneath my hipbone. The fabric is a deep midnight blue, the shape of the dress speaking louder than any pattern.

I find a pot of black pigment in a vanity drawer and use it to enhance my eyes and lashes. The vanity doesn't have my color rouge, so I decide against it. No one will be looking at me, anyway. I pull my bottom lip between my teeth before painting my lips just a touch deeper than their normal color.

I throw on a pair of simple black-heeled shoes before I change my mind and wear something more subdued. I've never been one to shy away from a challenge, and I don't plan on starting now.

Hapley advised us to come down as soon as we were ready, but when I step back into the hall, everyone else seems to have finished before me. I hear voices traveling from down the stairs, pulling me toward the revelry. When I enter the room, the sound drops several levels. Jaali is standing in front of Pearce, and even he stops mid-sentence to look up at me. Jaali jabs Pearce with his index finger and points in my direction. When his gaze locks with mine, an unfamiliar fire ignites in his amber eyes.

Conversation resumes with everyone but Jaali and Pearce, the latter still staring at me. His knuckles turn bone-white from their grip on his glass. I scan his face for any hint of annoyance, but for the first time since we met, I find none.

My eyes are molasses as they trail down over his outfit choice for the evening. His trousers swallow any light shining on them, a soulless black. The sleeves of the deep blue shirt he wears are rolled up a bit, exposing the veins in his forearms. Despite this being a party in a castle, the buttons on his chest aren't fully done. His marked chest peaks out from underneath the silk. Peppered under the scares are inked words that I don't recognize, and various rune-looking symbols.

In what feels like another battle of will, I walk directly toward the two men without breaking his stare, my face heating under Pearce's gaze. Jaali is the first to speak.

"Alright, Roan! Without the mask, you look great! I didn't know you had it in you. You look rosy and everything. I wish my bath did that," he chuckles.

The back of my hand meets my cheek to cool it down. So much for not applying any rouge.

His comment earns an unapproved snort from me before my hand can stifle it. "I think it would take more than a bath for all that," I retort, and he throws his head back in laughter.

Pearce shifts his weight uncomfortably from one foot to the other. His lips part and I fear that he'll comment on my appearance as well, but he says nothing. He simply takes another sip from his glass.

Someone taps a piece of cutlery on their glass, our cue to find our seats at the long table in the center of the room. I tip my chin down and gather details from the woodgrain when the Ladies of Caelfall enter the room hand in hand. They take the two empty seats at one head of the table, sitting together instead of separated. Lady Nymeria clears her throat.

"Thank you for joining us this evening, brave travelers. When we heard you would be trekking through Caelfall on your mission, we knew we must extend our hospitality. Tonight, we celebrate a great day for Spring: the commencement of our Spring harvest season." The room responds with a cheerful round of applause that we imitate.

"You've arrived on a magnificent day, as the meal we'll share is comprised of our greatest seasonal produce. So please, rest from your journey tonight. But not before joining us in celebration." Her eyes roam around the room, landing on me. Her eyes squint the slightest bit with recognition, yet she says nothing else and takes her seat.

Oh dear.

She leans over to Indigo and whispers something to her, inaudible over the chatter around the table. Neither of them looks at me again, and I calm my breathing. Maybe they don't recognize me after all. She could've whispered any number of things to her wife.

Pearce sits across from me at the table, Jaali to his right. Pearce is looking at the head of the table as well, and then his gaze shifts to me. A question sits on the tip of his tongue, I can see the fog curling out of his mind. Yet he says nothing and turns his attention to the food being placed in front of him. He's the last person I want to look at me too closely.

Dinner is filled with light conversation about our travels so far and what we're doing so far from home. Davian spins a false tale about us patrolling the Range of Unrest on our side to make sure no humans are trying to come through. Something close to the truth, but not entirely. If every species in Alunia knew of this journey, there's no telling what kind of feedback would make its way to the crown.

Once dinner is finished, the table is cleared of any used dishes and music starts to play from a piano I hadn't realized was there.

People get up and move about the room, some switch seats and others stand and make conversation. It seems like the formality of dinner is gone, and now a more casual gathering is taking place. My heart seizes when Lady Nymeria stands and starts to make her way towards me. None of the Spring natives seem concerned by this, not even sparing her a glance as she moves about the room.

Nymeria takes the seat on my right, which became abandoned once the music started. In a voice just loud enough for me to hear, she speaks. "Someone is far away from home, aren't they?"

Well, that's it. She's going to end my little charade and I'll be sent home. "I'm unsure what you mean, my lady."

The keeper of Spring glares at me from behind the warm brown curls lying over her brows. "Surely I would have heard from a certain Queen and King if they knew I should be expecting a royal visit," she says.

I attempt to slow my breathing, aware of Pearce's attention. "I'm sure you would have, my lady. They would certainly keep you informed," I try.

Lady Nymeria lets out a soft breath from her nose. "I am assuming they have no idea you're here, then."

Unwilling to continue maintaining my ruse with her, I let out an exasperated breath. "No, they don't. Please don't tell them, I've come too far to be sent back now." I finally look into her eyes, hoping the sincerity in them is enough for her to grant me this.

She purses her lips. "Your father won't be happy about this, you know. He forbade it this long for a reason, Raelenthia. And to disobey him like this?"

I look down at my hands, unsure of how to respond when the truth is presented to me.

"Wilder will be sad to hear he missed you." I look up to see her smiling softly.

"You won't send me home?"

"I'm not going to lie to your parents if they ask. But I understand your need to try. Don't tell me anything else. The less I know, the better. Be safe, please. Stay with the guards and don't stray off." She looks to her wife, still seated at the table head. I follow her gaze to find Lady Indigo with a smirk on her face, shaking her head at me. Lady Nymeria calls my attention back to her by saying, "You thought we wouldn't recognize that hair? How did you even make it this far without the guards realizing who rides with them?"

I chuckle softly. "Pure luck. The guards are from the outer portions of the kingdom, they aren't near the castle much. I doubt they've ever seen me in person, aside from maybe a birthday celebration decades ago. Our uniform consists of a mask and hood. They made it too easy."

She laughs as well, finding it just as amusing as me that I was able to make it this far. "Get back to your family as soon as possible. And for the love of Alunia, please check on that man. He's been boring holes into your head since you first entered the room." I don't need to look around to know exactly who she's talking about; his gaze is debilitating. He'll surely have questions about why the Lady of Caelfall would seek me out for conversation.

I feel blood rush to my cheeks as I recall all the infuriating things he's said since our meeting. "He's...horrible. He's barbaric and hard to read. I'll be glad to never see him again."

She looks over at him, and he averts his attention to the conversation happening to his left as if he had been involved this entire time. "We must be reading different books, then. I could pierce the tension with a pine needle. Men like that have a bigger bark than bite." She stands without waiting for a rebuttal and travels back to sit next to her wife. She takes Indigo's hand and places a sweet peck on her knuckles.

When I finally look at him, he is once again staring. The eyes that have previously only been merciless and unforgiving show what someone might mistake for yearning. I get the feeling the man across from me hasn't yearned for anything other than violence in his life. A pine needle... Lady Nymeria hasn't been around the buffoon long enough to know that he's impossible.

His jaw clenches, and I see his eyes flicker down. When he turns back to the conversation he keeps pretending to be involved in, I can't help staring for another brief moment.

Once the conversation idles among the group, Lady Indigo dismisses the party for the night and thanks us for joining their harvest celebration. She insists on shaking the hands of the entire party and now reaches for mine. When I place my hand in hers, she uses it to pull me closer to her. "It was good to see you, Raelenthia," she murmurs.

The corner of my mouth lifts slightly. "You as well, Lady Indigo." She releases my hand and exits the room with her wife, the evening officially over.

I turn the corner to exit the now-empty dining room and am met with a hard torso. I place my hands out in front of me to regain my balance, and my hands slip over silk fabric.

Gods...

I look up to find I'm standing face-to-chest with none other than Pearce. The sudden meeting makes my breath quicken, now ragged and uneven.

"They seemed to find you rather interesting. Why would they think that, huh?" he questions.

I hastily remove my hands from his chest and step back, putting any distance between us. I clear my throat and manage to regain some composure despite the heat I feel in my ears. "They expressed their joy over seeing a woman on a mission. They are the only noble couple of the same gender, so they told me to take pride in my position," I lie easily, impressing myself.

His tongue pokes his cheek as he nods, contemplating. "Right, right... Well, I guess I'll see you tomorrow."

He goes to turn away, and I snap my hand to his shoulder, holding him in place. A quick look around the immediate area is enough for me to have this conversation. He slowly turns to face me.

"What did you hear?" I say through gritted teeth.

"I don't think I know what you mean. I heard nothing of great interest, given the subject matter. Just...old colleagues catching up, it would seem."

This little...

"Care to explain how some *nobody* knight, new to the guard and assigned to her first mission, has Ladies as friends?" He sneers.

"Who told you this is my first mission?" I snap and rip my hand down from where it still sat on his arm.

The weasel smirks. "You did, just now. I had my suspicions but that all but confirms it. How did you get on this force, *Roan*?" His stare is unrelenting.

My breathing faults again, agonizingly labored. "I'm not going to answer that."

Pearce clenches his jaw, and outlines my features with his eyes, painstakingly slow. I can almost see the thoughts forming in his mind, and then he smirks. I start to walk toward my room, smacking my shoulder against his massive arm when I pass.

I barely make it a few steps away before he says too loudly, "But of course...*princess.*"

I freeze. This can't be happening. I turn slowly, my heart refusing to beat in my chest. He faces me directly, challenging me.

"I have no clue what you're talking about. These are serious accusations, and you should stop before we get in trouble."

"In trouble? Why would I get in trouble? I'm supposed to be here. You, on the other hand..."

"Keep your voice down. I'm not joking," I plead with him. It falls on deaf ears.

"Aren't princesses supposed to be rule followers? How would dear Mother and Father feel about their fragile little girl running away from home?"

"I'm not fragile. And I'm not a princess, so bite your tongue. This conversation is pointless, you're wasting your breath. We should both just go to our rooms."

He bows at the hips and replies, "Yes, Your Highness. Would you like me to escort you to your room, as well?"

"Pearce, I'm serious."

"So am I. Leave."

A hushed scoff escapes me. "You're out of your mind. We're so close, I'm not going back now."

He stands over me, brooding with his arms crossed over his chest. He says nothing.

I sigh, defeated. "You will mention this to no one. We'll finally be going into Baeton tomorrow and the last thing everyone needs is to be rattled about my *identity* of all things. Let me have this." He doesn't respond at first, just stands there, menacing.

"And if I do tell them? Will you send me to prison, princess?" The smirk on his face is unmistakable. He's thrilled to have something against me.

"Maybe I will," I bluff. "It would be in your best interest to cooperate." I hope he can't hear the fear that laces my words.

"What's in it for me?"

"I just told you; not going to prison," I say with all the gusto I can gather at the moment. He tsks and shakes his head as he stalks toward me.

"I think my silence is worth a heftier price, don't you?" He's toe to toe with me, peering down at me heavily.

Resentment bleeds into my voice, conceding. "What do you want?"

He takes a step away and then moves behind my back. He's circling me. I watch as his eyes slowly fall down my figure before dragging back to meet mine. "That's a dangerous question, don't you think?" I roll my eyes in response. "I want a lot of things." He surveys my features, gauging how far he can push this.

"Money? Title? Land? Just get on with it," I push.

"A favor," he says in a hushed tone. My brow pinches.

"A favor? That's it?" His mouth curls to the side, prideful. "You won't tell anyone who I am, in return for a *favor*. That seems a bit lackluster, to me, if I'm being honest. What's the catch?"

"Does there need to be a catch? I can't just do a good deed for a simple exchange?"

"I doubt anything with you is simple. You're extremely tedious," I groan.

"I get to decide the favor, of course. And I get to cash it in at a time of my choosing. Anything I want."

My mouth falls open. "That's ridiculous, I'm not agreeing to that." Does he think I'm that stupid?

He chuckles and shakes his head. "I'll need a bit more time to decide that, princess."

"Stop calling me that, someone might hear you." The back of my hand stings after I smack his shoulder with it. When I look up at him, he's smirking at me.

He's enjoying this.

"I'll let you know when I've decided." He sticks his hand out into the limited space between us and inclines his head. I look down at it but fail to comprehend the last minute.

"How do I know you'll honor this?" I utter, almost in disbelief. This man is not my ally; he's taken every opportunity to remind me how little he thinks of me. This seems like a bad idea.

"You have my word…Roan."

Apparently, I *am* that stupid. I place my hand firmly in his and shake. "Don't make me regret this. "

17

MY CLOTHES ARE NEATLY folded on the small wooden stool by the door of my room. I lift the top to my face and breathe in, notes of lilies and rainwater filling my nose. Laundered, just like they promised. I dress quickly in the stillness of the morning, absorbing the last few moments of peace before entering Baeton. As I'm finishing up, a knock at the door cuts through the quiet I've been wading in.

Davian's voice sounds from the other side. "Stables, now."

I throw Dessielle's bag over my shoulder and head out the door. The hall is empty, and I'm grateful I don't have to face anyone too early in the day after the events of last night.

Did the others notice the nobles' interest in me? If they did, they kept it to themselves. Maybe they don't want to cause a stir at the last stretch before enemy lines. I have the same wish, which is why I—Oh dear.

I promised him a favor.

What kind of favor would he even need? He'll probably want me to clean his home until the next solstice or tell my parents false tales of his bravery and secure him a title better than he deserves.

Except, he said he didn't want notoriety or land. What would someone like him bargain his secrecy for?

I quickly make my way over to the stables, but not before stopping by the kitchen to grab a last-minute muffin for the trip. It has chocolate bits in it, Roralei's favorite. My stomach clenches at the thought of my sister. Has she started the piece she said she'd make for me? I'll have enough stories to repay her for my absence.

The air is cooler on this side of Spring, being so close to Baeton. I didn't realize it yesterday because of the gradual temperature change from traveling, but after being in a cozy bed all night it's impossible not to notice.

The men are finishing up readying their horses when I arrive at the stables.

"I hope everyone slept well because that was the last night of comfort you'll get for a bit," Davian warns. "The Range of Unrest is exactly as it sounds. The field of mountains separates us from the humans. Terrainers made it to keep us apart for a reason, so passing through it is meant to be difficult."

Hart chimes in next. "Once we're past the range, there are no bridges. We avoided direct exposure by coming around this side of the line. We'll have to pass by a few surrounding villages, but our uniforms should be enough to keep them at bay; as long as they only see us from a distance. If they catch a glimpse of our ears they'll sound the alarms. Hoods remain up at all times."

I look around, and it finally dawns on me why we're wearing gray instead of the autumnal warm-colored battle clothing: these must be replicas of Baeton's guard uniforms.

Davian takes the floor again. "Our first goal is to get to the castle. They have slave quarters on the back of the structure that lead to working hallways. Royals don't use them, but other guards will be patrolling. You are to keep your masks on. Do you understand?"

We all nod, acknowledging the severity. "Good. Now hurry up, we need to get moving. We'll likely have to camp in the mountains tonight, so say goodbye to warm beds for a while."

I waste no time getting on Winnie and falling in line. The sooner we leave, the further we can make it in the mountains before nightfall.

The Spring scenery is beautiful. There are bright greens all around, rolling hills, and lush plant life. Spring has several islands just off its coast, a bridge connects the mainland to one of the islands. That island is where the pixies spend most of their time; they've taken over the marshes that dominate that landscape.

It doesn't take long before Jaali decides to start singing. He's not half bad, but it seems like the rest of the group would rather have their horses stomp on them repeatedly than listen to *Pixie Girl* one more time. In the short amount of time we've been back on the road, he's sung through it twice.

"Will you shut it, back there? I can't think over that nonsense," Hart barks.

"You'd like me to stop singing? Sure, I'll stop singing," offers Jaali.

And then he starts whistling.

"I'm going to kill him, Davian."

"You're going to do nothing of the sort. He's supposed to be a great fighter, we'll need him if things go south in the castle."

I lean forward to pester Jaali. "A great fighter, huh? Do you prefer swords or daggers?"

He scoffs and turns his head to face me. "I'm more of a hand-to-hand man. I'm trained in physical combat. It also helps that I'm wicked flexible," he says with a wink.

Pearce lets out what sounds like a mix between a scoff and a laugh. "Be forthcoming with your truth Jaali, tell her who taught you in the first place."

"Hmm... You know what, I'm not sure I remember. I think I learned in a dream or something—"

"You're going to dream deeply when I knock you unconscious."

I whip my head around to look at him. "Must you be so aggressive?"

He smirks at me, his eyes vibrant. "Always, *princess*," he says, mouthing the last word. I scowl back at him, angry that he's testing me, yet also flustered at the intensity of his stare. I turn back around before I can think about that last part too much.

"Will all of you just—think quietly to yourselves? Is that so challenging?" Davian pleads from the front.

Jaali falls backward in line, riding at my side now. My brows pinch, and he shrugs. "If Hart gets to have a buddy, I get one too. Grumpy-pants back there won't want me, so you're my next best option."

The right side of my mouth lifts. "Second place, huh? I'm flattered."

"Oh, you should be. It's an honor and a privilege, I'm sure."

We fall into a peaceful silence, no one humming or fighting. The occasional whistle sounds here and there, but only in quick bursts before a hush falls over us again. The mountains are becoming clearer, no longer a haze in the distance. The peaks reach just below the clouds, nowhere near as impressive as the Cosima Mountains near my home, but beautiful, nonetheless.

Around midday, we stop so the horses can have a bit of food and water. They only eat little by little, so we have to stop every few hours to make sure they're still alright to travel. Not like they could voice otherwise. I'd insist on it if we didn't.

In the distance to our left, I can make out faint smoke from the nearby village, Tarrin, if I remember correctly. Shades of green blend together in a blur after so long, which hopefully means we're covering distance quickly. We're set to reach the peaks by sundown; it's getting through them that will be the tedious part. There is no clear path through the mountains, we'll have to navigate through natural paths and guide the horses safely through the Fae-made formation.

We arrive at the base of the range as the sun dips below the horizon, hues of blue painting our surroundings through snow-capped peaks.

"We won't stop here; I want us to make some headway before retiring for the night. When I decide that it's too dark, we'll stop moving for the safety of our travel companions," Davian states as he strokes the horse beneath him. Without a response from the party, he starts forward again, leaving no room for rebuttal.

There are small, unmarked paths through the dirt and rock on this side of the mountain. Travel in either direction is extremely uncommon, which means no set road through the terrain has ever been established. The mountains in this part of the continent are lighter than the rest of Alunia due to the chill and snow from the other side of the mountains.

When it gets dark to the point of restricted vision, Davian halts us again. "This is where we'll stop. The area is flat enough, and we're far enough from the other side to not easily be found." We're about a quarter up the side of a mountain. Many are connected at different points with small bridge-like formations connecting the peaks at varying heights.

In the distance, I can see fires lit in Spring. This close to the kingdom's border, the temperatures are much cooler than any other part of the region. Aside from distant fire, the only light around us is the stars above.

The men decide that it's best to not risk a fire tonight because of our proximity to Baeton. It's because of this proximity, though, that they are in desperate need of a fire. My appendages protest every moment from exhaustion, but my fingers aren't frozen in my gloves like the males I travel with.

Hart's teeth chattering can be heard from my sleeping position, and I have half a mind to stuff his face covering into his mouth. In the darkness blanketing the world, I can see the breath leave my mouth. I grind my teeth, not from the cold, but from the heavy feeling of unease hovering over me like a storm cloud.

Jaali is close by with his back toward me. I can just make out the rise and fall of his body as he lies on his side, and I'm jealous that sleep seems to find him so easily.

I roll onto my back to gaze at the stars. Since I can't seem to get comfortable, I might as well look at the sky instead of the back of men who already seem to have collected a decent amount of filth in only a day. After a while of staring into the abyss filled with pockets of light, I feel a presence to my left in the dark. I tilt my head slightly in that direction, and I'm surprised to see that Pearce seems to be facing the same dilemma I am. He feels my stare on him and meets my gaze for a moment before turning away, putting his back to me.

I let out a small huff. "Really? You can't even bear to look at me in the dark?"

After a moment, he rolls onto his side to face me fully. "I'd rather lay elsewhere but Davian insisted we keep our traveling order during sleep in the mountains for whatever reason. So forgive me for trying to get some rest instead of staring at you like you seem to wish."

His words sting a bit, and I can't place why. Did I want him to be looking at me? Why *am* I irritated that he rolled away?

With an exasperated sigh, I move onto my back again and shut my eyes. "I don't know, Pearce. Never mind."

He stays on his side, though, facing me.

"Why did you come?" He whispers.

Eyes still closed, I respond with a question of my own. "Have you ever left Alunia?

"I have."

"Well, I haven't. I've never left. I've been here my entire life."

"Given your status, that sounds about right," he spits.

"I suppose it does. Or it *would* if my father was born Fae. I'm half human." He doesn't speak, waiting for me to finish my thoughts. "I've never been allowed to see where my father came from. Where half of my lineage stems. It's not common for Fae and humans to be together, especially after the Great War. It's also uncommon for there to be children born from those unions. I'm not the standard, I'm...the outlier.

There's an entire side to my life that I've never seen because my parents forbade it. I've heard the stories, I've read the history books; I know what happened. I know it's not safe. But I just..."

"You need to see for yourself." He murmurs more to himself than me.

A sigh leaves me. "Exactly." I roll over on my side, facing him again when his words hit me. "Why the sudden interest in me?"

A huff of air blows into the cool night. "Well, it seems that you're not leaving. You're impossible to ignore, you're relentless in your chatting."

I rub my hands down my face, exasperated. "There's just so much I haven't seen. I was reading a book before coming here about some utopia. Obviously, a place like that doesn't really exist, but it got me thinking... How do I know what isn't real?

I've seen so little of this world, there could be a perfect place out there for me. A place where I can have a purpose besides just being a princess."

He nods as if he understands. "Where'd you hear about this utopia?" he says.

The stars regain my attention, and I become lost in them as I recount the description the book gives of the magical place. The longer I speak of it, the further the cavern between his eyebrows becomes.

"What book is this, again?"

I pull my bottom lip between my teeth, trying to recall the title. "It was 'something plentiful'. Starts with a K, I believe."

Crisp silence settles between us.

"*Plenteous Kermera*?"

My head shoots back at him. "Yes, that's it. Have you read it before?"

His face hardens, and I remember this man is not my friend.

"What do you know about the people who live there?"

"They're just fiction, Pearce." I scoff quietly, not wanting to wake the others. "But not enough, I feel. The book isn't mine; I haven't had it for long. I stole it from my teacher's reserved collection, and I keep meaning to put it back but always forget."

"The princess is a thief?" His interest is piqued.

I chuckle softly. "Only on occasion. I knew she wouldn't let me take it, so I simply…forgot it was in my possession. And I've been forgetting that fact every time I see her." The smile that has wandered onto my face slowly fades. "I have so many questions. Questions no one will ever be able to answer, but I suppose that's the fun of fiction."

His voice is heavy with interest and something else. "Why are you so interested in them? You have enough going on, it sounds like."

"I'm fascinated by them. The idea that a community can live off the land like that. The way they sustain themselves and stay hidden for the safety and privacy of their people, I…" I shake my head. "I admire them."

When I look back at him, his eyes are trained on my face. I can't read him. One moment I'm sure he wants to throw me into the Veritas, and the next he's looking at me…like this. He tracks at the strand of hair that has fallen over my face and his finger twitches.

Pearce shifts on the ground and clears his throat. "Why don't we both try to get some sleep? We have a long day tomorrow." And then he turns away. I stare at the stars for a few more minutes before finally closing my eyes and getting some mediocre sleep.

18

I WAKE TO JAALI still sleeping, Hart and Davian crowded by the latter's horse, and Pearce is nowhere to be found.

Davian waves a hand for me to come over. I rise and join them, and they both look past me when I approach, gawking at Jaali snoring. How is he able to sleep so deeply in the middle of the mountains?

"I'm glad you're awake. We'll be moving through human territory today. Where we are now is about halfway through the range from what Pearce found this morning." So that's where he is, then: exploring the locale. "We can go directly to the castle in a day and a half, but the sun will be behind the peaks again when we arrive. We won't have much light," Davian determines.

"Which might work out better for us; the halls will be less crowded, and it'll be darker inside the castle. We'll be able to see just fine in the dim lighting, but it'll be more difficult for them to see anything we don't want them to," adds Hart.

"What's our escape plan?"

I jump, startled by Pearce's smooth voice coming from behind me.

"Careful, Roan. I could've been anybody," he says as he passes by too closely.

Davian continues, nodding. "Even though we'll be arriving after dusk, we need to remain alert. If we are discovered in the castle as unknown staff, we'll be reprimanded. If they find out we aren't human, we'll be slaughtered. So, keep your weapons close and ready, and don't get too close to anyone."

Pearce exhales loudly, earning a look from Hart. "Got a problem with any of that?"

"No," he growls. "But I asked for an escape plan, and I didn't hear one."

"You plan on needing a quick escape, Pearce?" Hart quips.

"Stop it, you two." Davian looks at Pearce. "Our escape plan is being stealthy. We already have an advantage by not using the most traveled portion of the region, and avoiding major roads and bridges. We'll get out the same way we get in. Silently. We'll leave the horses further away from the castle so we don't have to double back for them, and we can leave unnoticed. No one will ever know we were there. Does that suffice?" He stands directly in front of Pearce, but he has to look up slightly to maintain eye contact.

Pearce must realize the same thing because a small smirk appears on his face. "Got it." He turns away from Davian and goes to stand by Jaali, still snoring loudly. He leans down and says something to him, causing him to jolt up.

"You okay, Jaali?" I ask.

"Never better," he says with his usual chipper attitude. He punches Pearce on the arm, and Pearce chuckles at the attempt.

"Let's go, Jaali. We're back on the move," Davian calls. He readies himself with siren-like speed, and we're back to silent travels.

The winding nature bridges of these mountains are slim, only wide enough for one of us at a time. The horses are nervous, but Winnie keeps control while I soothe her mane. From our position in the peaks, I can see the white tops of trees on the other side. We'll have to travel further down the mountain to remain unseen by the villages below.

Late afternoon, after hours of winding between rock formations and underneath pieces of stone hanging on by a hair, we finally see a break in the formation. It leads directly into a forest; the same one we saw from above. The frosted trees are scrawny individually, but the woods are incredibly dense. Only thin streaks of light break through the trunks.

Davian crosses over the border into Baeton, and we hear the sound of crunching snow. He looks down and curses under his breath. "We'll need to lead our trail elsewhere if we want to return through this opening. Our footsteps will lead them right to the hole in their defenses."

My arms run into branches as we ride loops through the wood. Since we can't go straight from the mountains to the castle, we loop around different parts of the woods and retrace our steps a couple of times until we can no longer tell which way the steps came from.

Snow hangs on every outstretched limb, falling as our bodies knock into the fragile shelf. To our right, I hear sounds of life: children yelling and loud conversations carried quickly on the icy wind. Snow already rests on Winnie's mane and lashes. She's earned a lavish bath when we return home.

Davian must hear the sounds from afar as well; he holds his hand up to halt us. He inclines his hand at an angle to the left, letting us know our direction will shift moving forward. We continue through the woods until dusk, stopping for every snap of wood or crunch of snow to ensure we haven't been spotted. Finally, just after sundown, a break in the heavy forest reveals our destination: Castle Baeton.

There are knights scattered around the perimeter of the castle, in the same clothing as us. I release a sigh of relief that one thing on this trip has gone right. Davian breaks first from the woods, capturing the eyes of guards closer to the castle. They take in the lot of us and our appearance before they resume their conversations. No one speaks to us though as we move closer to the back of the structure to find their slave quarters.

As we pass by two guards, I unfortunately make eye contact with one. His brows lower, not in recognition, but in confusion. I break contact and try to glance around at the other guards when I realize none of them are women. Do they not have women guards in Baeton? My appearance is almost completely concealed, but that man looked confused when he saw me. My mask covers a lot, but does it hide femininity?

He doesn't say anything as we move further into the kingdom, but I feel the weight of his stare on my back. In the distance to our right, I can see the Peaks of Despair, the group of mountains in the human kingdom. I'm not sure if they chose that name for the peaks or if they were named when the humans settled here, but it certainly fits. They look rocky and treacherous and covered in snow. I wouldn't want to go through those.

The back wall of the castle is unassuming, although I imagine that's on purpose. When we move past the castle and back into the woods, I almost interrupt Davian to question him before I realize we're tying up the horses a bit deeper into the woods like he said. It's a smart idea, that way we can avoid any unwanted contact with soldiers at the stables. There's a small wooden door with black metal latches toward the left edge of the wall. A knight stands outside the door, tall and brooding compared to those I've seen here, yet small in comparison to the men surrounding me. His eyes widen as we approach, realizing the same thing.

Davian speaks for the group, reaching for the handle. "We've been directed to go down here and deal with some unruly rats," he says.

The guard looks him up and down, probably gauging if he could handle himself if he decides to retaliate. "Haven't seen you around before," he sneers.

"It's a big kingdom," Hart interjects. His head pops out from Davian's side. "I'd imagine there's a lot of people you haven't met."

The guard looks at Hart now, less threatened.

"Why do they need five of you for a puny write-off?" He looks from the two frontmen to the rest of us, snagging on Pearce and his sheer size. If he thought Davian would be his greatest threat, he isn't very observant.

Pearce doesn't shy from his stare, he holds contact. "It's not just one we're dealing with, it's a whole gang of them," he says in a husky tone.

The guard tries his best to maintain his gaze, but I can see him shifting his weight from one foot to another.

"Right," he manages with a gulp. "Well, be quick about it, for your own sake. Stay down there too long and you'll start smelling like the vermin." And he spits on the ground next to him. The way he speaks about these people is repulsive.

Davian twists the handle, light and snow pouring into the narrow pathway inside. As we move further down the steps, my eyes adjust to the darkness. Not even our prisons are so heavy with despair. The walls are made entirely of brick. Puny-lit torches are spread out on wooden columns along the wall. Metal grates are positioned in between each torch.

"There are...people down here?" Jaali questions.

Davian sighs. "I'm afraid so. But we have to keep moving, I don't want to be trapped in here if he comes looking for us."

We move quickly and quietly through the seemingly never-ending hall filled with iron, dirt, and little light. At the end of the hall are a few small stone steps, and a wooden door like the one we entered from outside. Davian pushes on it, and it cracks open. He nods his head at Hart, who has a disgusted look on his face. "*Me*?" He whispers.

Davian's head flinches, letting Hart know exactly what he expects.

Hart moves to the front, hand at the dagger on his side. He pushes the door open further into the hall and pokes his head out. After a moment, he steps out behind the door and shuts it softly. A minute or so passes before the door opens again, and all of our hands immediately snap to our weapons.

When Hart's face comes through the crack, we recoil. "Coast is clear. This floor is staff only; there's a kitchen to the left and a pantry on the right." He holds the door open for the rest of us as we pass through.

There is zero color in this hallway, if you can even call it that. The space is slim and barely brighter than the quarters, all gray.

"Top priority is finding their war room. We can't leave until we find every bit of information they have on Alunia. Anything you find needs to be copied, not taken. We can't leave any trace that we were here."

After hours of peeking behind doors and keeping close on corner turns, we make it to a full staircase. It's narrow, presumably meant for "lesser" folk usage to avoid contact with royalty. About halfway up the stairs, a creak sounds from somewhere in the distance. We all freeze immediately. Footsteps come close to the stairway and then seem to retreat again. Another door opens and closes.

"Let's pick up the pace. The last thing we need is to run into someone in this small space," Davian notes.

We fly through the rest of the steps and come to a landing on the second level of the castle. There's more character here, although not much. Dark brown wood covers all the walls, with little evidence that anyone lives here. Even the wall lights are dim like they were lit much earlier in the day and are running out of steam.

Davian looks to Hart and points back and forth between the two of them, and then to the left. He points Jaali forward, and then he looks at me and Pearce. He signals for us to move to the right. *Great.*

We split off into our groups with instructions to meet back by the slave quarters in six hours. Jaali moves cat-like down the hallway; his lithe body allowing him to glide from one step through the next. Pearce nods in the direction of our assigned hall and stands in front of me, leading the way.

He moves in a crouch, although staying low isn't at all possible with his stature. We come upon the first door in the hall, and he knocks lightly. No one calls from inside, so he cracks the door open. We hear water moving from somewhere further in the room, and Pearce closes the door soundlessly.

He knocks on the next and receives no response. When he pushes the door open, he peaks back at me and nods inside. We step quietly through the opening and shut the door behind us. Through the window, night has fully cloaked the continent.

The room has a few tables inside, all covered with maps. The air is stale and smells of old paper. I can't imagine how old these maps are.

I scope the room, my eyes flittering over the maps of several other continents. A map of Drennica sits on a table of its own, with small wooden blocks flattening each of the corners. I wave for Pearce to come over, and we both look at the large beige sheet.

"This is Drennica, and this," he points to a piece of wood carved in the shape of an anvil, "is Baeton. At least, where most of their forces lay. That's where we are now." I look at Alunia on the map and see another wooden figure.

"Is that a mouse?" I say in disbelief.

"Looks that way," Pearce sighs. "No need to hide your hatred in your own castle, I suppose."

"Do they mean to crush us? Us a small animal, and them a massive piece of iron?"

"It would seem so, princess."

I scowl at him from the other side of the table. "I told you to stop calling me that."

He rolls his eyes. "No one else is in here, stop whining." He pushes off the table and comes to stand beside me. "See this?" Pearce points his finger at a smaller anvil further from our current position, past a bridge that connects Baeton over a river.

"They have a group positioned in a forest outside the Range of Unrest."

My brows pinch. "Why is it so far from the others?" Unease settles in my stomach the longer I stare at the figure. "Why is it so close to..." My heart sinks as I realize. "They're moving troops to border Alunia?" I look over at Pearce, unwilling to accept what I see.

"It seems that way. They're stationed maybe a day's ride from the peaks, but the range is larger on that side of the Veritas. It would take them longer to get through it than it did for us on the East side. That would put them about..." He stares at the map, calculating, and points to the small town just on the Alunian side of the mountains: Tansmere. "Three and a half days from here, at most."

All the breath in my lungs disappears. "Why are they there?" I demand. "How long have they been there?"

"I'm looking at the same map as you, I have no idea. But we need to keep looking. There has to be more information in this room. Find something to write on, you'll need to make notes of this for Davian."

I scoff at his command. "Why do I have to do it? I'm the one who found this map," I scold.

"Will you just do it? Can you not fight me, just this once?" he pleads.

I let out a huff but do as he says. I look around the room and find a few blank sheets, a quill, and a half-used inkwell. It takes me a moment, but I roughly sketch the map before me. Bad day to be a poor artist.

We search the room a while longer and find a few more maps with varying locations of smaller anvils, none of which are consistent. They have several teams in rotation, and it looks as if they stay somewhere for a bit and then retreat when another team finds a different location.

Pearce looks over all of my drawings and points out where labels have to go and things I forgot to write down. Once we're sure there is no more to be found in the loose papers thrown about the room, we go back into the still-empty hall.

Every once in a while, we run into another soldier. We do our best to blend in and decide that sneaking around makes us look more suspicious than acting like we belong.

Am I supposed to salute them? Bow, maybe? I barely know anything about Alunia's army, let alone a human one. Their customs may be different. Every time we come across someone, I can't tell if their stares are due to our size difference and my feminine build, or our lack of acknowledgment.

After some time, I tell Pearce my suspicion.

"I haven't seen any other lady knights."

"What's your point? Feeling lonely?"

I swat his arm. He doesn't even flinch.

"No, weasel, I am not lonely. Your size is already concerning, none of them come close to you. And next to me? If they find out I'm a woman, surely that could be cause for issue."

The smallest hint of a smirk pulls at his lips.

"You're concerned with my size, princess?"

My palm splays over my face, defeated.

"I don't think I should be out in the open like this. I need to find somewhere to lay low, that way you stand out less. We don't need to draw any more attention toward us."

Pearce considers this for a moment. "Alright. I'll get you back to the slave quarters since that's where we're set to meet the men later anyway."

19

NOISELESSLY, WE RETRACE OUR steps to the rickety wooden door into the bleakest place in the castle.

Pearce sets off to go looking for more intel and tells me to sit tight and quiet. Sounds of bodies shuffling against the stone floor echo when I enter the room. I close the door behind me quietly and wait for my eyes to adjust again before looking around the room. It's filled with cells; pieces of hay pepper the floors. Do they sleep in here?

Once they realize I'm not here to antagonize them, the room shifts. Faces appear against the grates in the dim light. Old and young, human and Fae. All curious.

The face of a young human girl gives me pause. What on Drennica could she have done to end up here? Slowly, I make my way to her cell. The cold stone cuts into my knees as I crouch before her. "What's your name?" I ask her.

Nothing.

Her dull brown hair is caked with dirt, trails of past tears evident on her cheeks.

When I reach out to grip the bars, she jolts back and brings her hands to her hair, covering her mouth with it. This poor thing...

"My name is Rae," I whisper to her. I bring my hands to my mask and pull it down around my neck.

The girl's tired eyes grow wide as she gasps.

The closer she gets, the more still I become. I don't want to move too quickly and frighten her. A small hand sticks out through the bars, and I hold my breath. When her palm rests on my cheek, she says in a voice as quiet as a mouse, "Bee."

"Be what?" I whisper.

The girl takes her hand from my cheek and points at her chest.

"Ah, I see now. Your name is Bee?"

She nods slightly. "Beatrice."

"Well, it's lovely to meet you, Bee."

The ghost of a smile appears on her despondent face.

"How did you get here?"

Bee sits cross-legged just on the other side of the bars, and I mimic her.

"We were playing knights, and I smacked him with my sword. He got angry because I hit him too hard, and he told his father that I beat him."

"So they put you in this place?"

She nods. "His father is on the Guard."

I swallow, trying to keep a tear from slipping free. This girl is even younger than Roralei.

"I'm very sorry, Bee. You don't deserve this. You know that, right?"

Bee sniffles. "Mhm. I want to go home."

"I know sweet girl, I know. You'll get to go home, I know it. Just be patient, alright?"

It's all I can offer her. I can't break the bars of these cells, and beating them would cause too much noise; we'd be caught.

After Bee, I go to every other person in the room. Some of them are crammed with others in their cells, clinging to each other for any sense of connection.

When something knocks on the door softly a few hours later, all noise ceases and I pull my mask back onto my face. I blend into the darkness of the room and hold my breath as the door opens, only to release it when I see it's my party members.

They seem to take in our surroundings the same way I did. When we came through the first time, the blood was pounding in my ears so loudly that I couldn't hear my own thoughts. Now we all see it for what it is: cruel.

"What have you found, Jaali?" Davian keeps his voice low.

Jaali, still absorbing the sorrow like a sponge, takes a moment to respond. "Nothing of note, yet. I accidentally ran into some other soldiers and had to make conversation, but they aren't suspicious of me at all. They've been chatting about their workload like I'm one of them, so I'll pick what I can from them."

Davian drags his hand down his face. "You've been chatting with soldiers? Can't you make yourself sparse and stay in the background?"

"You think this face is good in the background? These are leading man curls, Davian."

Eyes roll around the room.

"What about you two?"

I look to Pearce, waiting for him to explain that I stayed hidden to not sabotage us, but he doesn't.

"We found some maps and made a fair number of notes. We'll keep you updated and give them to you once we're done here."

Davian looks at me for some kind of confirmation and then nods. "Nicely done. Do your best to use the night to our advantage. There are significantly fewer people moving about now, so we'll keep searching. If you need rest, take it wisely and be mindful of your position. We'll reconvene in the morning," and they all file out again except for Pearce.

He lingers near the door.

"Why didn't you tell him we split up?"

A shrug.

"I don't need him being worried about you. I can do more without you there, so it's just what's best right now."

I scoff. "Oh, I would just slow you down?"

"I didn't say that. I said I can do more."

Whatever that means.

"Go back to your treasure hunt, then. I'll stay out of your way."

"You'll stay here?"

My eyes turn to slits, and I give him a sly smile. "I didn't say that."

Pearce lets out an exasperated sigh and leaves the room.

I study the sullen faces around me.

"Do any of you know where I could find secrets?"

Bee makes a sound, her throat still hoarse from lack of use. "I know where the General's room is," she reveals. "They send me there to clean for him."

My heart drops into my stomach, but I ball my fists. I can do this. This is why I came.

She explains how to get to the General's bedroom from our position and tells me that he sometimes works late into the night; the room may be empty. I don't need to run into anyone on my own.

With my new insight, I set a course for the stairs. Two floors up I am met with a quiet, dimly lit hall. Perfect.

Eavesdropping once again, I place my ear to the wooden doors as I pass by each one. Every room casts no light under the door, except for one. The last door on the left. The flicker of flame dances out from the small opening near the floor. I listen closely but hear nothing.

I close my eyes and take a few deep breaths before gripping the handle and turning it as slowly as I can.

A cautionary glance around the room, and I'm standing in the chambers of a Baeton General's bedroom. Because I value my life, at least a little, I clear every area before taking a full breath. When no life is found, I drop my shoulders and start peeking around for anything useful.

The drawers are filled with nothing of note. Nothing under the bed. After clearing the main living space of anything important, I find the study. It's incredibly neat, with a small oil lamp on the cherry wood desk. The first stack of papers has nothing I need, the next is the same. Some of the small drawers are filled with random scraps of paper and bits of notes. When I reach for the last one, it doesn't budge. I pull on it a bit harder and the oil lamp rattles.

Being a sneaky child means I know a little about how to pick locks. My parents wouldn't let me hear the end of it when I broke into random rooms in the castle.

I take a pin from the coat of my uniform and slide it into the lock. Just when I'm starting to remember how to get it open, I hear steps outside. One set, determined. I immediately retract my pin from the lock and shrink into the shadows. There's no way I'll be able to get out without being seen, so my best option is to wait it out until I have an opening and make a run for it.

The door lets out a slight squeak. The steps halt. And then they get closer. The study door opens, and I see a man walk toward the desk while I hide behind a wooden room divider.

I'm holding in every urge I have to start trembling and give myself away. When he sits at the desk, I know I may be here for quite some time.

How lovely.

The man sifts through the pages on his desk, looking for something. When he looks from one pile to the next and stares at the last one, a blanket of cold settles over me. He readjusts the stack ever so slightly, misaligned from the other two.

He looks up into the black void of the room, and calls out, "Who's in here?"

I clench my eyes shut as if not seeing him will make it more likely that he won't see me.

A blade is removed from its sheath, the scraping metal filling the quiet study.

"I know you're in here! Show yourself!"

Shit.

I'm not nearly ready to go head-to-head with someone, let alone a General. The sword at my back suddenly feels like a burden.

The man begins circling the room, looking behind every large object in the vicinity. When he's far enough away, I see my opening and run. I'm not willing to pull my blade and risk losing.

Call it pride, call it foolish. I don't like to lose.

I barely make it from one room to the next when I hear him running after me, weapon at the ready. As I'm about to reach the exit, a body appears, filling it almost completely. Pearce's burning amber eyes lock with mine, and then they shift to the man rushing behind me.

Pearce takes in the situation in less than a blink. He makes just enough room for me to get by him and out into the hall, just as his fist connects with the jaw of the General.

I throw my hands to my mouth to muffle the gasp as his body thuds to the ground.

My eyes meet Pearce's, filled with question and disbelief.

"What are you thinking?!" I whisper loudly at him.

"What am *I* thinking? What are *you* thinking? Sneaking into a General's room? You're insane!"

"I don't know, alright? I wanted to be useful, I thought I could find something to help us."

He shoves the unconscious body back into the bedroom and locks the door from the inside. "Why didn't you pull your sword on him? You're armed, for fuck's sake."

"And make a fool of myself? No, thank you. I'd be gutted."

"Why would you make a fool of yourself?"

I avoid eye contact.

"Don't tell me..."

I tear the skin of my bottom lip with my teeth.

"You mean to tell me you snuck your way out of the castle, and you can't even use a sword?"

"I was taking lessons with someone! I just hoped I wouldn't need it..."

"We're not done talking about this. Right now, we need to get out of the area."

We scurry down the hall and are about to turn the corner when we hear a door open behind us.

"Excuse me, but what—"

"Nothing to see here, ma'am!" I say.

Pearce grabs me by the arm and yanks me around the corner, one hand firm around my bicep, the other covering my mouth. "Hush now, princess. Keep your mouth shut, or you'll get us both in a lot of trouble."

I try to bite his hand, but he evades it by letting go. "I feel bad, what if she heard something and now she's scared?"

"She'll be fine, let's go."

Before we make it down the hall, the same female voice shouts from her doorway, "Stop! What are you two doing?"

Pearce and I look at each other briefly before booking it down the hall toward our designated meeting place. We speed through the castle to where we last saw the others, dread creeping down my neck. Davian and Hart are pacing anxiously.

"There you are, we were about to come looking for you. Jaali hasn't come back either, did you see him?"

"No, we haven't," Pearce answers. "But someone definitely saw us." Understatement of the century. "We need to find him and take cover somewhere."

Davian curses under his breath and starts down the hall Jaali went down. He sounds off, volume hardly above a whisper, at least to human ears. "*Jaali!* Where are you?"

We reach the third door in the hallway and come to a stop. "There's noise coming from behind this door. I'm going to open it." He pushes it open, and the tension in his shoulders falls sharply with an exhale. "Dammit, boy. We thought you were discovered."

We enter the space hastily and shut the door behind us. Awe overtakes me as I look around the room. The walls are covered in maps similar to the ones that Pearce and I found. A large rectangular table sits in the center of the room with six chairs placed evenly around it. Sitting on the table are dozens more figurines like the anvils from earlier, but smaller. They're scattered throughout Baeton, and it looks to be a collective map of the individual placements we saw.

Jaali sits at the head of the table, feet up, looking down at something in his hands. "There you guys are! I think I found something," he says with a boyish grin.

"Good Gods..." Hart sighs.

We all freeze when we hear a fist pounding on a door down the hall. Steps, and then another knock, closer this time. "Who's in here?" A man's voice shouts, too close.

Davian snaps his fingers to collect our scattered minds. "We're going to exit the room with purpose as if we belong here. Head for the staircase that brought us here, and do not get caught." More knocking sounds from the hall.

Hart rips open the door and steps out into the passage. "I'll look this way, you go check the other hall," he shouts to the guard outside.

"Let me know if you find anything," the guard says, and Hart motions for us to exit one at a time.

We run as quietly as we can down the stairs to the slave quarters. The moment the door closes, a herd of footsteps moves down the hall. Sure-footed bodies move right past the door we're huddled behind, and we release a collective sigh of relief.

"Well, what now? They'll be looking for us, but we need to get back to that war room," Jaali says.

Davian rubs his beard in thought. "We'll camp out in here tonight. The guard from outside seemed to abhor this place. I think we'll be safe for now."

I break away from the men, desperate for some air. The darkness of night seeps through the slightest bit, but the prospect of getting clean air into my nose is impossible.

I kneel again before Bee. "Is there somewhere we can hide?" I ask her.

Her gaunt face nods, and she points to a small wooden door on the east side of the room. "Tunnels," she says with a croak. My eyes well with tears as I think of my little sister being trapped in a hell like this.

One of the men acts; something scrapes against the ground before the faint whining of a door. When I turn around, Davian and Hart are already moving into the pitch-black passageway, while Jaali holds the door open and Pearce looks between us.

"Thank you," I manage to get out.

She manages a faint smile, and it takes every ounce of strength I possess to leave her again.

Pearce eyes me as I walk to the tunnel, and I brush past him without a word. If he has something hurtful to say, I'm in no mood for it.

The tunnels are void of light. It takes a minute for my half-human eyes to adjust, and even then, endless nothing is all that's visible.

"Where do these tunnels even lead?" Jaali asks from where he moves in front of me.

"I've never been here before, Jaali. I don't know. Judging by the cobwebs I feel grazing my hands, no one has been down here in ages," Davian explains.

We stop moving when we enter a damp room, a stone crossroads. It seems that more tunnels lead in different directions, and now we're stuck with deciding which path to take. Davian looks around at the group and decides to section us off into our previous pairings, sending us on our own course.

Pearce moves first, taking the lead once again down the narrow hall. He does so with no argument from me; if I feel a cobweb, I may scream. I'm terrified of spiders.

A scuffle sounds from further down the tunnel, and Pearce reaches back to brace his arm in front of me.

When it approaches us, his arm falls back to his side. It's just a rat, so we keep pushing forward.

Hours of wandering through the same tunnel leads us nowhere except into our usual bickering.

"I can't believe you came here without knowing how to use a sword," he says.

"You said it before, I'm a princess. It wasn't exactly part of my lessons with Miss Woodstock."

I faintly see him shake his head. "That's ridiculous. How do they expect you to defend yourself?"

I shrug even though he can't see me. "They figure I'll always have someone to protect me. A guard, an army; it wasn't a skill they thought was necessary for me."

"And you agree?"

"Of course not." I scoff. "The last thing I want is to depend on someone else to fight my battles for me. Hence why I'm in these damn tunnels with a group of Alunian soldiers in an enemy kingdom."

"Point taken, I guess…" He's silent for a moment before he asks, "If you can't use a sword, what made you think coming here was a good idea? What if you were captured, or I hadn't found you before the General got to you?"

I purse my lips and become frustrated when I can't think of a better answer for him. "I think I just kind of snapped. Countless days watching everyone around me become more skilled and more sure of who they are and their place in the world. It wanes on me.

When I overheard there was an empty spot on a mission out of the kingdom, I couldn't stop myself. I had to see what I'm made of."

We continue with small squabbles until we reach a seemingly dead end. I can't hear anything from outside, but I assume the sun has started to rise after all this wandering.

Finally, after walking a thousand miles, we run into the others. One of them found an exit to the far side of the castle, the one closest to where we arrived. Conversation is sparse as we make our way through *more* tunnels, and I start to wonder who in Drennica's history would create such a painfully boring method of travel.

When we reach an unassuming door, we're astounded when it opens back into the working hallway. Finding our way back to the war room from here is easier given the number of times we paced through the halls. Since these halls were already cleared, all the soldiers who didn't rush outside are in other parts of Castle Baeton.

Once inside, the five of us split up and tear through every area of the war room. Maps, letters, travel plans, everything seems to be kept in this room.

"Don't use this time to judge what you think is useful, duplicate everything you see. We don't have time to filter," Davian commands.

Scribbling and shuffling papers are the only sounds as we copy down what we can before we're discovered. We finally find what we were looking for, and we're being flushed out. Our time here has been cut short, but we need what we came for. And we're going to get it.

Time drifts strangely as we draft everything we see, from army numbers to camp location details.

I flip through pages of notes until my eyes snag on the word *slave* scribbled on one, and all thoughts clear my head. Nearby, the word *control* makes me feel no better.

Then, the bells start.

Our heads whip up in unison before we all scramble to finish our current notes. Davian ushers us out of the room and back down to the slave quarters.

The halls are a storm of commands and armor as Baetonian soldiers continue their search for the unknown intruders, and the heavy quiet is a strange relief once we step back into the devastating room. That relief is taken away as they immediately head for the tunnels. I start to follow, but something prevents me from making the final steps to safety.

Bee is standing at the edge of her cell, eyes wide with concern at the clanging of the bells.

One final time, I kneel before her. "Do not be afraid. We will meet again, little Bee, I'm sure of it. You will go home, I promise."

Beatrice gives me a hopeful smile. "Thank you, Rae. Be safe," she says.

"You too, Bee."

I press a kiss to my fingers and place them on her forehead, a promise of a better future.

Her hazel eyes close, soaking in the little warmth I have to give her freezing form. Without another thought, I rip my cloak from my shoulders and push it through the bars of her cell.

"Take this. You need it more than I do."

And then I'm gone.

20

THERE IS ONLY A dusting of guards on this side of the castle. Many of them are probably manning the main entrances and searching inside the castle itself.

Sun shines onto the snow-covered ground, making all of us shield our eyes after spending so long in darkness. The few guards on this side are scurrying around, most of them too focused on their own tasks to notice us since we're still in their uniform.

The moment I start to think we've made it far enough to be without fear, the guard who eyed me down when we arrived turns a corner and locks eyes with me across the field of snow. His stare tightens, lines creasing his forehead. He starts running, and we head for the forest we came from.

Foolishly, I look behind us while running and see him reach for a bow. I immediately turn back and try to pick up speed, as if I can outrun an arrow.

My feet snag on a branch raised from the ground and I tumble to the powdered ground. I try to regain my footing, but the man is getting closer, arrow drawn. I turn and see Jaali look back for me, his eyes flying out of his head when he sees me lying on the ground. He starts running back in my direction and shouts, "Pearce, look out!"

I turn my head back to the man advancing me, and I see a broad body cut through the endless white, just as the arrow is let loose. The sound of metal piercing fabric and skin ricochets through my ears. And then another. Strong hands wrap around my forearms and pull me to my feet, lightly shaking me to bring my eyes to meet scalding ones.

"You alright, princess?" Pearce grunts.

I nod shakily, my eyes drifting from his to the arrows protruding from his skin. He grabs my wrist and signals for Jaali to keep moving forward. Pearce and I run as fast as we can to the horses and catch up with the others, but he's moving slower than he should be.

When we can no longer hear yelling from the castle, we stop briefly to take a breath and reconfigure our plans. I grab his bicep, my hand hardly wrapping around the outside half.

"What the hell? Why would you risk yourself like that?" I ask, filled to the brim with misplaced anger.

"I'm fine. You're *welcome* by the way," he says as he jerks his arm from my grasp. The wince that comes from him doesn't help his case, but we don't have time for that argument right now. I'll remove the arrows when we find safety, and there's no telling when that might be. We won't be able to go back through the Range of Unrest right away, it would give away our origin and put Alunia in immediate danger.

Baeton has no idea that we aren't human, only that something suspicious is happening inside the castle. The longer we can keep it that way, the better. None of us moved our hoods the entire time, and I send up a silent thank you to my forgotten Gods when snow starts falling, filling our prints as we head deeper into the Baetonian winter. We flee through sunrise and arrive at the base of a mountain range. From the grey color of the rock and the haze of fog that winds around the peaks, I know these are the Peaks of Despair. It's not the ideal place to lie low, yet it seems to be our safest option. They will most likely assume we went toward a dock for our escape, not the least welcoming place on Drennica.

Finding a safe place to hide out on a mountain is no easy feat, but we manage. On the other side of a large mountain by the coast, we break for a rest.

Once I stretch out my muscles and recover my breath, I set my bag down and stand beside Jaali. His back is facing Pearce, so I follow suit and face away from the man who seemingly took an arrow for me.

"Will he let you look at it?" I pry.

He scoffs. "Probably not. He's stubborn. He'd tell me he's fine, even if he isn't, and that I don't have to worry about him. I will anyways though." He chuckles softly.

"How have you been friends for so long with someone who shuts you out like that? Don't you get frustrated?" I imagine it would get old.

"He might be cold, but he's done a lot for me. A long time ago, I got into some trouble. Pearce had my back. He stood up for me and made sure I was alright when I came out the other side. Nobody else did but him. So, I stick beside him."

I sigh. "He sounds complicated."

"That's because he is. Don't take it personally." Jaali pats me on the shoulder, then stands to tend his horse.

I take a deep breath and close my eyes. He's just a man, I tell myself. How scary can he be?

My aching muscles protest as I move to stand in front of Pearce. He looks up at me with no emotion on his face and goes back to picking the dirt from under his nails.

I kneel in front of him so we're eye to eye. "I need to see your back," I demand.

His jaw clenches. "Leave me alone. I'm fine." He doesn't look up from his hands.

"I need to see that for myself, please. Let me look at your back."

The tension in his face eases as he says, "If you want me to undress, all you have to do is ask."

Heat rushes my cheeks, and I'm suddenly grateful we can't risk starting a fire. He would surely see the redness flooding my face that I'm certain is from frustration, and not any other reason. "The day I ask you to undress is the day the Veritas floods Alunia. Let me see the damage, Pearce."

He lets out a long sigh and reaches his arms behind his back to grab the neck of his shirt. With a groan, he pulls the fabric over his head and holds the shirt between his legs, which is when I realize he's already pulled the arrows out himself. In all the chaos, I didn't even notice. His head falls forward as he shifts so I can see his back. A small gasp leaves my lips. His back is completely covered in scars, some spanning several inches across.

Our skin heals rapidly, knicks and scrapes suture themselves within minutes. My eyes catch on his left shoulder blade. A pattern of darker skin paints the area in sporadic dots of scarred flesh, more black ink broken apart by the flashes of white. They almost look like teeth marks. The size of the creature that could've left such a scar would be monstrous. The beast must've bitten straight down onto the left side of his body. In between his shoulder blades, there are two puncture wounds. I reach out to touch the skin around the area, and he jolts the moment my fingertips graze his skin.

"He nicked me, I'm fine," he says as he starts to turn his back away from me. The tooth-shaped scars go all the way around the left side of his torso, his chest marked with the same injury.

I grab his shoulder and force him back around so I can see the puncture wounds again. "These should have started healing by now. They must have special weapons or coated them with something. I need to tend to these. We've been outside a while and you're not exactly the picture of cleanliness right now; they could become infected." I reach for my canteen and tear a piece of fabric from the corner of his cloak. It's not the most hygienic, but it's what we have. I turn the canteen over to soak the cloth and dab it onto the freshly damaged skin.

He hisses when the fabric hits his wounds. The muscles in his back flex as he fights to stay still. "Could you ease up back there?" He grunts.

"I've barely touched you. Stop moving, and it won't take as long." He grinds his teeth so hard I can hear them turning to dust. His skin is hot to the touch when I graze it with the back of my hand. Usually, I'm the one that's always warm. I clean the area as best as I can, rewetting the cloth a few times in the process. When I'm confident I've cleared any dirt and debris from his wound, I close my canteen.

"That may not prevent an infection entirely, but it's good enough for now. Turn around, I need to make sure there aren't any other wounds that should be looked at."

"There aren't. Go lay down." He starts to pull his shirt back over his head, and my eyes snag on the teeth-shaped scars.

"How did you get that?" I ask.

He pauses, the shirt halfway over his head. His chest rises and falls heavily when he peels the shirt back off. He wads it up and lets it fall between his knees when his eyes shoot to mine.

"A wolgeo." He says it barely louder than a whisper.

My stomach threatens to expel what little sits in it. I scoff. "Yeah, right."

"I'm not joking." He looks back down to his hands and rubs his thumb against his index finger roughly.

"Those aren't real. They're a—a wives tale told to children to—"

"To stop them from wandering into the woods alone? I know." He drops his head to look at his hands. "I thought the same thing until the wolf hybrid stood right in front of me seven years ago. I blinked, and its jaws were locked around my torso." A chill racks his body.

"You should put your shirt back on, you're shivering."

"It's not from the weather. I can hardly look at its marks. Not without being taken back..."

Neither of us speak for a long while.

"Thank you," I say into the night. It doesn't feel like enough, but it's better than nothing.

"For what?" He asks, clipped.

I roll my eyes even though he probably can't see. "You know what."

"Enlighten me."

"For jumping in front of me."

No response.

"And for hearing me."

Another pause.

"You're welcome." He shifts uncomfortably and pulls his shirt back over his head, this time uninterrupted. I finally stand, my knees aching from kneeling for so long. I settle down next to Winnie and do my best to get some rest.

After a night full of jerking awake at the slightest hint of noise, I feel exhausted. Given that we'll have to sneak back across Baeton today to move through the Range of Unrest, I guess a good night's sleep would've been too much to ask for. I look over to find Davian sitting on the ground drawing something in the snow with a stick, while Hart looks over his shoulder.

Pearce is still lying down, and I'm grateful he was able to get at least a little sleep; he needs to rest to fully heal properly. I shake my head, unsure of why I care so much about how the ruffian is feeling.

Jaali is tearing through his bag to find a snack, and I'm unsure if I've ever seen the man *not* be hungry. I wander over to Davian and Hart to see what our plan is for today.

"Morning, Roan," Davian says as he glances up at me quickly. Hart gives a curt nod. Looking down at the snow, I see points and circles, discovering Davian is no artist. He looks back up at me to find me smirking and says, "I'm using a stick, did you expect to see a master-piece?"

I shrug my shoulders and shake my head slightly. "I didn't say any-thing." I sit with them to let him finish his drawing, and eventually, Jaali comes to sit with the group. None of us dare to wake Pearce. The longer he sleeps, the better he'll be for travel today.

"This is where we are now," Davian puts his stick on the points I now know are meant to be the mountains we're in, "and this is the edge of Baeton. It's about a day's ride at normal pace, but we'll need to be quick, and we'll need to be quiet." He says the first part to me, and the second to Jaali. We both nod quietly, aware of our faults.

There's a river that cuts through the East side of Baeton, and it leads almost directly to the Range of Unrest. It's not as thickly blanketed by trees so there would be an increased risk of being seen, but it's also far enough away from the castle to hopefully avoid any guards. I relay this information to the group, and Hart disapproves of the path.

Jaali thinks the best choice would be back through the woods since we know exactly where the entrance back into Alunia is, while Davian insists that is the exact reason we shouldn't take that path: we could unknowingly lead someone right to it. He says when Pearce wakes up, he'll be our tiebreaker.

Right on cue, he clears his throat dramatically from behind the group. Our heads all snap in his direction, and I let out a sigh of relief at seeing him upright again.

"My ears were burning. Talking about me?" He seems well, his posture is normal, and he's rubbing the back of his neck. His range of motion has improved, which is a start.

Hart rolls his eyes. "We were just discussing our plans for getting back home. *Roan* here," he puts a harsh emphasis on my name, "seems to think our best option is to travel south and stay by the river—"

"She's right." Pearce's stare is cold, his tone unwavering.

Hart's brow furrows, aggravation obvious on his face. "We'd be more exposed than if we went back through the woods we came through. We should go that way," he insists.

"That's also the most likely place they'll check. They're sure to have dozens of guards in those very woods right now, probably hidden in trees waiting for any signs of movement, and then they'll shoot us in the back." He shifts a bit. He's surely healed now but the area will still be tender for a bit, more mentally than physically.

"A good soldier doesn't get shot in the back," says Hart. His head inches forward as he says it, almost daring Pearce to say something back.

Pearce doesn't retaliate the way Hart expects, though. He holds his stare and very calmly replies, "Maybe not. But a good soldier protects their team. They don't run away while one of their own is on the ground." He enunciates every word with precision, his contempt for Hart bleeding into his tone.

"A better soldier wouldn't be on the ground," Hart mumbles when he looks back down at the snow map.

Without flinching, Pearce says, "Keep it up, Hart. I dare you." No emotion is on his face, positive or negative. Maybe he's more injured than I thought.

Davian, sensing the tension rising in the group, clears his throat and gestures back toward his markings in the snow that are slowly being filled with more white powder.

After a lot of back and forth and smart quips from everyone in the group, we hash out a plan for skirting along the river bend. There are a few towns on the way from what we could gather from the maps we made, but we should remain far enough away from civilization so that we won't come in contact with anyone. Then, we're off.

Once we're on the side of the mountain that faces away from the castle, we'll be closer to the river while keeping ourselves out of the way of passing parties. These peaks are avoided due to their reputation which, after last night, makes more sense to me. The winds were brutal against the little of my skin that was exposed.

The sound of hooves crushing set powder is the only noise we make as we descend the peak. When we round the side of the mountain, a small village appears to our right. We'll tread near the outskirts of it, but from our current vantage point, it looks like we'll only be near a few isolated homes or shops.

The closer we get to the water, the colder it gets. The snow falling above us mixes with the draft coming from the water which means the winds are cruelly cold.

As we ride, I think over the last few days. Nothing makes sense. Set on getting answers, I turn around on Winnie. "Why did you help me?" I demand, quietly.

"Which time are you referring to?"

Arrogant weasel.

"Every time, I guess. Not telling anyone who I am, taking that arrow meant for me—"

"I didn't take it because it was meant for you. I saw someone who needed help, so I did what I thought I must."

"Right. Well, thanks anyways I suppose," and I go to turn around when he interjects—

"Don't. Just—," he sighs. "I don't need any of us getting hurt. That's all."

"That's a surprise," I sneer.

"Would you also be surprised to learn that I have no clue what to ask of you with that favor?"

I *would*, actually.

"What do you mean? It was your idea!" We're practically whisper yelling at this point, and he's moved to ride next to me instead of behind me.

"Only because I needed some kind of leverage. I'd be stupid not to take that opportunity. So now I'm trying to come up with something worthy of my secrecy." He sounds proud of his decision. I suppose he should be; I'll give him what he wants.

"Well, I hope you make it worth your while," I say with my chin high and look away from him.

"I'm sure I will, Roan."

Hours pass by uneventfully. The occasional snap of twigs and howl of wind makes us pause for a moment, but after we make sure the coast is still clear, we resume our traveling.

We come across two more villages, one on this side of the river and the other on the small island to the other side. Smoke billows from chimneys into the crisp blue sky. The village across the water is too far to see anything other than shapes. To our right though, I see a group of children running around, chasing each other. They're quite a distance away from their village, attacking each other with balls of snow. One of the children, a young girl, sees us and stops running. Her head inclines to the side as she stares. After a few seconds, she hesitantly lifts her hand and waves.

I lift my hand to wave back, but Pearce reaches over and grabs my forearm, his fingers reaching all the way around.

"Don't interact," he mutters.

"Why not? It's just a girl." It seems rude not to engage with her, she seems harmless.

"You never know what kind of spies they have in their employment. For all you know, that small girl could be a fully grown woman with stunted height. It's not like you can see her that well."

"Now that seems a bit dramatic," I jest. But when I look back over to the running children, the girl is gone. I look around the area to see if maybe she went back to playing, but I can't find her.

"That's strange, I don't see her now. Maybe she went back home."

"Or maybe she went to tell her commander of our location," he warns.

His idea sends a shiver through my body, exacerbated by the chill in the air.

"Cold?" He grunts.

"We're in the winter region, surrounded by snow. And I gave Bee my cloak..."

He looks like he wants to ask about what happened in the cells, but decides against it, reverting to his usual attitude.

"Should have thought of that before you left the castle, then. I bet your bed is much more comfortable than the ground we've been sleeping on."

"My bed is quite comfortable. I'll be very happy to be back to it."

"Maybe that'll be my price for our bargain. Your bed."

"You...want to sleep in my bed?"

A soft chuckle leaves him. "Alone, preferably. I'll have you drag it to my home yourself and watch as I roll all over my new covers and pillows."

"Wait, my pillows too? This is a hefty price you're talking about, now."

"Are you saying my silence isn't worth a hefty price? If that's the case," he clears his throat loudly, "Guys, I think Roan might be--"

I swat his arm. "Okay *fine*. Pillows too," I hiss.

The right side of his mouth curves up the slightest bit into a smirk. "You know, I forgot what I was going to say. Carry on, gentlemen."

Now seething, I look straight ahead and try, poorly, to forget that he's beside me.

"I don't think I'll take your bed after all. I need a bit more time to think."

"By all means, take your time. Take forever."

"Forever sounds too long. I don't know if I could stand *anything* forever. Especially a bed, that sounds dreadful."

When we finally come up to the base of the Range of Unrest, the tension in my body eases. I never thought I'd be so happy to see a giant mound of rock. We stroll alongside the range until the surroundings look familiar. One by one, we lead our horses through the small section of earth that leads into the maze of peaks.

"When you get through the opening, walk 50 paces, and then stop. Wait for the others to catch up behind you," Davian commands. He looks at Pearce. "Are you okay with staying in the rear for the journey back? I can have Hart swap with you."

Pearce's eyes shift to the side so quickly, I'm unsure if it truly happened. "I'm fine back here." Davian nods curtly before following Hart, who has already passed through.

"Why'd you do that?" I ask him. "I thought you'd want more re-sponsibility. To be a leader, or something." Get away from *me*.

"I'm fine where I am. Besides, I can't trust you not to get into trouble again," he says.

"Trouble? I was not in trouble."

"Then what would you call lying on the ground stumbling while someone runs at you with an arrow aimed at you?" His chest rises and falls sharply.

I look down at my hands on the horn of Winnie's saddle. "I'm not sure." I already know my defense skills aren't developed enough. I don't need a reminder from him, too.

His head dips a bit to the side, and he looks at me. "Did I hit a soft spot? Maybe you shouldn't have left your castle, princess. It's dangerous out here."

Although I know he's probably right, his words sting. He waves his hand in front of him for me to go through the opening after Jaali is through fully. I decide to bite my tongue and not respond to his comment. He's right, after all. I came out here thinking I was ready for this kind of challenge, but the longer I'm out here the more unsure I am. Of myself, of my skills, everything.

We make it through a large portion of the mountains before the sun falls from the sky and it's time for us and the horses to rest for the night.

"Everyone go ahead and find a spot, we'll be camping here for tonight," Davian says. Since we're getting closer to Spring, there are a bit more trees as we move through the mountain range. Jaali picks one to our left, throws his bag over a low-lying branch, and then hoists himself onto it as well. That man must be part creature. He moves unlike anyone I've ever seen.

When I look to my right, Pearce is laying out his cloak like a blanket for him to lay on. It's not a bad idea, we won't need these uniforms for the ride home, so we can let them get a little rough. I take a page from his book, peel off my outer coat, and lie next to Winnie.

"Copying me, Roan?"

"In the past eight days, you've had *one* good idea. Forgive me for wanting to have a more comfortable sleeping arrangement."

He turns from his back to his side so he's facing away from me.

I ready Winnie for the night and return to my makeshift bed.

The crack of a twig wakes me from my sleep. The sky is still dark, barely illuminating the bodies that lie around me. I look over and see Jaali still perched on his branch. Davian and Hart are lying a bit further to the right, sound asleep. Hart must have been exhausted because he's snoring quietly now. He didn't do that before. I look to my left to where Pearce—

Isn't there.

I snap into a seated position to ensure my eyes aren't deceiving me. Even with my only half-heightened Fae senses, I know they're not. I crouch-walk over to where his cloak still lays and place my hand on it. It's still warm. That crack really didn't wake up anyone else? So much for a group of trained soldiers. I get up slowly to prevent my bones from cracking and give away my movement. A small collection of pointed trees sits not too far from our location. When I start tiptoeing in that direction, I see a figure move and I freeze.

"*Pearce.*" No response. I'm whispering to the wind.

Fantastic.

The blur moves again, and this time I'm not sure that it's him. "Pearce? Is that—"

A scream attempts to leave me when a hand clamps over my mouth from behind me. I shorten my breaths to limit my movement against the body pressed to my back. The hair by my ear is jostled, and then he whispers to me. "Don't move. It might not have heard you."

My eyes close when I realize the body behind me is Pearce, not some human assassin. And then I tense again when I realize his proximity...and the fact that his hand is still over my mouth.

"Relax," he purrs into my ear. "The greatest danger here isn't me. There's a vaclik about 20 yards ahead of you, and it's been getting closer throughout the night."

I turn my head to look at him and he finally releases my face.

"You're serious?" I whisper to him.

"Deadly. I've hardly slept tonight. It woke me a few hours ago, so I've been going back and forth between checking its location and going back to camp."

"Why the back and forth? Why not just stay in one place?" That seems like more steps than necessary.

He shakes his head with a shrug of his shoulders like he's irritated I would ask such a thing. "I've been debating just killing the thing. But I don't particularly want to be marked as a vaclik slaughterer."

Dumbfounded, I ask, "Aren't they violent? Why not be rid of it?" Surely a *marking* or whatever he said would be worth the safety of a group of people.

Pearce's stare bores into my face as if just now noticing I'm maskless. "They're incredibly violent. But they also keep other unwanted creatures at bay. They're sort of a butcher for other violent things. Killing one is generally frowned upon, and the scent of those who kill them is forever altered. That way, anyone who comes near them knows they value their own safety above that of the public."

My mouth falls open. How have I never heard of this? When I ask him, he doesn't insult me like I expect. "You're not exactly out hunting wild beasts often, are you?" He has a point. "Anyway, I've been watching it to make sure it doesn't get too close to camp." He coughs quickly and quietly.

"Well, what do we do? Do we go back to camp?" I'm not sure how to deal with a creature like this.

His head whips back to the direction of the vaclik, and he puts an index finger over his pursed lips, telling me to stay quiet. He then aims that finger back to the group, so I slowly step back. He nods and several strands of dark wavy hair that have fallen from the bundle on his head fall into his face.

We make it back to camp soundlessly and we slowly pack up our things to make the process go smoother when the sun starts to rise. I can hear animalistic noises in the distance and each time they sound, my blood runs cold.

As more light shines from above, the quieter the beast becomes. Although I'm not an expert, I know that vaclik prowl at night. They are few and far between; practically unheard of in most of Drennica. The tall, thinly-haired creature has poor vision during the day, so that's probably why it was hunting last night. Because of the dimness at night, they can see a bit better, although still not well. Their hearing is what allows them to find prey, which makes Pearce's decision to quiet me the way he did more reasonable.

I hardly get any deep sleep, and each time Pearce gets up to check on the vaclik, I wake. The second the horses begin to stir, I make a scene pretending to wake up. The noise wakes the rest of the group, save for Jaali, and they collect their things without any idea of what almost happened in the night. Pearce comes around a tree then, and Hart questions where he was so early in the morning.

"Just doing a perimeter check. We're still close to Baeton, can't be too safe." His tone is deeper than when he spoke to me last night, and I know it's due to his general distaste of Hart, who looks Pearce up and down before going back to his tasks.

We call out to Jaali, who doesn't stir. I snap my fingers near his ear. Nothing. Pearce grabs a stick off the ground and jabs Jaali in the abdomen, who flails off the tree and lands on his hands and knees like a cat.

"Again? Are you guys serious?" He complains.

"You're like trying to wake the dead," Pearce grunts.

He rolls his eyes. "I'm far better company than the dead. Next time, try nudging my shoulder." He rolls his shoulder back and rubs the side of his arm from the force of the fall.

"Let's get going," Davian says. "We should try to reach the pixie marshes by the end of the day."

"We're not going back to the Spring castle?" Hart questions.

Davian shakes his head. "No, we're not. We have more information about the human army's plans now, and they'll ask questions we'll feel obligated to answer. We must keep this quiet until we can relay it to the Queen and King."

We all nod, accepting his direction. The Ladies of Spring *are* rather nosy. They would ask more questions than appropriate and their position may make it difficult to turn down their queries.

Without another word, we fall into our usual order. It's shifted from the start of this trek, no longer single file. Davian rides at the front with Hart to his left, Jaali rides behind them, then me, and Pearce hangs at the back. Or at least he did on the way to Baeton. Now, he trots up to ride next to me.

"Get bored back there already?"

"Trust me, being next to you is not my first choice. But since our backs are toward Baeton, there's strength in numbers. If something comes up behind us, I can throw you to them and get the rest of us to safety," he says with a slight smirk.

"Very funny. You could be a jester, the true unsung heroes." My parents have had the same jester since I was a child, simply because I loved them so much. They would flick water on my face and pull long scarves from seemingly nowhere; I thought they were truly magical.

"Real heroes don't call themselves heroes, they simply show up."

"You say that like you have experience," I poke.

"When my parents died, I promised I would keep an eye on those who found themselves less fortunate. I didn't have much, but I had heart. And a tiny sword I stole from one of the older members of the court." His voice is strong, but his eyes look distant.

"I'm sorry about your parents." I am, truly. My parents may frustrate me, and we may not see eye to eye all the time, but I don't know what I would do if they were taken from me.

"It was a long time ago." His jaw clenches, proving he's more bothered than he's letting on. It's not my business, but I can't help but feel sympathy for him.

"How did they die?"

I don't mean to ask out loud, it's meant to be an internal question. He's in no way obligated to share intimate details of his personal life.

"They died fighting for Alunia." My heart squeezes in my chest. "They weren't normally soldiers, but they were brave. I was seven."

"Do you have any siblings?" Another personal detail I have no right to know.

"Jaali is the closest thing I have to a brother. The other children didn't want to play with the quiet kid. Any other knowledge you require? Or can I stop dragging myself back through my childhood?"

I clear my throat. "No, I'm sorry. I didn't mean to pry." I did, but I didn't intend to make him so uncomfortable.

"Sure, you didn't," he scoffs. "You grew up in luxury with both your parents *and* a younger sibling. It's fine to want to know how the other half lives."

"I don't like what you're implying. Just because I grew up comfortable doesn't mean—"

"Comfortable? You grew up in a castle. With maids and cooks and everything else. You have a loving family. I'd say that's more than comfortable."

I let out a huff of air in response. He has a point.

He sighs too. Why does almost every conversation we have turn into...whatever that was? Just when I think he's coming around to me being a member of the team, he shuts me out. It's infuriating. I can't be that bad of company to justify his behavior.

I feel weight on the left side of my face. When I look over, he's already staring at me. His head isn't turned fully, only slightly, and his eyes are peaking down at me. When he sees me face him, he looks away. This man is insufferable.

21

WHEN THE SUN NEARS the horizon, we see the river surrounding the pixie marsh. A thick forest is just on the other side of the water, keeping the marsh mostly concealed from outsiders. Fae are usually friendly, but there is some slight tension between species. Pixies and ogres both enjoy wetlands, but despise each other. The pixies claimed the Spring marsh after the ogres settled down in the Summer swamp. They exist peacefully enough, when necessary, and I can't blame them for wanting a little privacy.

"We'll get to the river's edge before we break for the night," Davian announces. We arrive at that edge less than an hour later. I take Winnie to the water so she can drink her fill, and the others follow suit.

"You know the Ladies of Spring could find us out here, right?" I ask Davian. "We're not exactly concealed."

He chuckles. "Oh, I know. They probably knew the second we crossed back into Alunia. But as long as we keep our distance, their guards won't have a reason to approach us. We'll make do by the river tonight."

"Can we finally light a fire? Now that we're not in human territory?" Hart pleads.

Jaali chimes in with his enthusiasm for the idea. "Oh please! My body is still solidified after all that time in the snow. Some fire would be nice."

Davian looks between the two of them and then pinches the bridge of his nose. "Fine. But you two have to go find kindling since you want it so badly." Hart curses into the wind. Jaali hurries off into the woods, Hart begrudgingly following him. They arrive back with unexpected speed.

Once the fire is built, I decide to warm my frozen bones in the river with the light of the sinking sun. The garments underneath are plenty of coverage for a makeshift bath. Once all my heavy clothing is lying in a pile next to my boots, I step into the water and close my eyes. This is exactly what I needed. I reach down into the water with cupped hands and pour the water down my aching legs. Sweat and dirt mix in the fall down my leg as I wash off. I look up to see that the rest of the men have decided to do the same, and they've all found their own space to do it in. Jaali has his head fully under the water and whips it out, getting water everywhere. He shakes his hair out like a dog, and some of that water hits Pearce.

I don't mean to look at him. He's facing away from me, leaning down into the water to rinse his massive arms. When he stands to his full height, he peels his shirt from his back, balls it up, and tosses it with the rest of his things on the shore. Pearce then takes water into his hands and lets it fall behind his neck. I can see the muscles in his back moving as he does it. He's not cut from stone, but the sheer size of him is...impressive. His waist tapers in at the center, his shoulders and back spanning what looks like my arm's length.

My eyes latch onto his left shoulder blade. The teeth-shaped scars I saw before hold my attention as he lifts water onto his arms. Some of his other scars look like they were made with weapons: daggers and swords; maybe from combat. But others look smaller, more rounded. He turns to face me before I'm able to tear my eyes away. He's seen me staring, no point in shying away now.

I grind my jaw and maintain eye contact with him as I lower myself shoulder-deep into the water; underclothes be damned. I'll worry about chafing later. I dip my head back under the water, fully saturating my strawberry-blonde hair. When I come back up, he's still boring holes into my irises. His jaw is clenched, as are his fists. I stand fully, water falling at my sides from my now-drenched clothing. And then his eyes travel down, raking my body that is now fully on display, my soaked clothes clinging to every curve. I examined him and was caught; it seems only fair he gets to return the favor. Even from here, I can see his eyes trace the outline of my hips. He flicks his tongue out to quickly coat his lips.

Then he dips himself in the water. He had only been standing knee-deep until this point, keeping his shorts dry. When he rises, his thin shorts cling to his skin, the same as mine. He smirks, standing to his full height. I don't mean to break eye contact with him, but my desire proves to be stronger than my willpower when my gaze flicks down to his breeches, hung dangerously low on his hips due to the weight of the water in them.

The rest of the party seems completely unaware of the silent war happening in the river, all of them reveling in the temperate water that now feels scalding.

I shake my head to clear the thoughts currently crowding my brain and start to trudge out of the water when he puts his tongue to his cheek and chuckles. My step falters, shocked at the slightest joyous expression coming from him after something I'd done. I wring out my shirt the best I can as I reach the grass. When I turn around, Jaali tries to joke with Pearce but is shut down abruptly, who shakes his hands through his hair, droplets flying everywhere.

What the hell just happened?

"Did you fall in, Roan?" Davian says as he steps out of the lake.

"Yeah, sort of. Must've tripped on a rock or something." His brows rise with a chuckle, and he redresses.

When the men are dressed, Pearce's face is painted with frustration.

"What's got you so wound up?" Jaali questions.

"Don't worry about it," Pearce responds gruffly.

After a warm night of sleep from being near the marsh, we start the next leg of our trip. The goal is to reach Suncrest Heights in less than two days. It's a relatively straight shot, so that proves to be no problem. During our uneventful day, we pass the same villages as before. All of them the pictures of quaint family life.

The next night, the men find their positions for rest, and I step away with Winnie to let her drink from the Veritas. She's always loved this water the most, I think due to the temperature. The water in the middle of the continent is perfectly tempered due to all the seasons surrounding it. It's not too hot from Summer or cold from winter, it's perfectly pleasant.

We sit for a few minutes by the water, soaking in the quiet while it lasts. We're all tired of riding at this point, and still have more to travel if I remember correctly. When Winnie lets me know she's tired, I find a tree to situate her nearby. I step away from her, and she lets out a concerned noise. Winnie rarely gets spooked, so it immediately puts me on edge.

I decide to go look around the surrounding area and see if anything seems out of place. After searching for a few minutes, I find nothing. I start to move back toward camp when I see movement from the corner of my eye. It looks like a horse, but something looks wrong with it. As I move closer to it, it appears injured. Perhaps they hurt their leg or something while running. I approach the poor creature with an extended hand, and I call to it.

"Hi there, you poor thing." Its head snaps toward me, eyes irritated and strange. They almost look white, likely because the sun has fully dipped behind the mountains.

"Are you alright?" I call out to it again. It dips its head and starts to move toward me, strangely fluid. I've never seen a horse move like this. Its hair is wavier than any horse I've seen before, and it looks soaking wet despite being on land. The hair looks coarse. Not just the mane, but the tail, too. I retract my hand from the creature.

This isn't a horse.

This is a kelpie.

My heart races and fog fills my head. I told no one I was leaving, and now I'm alone with a deadly sea creature. I curse under my breath.

You've *got* to be joking.

I could call for help. One of them might hear me and get to me in time. but it could provoke the kelpie in the process. I slowly start to back away, making sure not to lose sight of the creature.

It takes a step toward me.

I've made a grave mistake.

"Hel-!"

22

PEARCE

"DID ANYONE ELSE HEAR that?"

I look around at the men sitting with me. They all shake their heads, looking at me like I have two of them.

"Hear what?" Hart mumbles from his place on the floor.

"It sounded like someone yelled," I explain.

Davian waves me off. "We're not too far from a village, I'm sure it was just some townspeople."

I look around the area we've set up as camp for the night, and my spine straightens when I don't see her anywhere.

"Has anybody seen Roan?" Maybe she ran off. Took her long enough.

"She left with her horse, I think she was heading towards the water. She'll be back soon. Why, you miss her?" Jaali teases.

I scoff. "Right. I'm going to see where she went." Hart shrugs, his distaste for both me and the princess apparent. Jaali is still smiling at his—what he would call—joke.

"Yeah, alright," Davian says with a wave.

Leaving the comfort of the fire we've set up already feels like a mistake, but I can't shake the feeling something isn't right. I stalk toward the water, listening for anything out of the ordinary. When I hear what sounds like something dragging, I freeze. Even with my enhanced eyesight, I can't see anything. But I also hear... Are those hooves? I look to my right and catch a glimpse of Winnie. But I still don't see *her*.

I'm next to Winnie in a blink, trying to soothe her while looking around for her rider.

"Where the hell did you go, princess?" I whisper to myself. That's when I hear splashing. A moment later, a single clap of thunder echoes through the trees. I angle Winnie toward camp and slap her rear to send her running there. My feet carry me to the water's edge, and I'm met with sloshing waves. A single thunderclap without a storm only means one thing.

This woman and water...

I push that thought to the back of my head. I'll tease her about putting herself in dangerous situations later. Right now, I don't have time to think about that. Or that I can't see to the bottom of the murky water. *Or* that my fingers are trembling at the thought of submerging myself in it. The river bath was one thing, I could stand in that...

I run through the shallow waves fully clothed, and plummet until I catch my bearings. By sheer force of will, I convince my feet to move.

Luckily, I can see through some of the water, but I'm terrified by what I find. With limited moonlight, I'm barely able to make out the horse-shaped figure moving about 40 yards ahead of me. I don't see Raelenthia from here, and the pit growing in my stomach doubles.

My feet kick as hard as my fear will let them as I cut through the water, closing the distance between me and the creature that seems to be in no rush. Like it has all the time in the world. They move through a faint beam of light coming through the water, and I see a gleam of long, strawberry hair floating behind them.

There you are.

The body of a kelpie is magically adhesive, making it easier for the beast to take their victims. I don't see any air bubbles coming from her face, and I pray to the Gods that she's just holding her breath for dear life, prolonging it.

I push with every muscle, past the mental blocks threatening to drown me, to get above the creature as it glides through the sea. As I approach, I see her atop the creature's back, eyes closed. My withering confidence threatens to collapse. She may be out cold, which means I'll have to get her unstuck myself. I grab either side of her arms as tightly as I can while moving forward and try to pull her up. She doesn't budge. I can't rip her from the thing while we're underwater, or her flawless, freckled skin will peel from her body. I'll have to reach the bridle to gain control of the creature.

I'm running low on air; I've already been down here a while. She has even less time. I use the last push I have to hover over the head of the sea devil and reach down to grip the bridle, avoiding its deadly adherent coat. The animal halts movement in the ocean. When I start to kick upward toward land, it follows. Its will is mine, as long as I keep hold of this damn thing.

When we finally break the surface and I can reach the sea floor with my feet again, I pull us onto solid ground.

"Release her," I command. "Leave us. You will not touch her again." The moment I let go of the beast, her limp body slides from its back without it even moving. I reach out and catch her before she hits the ground. The kelpie wanders back into the water until its head finally disappears into the black void.

I lay Raelenthia down on her side, keeping my hand under her head so she can cough up the water she inhaled during her struggle.

I push the wet hair sticking to her face and put it behind her ears. I never noticed before; their point is more subtle than mine.

When she doesn't move after what feels like forever, I start to panic. "Come on, princess, work with me here. I have a bargain to uphold."

Her body jolts, and she expels an ample amount of water. Her eyes don't open, likely due to exhaustion. I'll take her back to camp so she can rest and keep an eye on her throughout the night. I pick her up and cradle her gently.

As I walk back, shivers tremble through her. Her clothes are soaked, as are mine. I'll need to find her something to wear so she doesn't catch a chill in the night. I press her against my chest to provide some kind of warmth on the walk back to camp. Looking down at her face doesn't bring me any peace, she looks too pale. None of her usual fire is in her cheeks. Her lashes are fanned over them, not displaying her bright green eyes.

When I step back into the light of the fire, Jaali runs over to my side.

"What the hell happened?!" he shouts.

"She was gripped by a kelpie," I reply, a tremor running through my body.

Davian comes over and looks down at her. He raises the back of his hand to touch her face, and I instinctively pull her a little closer to my chest. Davian notices my hesitance.

"Is she alright?"

Obviously not. "She will be." She has to be.

The closest thing I have to family eyes me carefully from across the fire, peeling away the façade he knows too well. "You jumped in to get her, didn't you? Even though you—"

"Yeah." I sniffle. "Leave it alone, Jaali."

Jaali shrugs off his cloak at my request and hands it to me with too much understanding in his eyes. I bring her over to where I laid mine out earlier and take her jacket off before laying her down. She can't sit in wet clothes all night. Once she's free of the heavier garments, I cover her with Jaali's cloak. I eye Davian from across the small clearing until he offers his as well.

I grab the log I've been using as a chair and bring it close to her still body. Any hope I had about finally getting some sleep is long gone. At home, I spend most nights lying awake, staring at the uneven ceiling in my room. Since we've been on this mission, I've hardly slept. Tonight will be no different.

A strange gratefulness floods me at her not being able to tease me for staring at her. I have no idea how long I've been sitting like this, examining the rise and fall of her chest to make sure it's constant.

She has a knack for getting herself into trouble. Like this damned bargain I've trapped her in...

I didn't expect her to agree to it, let alone follow through. But she seems genuinely concerned that I'll use it to make her miserable, and that's not what I have planned. It sounded more ideal earlier in the trip, but now? I'm not so sure.

Whatever I decide, I need to pick soon. I've been away from home for too long already. The council expects Jaali and me back as soon as we're finished here. I suppose *finished* is a relative term, we didn't specify exactly how long we would be gone. I can send Jaali back with a message. If he'd even be willing to leave without me, that is.

Just...wake up, princess.

23

RAELENTHIA

C HATTERING ANIMALS FLOOD MY ears. The sun is up further than it normally is for our wake-up calls, so I'm surprised when I look around and see everyone sitting around the camp.

When I try to sit up, my head feels so dizzy I almost fall back down on the ground. Jaali jumps to my side and tells me to relax, and that I need to rest. Why is everyone still sitting around? I rub my temples with my index fingers and sit up slower.

"What's going on? Why are you all looking at me like that?" That, being like they've seen a ghost.

"How are you feeling?" Jaali asks.

My brow furrows. "Not great, now that you mention it. I feel a bit dizzy, and my body feels...heavy?"

Something shifts in my peripheral, and that's when I realize Pearce's stare is boring holes into my profile.

"You really don't remember what happened?" Davian questions.

I shake my head softly and purse my lips. "The last thing I remember is taking Winnie to the river for some water, and then I remember being cold during the middle of the night." I get a small chill and look down to realize some of my clothes are missing. "Where the hell are my clothes?" I instinctively lift the cloak I'm holding to cover myself even though I'm not naked, just missing a few key pieces.

Jaali tells me they're drying; they covered me with his and Davian's cloaks to keep me warm through the night.

"Why were my clothes wet?"

Pearce shifts again, leaning forward to rest his arms on top of his thighs. His voice is raspy. "A kelpie almost drowned you last night."

I gasp slightly. Looking down at my thinly clothed body, I pull the cloak tighter around me like it will keep those words from chilling me to the bone. "What are you talking about? I took Winnie to the river and then I..." I can't remember anything after that. "Why can't I remember anything after that?"

"That's probably a trauma side effect. That, or it could be from you being unconscious. Either way, you need to rest," Davian advises.

Pearce's jaw is tense, his teeth grinding like sandpaper. Hart shows the least bit of interest in this situation, while Davian and Jaali remain attentive but distant.

That doesn't make sense. Kelpies are adhesive. I wouldn't have been able to get myself unstuck, especially if I was unconscious.

I look around the circle of men, curious. "How am I alive right now?" I ask, my voice barely above a whisper.

Jaali looks down at his hands, suddenly more interested in his cracked knuckles than my near-death experience. Davian's eyes flick to the right so subtly, I almost miss it. They look to Pearce, who has turned as far away from me as possible.

"Pearce?"

He slowly turns his head, and his eyes refuse to meet mine. "You need to be more careful." His jaw ticks, and then he storms away.

After a while of peppering the remaining men with questions about the last 12 hours, I feel well enough to go after Pearce. I find him sitting on a worn boulder, half jagged and half smooth, worn by water over the years. I sit next to him but say nothing. He doesn't look at me, but I know he knows.

An exasperated sigh leaves him. "Don't start thanking me again," he gets out.

"I wouldn't need to if you stopped saving me." It's incredibly confusing that the man who's made me feel unwelcome on this mission is the one who keeps defending my life. I'm starting to get whiplash from Pearce's changing emotions.

"I wouldn't need to keep saving you if you didn't keep putting yourself in danger." When he finally looks at me, I don't see what I expect. I expect him to be angry with me, and he is, but there's something else there.

"I'm not doing any of it on purpose, I don't know why you're so upset," I confess while shaking my head.

He moves quickly to stand in front of me. His hands come up, begging the sky for reprieve as he says, "Can you manage to not do anything reckless for a day?" His chest heaves and his arms fall to his sides.

Feeling useless, I dip my head forward so it's hanging over my legs on the rock. *Can't.* "I can't stop getting into dangerous situations. I can't use a sword. I can't get away from deadly creatures. I'm not a good spy. I can't paint like my sister can, and I can't play an instrument like my best friend." I sigh, letting the stress that's building roll over me like a wave. "I can't do a lot of things."

He takes a step closer, his thighs almost brushing my knees. After a minute, he speaks up. "I couldn't read for most of my life."

My brows dip. "I allow myself a moment of vulnerability around you, and you make a joke?"

"It's true, I couldn't. My parents both died when I was young, and I went to an orphanage in a new and unfamiliar city. I wasn't as smart as the other kids, so I had to stand out in different ways. I became a fighter. A good one. No one cares if the big, rash soldier is intelligent. They're just fighting power. A body on the front lines to take brunt force." His eyes drift somewhere far from here before coming back to me.

"My mother made sure I learned when I was a girl. If she hadn't taken the care she did, I wouldn't be nearly as well-read." I chuckle softly under my breath, already too aware of the discrepancies between the two of us.

He's looking into my eyes like he's never seen me before. And maybe he hasn't. He inhales deeply and takes a step away from me, clenching his fists at his sides. His face looks pained as if the space between us is suddenly as difficult for him as it is for me.

"We should get back to the others," he says. He extends his hand to help me down.

I take it and jump from the rock. I can't place the feeling I get when he drops my hand, and my skin is met with the brisk air I hadn't even noticed before he touched me.

We make it back to camp in little time. Looking around, I see them all starting to pack up their things and I get a twinge of guilt for delaying our trip home. Jaali comes up behind me before I can say anything. "We're going to travel a little way into sundown tonight to help make up for lost time. The horses have been resting all morning, so they should be fine going a few hours later." I nod a brief thank you and pack up my things as well.

Winnie is happy I'm awake, her tail whipping around. I smile and soothe her with my hand along her neck. I can't imagine the stress she was under last night during the kelpie attack. My head falls against her neck and I wrap my arms around her. Winnie has been with me for most of my life, and she'll be around for a while longer if I can help it.

Another day is spent traveling through forests, and we cross through two barriers between seasons. Spring to Summer feels like opening an oven, while moving from Summer to Autumn feels like a stiff breeze on damp skin. One more night before we're back home and I'm forced to deal with the repercussions of my actions.

I don't expect my parents to be angry with me forever. I do, however, expect to be on lockdown upon my return. Whenever I tried to run away as a child to go on different missions, I never made it far. I was curious, and that often meant I got into trouble. I was always turned around before I ever left the stables. Except once, I somehow made it to the gate before I was noticed and returned to my father.

He knows how long I've wanted to see all of Drennica, including Baeton. I'd love to see the other continents someday as well, but right now I've settled for the nation that neighbors my home. He's told me countless times to stay away from other humans. They didn't all change their minds like he did.

We barely escaped Baeton, and not unscathed. Dessielle won't believe half the things I tell her. She'll want to know about everything that happened, and I'm unsure if I'll tell her about...

Pearce has hardly looked at me all day. I thought when we stopped for our halfway point to feed the horses that any conversation between the two of us would continue on like it did by the river, but I was, foolishly, mistaken.

I recognize some of our surroundings now, places Winnie and I frequent. I owe her a lot of love and care when we return, and even more treats. She deserves to go wherever she wants after the things I've put her through on this trip.

A trip that, after tonight, I'll be free of. It's sort of funny. I wanted to leave the castle so badly and go somewhere I'd never been, yet the entire time, I missed my home.

Our camp tonight is much cozier than any we've had before. We're all seemingly more comfortable in Autumn. Jaali came back with firewood a bit ago and made quick work of getting the flame started. He's quite the character, I'll miss him when he leaves. I think that's the only person I'll miss. Hart doesn't deserve the space in my head he already has; Davian is nice, but I doubt we have much in common. That leaves one other person.

Will he stay? He never even told me where he's from.

The men return to sitting in a circle like they do every time we take a long rest. I cozy up with Pearce's cloak—which I forgot to return—on a soft enough patch of grass near Winnie. In the distance, I can make out the light of fires sending smoke into the sky from nearby villages. I'm more than ready to be back in my cushioned bed with too many pillows and a lit fireplace.

Jaali looks at me and waves me over to join them. Hesitantly, I walk over and take a seat beside him. Davian asks Hart what he plans on doing when he arrives back home.

"I'll probably sit in my chair with a pint. After that, I don't care." His head falls back with a bark of a laugh before he swigs from his canteen.

Davian's brows pinch. "What about your wife?" Hart looks annoyed that she was mentioned, or as if he'd forgotten he had one.

"Yeah, I'll spend time with her too."

Charming.

Davian looks at Jaali and nods his chin at him to ask the same question. "I miss my mom. I haven't been away from her this long since she brought me home from the orphanage. I think I'll take her to see a show." He smiles sweetly while talking about his mother. I didn't know he lived in an orphanage, that must be where he met Pearce.

Pearce stiffens at the mention of the orphanage, I didn't think it was possible to look sterner than he already does. Davian sees the shift in him and takes it as a cue to answer himself instead of continuing around the circle.

"I'm going to go back to the pixie marsh after I rest for a while. My daughter has wanted to see them for a long time, and I think after meeting the Ladies of Spring, they could swing me a visit." He nods lightly to himself and looks down at the ground before him.

"I didn't know you have a daughter," I comment. It seems I don't ask enough questions.

The left side of his mouth curls up even more. "Emalie," he says. "She's six, and she's the light of my life. A curious little thing. She'd love to come on a mission like this. I think she'd look up to you, Roan."

My heart swells. "Me? Why is that?"

"You've shown a lot of courage on this trip. Things keep trying to take you out, and you keep surviving. I think that makes you a good role model for my little girl."

His confidence in me is flattering, although, I suddenly feel even worse for lying about how I got here. We're so close to the end that I decide to keep it to myself. Pearce has kept his part of the bargain thus far; I might as well hold out a little longer.

"What about you, red?" I trace the lines on my palm with my index finger while I try to piece together an answer that doesn't give too much away.

"I'll check on my little sister first. She's probably worried about me, so I'll need to spend a few days with her to make up for lost time. Also, my best friend. She'll no doubt make me sit and tell her everything that happened," I chuckle.

Davian's head shoots up. "Many things on this mission are classified. You can't tell anyone what we learned, not until after we tell the Queen and King, and they approve it."

"Of course, right. I know that. I just meant she'll have lots of questions about traveling. How I am, and whatnot." Not entirely a lie. She'll definitely ask questions, and I plan on answering them. The only thing I don't plan on telling her is what we found in the war room. That's the only piece that is strictly mission business. But my travel companions and their issues? I consider that fair game.

He finally looks at Pearce. "How about you? Any big plans?" His tone comes off as joking, which does nothing to lessen Pearce's intensity.

"Yeah, actually. I plan on making the most of being home. It'll be party after party. Lots of drinking and tomfoolery."

Hart makes a sound that's a cross between a scoff and a chuckle. "Really?"

"No." Pearce snaps his head toward him. "I'll return to work. I'm not all that social back home."

"Why is that?" I ask.

"A lot of people depend on me. I don't exactly have a lot of free time."

The crackling fire fills the silence his confession leaves in its wake. After a few minutes of us all warming our hands around the flames, we settle in for our last night sleeping in the woods.

Morning comes with new energy. We're all excited to finally be back home, whatever that means for each of us. The camp is packed and we're on the move within twenty minutes of waking, having fallen into a comfortable silence. When I see smoke coming from up ahead, I know it's Blackwood. Not long after that, I see the top of the castle come into view. There's no party waiting outside for our return since this mission was kept quiet from the Alunian people.

We lead our horses into the stable and return to the armory to piece together all of our intel before giving it to the King and Queen. I hand over all the maps I was able to make decent copies of, and finish off the ones that need adjusting. *I* can read my writing, but it may have been difficult for someone of sane mind. When I sense I'm no longer needed, I make a break for it. Davian turns away, allowing me to sneak through the wooden doorway into the hall. I make it around two corners when I bump directly into a soft chest. In front of me is Dessielle, mouth agape.

"Thank the Gods you're okay." She wraps her arms around me, pinning my arms down.

"I missed you! I have so much to tell you. What are you doing down here?" She finally lets go of my arms so I can look at her fully.

"What am I doing down here? Are you serious? I heard through a line of housekeepers that some soldiers were arriving back today, and I had *everything* crossed that it'd be you!" She puts her hands on either side of my face and squishes my cheeks. "I was so worried about you, I had to see that you were okay."

"I'm fine," I try to say through my puckered mouth. She lets me go so I can speak properly. "I have a lot to fill you in on. But first, I need to see my sister. And then I probably need to deal with my parents…"

She offers a dramatic frown. "Yeah, you might want to find Ro right away. I'm sure your parents heard the same thing I did, and I doubt they'll be far behind me to come down here." As soon as she finishes, voices travel through the stairwell from the next floor up. She grabs my hand and pulls me in the opposite direction. There are staircases on both sides, so we'll be able to avoid them this way. We run up the steps and exit the stairwell on the next level, breathless.

"Roralei was in the sunroom last time I saw her; I think you should start there." With a brief nod, I let go of her hand and slide from room to room looking for my little sister. I catch a glimpse of her pale blonde hair through a doorway, and I backtrack to look again.

"Ro!" I rush over to her, and she turns to face me just before I wrap my arms around her in a debilitating hug and spin her around. I think she may be in shock, she doesn't respond at first. Roralei pulls her head back to look at me, and realization sets in. Her eyes grow wide and she gasps loudly.

"Rae!" she finally exclaims. She wiggles her arms out from under my grasp and circles them around my neck. We stand like this for a moment before my arms start to ache from the weight of her. She's not the small girl I watched grow up anymore, she's over half the size of me. She'll probably surpass me when she's older.

With a final squeeze, I let her back down onto the ground. Disbelief pours from her. "Where have you been? You were gone for so long," she drones.

"I know, Ro. I'm sorry. I made a last-minute decision to go on a trip. I didn't tell Mother or Father, and I didn't want to tell you because if you didn't know, there would be no chance of you getting in trouble too." I reach down to cup her chin in my hand. "I'll tell you next time I do something reckless, I promise."

She looks up the bridge of her nose and right into my eyes. "If you get in trouble, I do too. You scared me leaving that way. I thought you were angry with me, or you didn't want to be here anymore."

Any resolve I have left shatters. I hadn't thought about what my leaving would do to Roralei, especially with no explanation. Releasing her chin, I nod and chuckle at her dedication to my cause. "Next time, Ro." She smiles back at me, content with my promise for the future.

"I should go find our parents before they find me. I suppose I have some explaining to do."

24

THE DOORS LEADING TO the joint office of my parents are massive. They're meant to show power, and they accomplish that very well. The dark brown double doors are at least eight feet tall, allowing for most diplomats from other regions to enter as needed. Approaching them now, they swallow me. I don't feel like a large diplomat. Suddenly, I am a young girl again, awaiting my parents' disappointment.

Inside, my mother and father are waiting on their respective chairs behind their adjoined desks. They insisted that one desk for a single ruler be made larger so they could demonstrate an equal distribution of power. At the sight of me, they both release a heavy sigh. I take a deep breath and open my mouth to start apologizing. Before I can begin, my mother bolts up from the chair and embraces me with the strength of an ogre.

Confused, I return it. When we pull away, she smooths her hand over my head and rests it on the back of my neck. "We're so glad you're alright."

I look between her and my father, who is still sitting at his desk. "Wait, you're not angry with me?" I ask.

"We're incredibly angry with you. You left on a private mission without orders into enemy territory without telling anyone where you were going." My father stands and slowly walks over to me, causing me to shrink into myself. He places a hand on my shoulder. "But...we're happy you made it back unharmed."

A tear threatens to fall over my cheek, and I quickly wipe away any evidence of it. I had been so prepared for them to be disappointed in my actions and fear for my safe return, I hadn't considered how much they would miss me. I wrap an arm around each of my parents and pull them into a hug.

"We've already discussed that your punishment for disobeying us will be assisting your mother with preparations for the Beltane Ball," my father explains.

Events take a lot of planning. I'll have to use a decent amount of my free time to make it happen. No lollygagging with Dessielle or sneaking off in the middle of the day to avoid my duties. It's not the most annoying consequence I've ever dealt with; they once had me fill a wheelbarrow with hay just to dump it out and do it again. They *loved* wasting my time.

After a bit of catching up, I leave the room and head back down to the armory in search of...I'm not sure.

Davian, Hart, and Jaali are all still debriefing when I arrive. Davian stands while the others remain seated on the bench. "I was wondering where you ran off to," he says.

I cross my arms and rub the outside of one with my hand. "I had to see to some things before heading out."

Davian nods and purses his lips. He holds out his hand for me to shake. When I do, he pulls me in for a brief hug. "If you want to be in the room when we lay everything out for them, you can." When I start to shake my head, he holds up his hand to stop me. "It's not required. I just figured you might want to tell your parents about what you helped discover." My mouth falls open, and he lifts his index finger to close it. He takes a step forward and puts his mouth a bit closer to my ear to avoid eavesdropping. "I'm older than I look. I've led countless missions out of this castle, and some of them were infiltrated by a little princess every now and then. I never forget a face, Raelenthia."

Heat floods my cheeks. That means he...*let* me stay? He knew who I was and instead of throwing me out and making me stay home, he let me prove myself. I throw my arms around his neck in a thank you, which he welcomes. "Not bad for a princess," he whispers with a wink.

Hart is leaning forward and trying to make out our conversation. Jaali is leaning back against the wall with his arms behind his head. He really could sleep anywhere. I walk over and nudge him on the leg and his eyes flip open.

"Where is he?" I ask. I don't have to clarify, he points to the door that leads outside; the one I snuck out of weeks ago. I take a deep breath before pushing it open and stepping into the cool autumn air.

I don't have to look far. He's sitting up against a large red maple tree with his legs bent in front of him. Without speaking, I sit next to him, mimicking his position. His head doesn't turn, but I feel the weight of his stare.

After a few minutes of silence, I decide to speak up. "So, what now?"

His head turns then. "What do you mean?"

I shift completely so my body faces his. "When will you be making the trip home? Wherever that is, for you." I try not to let hope bleed into my voice. I don't understand him at all. He's been cruel and harsh and hasn't hidden his distaste for me. But he also saved me. Twice. And I can't help but become more curious about him with each peek behind the curtain.

He looks back out to the lush landscape before us, trees and plants like a roaring fire of orange and red. "I have a few things I need to take care of before I can leave."

Something like relief rushes through my blood. I nod, trying to hide the ghost of a smile forming on my face. I shouldn't want him to be here still. Not after everything he's said to me. Yet somehow, I can't help but be thankful.

"Can you show me to my new bed? The one we talked about before?"

"You mean my bedroom?" I sneer, my eyes conveying unspoken vulgar language.

With a smirk, he says, "Yeah, that one."

"You're not taking my bed. We discussed that."

"I think the terms of our bargain can remain open, amendable."

"Even so, you're not taking my bed," I clarify.

"Okay fine princess, I'll stay away from your bed."

I spend the rest of the day walking around the castle with Ro. The trip to Baeton was the longest I've ever been away from home. I didn't realize that the structure has a specific smell. It slammed into me like a wave when I entered my parents' study earlier, and every room since has had unique undertones.

After Ro grows tired of wandering through the halls, I head up a few floors to my room. When I arrive in front of the door, my hand hesitates on the brushed brass ring. I push it open and find the room exactly as I left it. My pillows look untouched, although they look fluffier than I expected. I graze my fingertips along the covers of my bed. It's quiet in the castle, with no sounds from the usual hustle of people moving throughout the halls. Most of the castle staff probably were given the day off to limit the number of people seeing our party come back into town.

Speaking of which, I wonder if Davian has gone to speak with them yet. I look down at myself, still in my uniform, and debate changing my clothes. After staring at myself in the mirror for a moment, I kick off my boots and peel the uniform off my body. The undergarments that have seen too much water for my liking over the past few weeks fall to the floor. I quickly wet a cloth and run it over my skin. It's not ideal, but I'm unwilling to put even my least favorite gown onto skin that hasn't seen a real bath in far too long.

The doors of my wardrobe open with a creak, and I sort through the clothing until I find something that seems appropriate for a meeting like this. While I no longer have to hide who I am, I want to embrace this new side that I've discovered. Even if it's only the smallest bit.

Once I've readied myself as much as I can with little time, I reach for an old pair of boots instead of my usual slippers.

The halls lead me to another grand door. This time, it's Alunia's war room. I have a newfound appreciation for the creatures that draw maps after seeing the intricacy of the ones we found in Baeton. Upon walking in, I see the rest of the group already inside and seated before my parents. They keep several smaller chairs on their side of the large table in the middle of the room, usually occupied by members of their council. However, this seems to be a closed-door meeting. The only other person in the room besides the men and my parents is the commander of Alunia's armies, General Darcy.

All their heads turn when I enter. My parents look proud to see that I showed up after all. Hart and Jaali look the most confused. Davian gives me a small smile of approval and Pearce... His eyes look intense, but the rest of his face is emotionless.

Without a faltering step, I approach them. There are no remaining seats next to the men. I don't want to separate myself from those I traveled with, so I walk around the table, pick up an empty chair by its back, and bring it to the other side. My mother stifles a chuckle while my father drops his head with a pursed-lip smile. The closest place for me to put the chair is next to Pearce, so that's where I settle. I take my seat and swipe my hands down on my legs to straighten out my dress.

My mother clears her throat and addresses our group commander. "Please continue, Davian. You had just started explaining what you saw inside the Winter castle."

Davian leans forward slightly in his chair and nods. "Yes, Your Majesty. When we split into our groups for information collection, Hart and I were able to find a boardroom. After further investigation, it seemed to be a meeting place for the commanders of their forces."

"And what did you find there?" Father asks. I missed the warmth of my father's voice while I was gone. His beard looks a bit fuller, too.

"Well, My King, we found pages of notes filled with different methods of destruction. Some were about the different regions, which creatures populate the areas, and their weaknesses."

My father's jaw clenches as he nods. Davian continues. "All other regions on Drennica were included in their list. The topography of each one was noted, as well as any natural concerns for bringing large numbers through that area."

"So, they plan to march soldiers through Alunia?" My mother questions.

"It seems that way, My Queen," Davian answers sorrowfully.

She sighs with a heavy heart and folds her hands on her lap. "We'll go over those notes more thoroughly with you privately, Davian, thank you." He nods. "What else do you have to show us?"

He glances at Pearce from the center of our seated line. "I believe Pearce is the one who made it into their war room, Your Majesty. He has the map illustrations."

Pearce looks down at my drawings in his hands. He filters through them and finally settles on the first he'd like to display. Except he doesn't speak on it. Instead, he turns to me and hands me the stack of drawings before looking back at my mother. "Your daughter drew these, your majesty. I'd prefer if she told you about them."

I smile softly at him before taking the pages from his hands and looking at my parents across the table. Hart leans over to Davian, trying not to smack him for keeping secrets.

My father dips his head at me. "Well, Rae? What have you got?"

We spend hours discussing the layout of Baetonian troops and how they've moved around Winter. I try to interject when I can about what I saw on the maps, but Davian knows more about the meaning of their traveling from the notes he managed to take hold of.

Jaali speaks up about what he was doing while the other groups were picking through written information. He recounts how he moved silently through each room until he found a group of guards standing around and gossiping. One of the men told Jaali that he loathed his job, which was setting up enlistment opportunities for incoming soldiers. While he grumbled about his duties, Jaali nodded and expressed equal frustration about such tasks. The other men chimed in with the boredom of their respective jobs, and one of them mentioned that he oversaw the creatures they'd captured. Jaali didn't immediately ask what kind of creatures he was talking about to avoid suspicion, he needed it to come up organically. He says that after speaking to these men for a while, he discovered that the Baetonians have captured creatures from across the continent. Kelpie, ogres, even a few vaclik. Jaali says that when he asked what the need was for different kinds of creatures and not just one, the other soldiers looked at him strangely and insisted that he shouldn't be heard questioning the King.

Time flies past us; the next time I look around, sunlight no longer shines through the windows. My parents realize the same thing, lean in to speak with each other quietly for a moment, and then face us again.

"Thank you all for your help, this information is incredibly valuable," says Queen Calliope.

My father adds, "We realize it's late, and you may not want to travel to your homes until sunrise. If you wish to leave tonight, let us know and we will bid our goodbyes. Otherwise, rooms will be prepared for you for the night."

Davian thanks them but insists on getting home to his daughter. Hart accepts the invitation and asks if he can have alcohol sent to his room, which earns a concerned look between my mother and father and a hesitant agreement. Jaali only asks if he'll be fed, and when he learns dinner is soon to be ready, he accepts. Pearce accepts as well, although less enthusiastically.

My parents fill them in on where they'll be staying tonight and let them know they can bathe before coming down for dinner if they choose. The spit bath I gave myself earlier was nothing like I'd hoped for upon my return.

When I arrive back to my room, Willow is inside, sitting on the chair by my still-burning fireplace. The moment I'm through the door, she rushes up to me and squeezes all the breath from my airways.

"I was getting so worried, princess. Nobody knew where you'd went, they were searchin' the whole castle and couldn't find nothin'," she blurts out, her words moving so quickly it takes a moment for them to register.

"I'm sorry for the scare, Willow. I made it back safely though, I'm alright. Thank you for keeping an eye on everything while I was away."

She blushes slightly at the compliment and her eyes fall to the ground. "You're welcome, Rae. Had to make sure when you came home everything was nice and cozy."

Willow leads me to the bathing room, where the tub is filled with my favorite scents. I quickly undress without embarrassment and take a step into the scalding tub. When Willow realizes this, she grabs my arm and insists I wait a few minutes because it's far too hot, still. I look down at the water, which has steam rolling lightly off it. I hadn't even realized it was so fresh.

My only thought is that it will, hopefully, help with the layer of grime coating my body. The river baths on the mission did me no justice, and I am so grateful to be back in my large and *clean* basin. I spend far too much time lathering my body, and then doing it *again* until my skin is a vibrant pink from the scrubbing. I do the same with my hair, working my fingers into my scalp so roughly I can practically feel the bubbles breaking apart the dirt along the strands.

Finally satisfied with my cleanliness, I exit the tub and let Willow make me look a bit more presentable by braiding my hair back from my face. The gown I choose is simple since I'll only be wearing it for dinner before I retire to my room to sleep through the next several days.

It's emerald, with slightly darker embroidered leaves scattered all along the floor-length fabric. I put on my flattest slippers for the meal.

My feet lead me effortlessly through the halls until I enter the dining room. We're meeting in the formal dining room tonight due to the amount of people joining us. The table is set with a warm-toned cloth draped along the center, and glasses filled with what I know is harvest faerie wine, the deep berry color unmistakable.

Most of our party is seated, although I don't see Pearce in attendance. I look at Jaali with pinched brows and shake my head to ask him if he knows where Pearce is. He shrugs his shoulders, and one side of his mouth quirks to display his disappointment about the situation as well.

We spend the meal chatting about simple things like the weather between seasonal regions, and Jaali showers me with questions about being a princess. Hart tries to seem uninterested in the conversation but chimes in with small quips and comments. Jaali praises my courage for leaving the kingdom, making Hart chuckle under his breath and remark about it not being a smart decision. He's not completely wrong, but I refuse to let him know that his words get to me. So I continue without acknowledging him until we all finish for the night and return to our rooms.

On my way back down the hall, I find myself wondering why Pearce didn't show up this evening. My parents show their gratitude to us, and he stays in his room the whole time? The further I walk, the more my previous pity for him turns to frustration. Suddenly my feet aren't moving in the direction of my bedroom, but back down the stairs to his.

Before I fully think through what I'm doing, my fist is pounding on his door. It's not too late, so it shouldn't wake anyone on this floor. I don't hear anything from inside, not even the shuffling of movement. I knock once more, louder this time. When he still doesn't respond, I open the door. Looking through the entire room proves fruitless; he isn't in here. Where the hell would he be?

Something he said by the lake resurfaces in my thoughts. He said that a soldier didn't need to be smart, that he only needed to be a good fighter. The number of stairs I've taken today feels like it'll be a mistake come morning, but now my curiosity is piqued. I walk back down to the first level and through the grey stone halls that the training rooms occupy. I hear scuffling feet and grunting from down the hall, so I follow it. When I peek around the corner of the doorway, I see him.

His movements look fluid, like he's flowing through water. His sword comes down with incredible force, yet he follows through the movement without missing a step. It's sort of beautiful, the precision he has.

I can't help but notice he has no shirt on. When he glides through a move with his weapon, his deeply tanned skin molds over his muscles. I can see his arms flex even in the dim lighting of the room, large hands cutting through the air with ease. A slight sheen of sweat coats his scarred back. He's moving too quickly for me to distinguish the markings I've seen before, but I see the discoloration on his torso when he turns.

Unfortunately, when he *does* turn, he catches a glimpse of me, too. His movements halt and his sword lowers until it's almost scraping the ground. Since I'm no longer in hiding, I step fully into the room. He walks over to the bench at the side of the room where his shirt is lying and grabs it, pulling it across his forehead to collect the sweat building there.

"Don't make it a habit to spy on me, princess," he says coldly.

"I wouldn't need to if you showed up to meals," I respond just as blandly.

He holsters his sword and moves to stand back in the center of the room. "I wasn't hungry."

"That's ridiculous, you haven't eaten since this morning."

His brows raise. "Tracking my eating habits now?"

I grunt with frustration and tilt my head back with closed eyes. "Never mind. Forget it. Starve for all I care." I turn toward the door, but his hand catches on my forearm.

"Wait," he says. I turn to face him, and he lets go of my arm. I cross my arms over my chest, already finished with this interaction. "I just didn't want to be surrounded by people, alright? I wanted a little alone time after everything that's happened the past week."

I inhale deeply, my shoulders rising and falling dramatically. "It's rude to not say anything," I explain. "We were expecting you."

"Yeah, well I wasn't exactly in the mood to sit around and play pretend with someone else's family."

"Is this about last night? When we were all talking about who we're going to spend time with?" He stiffens. Clearly, I've struck a nerve.

"I don't care about that," he spits loudly.

"Then why didn't you come to dinner?" I ask, my voice rising with his.

"Because I didn't want to! Isn't that reason enough?" His voice is booming, but I refuse to shrink. Instead, I lift my chin and stand my ground.

"No. It isn't." I'm not sure why I'm pushing this fight, but at this point, I've dealt with his attitude enough that I refuse to put up with it right now.

"Then I guess you'll just have to be disappointed." He exhales heavily through his nose and lowers his volume.

"I guess so." I turn away quickly before he can stop me this time and make my way back up the stairs and through the halls to my room. I didn't intend to go in there and start an argument, but he ignites something in me that I can't place. Everything I feel around him is more intense.

25

I'M SITTING ON THE edge of my bed when Willow opens my door. She's coming to wake up my room for the day, but ever since I left home I haven't been able to sleep in as late.

She startles when she sees I'm not lying in bed. "My goodness dear, you scared me. You feeling alright?"

I chuckle softly while looking down at my feet. "Yes, Willow. I feel fine. I was a little restless this morning, that's all."

Willow walks across to the window and draws back the curtains. I didn't even realize I had been sitting in the dark until the light shines right in my face, my hand too slow to shield my eyes.

"Any big plans today, Raelenthia?"

I stand slowly, every muscle and bone aching in the process. "To lay in a freezing bath until my body no longer aches," I complain. All the riding and sleeping on the ground seems to be finally catching up with me, and every move is a struggle. The walk to the bathing room feels like dragging my feet through mud during a windstorm.

Anticipating my next move, Willow reaches around me to fill the tub. While the level rises, I start combing out my hair. I pull it around my shoulder to reach it all since it reaches the stool I'm sitting on. After I'm pleased with the lack of tangles, I put it in a simple twist to keep it away from the water in the tub. Last night's cleaning was thorough enough to last at least several more days.

Willow signals that the basin is ready and, although I told her I wanted a cold bath, I hadn't realized just how cold she could make it. I step in with one leg without thinking and am immediately in shock from the temperature. My leg jolts out of the tub, water splashing out. I let out a small yelp which summons Willow, who had stepped out of the room. Her step falters when she sees me, as I am fully naked and standing halfway out of the tub.

"You did say you wanted it cold, right?"

I nod with my lips pulled inside my mouth, making a thin line. "Yes. Yes, I did. Thank you, Willow," I say to dismiss her. This was my own foolish plan, and now I must deal with the ramifications of it. Cold settles in my bones as I grip the sides of the basin so tightly that my knuckles turn white. The sound of my teeth chattering in my head is the only thing I can hear when I'm fully submerged in my terrible idea.

After my chilling morning, I slip on a deep sapphire-colored gown with long, billowy sleeves. The square neckline conceals most of my upper half from the brisk morning air; perfect for a walk through the courtyard. The stone floor is covered with fire-hued leaves due to the open ceiling over the fountain. Scattered through the courtyard are holes in the stone where trees have been planted. A few of them are Dogwood, others Quaking Aspen; all of them equally beautiful.

A different kind of quiet fills the castle this morning. The only sounds are from trickling water in the fountain and small birds who seek to rest their wings inside the courtyard.

I sit on the fountain edge and watch the birds, settling into the quiet. Footsteps approach from behind and when I look, Reynard is coming right toward me.

"There you are!" he exclaims.

I offer a tired smile. "Here I am!"

He takes a seat beside me on the fountain and puts his arm around me for a weak hug. "I went looking for you while you were gone. Dessielle told me you were off with some stranger, but that didn't sound like you."

"Maybe you don't know me well enough, then," I drawl with playful eyes.

Reynard scoffs and tosses his hair. "Who would know better than me? Why someone else when you've got all this back at the castle?" He trails a hand swiftly down his body, which earns a hearty laugh from me.

"Good to see you still have your sense of humor."

He chuckles dryly. "Right... Well, now that you're back, maybe we can start training again? And you can tell me about where you went on your trip!"

My face twists, unsure. "I don't know, maybe you had a point." Thinking back on all the chances I had to stand up for myself in Baeton, I fell short. Pearce got hurt because of me. "Maybe it's for the best if I don't train anymore."

He nods. "That makes sense. Well, we can just hang out then. It doesn't have to be training, we can find something else to do together." He pats my thigh briefly before gripping the edge of the fountain.

Behind us, someone clears their throat. And right on the other side of the fountain, is Pearce.

My eyes widen in surprise. I open my mouth to speak, but no words come out.

Pearce stalks over and stands beside me. Reynard snaps up from the fountain, annoyance evident on his face.

"Who's this, princess?"

His torso almost touches the side of my arm as I stand, he's so close. I knew before that he was tall but seeing him next to Reynard makes him look like a monster of a man. The sheer width of his torso is impressive. The top of Reynard's head is only at Pearce's chin. He has to look up to talk to him.

I've never seen Reynard look small.

"This is Reynard. He's a royal guard, and my friend."

Reynard looks back and forth between me and Pearce. "And who the hell are you?"

Pearce takes in Reynard, slowly sizing him up. "Her new teacher."

Reynard looks as if I've physically wounded him. "I thought you didn't want to train anymore," he says, his eyes questioning.

"Not with you," Pearce answers for me.

It's my turn to look between them now. What does he think he's doing?

"Rae, who is this guy?"

"We met while I was gone. This is Pearce," I say as I tap Pearce's arm.

Reynard takes in the man before us and releases a short breath. "We'll talk later," is his goodbye before he storms out of the courtyard.

Pearce's stare follows him until he's out of sight. When he finally looks at me, his jaw is tense, and rage flickers in his eyes.

"Do all of your friends touch you so casually?"

I shake my head, confused. "We've been friends for years."

He cocks his head as if wondering whether or not he should go after Reynard. "That doesn't give him permission to touch you."

The intensity of his stare leaves me mute for a moment. When I can finally speak again, it's lower than I intend. "What did you mean, my new teacher?"

His eyes don't soften, but the tension in his face eases the slightest bit. "That's the man you were learning from?"

Answering my question with another is typical for him, and it only fuels my confusion. "Not for very long, but yes. We would meet after sunset and go over basic maneuvers."

The fire in his eyes only brightens. "Do you still want to?"

I sigh. "You saw how well I did in Baeton. I don't know if it's a good idea anymore. He made a decent point, it's not something I need to know."

He hesitates for a moment. Then, his gravelly voice utters the last thing I expect him to say. "I'll do it."

I shake my head slightly, thinking I misheard him. "You'll do what?"

"Teach you," he replies.

My heart comes to a halt, along with every thought that was bouncing around in my head. They all freeze. "You're going to...teach me how to use a sword."

He nods slowly as if coming to the same realization himself. A soft gasp leaves my parted lips. His eyes flicker down to my mouth at the sound and then quickly back to my eyes, his chest rising sharply.

"You can't be serious," I say through an unsure grin. "I already owe you one favor, I'm not further indebting myself to you."

He nods slowly before rustling his curls with his hand. "You won't owe me anything extra. Consider it a token of good faith."

With a slight bend at the waist, he leaves the courtyard. My feet have merged with the stone covering the ground. I'm unable to move from this spot for at least a few minutes before I turn to face the fountain and place my hands on the ledge for support. Whether it's physical or emotional, Im unsure.

I reach into the cool running water and place my hand on my temple. My face suddenly feels warm, but I have no fever.

I don't know if Pearce and I have ever been near one another for longer than five minutes and *not* gotten into an argument.

And I'm meant to train with him.

Once I've collected myself, I set off to find Ro. The time we got yesterday wasn't nearly enough, and a lot can happen in a short time when you're her age.

I find her exactly where I expect to, in the sunroom again. She's sitting cross-legged on a large blanket with a small easel in front of her. I decide to stand in the doorway for a minute to watch her. She makes a couple of brush strokes and then lays down flat on her back to look up at the ceiling. The *glass* ceiling, with sunlight shining directly through the panes and into her eyes. She holds up her hand and opens her fingers slightly, repositioning her hand to a few different spots over her face before sitting back up and making a few more strokes.

My curiosity gets the better of me and I walk over to the blanket and sit beside her. She doesn't jump, she remains focused on her canvas. A moment passes and she lays back on the blanket with her legs still crossed. I do the same thing to see what she's looking at. When she sits back up, I finally have to ask.

"What on Drennica are you painting, little sister?"

Without missing a stroke she replies, "The sun."

I smile at her whimsy and let out a chuckle. "How do you intend to paint the sun?"

She lays back down on the blanket, and I follow her once more. "Well not the *sun* sun, but what it looks like coming through the ceiling. It looks like lots of different colors when it shines through the glass, so I'm painting the colors I see."

All I can see is a blinding white light when I sit back up, blood rushing to my head with all the back and forth. Now that I'm closer to her painting, I can see what she means. When sunlight shines through the glass, the rays reflect different colors. Violet, cyan, cerise. She's capturing it rather well. It'll be beautiful when she's finished.

We spend the afternoon chatting about everything she filled her days with in my absence. "Miss Woodstock assigned a lot of reading during my lessons, and she kept getting interrupted by Lieutenant Aidman," she says with a shiver. When I chuckle, she explains further. "I don't like him. Something about him makes my teeth feel strange."

A boisterous laugh leaves me, and my head falls back with the sound. "Your teeth?"

She giggles softly. "I don't know, he just does!"

After a few more hours spent gossiping about our teacher, soldiers, and housekeepers, Roralei returns to her bedroom to clean off all the paint she managed to get on her skin. I take the time to search for Dessielle. There's so much to discuss, I'm unsure where to start.

When I find her, she's playing the harp. While she's capable of playing many instruments, the harp has always been her favorite. I know it isn't possible because I wasn't gone *nearly* that long, but her hair looks longer. Her dark mane sits in layers of coils, some framing her face and others trailing down her back. None of them are the same, yet they adorn her face with precision and chaos simultaneously.

Her hearing is exceptional, even for Fae. She hears my steps over the harp sounding beside her head and halts her playing when I step inside the room.

"Is it finally time for you to tell me about your rendezvous in the woods?"

A bark of laughter leaves me at her abruptness. "I did not have a *rendezvous*; it was an incredibly serious and important mission."

"Right," she says as her eyes shrink to slits. "And the tanned scruffy stranger has nothing to do with the strange energy in the castle since you arrived home," she accuses with a tilt in her voice.

I feel the blood rush to my cheeks at her implication. "Nothing happened, Dessi, I swear it."

She raises both brows, still not believing me. "Then why is he still here? Why didn't he go home?"

My head drops down to look at the floor and the skin around my fingers suddenly looks pickable. "We made an arrangement when he...discovered who I was. I couldn't have him telling anyone my identity, so I agreed."

"What did you agree to?" Dessi asks with a newfound enthusiasm.

"He hasn't told me yet," I explain. I fill her in on how the entire altercation went down. How he noticed my shift in behavior when we arrived at the Spring castle, and the attentiveness the ladies paid to me. After the story is finished, she doesn't speak for a moment. When she finally does, I almost don't believe it.

"You fancy him."

Another laugh leaves me as I continue to pick at my fingers. "Did you hear anything I said? I do *not*." Even as I say it, I can feel the color on my face becoming brighter by the second.

"And I'm an incredible baker. Are we finished telling lies now?" We leave the room she had been playing in and wander the halls, gossiping in low whispers.

"It's only lessons, I'm going to try and really learn this time. He seems like he'll be a serious teacher."

"I'm sure he *will* teach you some things," she says as she nudges my arm with her elbow.

"He's abhorrent. He made a point to verbally *and* physically attack me during the trip." I leave out the part where he saved my life...multiple times.

"I can see it now," she theorizes in a daze. "The two of you stalking around one another, sweaty and out of breath."

"Dessi, come on," I beg her.

"Alright alright, I get it. You can't tell me he's not fun to look at, though."

She's right, I can't tell her that. She can see it on my face when I hesitate to respond. We continue walking arm in arm through the halls until we bore of it. I tell her all about the incident with the kelpie as it was relayed to me, which does nothing to quell her taunting. After a while, my stomach rumbles loudly making both of us laugh. "I'm hungry too," she says. "Let's go find something."

With a full stomach, I say goodbye to Dessi for the time being and decide to spend the rest of my afternoon reading. I've hardly been able to truly rest since being home, and I'm unsure of when I'll have to return to my studies. I've spoken to my mother about when I'll be finished and won't have to attend anymore, but she insists that a lady should be educated. I'm well past the age that insists I remain in classes, but my mother's command is heavier than any status quo.

After seeing how women were looked at in Baeton, I have a new-found appreciation for the education I've been given. The only reason there *is* a queen in that kingdom is because it's historically expected. There were no lady knights like there are in Alunia, and that sits heavy in my heart. I can't imagine they allow young women an equal education, given how despised they are.

My bedroom smells of red oak trees when I enter, probably from the time I've spent around them since arriving back in Autumn. I find the bag I borrowed from Dessi and empty its contents so I can return it to her. Also, I'm looking for the book I borrowed from Miss Woodstock. I didn't have many chances to read it while on the road since there's hardly enough lighting for reading outside, and I'm ready to pick up where I left off. Although I can't seem to find it. Strange, since this is the only place I remember putting it. I sort through the bag again and am still, somehow, empty-handed.

I plop down on the edge of my bed and sit for a moment, trying to retrace my steps in my head. It can't have gotten far, I know I saw it not too long ago and I wouldn't have put it down somewhere outside. I have a vague memory of Pearce being near Winnie while I was sleeping toward the end of our mission. He wouldn't ha—

He definitely would have.

Without another thought, I grab the bag from where it lays on my bed and start toward his room. When I arrive outside, I pound on the door much like I did the last time I sought him out. I hear shuffling from inside the room, so I know he's here.

"*Pearce*," I say sternly.

The door flies open so hard that the tails of my hair fly in its direction, the wind pulling it from its styled position. He's standing on the other side of the door and I have the briefest flash of disappointment that, this time, he's fully clothed. That thought quickly gets drowned out by the sound of his deep voice. He's still staring at me, and he bobs his head in a way that shows both frustration and confusion.

"Well?" he asks.

"Did you say something?" Had he been talking while I was trying to swat away the image of his sweaty arms wielding a sword?

"Yeah, I asked what you wanted. I'm not in the mood for visitors."

With a small smirk, I reply, "Then I suppose it's the same as usual." I push past him and enter his room. He slams it behind me and follows me in, determined to stop me.

"You can't just walk in here, you know. This isn't your space," he complains.

"Well, then you should've thought of that before you took something of mine."

"I didn't take anything of yours," he replies with a furrowed brow.

"Yes, you did; my book. I know you took it, and I want it back. So where is it?"

Understanding dons his features, and he crosses his arms across his broad chest. I can see his forearms flex as he grabs onto the muscles there and my eyes linger for a brief second. "Oh." He walks over to a side table by his bed and opens the drawer. He pulls out the familiar-looking title and holds it against his chest. "You mean this one?"

My eyes widen in recognition as I reach out to take it from him. "Yes, that's the one."

He moves it behind his back at the last second. "This doesn't belong to you."

"Maybe not directly, but I'm borrowing it. I plan on returning it once I'm finished and to do that, I need you to hand it over." I hold my hand out, palm facing up. He doesn't put the book in it *or* stop staring at me.

"Who did you steal it from, again?" he questions.

With a crease between my eyebrows, I respond, "I told you; I didn't *steal* it. Don't be so dramatic. I fully intend on returning it when I'm finished."

"How far did you get?" Fantastic, another line of questioning.

I pinch the bridge of my nose and close my eyes in annoyance before relaying the last thing I remember reading.

He brings the book out from behind his back and looks at it. "I think I'll keep it a while longer. I want to do some light reading."

With a huff of frustration, I turn around to exit the room when he calls out from behind me.

"What did you think of it?" He says with more sincerity than I thought possible from him.

"Think of what?" I ask.

He takes a step toward me, closing some of the distance I had put between us. "This book. What you've read, what did you think of it?" The softness in his tone must be misplaced, but I try not to focus too much on it.

"Whoever wrote it had quite the imagination. An underground city? It's ridiculous. Interesting enough to read about, but it's all just nonsense in the end."

His brows dip slightly. Those broad shoulders roll forward, and his chest falls. Pearce seems struck by my harsh reality. He exhales from his nose. "Of course. How foolish of me."

"Pearce, can I please have my book back? I need to be done with it so I can return it before Miss Woodstock starts to think it's gone forever," my voice trails off.

His legs regain function, and he sullenly strides to me to place the book in my palm. "Enjoy your fairytale, princess."

26

DAYS FILLED WITH CLASSES and assisting my mother with tedious tasks pass by in a blur. I haven't seen or heard from Pearce since the dilemma with the book, which brings me more dejection than I care to admit out loud.

Jaali has made himself known, though. He's been practicing archery behind the stables at my makeshift range, and even following Ro around and pointing out different things she can paint. At first, she enjoyed the help, and now she says he just points at *everything* and says, "You could paint this," or, "Ooh, how about that?"

I fight the urge to see Pearce and check in on him. He's an adult who is fully capable of expressing his needs and vocalizing his feelings. When my thoughts finally start to drift from him to the other, more exciting, things in my life, I find a note just inside my bedroom door on the floor, seemingly pushed underneath.

Field behind the stables.

Before sunrise tomorrow.

My feet pad through the halls peppered with housekeepers and those with tasks to accomplish before the event my mother is hosting. I'm supposed to meet with her later today to adhere to my father's request. It's better than the punishment I thought I'd receive upon my return, and I'm not opposed to party planning.

I stand to go find Dessielle when my door swings open suddenly, warm air moving the floor-length curtains. She found me instead.

"Why did I see the mysterious man leave from the direction of your room not long ago?" She looks around the room. "Were you *alone* with him?"

"No, Dessielle, I was not alone with him. He left a note." I hand it to her and watch her eyes move like dragonflies across the parchment. I plop back down on my bed with a huff. "I'm expected to spar with him tomorrow. He told me to meet him in the field out behind the stables."

She eyes me heavily. "So, you're going to see him all hot and tired. Enjoy it while you're there, and then draw it from memory when you return, please."

I laugh at her intensity, and then lead Dessi out of the room. "I have no desire to be around him any longer than I have to. I'll see you for breakfast in the morning, and I'll tell you how the lesson went."

Dinner with my family now includes Jaali, who is still hanging around for who knows how long. Maybe since Pearce is still here, Jaali is here for him? I don't know why he wouldn't go spend time with his family but, given their past, he probably feels indebted to Pearce.

Pearce makes it down occasionally, maybe every two days. Tonight looks like one of those days in between.

Roralei and Jaali are going back and forth about the colors for the Beltane ball I'm being forced to help plan. Roralei is insisting that our mother choose purples for the upcoming summer season to lean into the plums that will be appearing in food and nature. Meanwhile, Jaali wants her to choose a cooler palette of greens and blues. Mother seems to be playing into both ideas, asking them what kind of décor would go with each color palette. Ro wins in the end, to Jaali's dismay.

Father looks like he feels bad for the man; his ideas are continually second best to his youngest daughter. His sadness fades when he looks at Ro and gives her a wink with a smirk. Ro tries to hide her excitement at being part of an adult conversation but decides against being humble as she sticks the tip of her tongue out at her opponent across the table.

Ro and I help to clear the table; she, because Mother is teaching her to be kind and helpful, while I'm helping to prolong going to sleep. The sooner I fall asleep, the sooner I wake up and meet Pearce to train. I'm not nervous, I gained some knowledge when I was training with Reynard. I'm more anxious about being alone with Pearce for over five minutes. Any time that's happened we've gotten in an argument, and I don't know if I have the energy to keep squabbling with him. But that's a problem for the morning.

My sleep is restless and fulfilling at the same time. I feel as though I've been resting for hours but also like I haven't slept a minute. I'm unsure of what to wear for training like this. My training with Reynard probably isn't a fair reference for difficulty or exerted effort. I decide to put on a pair of brown trousers that hug my hips nicely without limiting movement and a long-sleeved black tunic. I grab my boots from the back of my armoire and decide at the last second to throw on an olive-colored cape with a scarf enclosure instead of a button.

I trot down to the armory and training room to choose my weapon for the day. Since I'm up and moving at a Godsforsaken hour, my choices are endless.

The walk to the field is one I've taken before. I used to sneak out to this area to read when I wanted to ignore my responsibilities, even just for an hour or two.

I don't have to go far through the woods before I spot him. His dark hair and clothing stand out among the lush warm colors of the plant life. He's facing the tree line with a sword at his side. His head quirks the slightest bit when he hears me coming. Slowly, he turns to face me. His expression is unreadable, but I get the impression he'd rather be anywhere but here.

When I'm a few feet from him, he takes a step forward, causing me to halt.

"Show me what he taught you," he commands.

All the memories I have of my previous lessons disappear from my brain. I suddenly cannot remember anything I've been taught, and I pull my bottom lip into my mouth with my teeth.

With a nod, I assume the stance that Reynard taught me. When Pearce doesn't move, I realize he wants me to demonstrate alone. My cheeks heat and the pommel becomes slippery in my hand as I move through the few steps I remember. My movements feel dry and unpracticed, probably because they are. Pearce looks as fluid as a dancer when he swings his sword, while I have sand between my bones.

I finish the steps I remember and stand firmly facing him when I finish. He doesn't move or speak, so I move through drills I practiced those days with Reynard. They feel childish now, like I'm once again a young girl playing with a wooden sword.

Breathless with beads of sweat gathering on my forehead, I swing my arms around me to bring the sword against my invisible enemy. I jab the weapon forward periodically like Reynard taught me. I finish once again and stand directly in front of Pearce, chest heaving as I try to take in the chill air around me.

He takes his sword into his other hand and nods lightly. Slowly, like he's trying to find the words to describe how ridiculous that looked. He steps closer to me and places his sword underneath mine, angling it back up toward the sky from where it drooped beside me.

"Now show me what you've got."

"I just did," I say with a shake of my head.

Pearce turns from me and takes a few steps away. "No, you parroted what your *friend* taught you. Show me what *you've* got."

Confused, I ready my sword for whatever he's preparing to instigate. Pearce whirls around with startling speed and comes straight for me. He brings his sword down toward my right shoulder and I barely block his blow before he's aiming for the other side. I'm struggling with the weight of the sword to move it as quickly as he is, and my movements still feel impersonal. I'm not acting, only responding to his more advanced charges.

Once my arms feel so heavy that I can barely hold up my weapon, he lets me rest. I cross to the other side of the small clearing and sit on a moss-covered log. He looks at me for a moment and comes to sit beside me.

"I want to start somewhere else."

My forehead creases when I look up at him through pinched brows. "What do you mean? I know the steps, I just moved through them with no issues."

"You moved through them like you were doing them as someone told you to. You need to be able to act quickly and in advance. We'll be training strength in addition to defense."

I suddenly feel incredibly aware of every fiber of clothing against my skin. "I'm not weak," I say sternly.

"I agree. However, the sword you use today will be different from the next. And the next, and so forth. You need the ability to use any weapon around you, and for that, we'll be training to improve your strength. It's not a suggestion." He looks down at me. Not in a condescending way, but like he's trying to convey the level of sincerity in his words. And I believe he's telling the truth.

"What kind of training will we be doing?"

"Along with balance and stability, we'll be training strength in every part of your body."

I nod like I know what he's referring to. I exercise, I value movement, keeping my muscles intact, and staying fit. I've never considered myself an avid strength devotee, but I'm no feeblebody, either.

He remains staring at me when he continues speaking. "Each day we'll be focusing on a different muscle group."

"How often will we be doing this?" I have a life outside of this man.

"I expect you to train every day. I do the same, and I'll be holding you to the same level of dedication that I hold myself to. That way I know your progress is consistent."

"Every day? I can't guarantee that kind of commitment. I have other duties that are of a higher priority."

"That's why you'll be training with me at the same time we met today. Before everyone else is up and moving, and before you're required to be elsewhere." A small smirk appears on the side of his mouth and disappears when my eyes drop to it.

A sharp exhale leaves my nose as I realize this is where I'll be spending my mornings until further notice. My sleep schedule before the mission wouldn't have allowed for that. However, this new energy I have since being home will surely be put to the test.

"That's enough for the day," he says as he wipes off his blade from some of the kicked-up dirt that settled on it. "I'll see you back here tomorrow morning."

Without waiting for my response, he stands and walks back toward the castle. Fine by me, I need to bathe before I play princess today.

After a nice, warm bath, I go to locate my mother when I hear her voice coming from the great hall. She's talking about the swatches of the color palate she decided on with Ro. When I turn the corner, she waves me over for a second look.

"What do you think of these, Rae?"

In the hands of the housekeeper before her are two different collections of shades. The color families are the same, but the tones in the palate differ from warm to cool. I stare at them for a moment and try to imagine them cast around the ballroom and decide on the warmer shades. A lot of the wood in the room is a warmer brown color, so it seems fitting that the decorating colors be adjacent.

I point to the collection on the right, and my mother nods approvingly. "I think I like those as well. Thank you, dear." She thanks the housekeeper and dismisses her so she can distribute her choice to the decorators who take part in our events.

"Perfect timing, darling. I was hoping you'd come along with me today to go to the market and look at fabrics." My mother has a strong opinion about the clothing she wears due to her seamstress background. If she doesn't make the gown herself, she is included in the entire process of production from the design to the final product.

Already dressed for the day, I follow her out to the stables. She walks directly to her honey-colored steed that she's had since I was five. Amber was a present from my father on her 100th birthday, a large gift for a large milestone.

Winnie is happy to see me, as usual. I feel a stronger connection to her now after the travels we endured together. She has more confidence, and I think it's because it was the farthest she has ever traveled. She's more vocal now and isn't afraid to sass me when I don't understand her properly.

We start the short ride into town and make light conversation on the way. She asks more about the mission, what being on the road was like, and my thought process about going. My answers are short and clipped to prevent myself from sharing too much. I wasn't supposed to go, and talking to my mother about a direct abandonment of the rules seems strange. When she senses my hesitation, she confronts it.

"I'm not angry with you, you know."

Her words shouldn't surprise me, I know my mother better than to think she would shame me for any decision I make.

"I know that" I reply sheepishly. I do, but it still feels odd.

"I did many foolish things when I was your age, even older. When I met your father, I did *lots* of things my parents wouldn't approve of—"

"Oh Gods, Mother please, I don't want to hear about that." I refuse to listen to my mother's exploits.

Her head falls back with a hearty laugh. "Raelenthia, if you think I'm going to explain my intimate relations with your father to you, you are sorely mistaken." That's a relief. "I meant because of where he came from."

I know the bare bones of my father's history. I never want to put him on the spot or lessen his position as ruler in a Fae kingdom, so I leave the topic alone. What he chooses to share with me is his choice. Because of that, I don't know the entire story, and I know it's partly due to embarrassment.

"I know Father is from Baeton. It's part of why I went on the mission in the first place," I remind her. It wasn't anything they had done; I wasn't trying to run away. But there's so much I haven't seen, and I couldn't stand that I had never seen my father's home.

"Yes, but did you know we met after he deserted the Baetonian army?"

I almost fall off my horse. My father did what?

My silence is the answer she expects. She continues forward with a solemn expression.

"Your father served in their military when he came of age," which I did know. "At the beginning of the Great War, many didn't know what to believe. Many Fae still thought that all humans weren't evil, and many are not. But having those doubts at a time like that meant they trusted the wrong people, and they paid the price for it."

She continues, "I met him while he was on the run—"

"I thought you said you met at a market. That's what you told me as a child." I've heard the story a thousand times.

"While that's part of the truth, it isn't the entire story. He was on the run from his commander. He was instructed to deal with a family of half-Fae like yourself. He couldn't bring himself to slaughter innocent children, which was what Baeton was demanding from their soldiers. Instead, he gave them refuge. He got them out of the city safely and when he arrived in Alunia with them, I happened to be nearby. I witnessed his act of kindness and decided to help him."

My mouth agape, I stare at my mother's profile. This whole time, I had no idea my father had run away from his past life.

"Did he have a family there? How did he get away?" I have so many questions about the lives of my parents, that I'm unsure of where to start.

"It isn't my story to tell, Rae. I'll let your father tell you the rest when he's ready. But I thought it was only fair that you know the kind of relationship your father has with Baeton, with their mindset toward our kind. He only ever wants your safety. It's why he never wanted you crossing over." The weight of her confession sits heavy on my chest. I defied my father's wishes without fully understanding them.

I spend the rest of the ride in stunned silence, my mother content to let me sit with my thoughts.

The market is already teaming with life. Children chase each other through the rows of wooden stalls. Glass jars are placed in rows on some of them, filled with jams and honey.

Animals are welcome at events like this. Many shop owners sell things exclusively for them including treats, even accessories. I've gotten bonnets and hoods for Winnie in past years, some she still wears.

The cobblestone streets are covered in wooden buckets filled with goods, and tables with beautiful displays. Mother and I fit down the aisles together while on our horses as we take it slow and peruse the items around us. We both find small trinkets that we end up taking with us; hers is a small sunflower made of shaped glass, and mine, a wooden carving of a pixie's wings. Their wings are incredibly detailed, someone being able to recreate the image with such an unforgiving medium is inspiring.

We make it to the fabric shop and tie Winnie and Amber to a wooden post by the entrance. The comforting earthy smell waves out as we open the door. Inside, there are rows and rows of shelves topped with fabric samples. The moment we enter, the shop owner shouts from the back room.

"Just a minute!"

We wait behind the counter until they come out. Their small eyes protrude from their leathery green skin when they turn the corner and see the two of us.

"My Queen Calliope! How good to see you. And you as well, princess. Welcome, welcome." They bend slightly at the waist to offer a brief, informal bow. Kip and my mother have a long history.

Mother approaches the goblin and leans down to place a kiss on either side of their cheek. "Always a pleasure, Kip."

"What can I help you ladies with?" Kip says with genuine interest.

"We're looking for fabric for an upcoming event. I plan on making my own gown, and I brought Rae for a second opinion on my final choice."

The goblin's giddiness cannot be contained as they clap their hands together. "How wonderful! I can show you some of my newer patterns if you'd like, or you can wander about the shop first and look for something you fancy," they offer.

"I think we'll wander for a bit, but I will let you know if I have any questions for you."

With another quick bow, they return to the back room to resume whatever task we had taken them from. I split from my mother to walk down a different aisle to look at more patterns. I find one that's a deep eggplant color and hold it up over my head so she can see from over the top of the shelf. "What about this one?" I call to her.

"It's beautiful, but I don't want to blend into the décor too much." A fair request, so I keep looking. We go back and forth holding up different shades until we meet at the end of the shelves. On the endcap, there is a corner of a swatch peeking out from a pile. I reach for it right when my mother does, but let her grab it instead. It's a sandstone bronze square with a matte brocade pattern.

She looks at me with a twinkle in her eye. "I love it."

A sweet smile lifts my cheeks. "I thought you might. That one has my vote," I tell her.

She stares at the fabric in her hands and nods. We take the swatch back to the counter and let Kip know we'd like to purchase 10 yards of fabric. My mother isn't quite sure of her final design and wants more than she'll need in case she changes her mind. With a final goodbye, we leave the store with the fabric in tow. The color looks stunning against Amber's coat, the two almost twins.

When my mother notices the same thing, she looks at me. "I suppose I have a type," she chuckles.

We spend a few more hours walking to different shops and tents. We smell and sample every kind of wax there is, sip tea, and snack on homemade bread. With full bellies and souls, we ride back to the castle.

27

A FTER A FEW MORE days of hardly seeing Pearce outside of our lessons, I gain the courage to ask how long he plans on being here.

"Why? Would you miss me if I left?"

"Gods, no. I want to know when I can have my mornings back," I sneer.

His jaw flexes. "When you beat *me*. How about that? Seem fair, *princess*?"

I flinch the slightest bit at the pressure he puts on the title. "Yeah, right. Really, when will you be going home?"

He doesn't respond, only continues staring at me.

"Pearce, what do you mean I'm supposed to beat you? You've been training your entire life, and I'm only just now learning. That isn't fair," I bemoan.

"Isn't it? You didn't learn because you didn't need to. And now that you're training, you want to take the easy route."

"I am not, I've been training every morning!" He would know, he's been the one working me to exhaustion.

"And you're ready to be finished." His tone leaves no room for pushing him any further. He's decided my behavior, and there's no swaying his opinion on my devotion.

"I need to go meet my mother." I'm spending today helping her finalize the design for her gown so she can start sewing. She sews faster than any seamstress I've ever seen, so she'll finish in plenty of time before the party once she's made up her mind.

Pearce nods lightly. "See you tomorrow," he says shortly, and then he floats down the hall.

When we had dinner with the Ladies of Caelfall, we celebrated the beginning of their Spring harvest. We're nearing the halfway point between Spring and Summer now which is the reason for all the planning my mother has been instrumenting.

Since Beltane celebrates the midway point between Spring and Summer, preparing the bonfire and the maypoles are on my to-do list today. The two seasons blend beautifully in nature, and their representation on Drennica reflects that. Foods from both seasons are melded together for the feast that takes place. Chicken and goat are the main course Mother decided on, with my and Roralei's help, of course.

When I locate her in her office, we write down the final menu so that preparations can begin for sourcing the ingredients. Since Summer is our closest neighbor, we receive a considerable amount of our seasonal ingredients from them during other times of the year. With that finished, we can start on the final drawing of her gown. I'm not an artist like Ro, but I can take direction more clearly due to my age. We throw ideas back and forth until she finally decides on the outline. With that, we start cutting fabric.

She points me toward the pile of fabric we found in the market the other day. I hand her a section of it and look at the pattern she's made for us to follow. In silence, we cut through the brocade. I lay out the pieces as I finish so she can inspect them. The smile on her face is almost childish when she sees all the pieces laid out before her. "It's perfect," she says, a glimmer in her bright green eyes.

Finished with my part in this project, I leave her to her sewing. I stop with my hand outstretched toward the handle, and look back at her.

"Do you think Father would be willing to speak with me?"

Lost in the intricacy of her design, she says, "Of course, dear, he always has time for you."

"What I meant was, do you think now is a good time for me to ask him about what you told me? I feel I may owe him an apology." With a deeper explanation, I would have been more understanding of my bounds on the continent. My leaving most likely kindled more than anger.

Her head lifts, understanding in her eyes. "I think so, Rae. You're plenty old enough now, and you've seen the entire continent. While it may have been despite his wishes, it'll provide a deeper understanding of him. He may be hard to find, but try the archives. He might be there." She gives me a soft smile to ease my discomfort and looks back at her design.

I set out to find my father and pepper him with questions about his past. I don't mean to pester him but…so many years without knowing the truth about how my parents met. I understand they didn't want to share that information with me. They came into power before I was born. They didn't have to explain themselves to me, I only knew them as my parents.

As usual, my mother is right. He's exactly where she said he would be. He favors this library of sorts over our personal one with casual texts, and I never understood why.

I knock lightly on the doorframe to announce my arrival without startling him. He turns and smiles when he sees my face at the entrance. "Hello, dear."

"Is now a bad time?"

"It's never a bad time for you," he says as he closes the book in his hands. "Do you need me?"

"I suppose," I reply sheepishly. I feel like a little girl again, learning about the world.

I take a seat on the ottoman near his desk. I'm not sure of the best way to bring this up, so I dive headfirst.

"Mother and I were talking on our way to the market. She told me a little about how the two of you met—how you *really* met. And it brought up some things about your past that were unknown to me. I'd like to ask you about them," I confess.

The left side of his mouth rises slightly into an understanding and solemn half smile. "I was wondering when we'd get here," he says. My brows pinch in confusion, and he rounds his desk and sits next to me on the ottoman. "You were too little for the longest time. To me, you'll be little forever. But I suppose now is as good a time as any to let you know the truth about how I got here. Why I didn't want you going to Baeton," he says with a sigh. "What do you know about the Great War?"

"I know it lasted a very long time, and that many died; of every species."

He nods sadly. "Many died that didn't need to. None of them needed to…" He exhales sharply as if preparing himself to tell the story. "I lived in Baeton for all of my young life. My commander had instructed me to be on the lookout for anyone with non-human features: pointed ears, excessive size, eyes that seemed too vibrant, those sorts of things. The percentage of their humanity didn't matter; if they had Fae blood, they were to be dealt with. Executions were held in the streets, families were ripped apart.

One evening I was on my patrol route and noticed a young girl hiding behind a wall made of stone that wasn't quite tall enough to cover her. A wooden ball sat in the road, and I assumed it was hers. She didn't want to run in the street when she saw a guard coming. So, I dismounted my horse and picked up the ball to roll it back to her. When I stood with it in my hand, I noticed the slightest point to her ears. I didn't mean to freighten her, but I had a job to do. I was a soldier; I had a purpose. I asked her if her parents were home and she said yes, so I told her to bring me to them. She did, although she kept an arm's length from me. And then I found out why…"

He pauses for a while, and his breaths turn unstable. I place my hand on his to offer support. "If you don't wish to talk about it, I understand. I can—"

"No, it's alright." He pats my hands gently and sniffles before taking a steadying breath and continuing. "When I went inside the home, I didn't immediately see anyone else. Only when I called into the empty room did someone approach from the hall to take the hand of the young girl and pull her behind them. It was the girl's father.

The mother and another child were still in the hall, but I saw their faces peek around to see what was going on. I told them I found her in the street, and they needed to be careful. When he looked down at his daughter behind him, I saw his ears were pointed as well. I readied my hand on my sword, prepared to corral them and escort them back to the jailer to be dealt with, as I'd been instructed.

But when I looked down at the little girl cowering behind her father, and they didn't yell or try and attack me... A seed of doubt sprouted. There was no way what I had been told about their kind was true, that these were vicious and callous creatures.

Our heads were filled with information about the Fae. That they were evil. An invasive species that sought to condemn humans and conquer our lands. So, we retaliated. And struck them down one by one."

A small gasp leaves my lips, despite my trying to not make a sound. His eyes shoot to mine for a brief second before I nod gently for him to continue.

"I looked at the girl that had been playing in the street. I went into their home where they kept each other safe. Where they could be a family. And I was supposed to take that away from them?" A single tear slips down his cheek, and he wipes it away with his knuckle.

His voice shakes when he continues. "I couldn't do it. I knew I would be killed for sparing them, so I had to make sure no one knew where they were. I told them to pack as little as they needed to survive and that we had to leave right away. The sun had set by then, so we were able to move under the cover of darkness since human eyes can't reach nearly as far as theirs can. I brought them into the woods near where the Range of Unrest now lies. We rode through the night until we were far enough away that they could find someone to help them assimilate into society. It wasn't my place to separate a family. It wasn't my place to slaughter children." A sob escapes my father.

I wipe away the tears that have fallen on my face and place my hand back on my father's.

"I had no idea, I'm so sorry," I explain with a shake of my head. "I wouldn't have gone if I'd known, I swear."

He places his arm around my shoulders to comfort me. I should be comforting him; he defied his leaders to save a family of people he was trained to believe were his enemy. And instead, he helped them. "Is that when you met mother?" I ask to try and ease the storm cloud of despair looming over the room.

A flicker of happiness reappears on his face. "She found me; you know. I thought I was well concealed while watching them from the tree line but—" he laughs. "Your mother was, well *is*, incredibly stealthy."

I smile and daydream of my mother getting the upper hand on him. "Did she scare you?"

"Oh absolutely," he laughs. "She made no sound and appeared behind me like an apparition. She reached out to me, and her touch was so soft that I didn't realize until I turned around to swat away what I thought was an insect flying around me."

I laugh with him at the idea of him swatting at my mother. "Will you tell me more? About what happened after she found you?" I plead.

He nods his head gently. "I will. Some other time, though. It's getting a little late in the day, it'll be time for dinner soon."

Both of us teary-eyed, I hug my father. His strength doesn't go unnoticed in this kingdom.

I close the door softly behind me and lean against it for a moment to soak in all the information given to me today.

My father went against direct orders. He left his home and those he knew on an adventure he knew he had to take. It sounds kind of like me.

28

THE NEXT MORNING COMES too quickly. I stayed up reading my *stolen* book through most of the night.

I piece a quick breakfast together before heading to the field for our training today. We typically spend our mornings going through drills and strength training with minimal conversation. I feel a bit stiff, but I chalk it up to it being early in the morning. Neither of us wants to speak before we've had a meal, at least *I* don't. Today he seems more open to conversation, so I make a poor attempt.

"What are your plans for today?" I ask from the ground.

He glares at me from above with his arms crossed over his insane chest. "You owe me more pushups."

"My arms are tired," I complain.

"I'm sure they are. But weapons are heavy, and you need to be able to work with a sword for as long as necessary, no matter the size."

I attempt to stifle a laugh by poking the side of my cheek with my tongue. His eyes turn to slits in response. "What's so funny?"

"Nothing," I say too quickly. He doesn't believe me; I know he doesn't. Another laugh escapes and I clamp my hand over my mouth to prevent any more.

"Care to share with the rest of the class, princess?"

"Not really, no."

"Spit it out," Pearce demands, coldly.

I groan. Not helping.

I breathe out a long sigh. "You keep talking about *wielding* swords," I finally manage.

"Yeah, we're doing sword training. I'm teaching you to fight," he explains, still confused.

Tired of the embarrassment, I blurt out, "It sounded indecent when you said it like that."

He turns toward the makeshift log bench where our carafes are sitting and says, "I can assure you the swords we're using today aren't half as frightening as others."

A cough erupts from my throat, suddenly feeling very dry. "I'm sorry, did you just make a joke?"

Pearce takes a drink of water and looks back at me. "I guess I did."

Unsure of how to transition out of whatever that was, I ask if our training is finished for the day.

"If you're satisfied with your effort, we can be finished."

My brows pinch. "What is that supposed to mean?"

"It means we can be finished for the day if you're happy with the training you've already done. Do you think you've improved today?" It seems like he knows the answer, but he wants me to say it instead.

With a huff, I take one last swig of my water and return to the center of the field. We position ourselves in the same area every time we reset, so there's a patch of dirt in the center where our feet have trampled the grass.

He assumes his position across from me for sparring. We spent the entire morning building my strength by grappling and various prone movements. My arms already feel exhausted. I can't show him that, so I muster the remainder of my strength and put on the performance of my life.

Appearing weak in front of someone stronger is to accept defeat before you've even begun.

He'll be able to sense my doubt, and he'll attack with even more ferocity than originally planned. I can't deal with that yet. Maybe in a few more weeks, but I'm not ready for him to unleash his full capabilities. We both bow slightly at the waist like we do before every sparring match. He emphasized to me before we started training that it was necessary to let me know we were fighting with honor on an even playing field. As my skills increase, he fights harder. Dirtier. Until the only thing left to do is fight him as he is.

He pauses after bowing and waits for me to make the first move. He only does this when he's trying to read my movement, which only frustrates me further. I dip my chin and look at him through my fanned lashes. And I strike. I lift my sword toward his chest and he immediately swipes it back down. I cock my head to the side in frustration and take a slight step back. He follows me and extends his sword, and I meet it with mine. We clash and parry back and forth a few times before we both lower our weapons the slightest bit, when I fling my arm out and swipe for his face. He swerves his head out of the way and inclines it in surprise. "Really?" He presses.

"Whoops," I say with a shrug.

We dance across the field, kicking up dirt and filling the tree-encircled arena with clanging metal. We enter an unpredictable rhythm when he circles his blade around mine and uses that force to push me back. I fall to my backside before I have the chance to catch myself. He takes a large lunge forward with his weapon, but I defend the blow at the last moment, leaning my other arm onto the ground to prevent myself from being pushed flat to the ground.

With a heavy grunt, I shove myself from the floor and push forward with both hands on my sword, putting us in a lock. He pushes both our weapons down so they're at our sides. Both of us stand breathing heavily, refusing to look away.

"That's enough for today," he says.

"You said we weren't finished until I'm proud of my efforts. We can't end like that," I counter.

"I said that's enough." The rasp in his voice is strong, asserting this as his final decision. We're standing toe to toe, him looking down at me with stern features.

"Fine," I reply. I slam my shoulder into him as I pass him to retrieve the belongings I set on the bench. With full arms and defeat emanating from ragged breaths, I walk back to the castle.

29

Miss Woodstock spends almost the entire lesson going over the environment of the areas I went through on my mission. She's more nosey than anything really; she has a lot of questions about the areas we traveled through and the wildlife that resides in them.

I'm happy to answer her questions as it means we don't drone on through another boring lesson plan. Toward the end of our time, I ask if I can suggest a topic for our next class. Suspicious of my sudden interest in her lesson planning, she obliges, and I tell her I want to learn more about Kermera.

"Is that where my book went?" She inquires with a raised brow.

My lips curl into my mouth and my shoulders cave in slightly. "Perhaps..."

She exhales loudly and continues writing. "What more do you want to learn about them?"

Relieved that she doesn't press the issue further, I right my posture. "In the book, it doesn't mention anything about their leaders."

"That's because it's not real, Raelenthia," she explains without hesitation.

"I understand that," I huff, "but even in stories there are explanations for such things. This story seems unfinished."

When she finishes writing on the wall, she puts her utensil down and looks at me. "There are many different leaders given to the story. Maybe not in the book, but in different renditions of the tale. Some people have said that our late king and queen aren't truly dead. That they're ruling underground with a swarm of followers. Others have said that the people would rule themselves. It just depends on the person telling the story."

It's not an exciting answer, and it still seems strange that no ruler is mentioned in the story. "You can't expect to take your parent's place one day if you fill your head with nonsense."

A little defeated, I nod. I don't even want the position. My parents know that, but it's not entirely up to them. The current rulers have a large sway in who is given the crown, and the people of the kingdom have a say as well. If both parties deem me a ruler, I'm not sure I'd have the heart to turn them down. But I won't bear tomorrow's problems.

With our lesson finished for the day, I collect my things. As I reach for my bag, Miss Woodstock clears her throat. I look up at her and she waves me forward. I approach, and she grabs my hand to hold in both of hers. "You're a smart girl, Raelenthia. If you wish to keep the storybook, it's yours. It was collecting dust in here, anyways."

My eyes widen in disbelief. "Thank you, Miss Woodstock. I'll take care of it."

She smiles plainly and dismisses me.

Out in the hall, Reynard passes by my classroom just as I'm exiting the door.

"So, you *are* alive," he sneers.

Relieved to run into him after my lesson with Miss Woodstock, I smile. "Barely. I feel like I may fall over at any moment."

"I haven't seen you around since that *ruffian* stole you away." His voice is cold, clipped.

"He didn't steal me away, we're just practicing," I explain. "Mornings seem to be working with my schedule for now."

"How could I forget? You're so, so busy nowadays."

I nod, agreeing with him. "There's a lot to get done with this ball coming up. I can't help it, I'm sorry."

"Right, the ball."

I nudge his shoulder playfully. "You'll be in attendance, I'm assuming."

A hint of a smirk appears on his freckled face. "Wouldn't miss it."

Without another word, he continues his path down the hall.

The breeze moves harshly through the trees this morning. I look across the field and list their species in my head, one after the other.

"You know," I say into the silent morning, "that book I'm reading mentioned a tree I've never heard of before. Something called an Emerald Elm."

"I thought you gave that back," Pearce answers.

I shake my head, correcting him. "I don't have to anymore. Miss Woodstock let me keep it since I've been enjoying it so much."

His jaw ticks. "How kind of her."

"I think she's trying to get on my good side. Maybe she wants me to talk her up to my parents and get her a more impressive teaching position." I look over at him, and he looks lost.

"They're beautiful," he says.

"What is?"

"The Emerald Elms," he answers in a dreamlike voice. He seems to remember his whereabouts and shifts uncomfortably.

"They do sound beautiful," I say. "But I don't think there are trees like that in Alunia."

"I'm sure there is a lot of Alunia that you haven't seen," he says a smidge too loud to be to himself.

"Well, after our mission, I've seen every region on the continent." My chin lifts as I defend myself. "I've traveled through every region and have stayed for periods of time in all of them. If a tree like that existed, I think I would know about it."

We continue our training until my stomach sounds bounce off the wall of trees.

"What's next?" I ask with forced enthusiasm.

"Breakfast, hopefully. Your stomach won't stop begging for it."

I quickly gather my things, thankful to be finished. I've been much hungrier lately.

"Why do you seem bothered when I talk about the book?" He's been strange about it since I first mentioned it.

"I'm not sure how that book got into your teacher's library, but she shouldn't have had it. It's not meant to be here."

"Here in the castle? Why not?"

"Forget it," he huffs as he runs his tanned fingers through his wavy locks. "See you in the morning," he calls out before storming off.

Yet another conversation ended in a tedious clashing of heads. If it's not him ruining the moment, it's me. Maybe one day we can be civil but, given his line of questioning today, I doubt it will be any day soon.

After hurrying off, I enjoy a quick, calm meal with Roralei and Dessielle. My father is off doing who knows what, and my mother is most likely up to her knees in fabric trying to piece together her gown before the Beltane festivities. It's a relatively silent, yet relaxing, afternoon.

A few hours are spent practicing my steps before my next lesson with Pearce tomorrow and daydreaming about my, now *not* stolen, book. I wonder if the author has any other titles. Although, due to my hectic schedule lately, I haven't even finished this one yet.

The rest of my evening is filled with reading about how magical faeries were the ones to create the underground city in the first place. I wonder if these Fae are based on the kind of magic we have in Alunia.

The kind of magic in this book sounds so similar to the one in our world, so it makes sense it would be in a story written by someone on the continent. I lay on my back and close the book before putting it away for the night. I've stayed up far later than I intended to, and I know it's going to affect my performance in training. When I go to place it on my bedside table, my hand trails along the gold script on the cover. I brush along the title once more and blow out the candle that has been allowing my late-night reading before drifting off to sleep.

30

PEARCE

The cracked skin of my knuckles scrapes against my strained eyes. Another night of tossing and turning restlessly just in time for a training session. Rae might have a chance against me today.

She stands a chance against me every day, really. I didn't expect her strength to be so powerful, although I suppose it shouldn't come as a surprise. She's as strong-willed as they come on Drennica, the stubborn gripe. And I've met *plenty* of stubborn women. Raelenthia has a tenacity I've never seen before. She's more talented than she gives herself credit for, though I'd never tell her.

I take care of my morning tasks before heading downstairs to grab the miscellaneous things we'll need for training today. My sword stays sheathed at my hip when I'm not clashing weapons, or words, with her, so I don't stop by the armory.

She hardly listens to me as is, but I wish she'd carry something with her. She walks around with no weapon. The least she can do is carry a dagger. She's been wearing those damn boots almost every day since we returned to this castle, so I know she has somewhere to stash it if she doesn't wish to wear a belt. Maybe I can make that part of our lessons this week. She could use a little homework. And if she's smart, she'll listen to me.

Mist covers the field this early in the morning, which doesn't slow me down in the slightest. I know where our log bench is by now. My feet kick into the floor-level cloud and I place my things down softly, not ready to disturb the little quiet I'm able to find in this place. I decide to warm up since I still have a decent amount of time before she comes downstairs. I always arrive early. The settled mist and the density of the trees surrounding the area remind me of home.

Jaali has been pressing me about when we'll return. I've already been gone a substantial amount of time, I should have returned by now. I told them I'd be back as soon as I could, but that timeframe has been unexpectedly lengthened. My people expect me home. The council has requested my return several times now, which is why Jaali has been so persistent. I can't even tell him why I feel pulled to stay here. It's certainly not the food or the weather.

And it's certainly not...

Raelenthia turns the corner, cutting through the mist in those same brown lace-up boots she wears every morning. She typically sticks to a certain color palette: green and brown for the most part. Today she's wearing a long cerulean tunic and black pants. Small black gloves reach a lighter blue puffed sleeve beneath her tunic, providing an additional layer between her pale pink skin and the brisk air of the morning. She won't be needing the additional layers, I'll get her warmed up in no time.

"You're here earlier than normal," I call out to her.

"Are you always out here at this time? What are you, an owl? If we need to move your bedroom outside, let me know and I'll make it so." That smart mouth.

"Some of us like to get an early start on our day. How lovely of you to join me," I sneer. She sleeps like the dead. I've had to have Willow wake her a few mornings since we've started training and I'm sure I'll have to do it again.

"Well, I'm sorry for not wanting to train on an empty stomach."

"You'll wish you had left it empty after today, princess."

Her nostrils flare the slightest bit at the nickname I've refused to give up. It's not clever, but I like it. It stuck while we were on the road, and it's certainly fitting. Her face alone is regal. Her chin kicks to the side in frustration, and I do my best to fight the smirk surfacing on my face. "Ready to get your ass handed to you?" I say as I reach for the belt of my sword.

She huffs, but nods firmly and takes her place in the center of our earth-given arena. We'll be starting our session a little differently today, and she catches on when I take the holster with my sword and place it on the log with the rest of my things. "Today we're starting with hand-to-hand combat," I announce.

Her head shakes slightly. "Your job is to teach me to fight with a sword. I don't need to fight with my hands if I have a weapon."

She has no idea how wrong she is.

"Like hell, you don't. My *job* is to teach you to defend yourself. What happens when your sword gets knocked out of your hands because you were caught off guard? Will you let an opponent beat you that way? Without a real fight?" I don't hesitate to attack her pride. It's the fastest way to get her riled up; I know she'll respond with that fire she tries to stamp down.

She grinds her teeth, making her jaw clench. She tosses her sword onto the ground with her belt, which makes my eyes roll. The brat. Why couldn't she just walk over to the bench? It takes one second, and now the blade is filthy.

I stand across from her in the dirt patch we've created with our pacing and circle her. Prey and predator, we shuffle around one another, waiting for the other to strike. I reach for her wrist to pin it behind her, but she's fast; much faster without a sword in her hand. She drops beneath my grasp and when I reach out with my other hand to her new height, she's already moved behind me.

Refusing to keep my back to her, I whip in her direction and block a shockingly solid punch she was aiming at my ribs. My hand fits around her fist almost completely. Her eyes pause on it the moment mine do, and she rips them apart just to feign an attack on the other side. Wrong move. When she shifts her weight from one foot to the other, I kick my leg out and sweep her feet out from under her.

She knocks backward completely, a cloud of dirt flying out from underneath her solid body. She coughs and, for a moment, I feel bad for knocking the wind out of her...which is ridiculous, I'm doing my job. She should have kept a closer eye on my movements. Still, I can't help reaching my hand down toward her and pulling her upright.

When she stands, she brushes off her backside and claps the dirt off her hands. "Yeah, you were right... I shouldn't have eaten this morning," she admits as she places her dirt-covered hand over her mouth to keep the bile down.

We continue hand-to-hand for a while before I let her pick up her sword again. Physically, she looks small next to it. But her presence is much larger. It makes her as big as me, which is no easy feat. Her steps have been much smoother recently, flowing from one move to the next with an ease that wasn't there before. My methods might not be her favorite, but they're doing her a world of good. If only I could give her lessons to quell her attitude. *That* would be life-altering.

Lost in my daydream, she slices her sword across the outside of my left shoulder. It doesn't hurt enough for me to stop training, but the look on her face is priceless. "Not a bad lick, princess. Let's keep going."

"I—I didn't mean to do that," she rushes out.

My brow rises. "You didn't mean to hurt me...in our sword fighting lesson? Let's be honest with each other, shall we?"

She exhales a large breath, her lips blowing out comedically and she nods. "You're right, okay."

We resume our initial stance and clash after clash, our weapons strike. The mist around us has mostly dissipated from our constant movement, and a bead of sweat sits just above her brow. I knew she wouldn't need those layers.

Her strikes have more force this time. She's tapping into her energy reserve, and I can tell she's throwing everything she has into this back-and-forth.

Finally. Give me a challenge.

Grunts escape us as we each take swings at the other, only to dodge them at the perfect moment. A second of quiet passes and our next swings are more lax as we pause to breathe and read the other. I push forward causing her to step back and absorb my blows with more precision. She swirls her blade around mine and pushes me back, no longer content with being prey.

That's it, princess.

The left side of my mouth quirks up at the chance of a real fight. Neither of us holding back, we dance in a battle of steel. Our steps, now perfectly in tandem, feed into the momentum of our swings. Her elbow raises slightly, giving away her intent to strike low on my body. I lower my arm in response to preemptively block her blow. But she doesn't strike where I expect.

Instead, her sword comes straight for my face.

And I'm too late to evade it.

The deadly metal connects with the side of my cheekbone, slicing through the skin.

She freezes immediately.

I've never seen the whites of someone's eyes appear so quickly. She doesn't realize the skill she's just shown, all she knows right now is that *I* have a flesh wound and *she's* the one who caused it.

If I wasn't so impressed, I might be aroused.

What can I say? A dangerous woman has always done something to me.

I lift my hand to the slowly falling stream of blood and swipe it with my fingers. The crimson covering my hand sets my nerves on fire as I rub my fingers together, trying to contain myself. Then, I look at her bright green eyes that are as wide as they can be.

"Fuck, Pearce I-I'm so sorry. Let me—"

Her eyes track my fingers as I bring them up to my open mouth and trail the pads across the flat of my tongue.

"You really shouldn't have done that."

Her breathing hitches and her cheeks flush.

I lift my sword and bring it crashing down on hers, which she barely lifts in time to defend herself. Our weapons swirl around us with light gleaming off them from the further rising sun. We're out here later than usual.

Fine by me.

I block her next blow and push inward, and she does the same in an effort to right her balance. Before I realize it, we're in a lock. Our swords pushed up against each other, our chests heaving from exhaustion. Her face rests right behind the conversion of our weapons. Her soft angled chin has a slight dimple in it that I never noticed before. If I dropped my hold on my sword even the slightest bit, I could move closer to her. My eyes flick down to her parted pink lips, and I stare for longer than I intend to.

Her eyes seem to trace the lines of my face like she's never seen it, before landing on my lips as well. Another heavy breath leaves her, and her chest grazes the outside of my knuckle, sending a wave of desire through me. The urge to chuck this sword into the woods and peel the absurd number of layers from her hits me harder than stone.

What am I doing?

I start to let my guard down when a familiar voice cuts through the staggering quiet.

"Princess, you're running late for your lesson this morning!" Willow calls out from across the field.

Raelenthia jumps at the intrusion, as shocked as I am at the appearance of another person in our clearing. She closes her eyes and lets out one more heavy breath. "*Shit*," she whispers. "Coming! Thank you, Willow."

Willow nods and lets her stare rake over us one last time before heading back toward the castle.

"I'm sorry I cut your face," she whispers to me.

I resist the urge to smirk at her admission. "I'm not," I admit. "I want to see that same fire next time we train. Don't disappoint me."

She nods sharply at my request before rushing over to the bench to collect her things. She walks briskly out of the field, my stare glued to her as she moves. Before she's out of my sight, she steals one final glance at me, blushing when she realizes my vision hasn't strayed.

Don't worry, princess. I see you.

31

Raelenthia

I HAVEN'T HEARD ANYTHING Miss Woodstock has said this entire lesson. I can't get Pearce's eyes out of my head. The heat they held in them when he looked at the blood smeared on his fingers struck me in a way I didn't expect. And now it's all I can think about.

Miss Woodstock stares right at me with a raised brow. "What?" I ask.

"Are you going to answer me, Raelenthia?" She says without hiding her annoyance.

"Could you repeat the question?"

Miss Woodstock sighs, exasperated, and continues. I'm trying to keep up, but she's piling on information faster than I can comprehend it. I spend the rest of the class trying to think of healthy ways to release the tension building in my body. My knuckles are white, and my mind is racing wildly all because of...

Him?

This is ridiculous. Sure, I'd be a fool not to find him *physically* appealing. He's tall, broad, and strong; his eyes could melt the Peaks of Despair. Never mind that a lock of his dark wavy hair escaped from the tie he had managed to put most of it into and stuck to his temple this morning.

He had his sleeves rolled up today, something he only does after working up a sweat. The veins in his forearms were on full display while we practiced. The layer of stubble on his jaw is thicker now than when we arrived. It looks good on him.

What am I doing? He's leaving. However long it takes him to tie up this loose end, cash in his bargain, and then he'll be done with me. A debt to be paid. And once it's done, so are we. And *we* aren't even anything. Gods, the man tried to get me kicked off the mission and sent back to the castle before I had even gotten a chance to prove myself. He threatened to *drown* me. He exploited my life for his own twisted, personal gain. He's barbaric and rude.

I'll be glad when he's gone.

For now, I'm due to meet my mother for party planning. This is the strangest punishment I've ever received from my parents, but I'm incredibly grateful. I know my father wanted me to understand the gravity of what I did without dulling the confidence I found outside my title.

Mother's dress is almost finished, she's been working on it tirelessly for days now, which is perfect because Beltane is approaching quickly. I find her in the parlor sipping on her afternoon tea.

"Taking a break from sewing, mother?"

She places her cup on its saucer and drops a sugar cube into it. "Yes, my hands deserve a break after all my tedious and intricate work."

"Always so humble," I chuckle. She has every right to be proud, but I love to push her buttons. She rolls her eyes at me playfully and we chat about our days as she empties her cup.

"So how are your lessons going, dear?"

"They're fine. I've been doing all my reading, and I asked her for a bit more of a challenge in our map reading."

"Mm, I'm glad to hear it. And what about your morning escapades with the brooding stranger?"

Suddenly my throat is filled with gravel, and I cough when I fail to catch my breath. "I'm sorry, what did you say?"

"Oh, come on Rae, tell me about him. Yes, I know all about your little meetings. Nothing happens in this castle without me knowing about it," she tells me with raised brows.

"It's nothing. I wanted to learn how to properly fight with large weapons, and he was willing to teach me."

"Is that so? He doesn't strike me as a selfless teacher. He offered to help you train out of the blue?" The lilt in her voice implies she knows more than she's letting on but wants to hear it from my mouth anyway.

"I was having Reynard teach me before I left for Baeton. I hadn't known I would leave yet; it was just a skill I thought would be helpful to learn. When we got back, Pearce overheard Reynard and me talking about picking up where we left off. He stepped in and insisted he teach me instead."

"Ahh, alright. That does make more sense. Men are such proud, foolish creatures. He probably didn't want Reynard near you, so he put himself between you."

"You're implying that he was, what? Jealous? Really, Mother, that's absurd."

"Is it? He may be a little cold, but sometimes those are the ones that—"

"I am not having this conversation right now. Don't we have something else to discuss? Anything else?"

She throws her head back in laughter and pats her hand on my lap. "Alright, fine. Let's go finalize the menu and plan this party, shall we?"

"What do you think of this one?" I ask Dessielle as I turn the corner of the dressing wall.

A sharp gasp leaves her lips, and her eyes widen.

"Rae... If you do not wear that gown, you may as well not go."

I give her a look that expresses disbelief in the severity of her statement, but she doubles down. "This is the prettiest dress you've tried on today. I think you should pick this one."

I turn to look at myself in the full-length mirror. The plum-colored silk fabric drapes onto the floor in a wave. The bodice fits my core perfectly, accentuating the dip of my waist.

"It's not too much? My chest feels a little...on display."

"You're a princess. You're *always* on display. You might as well make it an interesting show, right?"

I shake my head with a chuckle and look back at the mirror. The purple is mixed with a warm red, like blackberry faerie wine.

The small freckles that cover my arms are fully visible in the sleeveless gown, and I trail my fingers on the outside of my arms.

"Stop fidgeting," Dessi commands.

"Yes, ma'am," I respond with a stiff salute.

I drag my hands along my sides and stare at the dress a second longer before finally giving in. "Alright, I think this is the one."

"Eek! Good, because if you didn't choose this one, I would have to wear it. And it wouldn't look nearly as good on me."

"What are you wearing, anyway?" I ask from behind the dressing wall again.

"Something teal, I think."

I shrug off the fabric and put on my green pants and navy tunic, as well as my trusty brown boots.

"Do you think Pearce will come?" I don't mean to ask. It simply slips free.

"I'm sure he will," she says. I'm not sure if she genuinely believes it, but it helps, nonetheless. "Have you two finally settled? No longer at each other's throats?"

I laugh to myself at her choice of words. I haven't told her about yesterday morning in the field, simply because I don't want to have to explain why him with blood on his face made me aroused. Or the fact that if Willow hadn't interrupted us, I may have let him lick me the way he did his fingers.

I don't dare to have that discussion with myself right now, let alone with the most sexually confident woman I know. I'll address it later. Or never.

Never sounds good.

Once I'm back in my clothes, I take a seat beside her on the ottoman.

"So, what's next for you, Rae?"

"What do you mean?" I ask as I lace up my boots.

"You go on this big journey of self-discovery and come back to your normal life? That doesn't seem fulfilling. It also doesn't sound like you," she explains.

I whistle a sigh of uncertainty. "Thanks for putting it all out there, Dessi."

"Oh, come off it, Rae. You don't want to be taking lessons with Miss Woodstock still, you're well past the age for it. I know you want more. You've traveled now, you've seen things I know you can't fill me in on, and even though I've come to terms with that, I'm still not okay with it. My question stands. What's next?"

I use the time it takes to finish putting on my boots to think about her question. What *is* next? I haven't thought about it, to be frank. I expected to be able to fall into my old life without really thinking about what that would mean for my future.

Do I want to rule Alunia? Not particularly.

I don't know many other options for me. What I *want* is to be of use. I want purpose. Maybe I could become a warrior. Pearce would probably laugh in my face if I told him that, given my track record in our training sessions.

But how am I supposed to become better at something if I don't practice?

This seems like something worth discussing with my parents. Am I even allowed to turn down a position in the court? The position is technically elected, but since the current rulers have children, the kin will likely be thrown into the mix when it comes time to select a new ruler.

My parents are still young as far as Fae age goes. My father stopped aging after he and my mother were married. We don't live forever, but our lifespan certainly makes it seem that way. Since my parents had Ro and me after my father's age was halted, we have a drop of mortal blood without the lifespan.

Because of that, their rule will come to an end when they decide they are ready to give up the title, or if requested by the people. And I don't suspect the latter will happen; my parents are incredibly adored.

Dessielle snaps her fingers before my face to pull me back to reality. "I'll take that as an 'I don't know,' then, I suppose."

Embarrassment raises blood to my cheeks. "Sorry, Dessi. I guess I have been a little lost lately."

"You need to get out of your head. Too many thoughts can drown out your sanity and make it feel like you have none. Like you're...treading water. You need to let it out. And if you ever decide to talk about it, you know where to find me." She places a kiss on top of my head and stands while I offer a silent thank you.

Before she exits the room, she says, "I'm meeting someone tonight, I'll let you know how it goes."

"You can't just say something like that and expect me not to have questions."

"I have a lot of hair and not a lot of time. She's amazing, you don't know her, yes, and no."

"You don't even know what I was going to ask!" I laugh at her gall.

"We've been best friends for half our lives. Trust me, I do." With a wink, she glides out the door.

She's right, I always ask the same questions: Do they treat you well? And do you need a chaperone?

I think back to the man I saw at her door before I left for Baeton. I guess she's not seeing him anymore. She's always preferred women, so I'm not entirely surprised.

The next few days go by in a blur. I train with Pearce a couple of times, and he seems even more tense than before I cut him, which I would've thought impossible. The skin is mostly healed, although not entirely, which surprises me. Something of that size should have sealed by now.

How strange. I'm almost sad to see it go.

I can't imagine our moment in the clearing affected him the way it did me, he would have said something.

Who am I kidding? He's ready to be back home. He can't stand me just as much as I can't stand him. Maybe more. Me slitting his skin probably stoked the fire of his distaste. Hopefully just a while longer, and he'll be gone. I'll be glad for it.

Roralei has kept me busy lately with all of her questions about the other regions. She hasn't been to all of them yet because of her age, our parents didn't want to take her out of her studies. She's seen Summer due to its proximity, but Spring is a bit more of a task to see when you're traveling for pleasure.

She finished the painting she was making for me while I was away. She chose to paint a scene with a large window in the sunroom. There's a small chess table in front of it, and her ability to capture the likeness of stationary objects is incredibly impressive, especially for her age.

I walk into my room and graze the finished painting with my fingertips. It sits on the small table outside of my armoire, next to a small candle I refuse to light. It was a gift from Wilder when we were children, and I want to ensure it lasts as long as I do. I pick up the braided, skinny rod and hold it toward the light of the fireplace. The wax is pale blue with a shimmer that swirls deep inside it like an endless cavern of life.

When I put the candle back down on the table, I see small, finger-sized dents in the side of the wax, the ridges of my fingers pressed into the figure. Did I squeeze it that firmly? I chuckle out loud in my empty room. Dessielle's truly going to think I've gone mad.

The Beltane festivities start tomorrow. I'm unsure that I'm ready to face the kingdom after learning what I have. My mind has been occupied with less important things like classwork instead of the notes I relayed to my parents.

Will they make an announcement tomorrow night? Everyone will be gathered for the ball; it would be the perfect time to address as many people in one place as they can. I make a mental note to ask my father tomorrow morning about his plans to move against the humans. We know they have *something* in the works, even if we don't know exactly what. The large creatures they have detained are of great concern as well. Are they torturing them, or are they being used as weapons?

There's so much I'm unsure of about the near future. But I know two things for certain: We need to defend Alunia against Baeton, and I want to fight with our army when that time comes.

After the past few weeks I've had, some alone time in the courtyard seems like the perfect remedy. I haven't been by myself in ages. My boots slide on effortlessly now, the well-worn brown leather the perfect mold of my feet. I've barely closed the door when my soul jumps from my body.

Right outside the door, leaning on the wall is Reynard.

"Hey, Rae," he says with his arms crossed, looking aloof.

My hand shoots to my chest to ensure my heart is still beating. "Well, hey," I say with a sigh.

Reynard falls into step beside me.

So much for being alone.

"You've been keeping some interesting company lately."

I slow my steps, unsure of where this animosity is coming from. "We're still talking about this? While I appreciate your concern, I think you're being a bit dramatic."

"Am I? As a guard of Alunia, should I not be concerned for the safety of the princess?"

I huff a breath through my nose, trying to understand my concerned friend. "He's not going to hurt me, he's helping me."

Reynard's tongue pokes out against his cheek. "I don't like him."

"You don't even know him." I continue through the halls, delaying my arrival to the courtyard.

"Do *you* know him, Rae? Where did he come from anyway? I asked around. None of the other guards know who he is. Running off for weeks and then showing up again with some stranger isn't the best look for a princess if you ask me."

"You need to relax. Pearce is just passing through; he'll be leaving soon."

Reynard's shoulders seem to ease. "I'd still be careful if I were you."

32

T HE BALLROOM IS DECORATED beautifully. Jaali and Roralei have been following my mother around all morning to ensure the colors and décor are up to their standards. Jaali might be having more fun than Ro, and that's a sight unseen. Summer and Autumn are both filled with warm colors, so those are the hues that adorn the wooden banisters and the golden metal chandeliers. The room is currently filled with much more light than we'll be graced by this evening, sending shadows along the marble flooring.

The centerpieces I chose look beautiful in the space. Large sea glass cat tails, periwinkle combs, and raspberry-stained stonecrops sprout from every table to create the perfect Summer setting.

All that's missing are the guests.

I didn't train this morning. I have a lot to take care of today that doesn't involve getting covered in grime, and potentially blood, with a boorish man. The coming of Summer means the typical chill in the air will be a bit warmer. The decorators worked with the purple tones my mother showed them and incorporated the Summer colors rather well. I'll have to tell them how beautiful their efforts turned out.

Willow does an immaculate job with my hair and cosmetics as usual. We decided on an updo since the back of my dress trails rather low. The majority of my hair is pinned in a spiral, with two loose braids draped over it. I'm more excited than I expected to be for a holiday like this. I've celebrated Beltane before, but this is the first time it's been with new friends to help put it together. I think the people need an event to look forward to, so hopefully it's successful for all of us.

I look at my finished appearance in the mirror and have to keep myself from touching it to ensure I'm real. I look like myself but elevated. I quickly put on a pair of heeled slippers to walk with the long skirt of the gown I chose. The fabric in the skirt is gathered onto my left hip, letting it cascade down my thigh. My breasts are perfectly cupped by the taut fabric that crosses in the back halfway down my spine.

It's not a typical gown for a princess, but I am no typical princess.

I take one last look at myself before going down the hall to find Roralei. She's in a cool blue gown, like a cloudless sky, finishing up her braided crown when I enter her room. Her eyes connect with mine through the mirror as she asks, "What do you think?"

"I think you're the most beautiful princess on Drennica on any given day. You look incredible baby sister, very nice job with your braids today." She smiles at me and walks over to her wardrobe to grab a simple black pair of shoes and slip them on. Her dress is floor length so you can't see them anyway.

She looks up at me through her icy-colored lashes and holds out her hand. "Ready?"

I place my hand in hers. "Always."

We head down the stone staircase to the main hall and take the connecting bridge to the ballroom currently filled with guests. We wait at the top of the staircase for Mother and Father, as there will be a formal receiving line once we take our seats on the dais. They round the corner not long after we do, hand in hand. Mother's finished look is extraordinary. The amber gown has golden chain epaulets and a matching gold lining along the bust. Her necklace is the same shade and material as the sleeves. I give her a curt nod and a smirk to let her know how proud I am of her and her work. Father looks dashing in a deep blue velvet coat with pants a few shades darker. His medals from his time in service are along the left side of his chest. The right breast pocket holds Mother's favorite flower, a marigold. We make quite a stylish family.

The music from down below comes to an end and transitions into a slower tempo. Father gives me a small nod, and I squeeze Ro's hand to get her attention. We move around the corner to the center of the staircase and look down into the full ballroom. It looks even better with people inside. When the music picks up, we start our descent into the crowd.

About halfway down, I lock eyes with Dessielle and take a deep breath. She did go with something teal, and her hair is in locs down her back with gold bands woven throughout. I look briefly around her for any sign of the woman she mentioned before I realize I don't know who I'm looking for. Not far behind her, I catch sight of Reynard, who is here on duty. The uniform consists of autumnal colors, so he's still dressed for the occasion.

When we reach the bottom of the stairs, the mass of guests before us is already parted and we make our way to our thrones upon the dais. Ours sit outside the Queen and Kings, mine a deep, shiny copper and Roralei's is a brighter white gold. When the music announcing the princesses comes to a halt, the crowd looks back to the top of the stairs, to Mother and Father. They look from one another down to the sea of Fae and other various creatures below them and descend the same path as us. They stand in front of their own thrones, both a true brushed yellow gold, and turn to face those gathered before them. Father raises his hand to quiet any lingering chatter.

"Hello everyone, good evening!" he says with a chipper expression.

"And happy Beltane to all of you," my mother adds. "Thank you for joining us tonight to the midway point between our two sisters, Spring and Summer." Applause erupts through the crowd.

"After the formal festivities, you are welcome to stay for the bonfire and the following smaller activities throughout the night. We have plenty of food and rooms to house anyone unable to make it home before dawn," Father says with a wink. Hooting and whistling fill the space in response.

Mother's expression turns somber, and I know what plans to discuss next.

"We stand before you tonight to keep you as educated as we are. A team of brave soldiers went into Baeton to gather information about a potential threat." Scattered whispers rise. "While there is no imminent danger to us, we ask you that, moving forward, you stay away from the Range of Unrest as much as you can manage."

Father regains the crowd's silence by waving his hand above the sea of heads. "This won't be forever. Only until we figure out what moves they plan on making, and what further steps we need to take to keep Alunia as safe as ever."

They always know how to calm a troubled mind. A few troubled citizens come up to them privately with questions once they dismiss the masses, and the music swells again.

I can't stop myself from looking around the room for a man I know I won't see.

Dessielle pulls me aside and chats my ear off for a while, something I happily welcome to calm the swarm of nerves. Jaali comes down the stairs then, the straggler. He was probably napping and didn't realize the time. He comes down to meet us and bows slightly at the waist.

"Well, well, princess. Look at you! You look stunning, Rae." He pulls me into a tight hug, pinning my arms down at my sides.

"You don't look too bad yourself, Jaali." He swipes the invisible dust from his shoulders and cocks his head.

After a lull in conversation, I muster the courage to ask him. "Is he coming?"

Sympathy bleeds into his face. "I don't think so, red. Parties aren't typically his thing."

I wave away his sympathy in the space between us. "Oh, of course, I know that. I didn't expect him to, I just wanted to know if I needed to brace myself for his arrival. You never know what kind of mood he's in, you know..." My voice trails when I look down at my feet. I try my best not to look disappointed. I have no reason to be, I know he doesn't enjoy this sort of thing. It's not like he told me he would be here. Or that I even want him here.

It's best that he isn't, I tell myself. I don't want to see him anyway.

I find a seat that isn't on the dais and do my best to blend in with the locals. I snatch a glass of faerie wine from a tray and waste no time downing the entire thing. I'm a much better dancer when I've had a glass or two, and I figure I might as well start now. The blend of berries goes back easily despite being a little bitter for my taste. I place the glass back down, lock eyes with Dessielle across the table, and nudge my head toward the dance floor. She holds up a finger to halt the conversation she had found herself in and meets me before the floor with an extended hand.

We used to steal each other for entire nights when we were younger. She was my only dance partner until we branched out to people we were interested in romantically. We learned quickly that dancing with someone is a good way to gauge your chemistry. If you're able to ebb and flow with the other person, it's more likely you'll be a good match. A silly observation, but it's served us well throughout the years.

Dessielle and I are rather clunky when we dance together. We both try to take the lead and make wrong turns, and sometimes we step on each other's toes. The stakes are low, so we simply float with the music and ensure we have a good time above all else. We fall into place with the other couples and a cheerful, medium-paced song begins to play.

A flurry of dresses and hair moves about the room. Warm and bright colors reflect with light from the candles scattered throughout the ballroom. We dance madly with unwarranted confidence until the song finally ends and we retire to our seats. A slower ballad starts, and the dancing becomes more intimate.

When I'm halfway through another glass of wine, Reynard finds me. "I had someone take my post for a minute. Care to dance?"

I place a hand on my stomach full of wine, the idea of more twirling enough to make me sick. With a groan, I decline. "I think I'm going to rest for a while. Give my feet a break, take a breather."

His jaw tenses briefly. "Sure, I get it. You never could hold your alcohol," he says with a breathy chuckle.

"I'll find you later though?"

He nods with a close-lipped smile and leaves to return to his post.

I sit in awe as couples drift by, skirts and laughter spinning out around them. Song after song, I watch them in a daze. They make it look so effortless.

Part of me wants to fill another plate with snacks. I flirt with the idea for a few minutes and finally look over toward the large wooden table covered with food when something spikes my pulse.

Leaning against the wall with a glass in his hand, he looks devastating. His dark wavy hair is neatly styled, yet still roguishly handsome. He's wearing a black tunic that exposes the slightest bit of his muscled, inked chest. A raisin-purple vest is buttoned over it, emphasizing the width of his torso to his waist. Black pants that can't help but yield to the thick muscles in his legs meet with dark leather dress shoes.

One leg is slightly crossed over the other, his index finger tracing the opening of the glass as his eyes connect with mine. When he realizes I know he's been staring, he prowls across the dance floor. He cuts through the slowly twirling couples with ease, as if they aren't in the room. His gaze is unwavering. I feel the stares of those around us, his only friend in awe of what he's witnessing.

Pearce extends his hand before me. "Would you dance with me?"

Stunned, I pause. He holds his position, not flinching at my hesitance. I don't even see him breathe. I clear my throat, trying to find my voice. "Okay," I say before placing my hand in his. I stand and follow him to the middle of the dance floor, suddenly all too aware of my hand in his. Every touch point feels like they're ignited. His fingers brush along the exposed skin of my spine, leaving trails of fire in their wake before settling on the small of my back. I inhale sharply when he pulls me closer to him, and I place my hand on his shoulder.

If we weren't dressed to the nines, I would think we're back in the clearing. Our steps seamlessly bleed into one another. Before I know my next move, he's already responded to me and leading me into the next one. It feels as though we aren't moving, but the background blurs together with every twirl and stride.

Pearce takes a step back before spinning me out and back into him. My hand rests on the crook of his neck, while his is back on my waist as we step slowly. He turns me away from him again, and this time when I return, his grip is firmer on my waist. Searing. Possessive.

Our steps slow as we move in unhurried circles. We inch closer and closer until we're practically on top of one another. We come to a stop despite everyone still dancing around us, our fingers having locked together at some point. Chest to chest, I look up into pools of fire and honey and soundlessly beg for answers I know I won't get.

When those same eyes flash to my lips, I can't stop myself from taking the bottom one lightly between my teeth. His eyes darken at the movement. His chest expands in a deep breath, pushing our bodies flush with one another. My lips part slightly in a gasp when his head inclines. My lids flutter closed as I decide to throw caution to the wind, lean into him, and—

"Attention everyone, the fire will be started shortly. If you wish to watch the lighting, please feel free to join us outside," calls a server. Pearce and I jolt at the outburst and my heart races in my chest. The server taps a knife against a glass and repeats the message. Guests start to pour out onto the terrace and down below around the fire pit.

We take the cue of those surrounding us and take a challenging step apart. His hand doesn't drop from my waist. It falls slowly, briefly grazing the roundness of my backside.

Our eyes are pulled to one another, and I decide to break the silence.

"I suppose we should follow the crowd."

He clears his throat. "As you wish."

I already regret my suggestion. Being in a large crowd is the last thing I want right now. We've barely made it off the dance floor and I already want him to swoop me back into his arms and spin me around regardless of the music no longer playing.

I melt when his hand lands on the small of my back, guiding me toward the fire outside. Every time his skin brushes mine, a current rushes through me. I curse under my breath at my body for behaving out of sorts. I need to snap out of this. When he's finished with me, he'll leave. And my life will go back to the way it was. Back to normal.

If normal is what I want anymore... I don't want a higher position in the kingdom. I'd prefer putting my new skills to good use and fighting with the rest of our army.

My parents would never allow it. Although...they didn't allow me to go to Baeton either, and their response was not the one I expected.

Pearce isn't what I expected, either. His showing up here tonight is enough to prove that. I truly expected him to stay tucked away in his room for the night. Or if he did leave, he would be in the training room.

Neither of those happened.

I glance beside me to ensure he's still there, that I'm not dreaming. He catches sight of my poor peeking, and his eyes flick down to the ground. He's not blushing. He's probably just warm. We *were* just gallivanting around the room. And now there's a massive fire being built.

A small countdown comes from the crowd, and a torch is placed at the base of the massive fire. The flames slowly travel up the large logs in the peak until the entire structure is engulfed. Cheers sound all around us, and applause fades into crackling firewood. An announcement is made saying that the music will resume shortly, and various Beltane activities will be happening late into the night. Others will take place tomorrow morning when the avid partiers are still in their beds after the eventful night to come.

Pearce and I wait out on the terrace as the onlookers slip into the building or down the stairs for their chosen pursuits. Before I realize it, we're no longer surrounded. Completely alone.

"Thank you for coming," I blurt out.

"You did a wonderful job; it came together seamlessly." The low pitch of his voice sends goosebumps up my forearms despite the heat rolling off me.

"It was a group effort. I didn't do all of it, I hardly touched any-thing." I reach up and put a loose strand of hair behind my ear.

"You don't need to touch something for it to be affected by you," he says, his eyes boring into my profile.

I look at him a second too late to catch the emotion on his face. "It's just a party," I whisper. "It's silly. Really, it's nothing."

"Everything you do is *something*," he counters.

"What are we doing out here, Pearce?" I fully turn to him now, and my torso is so close to his arm perched on the balcony that a slight adjustment would make us touch. I barely resist the urge.

"We're having a perfectly fine conversation."

"Yes, but *why*? We've hardly had one in the weeks I've known you."

"Forgive a man for trying to have a better attitude." The cock of his head and the way his eyes turn to slits tells me I've ruined what *was* a fine conversation. He shakes his head slightly and lets out a deep sigh. "Never mind, then." He starts to turn away, but I grab his forearm before he can.

"Wait," I say. He halts but doesn't turn.

"I'm sorry," I huff. "I don't know why I had to turn that into something...ugly." He must sense the vulnerability in my voice because he faces me without ripping his arm from my grasp.

"Don't go soft on me now, princess." The eyes that are usually ice cold are now as blazing as the pit below. "Tell me what you really think." His usual challenging tone is back once more.

"What I really think of what?"

"Of me. You said so yourself, we've hardly had a pleasant conversation since we met, and you just ruined one. Since we're being vulnerable, let me have it. Tell me."

"I don't think you want that," I say.

"You have no idea what I want."

He's right. I gather my courage and tuck away any remaining common sense to avoid this situation. I lean into the fire and stew on my next words.

"You're a brute."

"Excuse me?" He takes a step closer, his forearm still surrounded by my barely-fitting fingers.

"You heard me. You're rude, inconsiderate, and cold. First, you were cruel to me for no reason in the woods, and then you repeatedly saved my life. Your attitude is constantly flipping, and you do things I don't expect."

"Like what?" He challenges.

"Like coming here! Dancing with me, praising my efforts. It doesn't make sense, and I can't keep up with your constant back and forth."

"I've done nothing that wasn't warranted," he says down his nose at me.

"So, being boorish is warranted all the time? I wish I'd known that on the way to Baeton."

"Speaking of Baeton, I'm not the only one here with a spotty track record. You snuck out to go on that trip, and who knows what you had to do to get the position."

"I don't like what you're implying," I say through gritted teeth.

"Oh, I'm sorry, let me not imply. I think you went on a mission you weren't invited to or ready for and expected everyone to welcome you with open arms. Some of us have real consequences for our actions. I shouldn't even still be here," he says, almost yelling the last bit.

"Then why are you still here?" I match his volume.

"You know why," he growls with wide eyes. I finally let go of his arm and let out a frustrated sigh. "I should have left the very night we arrived. But I stayed here instead because I wasn't ready to leave yet."

"Oh, please. And why is that?" I ask as I roll my eyes.

"Because of *you*, Raelenthia! I stayed because of you!"

33

HIS WORDS HIT ME like the crash of a wave against a barricade.

"For whatever reason, I wasn't ready to leave you yet. I can see now that was a mistake, and I should've left a long time ago." He rubs his hand down his face in frustration, and I scramble to collect my thoughts before he tries to storm off again.

"Why would you stay for me?" I manage in a whisper.

He runs his fingers through the dark curls falling into his face after dancing. "I don't know. I suppose I thought maybe we could find some common ground and not be so...hostile." He scrubs his hand down his face.

"Well, I guess you were wrong."

"I guess so." He starts to walk away again, and this time I don't stop him. He heads back toward the hall to go anywhere but here. Probably to pack and finally leave this place.

I've received a decent amount of training; I'll make it work. I did nick Pearce the other day, so that must mean *something*.

Thinking back on that day, I can't believe I was so blinded by lust that I thought he might feel the same way. All I cared about was ripping into his clothes and having him right there on that field. Thank the gods that Willow came to grab me, otherwise I would've made an utter fool of myself.

Still out on the terrace, I take a calming breath. I don't know how much time has passed since he left. I straighten my shoulders and let my feet carry me back toward the masses to find Dessielle. If I go to my room now, I'll spend the rest of the evening wallowing and I'll never hear the end of it. She's sitting on a chair next to Jaali, laughing. I slide onto the seat next to her and lay my head back against the chair.

"Back so soon?" she chimes.

"Very funny," I groan.

Jaali cuts in with childlike enthusiasm. "I've never seen him dance that way; I can't believe you got him to do that!"

"I didn't get him to do anything. He asked me, not the other way around," I mumble as I pinch the bridge of my nose. "Besides, he went back up to his room," I sigh. "You both will probably be going home soon if I had to guess. He's finished here."

Confusion blooms on both of their faces, but it's Dessielle who speaks up first. "What do you mean? We just saw the two of you together, you danced like you've been partners for years. We came back inside with everyone else to give you some more privacy."

Jaali's confusion turns to concern for a friend. Whether it's for Pearce or me, I'm unsure.

"We got into it again. Surprise, to no one." I roll my eyes.

"What did he say?" Jaali asks.

"No offense you guys, but I don't want to talk about it right now. I'd like to sip a glass of wine, make a maypole, and maybe have more wine." With my head still back on the chair, I peek open one eye to read their expressions. Dessielle looks worried, and Jaali seems frustrated. Both of which I didn't expect.

Dessielle stands and extends her hand toward me with a solemn smile. "Let's go get you that wine, then." I don't miss the incline of her head at Jaali. I manage a small smile back at her and look to Jaali to see if he'll be coming with us.

"I'm going to head to my room. I've got a few things to tend to, you guys have fun."

"What things? It's late," I say.

"I know, red. We'll talk later." He pats me on the head as he walks by, and I stand with Dessi.

We wander over to the drink table and spot a tray of half-filled glasses of different shades of purple and pink. I look around the immediate area to ensure no one is coming back to pass them out, and I pull the sterling into my arms. Dessielle grabs a collection of bread and meats from the next table over and nods toward the large open doors leading to the terrace. Moving quickly, we weave through the scattered tables and receive a few strange looks from guests still inside the ballroom.

Outside, it's a bit more crowded. Chatter from the festivities below travels up to the balcony and fills our ears as we sit on the ledge. No one will yell at us, I *am* the princess after all. No matter how I feel about the title. We fall into a comfortable silence, picking from the board of diced food and sipping the various flavors of stolen wine. After a while, she looks over at me. I'm tipping back the last of a glass to get every droplet when I feel her stare.

"What?" I ask, muffled by the glass still against my mouth.

"Just looking at you. I missed you when you were gone."

"I've been back for a while now, Dessi," I say with furrowed brows and a small smile.

She nods and looks back to the fire. "I know you have. You came back different, though. Stronger, more determined. I know you've been in a mental battle with yourself for a while about your future. And maybe I'm wrong, but it seems like you've been surer of yourself since he's been around."

I groan, frustrated that we're back to wasting breath about a man. "Dessi please, I don't want to talk about him."

"Okay fine, *I'll* talk about him. He didn't have to dance tonight. Coming here was enough of an announcement that he's not a complete wretch, and he could have stopped there. But no, he whisked you away and you two danced beautifully and intimately and I know you have more feelings than you're letting on.

Maybe it's time you sit and think about what you want, and what you're feeling. Some introspection could do you good."

I hate that she's right.

"Stop doing that," I tell her.

With a smirk, she says, "You know I'm right. So, let's finish our snacks and get you to bed, shall we? It's been a long night and I'm due for a bath."

"I'm glad you said that." I toss the glass back once more to try and get any last bits of the sweet liquid. "I was going to say something earlier, but it didn't seem like a good time."

She reaches between the two of us and punches the outside of my shoulder lightly. "Oh hush," she says with a laugh. She looks at me stealthily before saying, "You certainly had lots of eyes on you tonight."

"That's sort of my life."

"It had to feel good though, being on the arm of the biggest man in the room." She zones in, violet eyes prying.

"Okay, it felt amazing," I confess with a laugh.

We clean up what little mess we've created and put everything back in its right place. Dessielle and I walk unhurriedly through the castle, stopping in front of photos and pointing out the things in them we find interesting or funny. The sound of revelry gets quieter and quieter as we move away from the ballroom through the halls to my room. She drops me off at the door of my bedroom and brings me in for a tight hug. Before she lets me go, she pulls back and looks at my face.

"Whatever you choose to do, I'll be behind you. If you want to step down from the crown and become a soldier, you do that. If you want to take the position when your parents step down, you can do that too. Just don't get stuck in your head, alright?"

She pauses and gives me a stern look. She knows I often refuse to ask for help.

"You need to talk these things out with the people who care about you. The world can feel like it's ending in your own mind. Share it with others, and the burden becomes lighter."

I sniffle to try and hide the tears brimming in my eyes before pulling her back into my arms. "Thank you, Dessi. I love you."

"I love you too, Rae. Get some rest, alright? You've had a strange few weeks."

I nod and open the door to my dimly lit room. I forgot to light the other smaller candles earlier in the day, and I told Willow to leave me to my own devices tonight so she could enjoy her evening. She listened, and now the only light in my room is from my fireplace. I plop down on the edge of my bed and start to take off my shoes. About halfway through, I find myself staring at the flames in the hearth. They're flickering about, but nothing in comparison to the giant fire ablaze in the courtyard. It'll burn throughout the night if it's not dampened.

Barefoot, I go into my bathing room to undo all Willow's hard work. She usually puts my hair in some kind of simple braid to prevent it from getting too wild while I sleep, but without her here, the task is mine. Typically, my arms get tired during the process due to the amount of hair I have, but all of my training seems to be paying off. My shoulders don't ache in the slightest while I cross the hairs back and forth again until I run out of hair to style.

A small thank you to Pearce passes through my mind, but I quickly swat away the thought. He doesn't deserve the space he takes up in my mind. I decide to think about other things that confuse me, instead: mathematics, the creatures Baeton is holding captive, men in general, and Miss Woodstock. I'll never understand that woman.

I start to unlace my dress. I'm about halfway through when I hear knocking at my door. Dessielle probably left something in here the other day or has something else to say.

"Back already?" I call out from my bed. I walk to the door with my dress unlaced behind me and joke, "I thought you said it was time for me to go to bed." I whip open the door expecting to see my friend, when I break out in goosebumps. It's not Dessielle standing outside my bedroom. It's the man I've been trying, without success, to avoid thinking about.

"Pearce? What are you—" He steps right past me and into my bedroom. "Wait, you can't just storm in here like—"

"Like you did to me?" he says. Fair point. "I don't like how we left things," he says to my bedroom wall. I close the door gently to avoid waking any guests who may be sleeping here for the night.

"It's how we usually leave things," I reply without hiding the frustration in my voice.

"And that's ridiculous. We're both adults, we should be able to have a normal conversation without it turning into something obnoxious and ugly."

"It wouldn't get so ugly if you didn't shut down."

"I wouldn't shut down if you weren't so invasive."

"You think *I'm* the problem here?"

He runs both his hands through his hair, and a single curled strand falls back onto his forehead. I hate how good he looks when he's angry. "I think *we* have some issues to work through. And I'm not leaving this room until we've discussed them."

My eyes widen in disbelief. "That's ridiculous. This is my bedroom and if I want you to leave, you will leave."

He crosses his arms as well as he can over his broad chest and takes in a large breath. "Do you want me to leave?" He asks.

I hesitate for the briefest of moments and a smirk appears on his face. "I didn't even say anything," I squeal in an attempt to defend my clearly confused actions.

"You didn't have to, princess."

"I told you to stop calling me that," I say with clenched fists.

He notices the movement and raises an eyebrow. "Did you? I'm sorry, I don't listen to whining."

I stomp my foot on the ground without thinking, only to prove his point, and a ghost of a smirk appears on his face. The little weasel. "I thought you'd be leaving after our altercation earlier."

His head cocks at my assumption. "A real man doesn't act out simply because his ego is bruised. We weren't finished. I thought I would let you cool off and come back later. By the look of you, it seems you had an eventful rest of your night." My body warms in every place his eyes trail, which is all of it.

"What is that supposed to mean?" My voice comes out lower than I wanted it to, like what he says affects me. It shouldn't, but it does. And I can't let him know that.

His jaw clenches as his eyes travel back up my body to meet mine. Every nerve is on fire right now, and I'm unsure if the Veritas Sea could put it out at this point. "Is there a reason you're partially undressed?" he asks, voice strained.

"I was in the middle of getting ready to sleep when you so rudely showed up at my door," I inform him. "I'm tired. I don't have time for whatever this is." I start to walk toward the door so I can open it for his exit. He's fast though, up and moving before I realize it. When I turn the handle and crack the door open, his hand is on the wood pushing it closed with a loud thud.

"Pearce, *please*, people are trying to sleep."

"I like it when you say that."

My heart drops into my groin. "S-say...what?" I stammer.

His head drops right next to mine so he's whispering in my ear. His breath tickles me as he says, "*Please*. It's so rare that you have manners, I didn't know if you remembered the word after our little tiff in the woods."

I turn around to argue his point and am reminded that he's right behind me. When I pivot, I'm trapped between the door and his chest. His arm is pinned beside my head and he lifts the other, blocking me in on all sides.

"I can't keep doing this," he practically growls.

My throat bobs, and his eyes drop to my throat. "Doing what?"

When his eyes flick from my throat up to my lips, I know what he intends to do. I should stop him. I should tell him to leave so I can go to bed, and he can go back home.

But I don't.

"Resisting you," he utters. And then his lips come crashing down on mine. Despite the intensity of pressure, his lips are soft. His hands suddenly aren't on either side of my head, but on my hips as he pulls me deeper into him. I loop one arm around his neck while the other hand finds his cheek.

For a second, I think about pulling away. But then he removes one of his hands from my waist and puts it at the nape of my neck, his fingers twining in my hair. He tugs on it sharply, causing me to gasp against his lips. He takes the opportunity to deepen the kiss, and I lean into it. My body melts against his and a sound emanates from his throat that would light the hearth if it wasn't aflame already. The stubble on his face scratches against my chin and I feel like a cricket, rubbing my legs together to try and lessen the heat growing between them. I flex my fingers at the nape of his neck and dig my nails into his skin. I only notice when he groans again and tugs harder on my hair in response.

"Keep doing that, princess, and I can't promise the safety of this dress," he murmurs into my lips. His hand drifts down to the open laces at my back that I had forgotten were undone. His knuckles graze the exposed skin there and send a shiver down my spine.

I pull back just enough to say, "If you rip this dress, I can't promise *your* safety."

He smirks. In an instant, both his hands are gone from my hair, and I immediately miss the weight of them. But then they're on my hips, and he spins me around with wild speed. My chest is pushed tight against the door as his hands start meticulously unlacing the rest of my dress. "Do you always need to wear such complicated clothing?" he says in a huff.

"Is now really the time to criticize my fashion choices?" I counter, waiting to be flipped back over.

"You look exquisite, but maybe next time pick something not so difficult to get you out of," he says before pulling the straps over my shoulders and pressing a scalding kiss to my shoulder blade. His lips are a brand against my skin, melting away the night air seeping through my cracked window.

The soft straps of my dress hang around my shoulders as he pushes my tailbone until I'm flush with the door. He pulls apart the last few sections of lacing and his calloused hands push the fabric down my arms, baring my front to the door.

His hand finds its way to my neck, and he uses it to pull me to face him again. Those molten amber and honey eyes lock with mine and he places his fingers around the width of my jaw, his palm pressing against my neck.

"You say the words, and this stops entirely. Do you understand?" His words come out breathy. I nod feverishly. He shakes his head and says, "I need to hear you say it, princess. Use your words." His stare is blistering.

"I understand," I manage from under his commanding grip on my throat.

"Thank the Gods," he rushes out before descending on my mouth again. His full lips meet mine with a hunger I've never felt inflicted upon me before. The hand on my throat wraps around it entirely with mouthwatering pressure and his other latches onto my waist, his thumb swiping against the exposed skin. Our lips move against each other slowly at first, with more intensity after each breath. I pull back to try and get some air in my lungs, and his mouth travels along the edge of my jaw to my neck. He nips at my ear which earns him a small yelp that he devours with his tongue on mine. I feel his hands trail down the outsides of my arms, and he collects my wrists together in front of me with one hand.

Pearce pulls his mouth from mine, and I lean forward to follow those lips when he pulls me toward my too-empty bed. He sits on the edge of it, facing me and my exposed breasts. His fingers hook into the dress sitting around my waist and he pulls it, painstakingly slow, down the rest of my body, trailing hungry kisses down my stomach as he does. When the dress gets to my knees, he falls from the bed to the ground before me. From his knees, he pulls the dress the rest of the way down my legs. I move to step out of it, but he's back on his feet and scooping me into his arms. Before I can process being bared to him and in his grasp, he places me on the bed. Laid out before him in nothing but my dark green undergarments, he licks his lips as he stares at me from above. I try and sit up to reach him. Now *he's* the one wearing too much clothing.

"Let me take the vest off," I say from the bed.

A heavy, sultry chuckle leaves him. "I guess the Veritas has flooded Alunia."

The hint of a scowl flashes on my face before I decide to drop it. I lift my hand to his stomach and reach for the first button when he grabs my ankles and yanks them further off the bed. My feet barely reach the ground, and my hips are teetering on the edge.

"Not until I'm finished," he utters.

"How will you finish if you're fully clothed?"

His eyes darken and a smirk pulls at the corner of his mouth. "That's not what I meant, princess." In one quick movement, he rips my underwear from my hips, the tattered pieces gathering around my knees before he flicks them to the side. Looking up only reminds me that I'm incredibly nude while he's still fully clothed. I bring my legs closer together in an attempt to hide the evidence of my arousal, but he places his knee in between them.

"Mm-mmm," he sounds. His hands clamp down on my thighs. "Keep these strong legs open for me."

A shudder rocks through my body when he skates his knuckles directly up my center. He falls to his knees again and starts slowly lapping at the bud of nerves at my core. His tongue adds to the slickness of my pleasure, sending shockwaves through my legs. I place them on his shoulders; an action he rewards by reaching one hand up to put delicious pressure on the pink bud of my breast. He pinches softly, forcing a soft moan from my throat.

"There she is," he purrs in between my thighs. "Let me hear you." Before I can begin to process his command, he places a finger at my entrance and my legs tense, twitching inward. He pulls his mouth away and swats the skin on my inner thigh with his palm. "What did I tell you?" I jerk them apart as quickly as I can. Anything to keep his mouth on me. My silent pleading is answered when both his tongue and his finger begin to work on me in tandem. He curls his finger inside of me while he flicks his tongue onto the sensitive button and finds a perfect rhythm that causes me to roll my hips.

He chuckles a warm exhale onto the slickness of my core. "Greedy little ember," he teases, and he returns to the devilish pattern he's created with two of the three weapons at his disposal. Pearce feasts on my most sensitive spot until every muscle in my body is tense, and my thighs are squeezing either side of his head. My fingers have made their way into the dark waves at his crown, and I pull on them unabashedly as I reach the peak of my pleasure, letting the tension of the past weeks come crumbling down around us.

Pearce stands from his place between my legs and licks his lips, collecting any bit of dew he may have missed. He crawls onto the bed and positions himself above me. When he kisses me this time, it's slower. No less intense, but the abrasiveness of our earlier connection was just released by his mouth. I reach up and start unclasping the buttons on his vest when he stops me. I look up at him confused.

He cranes his neck to nip at the skin underneath my ear. "I think we should finish this some other time," he drawls.

"What, why?" I say as I try and cover myself with the cover spread out beneath us, suddenly too aware of my nakedness.

"When I have you for the first time, it won't be with any liquid courage. You'll beg for me sober." His fingers trace the outside of my face, and my eyes close as I turn to his touch. Then, he's off me and rebuttoning his vest. Before I can argue that I'm of sound enough mind, he places a finger against my lips. "I'll see you bright and early for training tomorrow, little ember." And then he's gone.

34

PEARCE

I CLOSE THE DOOR behind me softly. At least, I think it's soft. I have no idea how loud anything is at the moment. My heart is pounding too loudly in my chest. For a moment I fear that it might be beating *too* quickly and I might die in a hallway after feasting on a beautiful woman.

Wouldn't *that* be a way to go?

My hands unclench at my sides, and I stretch my cramping fingers. I didn't realize how hard I'd been clenching them while exiting her room until the curved moons of my nails finally bit into the skin of my palm. The look on her face, when I stood from between her thighs, will be permanently engraved into my memory. Her pale pink skin more flushed than usual, her braid of long strawberry waves falling behind her shoulder when she sat up from the bed.

Why did I leave again?

Damn wine.

I know she's mostly come down from it by now, but there's no chance I'm risking my first time with her not being...her.

If there ever even *is* a first time with her.

I don't know how long I can convince Jaali I need to stay here. He's been hounding me about getting back home, and I understand his rush. I do. People are expecting us and we have matters to deal with that cannot be handled from the inside of this castle.

With one last look at the door separating us, I imagine her still sitting on the edge of the bed, now with her sheet wrapped around her. It's enough to draw me back in, but not tonight. Tonight, I have to speak with Jaali.

I know he's expecting to hear from me after my behavior at the ball. Parties aren't my thing. Neither is dancing, so I know he's sitting on a mouthful of choice words about how I'm acting out of character. And he's not wrong, which is the most annoying part. He's usually not, although I wouldn't ever tell him that; his head is already too large.

I stalk through the halls until I reach his room. I know he's itching to get back to his bed, and I don't blame him for it. This castle is beautiful, but home is everything. I don't bother knocking and decide to enter the room unannounced.

"Where are you, man?"

His lean torso is on full display as he walks out of the connected bathroom with no more than a cloth wrapped around his waist. "Oh, sure. Come on in, Pearce," he grumbles.

"We need to talk," I say as I sit down on a small, padded bench near the window.

"Like hell, we do. How long do you expect me to fill my time, day in and day out? We should be back home putting together our plan for Baeton. Ke—"

"I know what we need to be doing. I haven't lost my mind." His brow lifts at my statement and I scowl at him. "I've just been a little distracted."

"You're telling *me," h*e says while carrying on with his nightly routine. I'm surprised he has time for anything else with all the primping and grooming he does. He takes an immense amount of time trimming the already perfect hairs on his face.

"I just need a little more time," I tell him. I don't know why I feel obligated to explain myself to him. If we had a typical leader-subordinate relationship, he wouldn't be questioning me. But we're more than that, we always have been. Jaali is like the brother I never had, which makes his opinion matter even more when I'm being reckless. Like right now.

"How much time is sufficient, Pearce? We've been away long enough. They're expecting you and are probably growing impatient while they await the information we left to find in the first place."

I pinch my brows, frustrated that he's right once again. "I know. Trust me, I know. We'll be gone soon." I look at him as he's pulling his shirt over his head.

"One more week. I need to hold you accountable, I'm sorry. I like her too, but we have to go. Don't get too comfortable, alright?" I sigh when he leaves for the bathing room again.

I'm afraid it might be too late for that.

Leaving Jaali to enjoy the remainder of his night in peace, I return to my room. I pull off my shoes and start the task of undressing, a task I wish I had let her do in that room. I'll forever kick myself for that.

She's the most determined woman I've ever met. I'm drawn to her, despite what she may believe. I would hope that, after tonight, she doesn't still think I can't stand her. But I honestly couldn't blame her if she did.

That first day we met in the stables put me on my toes. Jaali and I had scoped out the group and knew who we would be traveling with so we could plan around them. We secured our spots and found the right clothing, only for one of the members to be changed before we even left the castle.

Raelenthia is full of a fire I've never seen in anyone, despite her being raised to be dormant all her life. She's filled with sass and has a smart mouth; one I don't know if I'll be able to keep myself from grabbing and kissing before we leave here. Gods help me, this woman cannot be my undoing. I've worked too hard to be interrupted now.

Light comes through the large window across the room and wakes me. I'm still not used to so much morning light. I dress quickly in my usual attire: a black fitted tunic and pants that allow me plenty of fighting room. After she nicked my face, I knew I needed to step up. Raelenthia has shown serious improvement since we started, and it fills me with rage thinking about her *friend* putting doubts in her head. He's been smart enough to avoid me since that day, and if he weren't a snake, I might respect him for it. As long as he stays away from her, that issue will remain our only one.

The halls are empty as I make my way to the kitchen. I may have given her a hard time for doing the same before a lesson, but that's because she ate so close to training. She didn't make time for it, and that was her mistake. I pass by Willow on my way out. We dip our heads in acknowledgment but otherwise say nothing.

I leave the room with my muffin in tow and make it nearly to the stairs to the armory when I hear footsteps behind me. I whip my head in their direction and see Willow come around the corner. She doesn't cower and hide when I see she is following me, which I respect.

She straightens her back, her chest lifting a bit. "You be careful with her," she demands.

My intense stare softens. "I've got to rough her up a little to be a good fighter," I explain. I know what she means though, so I say, "Other than that, you have nothing to worry about from me." She nods sharply and holds her hand out in front of her. I cross the distance between us and shake it firmly, and she heads back to the kitchen. I stand in the hall for a moment more and think about her words.

I only have a week. I can't let her think I've just up and left, but how am I supposed to tell her I was summoned by the council the moment we arrived back in Autumn?

As much as it pains me, I know I can't pursue her any further. Last night was a one-time thing.

It has to be.

One I'll think of in comparison to any future partner, though there hasn't even been a *potential* one in a long time. Raelenthia is the first person to challenge me in a way that sets my soul on fire. And I respect her too much to toy with her. I have to go home, and she has to stay here. I'll tell her today that I plan to leave, and that will be that. We'll train every day until then. Hopefully, that will be enough... For both of us.

I waste no time collecting the weapons we'll be using for training today. Now that her strength and stability have improved along with her swordsmanship, I'm steering our path toward real fighting. Jaali has filled me in further about what he saw and heard around the other guards in Baeton, and I need her to be able to protect herself. I don't doubt that she would go out with a fight, but I need more than that from her. I need survival. So that's what we'll be going over.

She's been picking up her own fighting style, which is typical. But I have to teach her that it's okay to not always fight with structure. She needed to understand that first before we could get to this point, and now that she has, I can't wait to see what she'll do with the right guidance. She'll be an unstoppable force on any battlefield when she's finished with me. Which I had, foolishly, hoped would be much further from now. Not for her sake, but my own.

I've grown rather attached to her, and I can't put my finger on any single reason; there seem to be dozens. But once I go home, my interest will surely fade, and I can go back to working with my council for the good of my people. Once I fall back into a routine, I'll be better. I won't think about her when I wake up or when I fall asleep. I won't hear a laugh from somewhere in the castle and compare it to hers. I won't do any of that, and life will go back to the way it was—except for the brewing war. Jaali would have my head if he knew I let her flood my thoughts about our war strategy, so I make a mental note to avoid discussing her in the future.

With Baeton now at the front of my mind, I sharpen my focus on their army. My purpose here is to teach her to hold her own and take out as many enemy troops as she can when that time comes. And it will.

Jaali informed us as a group that the Baetonians have a multitude of creatures locked away in a separate dungeon. Their minds have most likely been altered to make them into dangerous beings since their first instinct would typically be to retreat to their own homes when faced with Fae from the surrounding regions. I have to make her into a weapon so strong, no one would dare pass through her. She needs to be unstoppable. So that is what I'll make her.

Just when I've collected my thoughts and warmed up, I see her tentative steps coming toward me. I hadn't thought about the rush I would get from seeing her again after being kept between her thighs, and the wind almost knocks out of me, even at this distance. Her eyes don't pull away from mine, and a heady cloud fogs the mind I've spent so much of my life building walls around.

She's dangerous. Not only with a weapon, but she's *becoming* one to me. Something that I've told myself doesn't exist, that could alter my life forever. Something that I don't deserve.

I still think that, regardless of my actions with her last night. I won't be speaking about it unless she does. I can't give her any inkling that she has affected me so heavily, or I lose all of my influence as her teacher.

She has on a different dark blue tunic with pants a few shades lighter. Her boots are caked in mud from all of the rain that's graced the region lately, and my mind briefly projects an image of us both covered in it—me pinning her down, and her using all of her might to break her arms free of my hold, and she would succeed because she's a tiny beast.

I'm brought back to reality when I hear the slice of moving metal cutting through my thoughts. She's unsheathing her weapon, and I hold out my hand to stop her. "Not so fast. We're starting with a bit of a different method, today."

To my surprise, she doesn't question me. She slides the sword back into its place and takes off the belt it's attached to. I watch her walk to the center of the field, awaiting her next instructions. Something is wrong. She's being too accepting; I see no sign of her usual defiance. "Something the matter?" I ask her.

Her head shakes from side to side slowly, but something else flickers in her light green eyes.

This simply won't do.

"Get on with it, princess."

"What are you talking about?" she questions.

"Whatever you're holding in that is affecting you so heavily. Spit it out, or I'll work it out of you myself."

Her breath hitches and her fists clench at her sides. "It's been a strange couple of days," she confesses.

"Strange how?" I ask, knowing damn well I'm the cause of her frustration. I've been quite difficult to work with, and then I threw everything she knew on its head last night. I'm not surprised she feels this way right now, but I am surprised she would let me see it. I won't look too far into that.

"Can we get on with training, please? I don't want to talk about this right now."

I don't hide the smirk that spreads across my face, and her eyes widen. "As you wish," I comply. I lunge at her, my hands reaching to pin her arms at her sides. She comes to at the last second and barely avoids my hold. Her fist comes straight for my jaw, and I jump backward to avoid the blow.

"Is this what you need? To hit me?"

Breathing heavily, she cracks her neck and looks at me with fierce eyes. "Maybe, yeah. Might feel good."

"Bring it on then, princess. Make yourself feel good." That earns a snarl from her pouty pink lips, and she runs full force at me, reaching for my waist. Her shoulder connects with my lower abdomen and knocks me back a step, and I have to snap myself back into the moment. She truly is angry with me.

Fair enough.

I reach down and wrap my arms around her waist, flipping her with all my strength. Her legs come up toward my head, and she's now dangling in front of me with her back to my groin.

"*Pearce*, let me down! This is ridiculous!"

"You can be let down when you deserve it, little ember."

"Don't call me that," she cries.

"Would you rather I call you princess? I figured I'd give you a reprieve."

"Don't call me anything," she answers. "Just let me go."

My grip falters for a moment around her midsection. She reaches far enough to grab onto my feet and kicks her legs down with enough force to separate us, righting herself. I barely stifle a laugh, and she looks even more angry now. Her head is beet red from being upside down, and it's incredibly cute. Small hairs around her face are sticking out and I know she would be livid at me seeing her this way. But I kind of like it.

"Feel better now?" I ask the tomato standing in front of me.

She lets out a heavy breath, turns away, and starts walking towards the castle. We're not finished here.

I run up behind her and tackle her to the ground, trying to land with mostly my body hitting the floor. I don't want to crush her under my weight; she would turn into pink and blue leather.

"I'm not letting you go until you tell me you won't run away."

Her body goes still within my arms. "You're acting insane."

I look down at her as much as I can in our current position. "Am I? Well picture me as a truly insane person and fight me back." I think hard about how to get her to stay and fight. I don't want to do this to her, but I go for what I know will set her fuming. Her ego.

"You want to be a warrior so bad, but won't even fight someone who takes it easy on you?" She thrashes a bit but doesn't respond. I have to keep going.

"Is that all the fight you had in you? I expected more, I'll be honest." At that, she jerks her lower body with enough force to break free the slightest bit. When I firm my grip on her, she freezes once more.

And then she bites my fucking arm.

I let her go instantly, and she crawls away from me, assumes a fighting stance, and wipes away the blood that smeared onto her lips.

Why the fuck am I hard?

Seeing her in a frenzy like this is doing awful things to my head. I need to get us back on track, and fast. Before I take things further than I left them last night.

When she lunges at me, I place my hand out just in time to catch her shoulder and stop her. Her arms fling out toward me, trying to get ahold of anything she can use to take me down. To her dismay, my wingspan is much longer than hers. She looks adorable like this.

I shove her back, causing her to stumble before she rights herself again. "Are you done?" I ask her.

"Are you?" She says with more attitude than a small child.

That smart mouth.

"We have some actual training to get through today, so I'm calling for a truce." I raise both my hands in surrender and wait for her defensive stance to dissipate. When it finally does, I hand over her sword and walk to the center of the clearing.

"I want you to come at me full force," I tell her.

"Are you sure about that?" She asks and cocks an eyebrow.

"Incredibly. Give me all you've got."

She's strong. I knew that before her weapon came barreling down toward mine, but it's nice to see it in action. We hold that stance until she finally bends and circles her weapon back around to regain the upper hand. I knock her sword down and she comes back for the left side of my torso. I have to physically jump out of the way to avoid her blade. We continue like this, slice after strike, before I send a blow that knocks her weapon from her hands. It lays in the dirt before her, and she raises her hands. My weapon is at her neck, just inches away from her rosy flesh.

"Again," I tell her.

"Already? I need time to recover first."

"Your enemy won't give you time to recover. You need to be able to withstand fighting for long bouts of time." She needs to get her head on right.

"Okay fine, but this isn't a war scenario. We can take rests as needed."

"You won't have that luxury one day. We need to train you for that, not your everyday life. Now pick up your weapon and get your shit together." She flinches at my harsh words.

I take a deep breath to try and collect myself. There's no real reason I should be this angry about something she's right about. But when I leave at the end of this week, this will be all the truly helpful training she'll have. She needs to understand the severity of what she wants, and what it will take to get there.

"Consider me your enemy," I say in a low voice.

She pulls her shoulders back and collects her weapon. "Easy."

The two of us move at each other with our full strength. I may be stronger, but her lean and agile body means she can be faster. Our chaotic yet controlled steps kick up dirt all around us until our feet have carved a circle in the ground. After a few minutes of constant movement, I try and cut my sword in a way that will halt her pattern. I aim for lower on her body in the hope that she'll drop her arms to block, but she doesn't even consider it. She shifts her original path to aim for my torso, and we pause with her pointed right at the center of my chest. Too close to my heart for comfort.

She freezes, not pushing the sword any further into my chest. I lean forward, into the tip of the blade. "Do it."

Her eyes falter the slightest bit. Not long enough to show the emotion underneath, but enough to notice the movement. "What?" she asks, confused.

"I said do it. I'm your enemy, so push." When I try and lean even further, she pulls the weapon further away. It's still pointed at me, but the metal is no longer piercing through to my heated skin.

She tends to raise my temperature.

"I'm not doing that," she says and lowers her sword. She strides over to the log bench to collect her things and turns back to me looking flustered. "I have to go meet with my parents."

"About what?"

"How should I know? I was only told this morning." And then she walks back to the castle without giving me a second glance.

35

RAELENTHIA

THE LARGE WOODEN DOORS creak as I push into my parents' meeting room. They're both seated in their respective chairs, and there are three more seated on the other side. I take the one in the middle to be directly between my parents. We make small talk for a few minutes before I ask them why they've called me in today.

"Just a few more minutes, dear, and we'll get to it."

What are we waiting for? I rushed to my room after my training session to bathe before grabbing a sorry breakfast and coming here. They could have at least told me a later time if they weren't ready for me...

A knock sounds at the door. "Come in," my father calls.

Jaali's perky smile appears around it, and he strolls over to sit at my left. "What are you doing here?" I ask him.

He shrugs nonchalantly. "Don't know. I figure I'm about to find out, though."

"Is he with you?" My mother asks Jaali. The crease between my brows deepens. Who else is coming?

"I think he was right—" The door creaks open once more and the same devastating face I battled this morning steps inside. My entire body goes cold, my mouth bone dry.

His eyes are on me the moment he enters the room. Pearce approaches the final open seat on my right, sits down soundlessly, and laces his fingers on his lap. "Sorry I'm late," he says to my mother. She dips her head and motions to my father for him to address us.

"As the three of you know, Baeton has been stirring up a bit of worry throughout the kingdom. The fact that they have creatures native to Alunia does not sit well with us, and we're concerned that there is a darker intention for their possession of them. We called for Davian, but he could not get here on such short notice. We are going to move forward with you three to discuss our plans."

Jaali shifts uncomfortably in his seat while Pearce goes as still as the dead. My mother looks at them both but continues. "We want to bring the creatures home obviously, but our main goal is to avoid as much chaos as possible. This kingdom has suffered enough loss and turmoil since its creation, and we want to limit it where we can. We'd like the three of you to, once again, go through everything you remember about what you heard and saw so we can draft a peace treaty."

"A what?" Pearce asks, dumbfounded. "They kidnapped beings from Alunian soil and have been sending soldiers to scope out entrances to the kingdom. They would laugh at a peace treaty."

She sighs and looks to my father to back her up. "They've shown mercy with other kingdoms and have treaties with them. They *have* allies, we're just not one of them. I think they're scared, and I think they're letting the past guide their actions. They feel threatened by things that they don't understand. That doesn't mean we have to fight them," he says.

I nod slightly, considering his words. My father has seen both sides of this. He would be the most understanding party here, given his history. "It might work," I offer. "We could always try, while still being prepared for the worst-case scenario." I feel Pearce's eyes land on me immediately after I finish.

Mother smiles softly, hope shining in her familiar eyes. "We thought so too, dear. That's why we hoped the three of you could relay all of your previous information again, so we can discuss the best way to approach both sides."

Jaali starts first, recounting the story of the worried guards. He doesn't miss a single detail, it's almost word for word the same thing he said the day we arrived.

Pearce goes next, obviously disagreeing with this plan. He stresses the importance of striking first and striking hard. He gives his side of our trek through the castle and relays what the security was like.

When my turn comes, I decide to focus on the maps. I remind my parents where each camp was placed and where they relocated to. We talk about whether we noticed any camps out in the woods while we were there, or if maybe all their soldiers were at the castle after returning from scouting. None of us can recall, so we go back down the line to share any final details we find vital. Once my parents are satisfied with the information presented, we're dismissed. Mother and Father lean in and whisper to one another, while Jaali stands up hurriedly to probably go find some food in the kitchen.

Pearce and I stand at the same time, and I crane my neck in a useless attempt to keep my parents from hearing me. "You didn't tell me you'd be here."

"I didn't know until I was summoned not long after you left. I guess they recognize intelligence," and he winks.

The chill that runs down my spine is ruthless as flashes of last night blind every other thought in my head. I stomp out of the room in a blur, needing to be anywhere but here.

I find myself walking to the library. The smell of books evens my breathing and slows my heart rate, so I look through the shelves and filter through every title and author we have in the massive room. After finding a title that seems interesting enough, I take refuge in the large wingback chair by the window. There's a kettle bowl in here since Mother usually takes her morning tea with literature. I pour myself a cup and settle in to read.

I'm a few chapters in when the hairs on the back of my neck stand up. I place my cup back down on the table and mark the page before putting the book down. I hear nothing coming from the hall, so I walk over to the door and close it. Before I can, a black boot shoves its way between the door and the frame. I gasp, startled. I'm even *more* startled when I look up to see Pearce eyeing me like he may destroy me.

He wasn't happy in the office; he wants my parents to take a more ruthless approach. But I agree with them, we should exhaust all efforts of peace first.

He uses his knee to push the door back open. "Hiding from me, little ember?"

"No," I scoff. "I have no reason to hide, I've done nothing wrong. You're not as scary as you think."

He cocks a brow and strolls over to the chair I had been lounging in. The man picks up my tea, sips it, and moves to pick up the book too. "Excuse you, those are mine."

He pauses, his hand still on the cover. "I thought this library was open to everyone in the castle. I'm within my rights to be here." And he picks up the book.

Who does he think he is? I march over to him and reach for the book so I can rip it out of his hand, but he wraps his fingers around my outstretched arm and pulls me down so we're face to face. If I lean in just a few inches, our lips would connect. I exhaust all effort to not look down at them. I fail. And he sees it.

A heavy groan comes from the back of his throat, and he places the cup back on the table without looking away from me. "Is this your seat?" he asks, gravel in his voice.

I nod shakily. He tsks and cocks his head slightly. "Tell me."

I swallow as best I can while in this position and clear my throat. "This is my seat." He smirks, and I regret confirming. In a split second, he stands from the chair and flings me into it, his hand still wrapped around my wrist. He looks massive with my legs on either side of him. The heat in his eyes is enough to warm the tea in my now room-temperature cup. I try and close my legs, but he doesn't move for me to do so.

He kneels.

"Pearce, this is a library."

He looks up at me from under his dark lashes. "Then I guess you need to stay quiet." My eyes dart to the door, only to see that he locked it behind him after entering. His fingers skate along the skin at my ankles and move slowly up the outside of my legs. He lifts the skirt of my dress up around my waist and places small kisses along the inside of my thighs.

I bite my lip to keep a soft gasp from coming out, and my hand finds its way to his hair of his own accord. He must sense my sudden eagerness as he places another kiss on the bud of nerves there over my underwear.

"You said you didn't want to," I manage in a low voice.

"I said we *shouldn't*. You're misremembering. You're of sound mind now, correct?"

I nod, and he raises his brows at me expectantly. "Yes, I am," I clarify.

He moves his lips back to the ones in front of him and says, "Much better," before pulling the cloth to the side and trailing his tongue through the entirety of my center. A moan escapes me before I can silence it, which fuels his eagerness. He starts sucking and licking at the wetness gathering there and I *swear* I feel a few small bites. My head starts to fall back against the chair, and he grips the inside of my thigh. My eyes flutter open and he pulls just far enough away to say, "Eyes on me while I'm between your legs, little ember."

A heavy blush covers my body, and I wouldn't be surprised if my skin is the color of my hair. His arm reaches up to splay over my stomach. His palm covers my lower abdomen, and he pushes down on it slightly, just enough to ground me. He groans and stands swiftly. For a moment I think he's backing down again, but I'm wrong. He grips my biceps and hoists me from the chair to stand on trembling legs. I'm spun around and pushed forward; I have to put my arms out to brace myself on the seat.

Pearce makes quick work of the laces on the back of this dress, much simpler than the one from the ball. He pulls me by my hips and places his hands on my shoulders, pulling down the fabric there. He slides it down my arms until the peaks of my breasts pop free. His sure fingers guide it down until it puddles on the floor beneath me, and I step out of the sea of teal fabric. I turn back to him, and his eyes take me in fully. They linger on my chest and travel down the curves of my waist, all the way down to my toes.

He pushes me back on the padded chair, and my breath hitches when he returns to his previous movements with his mouth. Now that I'm exposed to him, his hands travel up to my breasts and he squeezes firmly. My hand is fully in his hair, keeping him in my most sensitive area. Although, I don't know if anything could make him leave. His rough hands roam over my soft skin, his callouses leaving goosebumps in their wake.

One hand grasps onto his wrist as he puts dangerous pressure on my apex, my nails digging into his arm. With the other, I pull at the dark curls of his crown. I gasp and moan softly into the quiet space, trying my best to keep from squealing in one of the quietest rooms in the castle.

Here, of all places.

Really?

When I manage to catch my breath, I feel his fingers slide through my folds and enter me with a gentleness I didn't foresee. He moves them in and out of me steadily, building pressure in my core. His wrist twists and those fingers curl inside of me, hooking themselves into my psyche and bleeding every ounce of hesitation left in me dry. I take a deep breath as his mouth descends and works in tandem with his fingers. The pressure and stimulation cause me to close in on myself, but he pushes my knees back apart with his free hand and shoulder.

The nerves in my body become fully charged as I feel pressure building around his hand. I'm not going to last much longer at this rate, and I think that's his end goal.

A never-ending cycle of drawing me in just to push me away. But right now, I don't care as my back bows. I release a moan much louder than anticipated and come apart on his tongue. He doesn't stop moving in me until my breathing evens and my hold on his hair softens. He licks his lips before taking his fingers, the ones that were my undoing, and licks them too.

Pearce puts his hand around my neck and pulls my face to his with another hungry kiss. When he pulls away, I look up at him and reach for the waist of his black trousers. He doesn't block me this time, he helps me pull them the rest of the way down before they gather around his ankles. His cock flicks out and hangs between us, and I think I may have a heart attack. His tan skin stretches over the piece beautifully. Pearce takes it in his hand, rubbing it softly. He eyes me from above, and I nod. "Remember little ember. You say so, and everything stops immediately."

"I understand," I say in a whisper. His eyes turn ablaze and shift to a shade darker. They'd undress me if I wasn't bare already. He pushes me back down onto the chair and aims himself at my parted lips. The flat of my tongue trails across the angled tip before I welcome him into my mouth. His hand knocks itself at my roots, pulling my head back the slightest bit so he can look into my eyes as my tongue swirls around the length of him.

The force at my neck pushes me further onto him. When I hear his heavy sigh, I look up at him through hooded lids and hold his gaze as I use my hand to build his desire, bobbing up and down in tandem with my tongue. He thrusts in and out of my head with a cruel rhythm, controlling his pleasure. His other hand finds its way to my face where his fingers latch onto my jaw, holding it open as he pushes even further.

His head falls back with a moan as I inch my lips further down his shaft until my eyes water. When he's fully sheathed in my throat, he pulls out slightly and thrusts back into my mouth in short bursts. I don't even realize I'm touching myself until I hear him hoarsely say, "That's it, little ember. You're doing so well."

I hollow my cheeks to let him push into the deepest part of my throat, all while dragging my tongue along him as he thrusts in and out between my lips. His fingers bruise my jaw before he moves them to splay along my throat, the other pulling my hair together at the base of my neck. Pearce's pace turns dangerously jagged and I feel him freeze before telling me, "I'm going to finish down your throat, princess."

Not a question.

His fist tugs sharply on my hair before he pushes himself fully against the back of my throat when he groans his release. I don't dare stop meeting his thrusts until his cock no longer twitches against my tongue.

When he finally separates us, he leans down and rests his lips on my forehead. Heavy breathing fills the space, and I hear him mumble something against my skin.

"You're going to ruin me."

36

THE REST OF THE week flies by in tension-filled training sessions, listening to Miss Woodstock's voice falter in and out of my ears as my attention wanes, and Dessielle peppering me with questions about Pearce. The frustrating part is that I don't know the answers to most of them. I hardly know anything about him, or his life. I don't even know where he's from since he's never explicitly said.

In my free time, I've been delving more into reading. I've almost finished the novel I now own from Miss Woodstock's library. The more I read from it, the more disappointed I am that I'll never see it for myself. It sounds like the ideal system, where things are left on their own to thrive and be themselves without outside intervention. It's a shame it's not a reality.

I spoke with my parents about my fighting lessons. I told them about how much I've improved since the beginning and what I'm capable of thanks to my teacher. Mother's eyes showed her suspicion and curiosity at the mention of him. She tried to press deeper about the relationship like she did previously, but I wasn't willing to share any additional information. She knows I've had partners before, but discussing in intimate detail courting and romantic quests is too far for what I deem necessary shareable information.

The weekend will most likely be filled with reading while Roralei works on her paintings. She plans on having a few friends come to visit, I'm excited for her. Since it's the end of the week, I won't have classes with Miss Woodstock, and I gave Willow those days off to spend with her family. Things have been slow lately, flowing along day by day.

When I arrive in the weapons room to find Pearce sitting on the bench with no weapon, I'm confused. The look on his face isn't one of happiness, and for a moment I'm scared that he's going to fire me as a student. I feel that my skills have improved greatly, so I hope that's not the case. He pats the space next to him, and I take it.

"I know things have been...strange between the two of us."

"That's putting it lightly," I jest. He doesn't look amused, and now I'm even more sure that he has bad news.

"Whatever it is between us, I respect you enough to tell you that I'm leaving soon."

My hopeful heart shrivels up like a dried fruit until only the husk remains in my chest. I knew he'd leave eventually but I just...thought I had more time. I nod slowly and look at the wall. Anywhere but his eyes that I feel burrowing into my soul.

"Alright. How soon?" Maybe we have enough time to squeeze in another lesson, although I know how selfish that sounds.

He wants to go home. He's been away for a long time, much longer than the other soldiers that traveled with us. It's probably time. I try not to let my disappointment show when he says, "In a few hours."

My eyes widen in surprise. A few minutes of silence pass before he places his hand on my shoulder, pulling my attention from the stone wall to his roguishly handsome face. A face that I won't see again after today.

"I'm not happy to be going, you know."

My brows pinch. "You're finally going home. You've said you want to return for as long as you've been here."

He nods slightly and purses his lips. "I have, that's true. But I've since become...fond of this place, I guess you could say." That husk in my chest swells the slightest bit at the idea of him coming to love my home as much as I do. I understand why he has to go, I just didn't expect to be so upset by it.

"It's a lovely place. I'm unsurprised," I offer with a small smile.

"It's a fine place. The people here are alright, too." His hand falls from my shoulder to my hands clasped on my lap. He squeezes them and dips his head to coax my eyes to his.

I look at our joined hands and try not to let my emotions interfere too much. He's going away, and I have to prepare myself for that. "Thank you for telling me. I'll leave you to finish getting ready for the trip home." I stand and exit the room with no other words from Pearce.

The small hope I had that he might stay longer, whisked away with a few words. It was an unfair wish to have.

He should go. We aren't together, we're barely friends. I don't know why I expected anything else.

My bedroom welcomes me warmly. The fire is still lit from last night, and I'm always amazed by how long it lasts in here. Roralei has told me that the fire in her room goes out sometimes in the middle of the night, or at least while she gets ready the next day. Meanwhile, mine burns for days on end. Willow says it's because my soul is full of fire. She's always been one for a good story.

I decide to spend some time tidying up my room while Willow is with family. I hum while putting away stray shoes and cosmetics. I fold my towels and place them by the bath, and even go through the items in my wardrobe to see if they are still to my tastes. When they aren't, I sometimes alter them and give them to Roralei. If they don't fit the way I wish they did, I give them to Dessielle. Anything that doesn't quite look right on me typically looks like it was made to fit her curves.

I'm so caught up in my spinning and humming while cleaning that I let out a sharp squeal when I bump into that damned muscled chest. The last time Pearce was in my room, he ended up feasting on me like he was a dying man, and I was his last meal. And then he left without servicing his own needs. A shiver racks my body causing me to brush against him, and his nostrils flare.

"What are you doing in here?"

"I thought I'd come say goodbye."

My throat bobs. "It's time already?" I didn't realize how long I'd been up here.

He nods solemnly. "I am. I figured I would stop by again and let you know; to thank you for everything, and I hope that I see you again."

My brow rises. "Really?"

He makes a sound like a scoff but mixed with a laugh like he can't believe it himself. "Yeah, I guess I do." He leans his head down, and my eyes fall closed when I feel his lips brush against my forehead. Pearce places a soft kiss and pulls away with sad eyes. Eyes that almost make me believe he's going to miss me. But I know better, so I don't stop him when he starts to turn for the door.

He stops himself.

I brace myself when he turns around and stalks back toward me, leaving little to no space between us. His hand settles on my cheek, and he meets my eyes with gut-wrenching sincerity.

"Fuck it," he growls, and then his lips are on mine in a devastating kiss. My arms loop around his neck and fabric flies around us until our skin is touching and my body is on fire. The softness of my bed meets my back as he trails his hands down my bare chest and abdomen.

He reaches down and angles himself toward my middle, coating his tip in my arousal. He reaches across our bodies and places a hand against the side of my neck, his thumb rubbing my cheek. "You know if you change your mind--,"

Before he convinces himself otherwise, I kiss him once more and say, "I know." Our lips sealed together, he knocks at my entrance and begins to push through. I open my legs wider to welcome him as he starts to move slowly. He pushes forward an inch, and then retracts before pushing back further. His hand on my neck turns from gentle to slightly bruising. It's nothing I can't handle, I won't stop him.

His hips rock forward more surely, his thrusts more even and taking. I reach up to his hips and grasp the skin there, pulling him forward with each thrust. Pearce reaches between us and rubs his thumb against my center at the same pace as his movements, and my mouth falls open in a silent scream. His grip shifts from my neck to my breast and he squeezes brutally, picking up the pace of his hips until I feel like I might explode. My feet lock around his waist to bring him closer, and he growls when he becomes fully sheathed inside me.

Pearce grabs my chin in his strong hand, his fingers pressing firmly into my jaw to lock my eyes with his. It's not painful or demanding, his touch *just* forceful enough to command my attention and send sparks through my skin where his fingers connect with it. I watch him grind his teeth as his head falls forward, and then I'm met with his absence and a warmth on my stomach.

Before I have time to overthink what we've just done, Pearce reaches down to gently toy with my slit, not allowing me to get ahead of myself. He knows how to bring me back to the moment.

Chest heaving, I reach aimlessly for any bit of bedding to grip onto. Pearce uses his other hand to latch onto my hip, gripping my side in a harsh contrast to the delicate fondling between my legs.

As I start to reach the peak of my pleasure, he grips my face with a seductive gentleness. "Take a deep breath, princess," is the warning I get before he sinks back into me. The swell of emotions mixes with my roaring release, and Pearce rides the wave back down with me.

He releases a breathy moan mixed with a sigh, his heavy breaths stretching his skin over the striations of his pecs and shoulders. Skin to skin, we lay bare with one another, the sound of our slowing breaths the only noise in the room. His hand trails from my jaw to my neck, where he rubs lazy circles with his thumb.

His eyes look satiated, content. Like he had previously been rattling around in his mind like a caged animal. His brows are creased, and his lips are pursed like he's contemplating something. Pearce speaks first, breaking the steamed silence. What he says nearly makes me fall off the bed.

"What if you came with me?"

Unsure if I heard him correctly, I shake my head before quickly asking, "What?"

"What if you came with me? You said so yourself, you're curious about where I'm from and, despite my better judgment, I can't seem to part with you yet."

"I... We're not—"

"Look. I can't explain why, but the idea of leaving you here for the foreseeable future doesn't sit well in what little remains of my soul. I'm not asking you to leave permanently. But can you look at me and tell me you don't feel things for me?"

"You have no idea what I feel."

He looks at me like he's stripping me not of my clothes, but my being. Like he's seeing through my sarcastic façade, behind the walls I've struggled to maintain. "I might not. But if you have even the smallest hesitation about me leaving today, I want you to come with me. Just for a few days. And then if you want to leave, I'll take you home myself."

That confuses me further. "You'd ride home, and then ride back with me, just to go back home again?"

His body stiffens. "I'd see you home myself. No other man is staying with you that long in close quarters. So yes, I'd take you back."

I can't help the heat that rises to my cheeks. I probably look ridiculous, yet he's still staring at me with hope shimmering in his eyes. Hope that I'll say yes. I can't believe I'm even considering this...

"How far away did you say it is?"

"I didn't."

I roll my eyes at him. "Okay, then how far is it? You said I wouldn't know where it is, so it's probably far enough."

"It's closer than you're imagining. It's just a bit closed off from the rest of the kingdom. We like to keep to ourselves there."

"You? Keeping to yourself? I never would have thought that," I say with feigned surprise. Now it's his turn to roll his eyes.

"Don't make me retract my offer."

I have no doubt he would do that. He's proven he's a man of his word. I hardly trust someone so soon, but something about his request seems...genuine.

I take a deep breath, exhaling all of the negativity peppering my thoughts about how this is a bad idea that can only end in heartbreak. When I find my voice, I look at his waiting face and say, "I'll go with you."

The smallest smirk blooms on his lips and I have to fight the urge not to kiss him again. He's finally extended an olive branch to something real. I won't ruin it by being overbearing.

I have a tendency to be *too much* for some people. By the time I realize it, they've reached their limit for tolerating me while I try and piece together what I did wrong. I don't want to overstep. I'll keep calm...wherever it is we're going.

I move around my room soundlessly, throwing things into my luggage. When he realizes what I'm doing, he tells me to pack warm. "It's not that cold outside," I reply.

"The climate there is a little bit harsher. Don't fight me on this, little ember. You'll want to bring some thicker clothing." When he's confident I'll heed his advice, he heads for the door. "I'll fill in your parents on where you're going."

"Oh please. There's no need for that, I can handle it."

"You have a bag to pack. We'll be leaving soon, and I have a feeling you don't pack light." We scowl at each other before he exits the room. I hastily throw some clothing together and am swarmed with gratefulness that this journey won't be like the one to Baeton. I'm going as myself, not a pretender.

After I pack what I hope is well enough, I head down the hall to find Roralei playing in her room with the girls she brought over. I pop my head in the room and wave her over with a finger. I tell her about the trip I'm going on to a surprise location with the new friends I made on my mission. At the mention of Jaali, she asks me to tell him to "keep the rosebud." Apparently, he'll know what that means. I guess they said their own goodbyes, and I'm sad for my little sibling that her friend is leaving. Sure, they might not have gotten along at first, but that can be said about other people in the castle as well.

Dessielle is more prying about the situation. She insists I tell her exactly how it all happened in graphic detail. When I stumble trying to collect my thoughts, she just giggles and teases me. "Someone finally pinned down my girl, huh?"

I release a laugh mixed with a scoff. "I am not *pinned down*, Dessi, that's a bit dramatic. Call me curious. I'm not ready to lose my teacher yet."

"Not ready to lose the teacher, or not ready to lose the man?" I purse my lips, unsure of my response. I decide not to answer, and instead change the subject to the outfits I packed, and her duties as surrogate sister for Ro while I'm gone. She's never let me down before, and I don't expect her to, ever.

"You're not getting out of this conversation, Rae. I need a minute-by-minute retelling when you get back!"

After leaving her room, I pad down to my parents' office. I know Pearce said he'd handle them, but I don't need him to fight my battles for me. Not that this is a battle, but I want to see them before I go. I crack the door open without knocking and find that Pearce isn't inside with them. Upon my hesitation, my mother smiles and waves me in.

"He already left, dear. You don't have to hide."

My father pulls his small glasses from his face and places them on his large mahogany desk. "Are you sure you want to go with him? I can have the guards lock him up downstairs. Or I can leave him tied up outside the border of Alunia for the—"

"Father, my Gods! I'm not leaving forever, just a few days. Maybe less than that if I grow bored of the place."

"Where are you even going?" My mother asks.

I rub the outside of my arm, once again embarrassed that I don't have the answer. "I'm not sure exactly. He told me I wouldn't know it, so I guess it will be a surprise."

My father huffs. "Seems strange to me." Mother swats his shoulder playfully and he looks at her from the side and winks. She doesn't even try to hide the blush on her cheeks.

"She'll be fine, Aidmar. She's an adult, fully capable of making her own choices."

"Doesn't mean I have to like them," he grumbles.

"And besides, she's a swordsman now. She can take care of herself."

I smile gratefully at her. "Thank you, Mother. I'll see you both in a few days." I peck them both on the cheek before heading back to my room to grab my bag. When I get in the hall, Pearce is already standing there with my bag in his hand.

"Did you go in my room?"

He shrugs. "I knocked, no answer."

I shake my head at him while trying to hide the smile spreading on my face.

We make it down one set of stairs before a figure blocks our path.

"Leaving again?"

Reynard has his arms crossed against his chest, his eyes seething.

"I'm just going on a little trip; I'll be back soon." I move to step around him, and he cross-steps to cut me off.

Pearce's arm flies out in front of me, putting a buffer between us and Reynard. "Watch yourself," he hisses.

Reynard's arms flail out in confusion. "Him, Rae? Really?"

"What is your issue with him?"

"You didn't dance with me but accepted his offer, and now you're running off with him. What about me?"

I release a sound that's part chuckle, part scoff. "What *about* you, Reynard?"

His head falls, shaking. "It's like I don't know you anymore." Before I can make sense of him, he storms off, ending any further discussion.

Pearce slides his defensive hand around my waist.

"Are you alright after that?"

My eyes linger on the last place Reynard stood. "Yes, I'm fine. He'll get over himself. I'm not going to let him ruin this."

This time when I leave Alunia, it will be as Raelenthia.

No more hiding.

37

THE HORSES ARE ALREADY prepared when we arrive at the stables. This is all happening so fast; I hadn't expected my parents to be okay with me leaving again. I didn't expect them to be okay with my sneaking out either, though. They constantly surprise me.

Jaali doesn't seem to be his normal excited self. If I didn't know better, I would say he's anxious about his return home. Pearce has his usual expression glued to his face, one of disregard. I've peeked under that exterior, though, to the bit of softness that he hides underneath. I can only hope I'll discover more before I return home.

I can't keep running away. I'll have to commit to a path soon, and I'm still unsure of which direction I plan on going in. But I think I might like this one.

We head south past the local farms, but not to the Blackwood. Instead, we head a bit more west. There's nothing this way except for trees and wildlife, so I assume we're taking the scenic route to wherever it is we're going. We spend almost the full day riding with light conversation and small yet comfortable bouts of silence.

"Are we going to Summer?" I ask after a while.

"No," is all Pearce says in response. Nothing further.

When the sun is low in the sky, we arrive in a small clearing. Jaali dismounts his horse and brings it over to a giant collection of rocks. Some are larger than others, but it looks like boulders were displaced after the separation of the continents. They're covered in moss, and caked with dirt.

"Are we stopping?" Confused, I stroke Winnie's mane.

"Yes, we are," Pearce says. "We're here."

I almost laugh. "You're joking now, huh? You really meant it when you said you're from the middle of nowhere. This isn't a city, Pearce."

He chuckles under his breath and then softly says, "No."

Jaali places his hand in front of the largest moss-covered boulder and traces his fingers through the air in a pattern I can't distinguish. The space around his hand shifts, light reflecting off the nothingness. Pearce hasn't stopped looking at me, but I can't tear my eyes from the ripple of light.

After a moment, a large opening appears in the boulder, and I watch as what appears to be a cave materializes in front of us. I've seen magic before, but nothing like this. Jaali looks back at the two of us and waves us forward, apprehension still showing in his eyes. Pearce motions for me to go ahead of him. I move slowly toward the strange opening and take one last look at my surroundings before entering the dimly lit space.

We walk down a seemingly never-ending ramp made of dense earth before coming upon a stone staircase. Jaali continues down without the slightest hesitation. I pause Winnie at the top and dismount, now fully convinced I'm being led to my death.

Maybe that's why Jaali was acting so strange; he feels bad about killing me.

I look back at Pearce who is trying his best to hide the smirk on the corner of his mouth and failing miserably. He ushers me forward with a wave of his arm and I take a deep breath before guiding Winnie down who knows how many stairs.

By the time my legs grow tired, I decide to question our intentions. "Do you mean to kill me?"

A chuckle comes from behind me. "What are you saying up there?"

"Nothing, just that this seems like quite extreme measures if you intend to kill me. Take me to bed to get my guard down and then lure me to a tunnel in the ground where no one can—"

Pearce's hand closes around my wrist, spinning me around to face him. His face is marble, the minimal light making him even more ominous. He lowers his head until his lips graze my ear. "I took you to bed because I wanted to. And I plan to do it again. Now turn around and keep walking, little ember," he drawls, his voice thick with abrupt desire.

I find myself wishing there was no light in this place. What little peaks in is *certainly* enough for him to see the embarrassing shade of red my face has become.

A haze of blue light appears in the distance, closing in by the minute. When we finally arrive at its source, all breath is stolen from my lungs.

Row after row of stone paths and buildings. Interconnected stairways with moss covering large portions of the chiseled rock, and warm lights placed in glassless windows. As far as I can see in the dim light, massive columns hold up what look like homes. The structures vary in size, some stand alone while others are stacked several stories high.

"Pearce…" I manage after I find my voice. "What am I looking at?" He and Jaali stand on either side of me, looking out over the maze of stone.

"Our home."

I say nothing for a long while. I don't move either. I can't seem to pull my eyes from this anomaly that looks like an underground—

"Where are we?" I whisper, already knowing the answer.

Pearce's stare sits heavy on my face. "This, princess…is Kermera."

Every ounce of blood freezes in my veins.

The story.

His obsession with my book.

My mouth falls open and I shut it repeatedly, unsure of which words mean to come to the forefront.

"Take your time," he says softly. "I know this is a lot."

"This is… This is insane. You mean all this time—it's just been here?"

He purses his lips. "Not for forever, but since the Great War," he explains. I nod slowly, failing to process even the smallest grain of information. After another deep breath, I pull my shoulders back and tilt my chin in his direction.

"Alright, I'm ready."

A light huff. "Are you?"

"I'm not sure. But I'm trying to be," I offer with a weak smile.

"Very convincing, little ember," he says at full volume.

I glance over at Jaali who seems unbothered. "He's right there. Must you use that name right now?"

His eyes darken at my plea. "If you're embarrassed by a little name-calling, you should remember how we spoke when we met. Besides, Jaali isn't dense. He knows something is going on between us."

My brow cocks. "There is, is there?"

I can't tell if he looks like he wants to push me off this ledge or throw my clothes off the side of it. "Do you need me to remind you of this morning?" My face flushes, and I don't try to hide the smile his words bring me.

"If you're truly ready, we'll move further into the city. But if you need more time to process, let me know."

I start to nod and he raises his brows at me, expectantly. I roll my eyes and say, "I'll let you know if I need a moment."

Pearce takes a deep breath and exhales it sharply. "Right this way, then." Jaali offers me an empathetic smile yet says nothing.

We begin walking down a stone slab pathway toward the maze of buildings. The path slants down, steadily descending until we arrive before a fountain at the base of a massive structure. It looks like some kind of temple or meeting place, with large columns and an archway that could fit an ogre. I look to the men beside me to question our next move, but they don't stop when I do. Instead, they make a left and tie up the horses near the fountain, avoiding the building entirely.

As they lead me away from the strict building with the fountain, I soak in my surroundings once more. The yellow glow I saw in the holes of buildings are candles filling windowsills with warm light. The closer we get, I see the silhouettes of people in their homes. I pull my focus from them when I notice various colored lights lining the ground before us. Jewel tones glisten, burrowed in the ground, each one a kaleidoscope of vibrancy as candlelight flickers against their edges.

Pearce leaves my side to speak with Jaali. After they whisper back and forth for a moment, Jaali nods curtly and turns to me. He places his palm on my head and wiggles it like you would a child. "You stay with Pearce, red. I'll come find you guys in a bit."

"Where are you going? We just got here," I say, a bit annoyed. I'm not sure I can handle the intensity of Pearce's stare once we're alone again.

"I'm not going far, I promise. I'll see you in just a little while." And with that, he moves through the crowd in front of us.

I look back at Pearce who has his hand out in front of me. I look down at it, and then back to him before hesitantly placing my hand in his. His large fingers intertwine with mine while his thumb moves back and forth in a soothing motion. I allow him to lead me into the same crowd Jaali went through, except we move with less intention.

As we pass by both aged and young faces, my thoughts flicker back to the fact that I am seeing people I thought didn't exist. Not that they're a different species; so far, the people I've seen are creatures I'm familiar with, but their living in this place makes them Kermerans.

They live in a place I believed to be a fairytale. Until today.

I gawk at the greenery climbing up the buildings and make a mental note to have Pearce show them to me more in-depth later. Right now, I want to see this bustling city for what it is. We step around a collection of people and come face to face with a seller of what looks like tiny crystals and other small bobbles.

Colored glass, textured patterns, and weathered stones cover the table before the light-haired man. Upon seeing us, the man stands to his feet abruptly and greets Pearce, who offers him his hand to shake, and the man gratefully takes it. He then looks at me and smiles brightly before showing us his wares and going into great explanation about all of them. Where they come from in the city, how he smooths them, and how his daughter picks out every stone they clean. He points to a small girl with ribbons in her bubbled hair, and she waves before going back to playing.

I pick up a particularly beautiful blue stone and turn it over in my free hand, the one not latched onto Pearce, and return it to the table. Before I get the chance, the man puts his hand out to stop me.

"No, you keep it."

"I don't have anything to trade you, I'm afraid." If I'd known there would be a market, I would've prepared.

"Please take it. Consider it a gift," and he smiles between the two of us. Pearce dips his head, thanking the man for his kindness, and we continue down the rows of stalls.

We spend hours talking with strangers on the street. Some of them sell things they've made or cooked, and others are simply there for the revelry and community. Each one of them has a kind smile and sweet words.

I almost forget we're in a fabled place that has thrived underground my whole life without me having any idea.

Every time I start to spiral on that fact a little bit, Pearce squeezes my hand to pull me back to the conversation with ease. He can tell I'm still freaking out a bit, but I feel better as time passes.

With each introduction to another citizen of Kermera, my posture softens and my mind eases. When Jaali finally returns to us, he pulls Pearce aside and they share a brief discussion that I'm, once again, not privy to. He can't take him far because he refuses to let go of my hand, so instead of walking away, they use hushed whispers and move only a step from me. Once finished, we start the walk back to the large building with the fountain.

Instead of marching right up the front steps, we take a small path to the right of the building that leads to its backside. We enter through a tall, dark wooden door, covered in a clinging plant. Pearce reaches for the clasp of my cloak and undoes it before removing it from my shoulders and hanging it over his arm. "I'll take you up to your room for the night." He motions toward the stairs positioned against the back wall while I crane my head around the room.

"We're staying here overnight? Why not just go to your home?"

"It's a bit complicated, but I promise I'll explain soon, alright? For now, let's just get you upstairs."

I begrudgingly follow him up to another wooden door, this one with a beautifully earthy room behind it. I gasp softly at the lit candles in their bronze metal holdings, and the candle chandelier hanging from the ceiling. An ornate bed sits in the corner with dark blue bedding and lush pillows. A fireplace with twin molding to the bed is next to it on the wall. This room makes me want to fall asleep for years or read a book with a cup of tea. Preferably both.

I walk further into the room and then look back at Pearce. "This is where I'm staying?"

He nods. "Is it alright? Do you like it?"

I smile brightly to reassure him he picked the perfect place. "It's lovely, thank you." After a moment when he doesn't leave, I ask, "Where will you be staying?"

His tongue pokes the inside of his lip in a failed attempt to hide his amusement as he crosses his thick forearms against his chest. I clear my throat.

"Oh... Alright."

"Is that okay with you, little ember?"

I take my bottom lip between my teeth out of nervousness and release it when his eyes snap to it. "You're a grown man, you can do what you'd like," is my response.

He chuckles and strides toward me. His hand settles low on my back and pulls me so close, my eyes immediately drawn to his.

"In that case..." He leans down and places a soft kiss where my neck meets my shoulder. A shiver runs through me at the intimacy of it, and I place my hand on his chest and push against it slightly. He pulls away immediately to read my face and ensure he hasn't crossed any boundary. "I'm hungry," I whisper.

"Me too," he whispers back with a wink and returns to my neck so quickly that I laugh.

"I'm serious, my stomach is going to start wailing if I don't eat something soon."

His hand lifts to brush a stray piece of hair out of my face and behind my ear. "Why don't you bathe and change, and we can go out. The market will be going late into the night, and we can eat there."

My stomach growls loudly in response. "I would love that!"

He releases me before grabbing my hand and pulling me to the attached room I now see is a bathing room. "I'll leave you to get ready. I have some things to see to before I can settle for the night, but I'll be back before you're finished." He lifts the hand he's holding and places a kiss on my knuckles before leaving the room.

Left alone with my thoughts, I run the bath and fill it with all sorts of oils I find on a side table. The tub smells of honeysuckle and moss, and it's grounding. I chuckle out loud to myself at the fact that I'm currently underground. As I lay in the warm water and wipe off the stress of today, I think back to all the things Pearce said before that didn't previously make sense.

The fact that he doesn't live far—but I wouldn't know where—comes to mind. His interest in that book should have been an indicator that something else was going on, but, well... It did truly seem like a fairytale.

And now I'm living in it.

I'm in a secret city with a devastatingly good-looking man, going to a busy market with vibrant people, and will experience food I've never tried before. This really *is* a fairytale, isn't it?

I finish bathing quickly, and only when I'm standing naked in the tub do I realize I have no other clothes. I left my bag with the horses.

I walk back into the room after getting myself mostly dry and see a dress lying out on the massive bed. I stare at it, perplexed, and then realize there's a little note beside it.

The rest of your things are in the drawers by the door. I unpacked your bag for you, I hope that's alright. I know you said you might not stay but I figured one more item of clothing wouldn't hurt.

Wear this dress, little ember. The color will look stunning on you.

He's not even in the room and my face heats while goosebumps cover my arms. I trail my hand over the dress that's just a few shades lighter than the linens on the bed. It has capped sleeves and a square neckline. It cinches in under the bust; the rest of the skirt isn't tightly fitted, more flowing. I catch myself biting my lip again before I pull the dress over my still-damp hair.

It somehow fits perfectly, as if made to fit my body. A large mirror is hung on the wall opposite the bed and fireplace, and I twirl back and forth in it to watch the skirt flow around me. I spin around the room barefoot, letting it fly out over the cozy rug beneath my feet. I slow when I catch a small movement out of the corner of my eye, and halt when I see Pearce standing in the doorframe.

He has his arms and legs crossed nonchalantly, but his face shows his amusement at what he's caught. "Please, don't stop on my account." He moves to stand behind me and turns us so we both face the mirror.

His hand rubs the outside of my arm as he eyes me fully in our reflection.

"Do you like it?" he asks, quietly.

"The dress? It's beautiful. But how did you—"

"Know your sizing?"

I nod.

He shifts my hair behind my ear and brings his mouth so close I feel his next words in my soul. "I've seen every part of you, little ember. Measurements are no match for my memory of you."

Pearce spins me away from the mirror so that I'm buried in his chest. The hand on my arm travels up to cup my face, forcing my eyes to his. "You shouldn't keep looking at me like that. I'm starving," I say, flustered.

In a low groan, he says, "So am I." My eyes flutter closed as he brings his lips to meet mine. My hands twist into his hair and lock into the curls at the base of his neck while his travel down my sides to pull me closer by my waist. Before we get too carried away, he breaks the kiss and places a small peck against my hairline. "Come on. Let's get you some food."

We reluctantly pull ourselves from each other and head back down the stairs and towards the market. Some of the families and older citizens have gone home, and younger couples and groups of friends fill the streets. Music pours from large string instruments. There isn't a concerned face in the crowd, they're all enjoying each other's company.

We take our time moving through the collection of people and look at each option for food at the stalls. Some are meals I recognize, while others are completely new to me. A loaf of mushrooms and dark meat sits on the table in front of us, my mouth watering at the savory smell. Meanwhile, the stall next to us has a broth with herbs and spices, and grains that look like small waves.

Every stall has small lights hanging above in various colors, shades of blue, purple, and green, similar to the ones peppering the ground. They almost look like stars.

Bodies brush by me as I take a step away from the stall and into the center of the pathway. My head falls back as I stare at the ceiling of the massive cavern. It's too dark to see the top, I have no idea how large this place is. Pearce says my eyes will adjust after being down here for a while, and I hope he's right.

The darkness of the rock is the perfect background for the twinkling lights. It reminds me of when Roralei and I used to climb onto the terrace when she was younger and look at the stars while we were supposed to be sleeping. Mother caught us one time. She stayed with us until we started to fall asleep, then helped us both into my bed.

Pearce's strong arm brushes mine as he stands next to me, mimicking my movement. I see his tall frame in my peripheral and chuckle at him with his neck craned back. He catches me staring at him and bumps me with his hip before grabbing my hand and pulling me back to the food stalls. "You need to eat," he whispers close to me. "You've had a long day."

"How am I supposed to eat with you staring at me like that?"

"Very carefully," he says with a wink.

I decide on the meat and mushroom dish we saw earlier, and we continue to walk while eating. It's nice, not sitting at a huge table and having to make small talk. It's exciting to be in a place I'm unfamiliar with. And being here with someone just as unpredictable makes it even more entertaining.

After finishing our meal, we find that some musicians have gathered to play: one with a lute, a harpist, and a mandolin player. They fill the night with cheerful music as couples dance in the street, children carelessly weaving through the revelers. Eventually, a collection of single dancers join together and all dance with each other.

My wide eyes meet Pearce's before glancing over at the party happening around us. I slowly back away from him, swaying my skirt as I go. Hips first, I push into the line of twirling bodies and let myself flow with the music. To my surprise, I see him trying to emulate the dancing he sees around him. I let my rhythmic steps carry me to his side.

"What are you doing? I've seen you dance before, you're good. You look stiff."

"This dancing is different. Ballroom is something I'm good at. It's controlled and taught, not so free-moving. That's not really my strong suit."

I scowl at him for a moment before taking his hand and yanking him sharply into the center of the large circle that has manifested in the road. I sway my hips to the music, letting my arms flail out to my sides with the beat of the song. I catch his eye and nod for him to follow along. The simple movements look a bit stale on him at first, but he slowly starts to warm up and loosen his limbs.

We dance and weave through the circle, each member of it getting their chance to shine and then moving back in sync with the person next to them. A girl who looks about my age steps into the center and grabs my arm, pulling me forward to join her. Without a hint of grace, we spin and kick and clap along with the rest of the dancers, making a true spectacle of ourselves in the square.

When I find Pearce again, he's stepped back from the group, but no less invested. He looks more at peace than I've ever seen him. The creases in between his brows are less noticeable here. His eyes are brighter.

The crowd of dancers and the audience we've gathered start to split up. Some spin off with their partners to move alone, and we follow suit when the music slows. Couples hold each other close, their partner a buoy in a raging storm. When Pearce pulls me to him, it puts me back in the ballroom at home. The feeling of every eye on us, some heavier than others; yet at the same time like we were the only two here.

He squeezes my hand in his, pulling me back to the moment. The calming music reminds me of a string-filled lullaby. Something to signal the descent of the night and the slowing of the chaos of the market. Around us, stalls take down their lights and clear their tables. Couples leave the area and make their way back to their homes. I don't realize how tired I am until our swaying stops, and my eyes struggle to open. My head had fallen on his chest and laid there, content.

When he feels me stir, he pulls away enough to look at me. "Let's head back," he says and guides me gently out of the remaining dancers. I don't remember the walk back to our room at all. The next thing I know, I'm in what must be Pearce's shirt and am lying snuggled under the covers, pulled against his body.

So much of this man is a mystery. I seem to forget that as I fall asleep on his rising chest to the sound of his soft breathing.

38

THE ENTRANCE WE CAME through yesterday didn't give away the extent of the internal architecture. While the expansive hall I'm standing in is made of stone, the wide, weathered stairs on either side of the room are not what I expected.

A circular window the size of a small home sits on the back wall behind the stairs. More steps lead off either side of it to halls I cannot see. Greenery is abundant inside, with large plants and fern-looking leaves along the walls and stair railings.

Pearce insisted that I be brought breakfast in bed and refused my help in retrieving it. I've essentially been told to stay put since we arrived back in the room last night, but now he's giving me a tour of the building.

I can't help but wonder about the salaries people receive in this place. Pearce is a soldier and, if this is an inn, it's one of the most intricate I've ever stayed in.

I'm still unsure of *what* this place is exactly, and he hasn't been much help in answering my questions, which I find incredibly frustrating.

"I came all this way, and you won't even tell me where I'm staying."

"It's not relevant," was his response. I disagreed, but he proceeded to get dressed and tell me we were going out, so I stopped pushing it.

My interest is piqued again, wandering the halls. As we walk past the lowest staircase, voices travel from the upper level. I can't hear anything specific, just enough to know there's a group of them. "Who else is staying here?" I ask him "I can't imagine what travelers would be stopping in."

"I told you not to worry about what kind of building it is, little ember. Now let's go before the roads get too busy."

Instead of following him toward the back exit, I quickly change directions and head up the stairs. It takes him a moment to realize and when he does, I'm already on the second flight. He forgot I'm faster than him. His mistake.

Giggling, I take the steps quickly, skipping some and speeding up until I arrive in a hallway with dark wooden doors along the walls. There aren't many, maybe five total on the entire floor from what I can see. I hear the voices coming from the third one on the left, so I head to it.

He turns the corner after, sees where I'm headed, and begs, "Don't open that."

But I'm already twisting the curved brass handle and pushing open the door, a teasing smile on my face. "Come and stop me," I taunt. And then I screech to a halt. Upon entering, all conversation ceases. Unfamiliar faces look at me in confusion and contempt for interrupting what I now see is a meeting.

An important one, it seems. *Gods.*

Pearce steps in behind me and their eyes fall to him instead, surprise replacing the confusion I created. I can't help but notice the smile that appears on a young brunette woman's face across the large table in the center of the room. She's staring at Pearce like she knows him. They all are.

"There you are! My goodness," says an older woman with greying hair. She must be incredibly well-lived for her hair to show her age, given our lifespan. "We were wondering if you'd ever come back," she finishes.

"She's right," a masculine voice calls out. I look for where it came from and find a red-haired man maybe a little older than Pearce. "It's about damn time you show up," he says and playfully punches him on the shoulder. Pearce hugs him and they exchange pats on the back.

"You really shouldn't be away that long, my lord." The grey-haired woman comes to share a hug with him while I'm frozen in place.

"Your...what?" My head shoots toward Pearce, who's already looking at me with a sorry expression.

"I think we should step outside." He tries to reach for my arm, but I pull it away and walk out to the hall myself, not holding the door behind me.

"Tell me what they're talking about." My voice is clipped, my jaw tense.

He hesitates, tripping over his words before releasing a long sigh and looking at the floor.

"When did you plan on telling me? Were you ever, or were you going to have your fun and then send me home with me being none the wiser?"

"Of course, I was going to tell you. There just hasn't been a right time."

"*Any* time would be better than what just happened. I've made a fool of myself, haven't I?" I lift my chin and look in the direction of the meeting room, feeling their stares on me even now. The stunning brunette barely glanced at me before looking back at Pearce.

Feeling embarrassed, I turn sharply down the hall and head back down the steps. I don't know where I'll go. I'll walk the streets or—or I'll go back to the room and lock the door. Anywhere is better than being made a fool in front of strangers.

I know even less about him than I thought I did.

I slept with a man I knew nothing about.

And while it wouldn't be the first time, it *is* the most embarrassing.

Before I know it, I'm at the fountain in front of the building. Pearce probably isn't far behind me, and I doubt there's anywhere I could go that he wouldn't think to check. This is his home, after all.

His territory.

Any stone I choose would be turned by him. The water ripples out from my hands as I dunk them in and splash it onto my face. I feel warm. Flustered. Stupid.

He makes no sound, yet I know when he's behind me. I can feel him.

"Raelenthia, can we talk about this please?"

"Talk about what? How I know *nothing* about you? Why don't we talk about all the other things you've kept from me?"

"Anything I kept from you was either because I had to, or because it wasn't safe for you to know yet."

"Why is it your place to determine what's safe for me?"

He throws his hands up in frustration, and motions to the space around us. "This place is under my protection. I'm not going to apologize for not telling you about it sooner, or for waiting to tell you until now."

"Then what *will* you apologize for? Because something about this feels wrong."

He sighs. "You're right. It does." He sits on the edge of the fountain and motions for me to do the same.

"Why were you even on the mission to Baeton? They wouldn't have contacted you here." No one outside knows Kermera exists, let alone how to contact its ruler.

Pearce pulls his lips into his mouth. After a moment of contemplation, "Jaali and I took the place of two other guards that were...unable to attend."

I glance at him sideways. "What is that supposed to mean?"

"There was information in Baeton that we needed. So, when our spies discovered a chance to get into the Baetonian castle, we took it. The guards who were assigned to go were suddenly unable to make it, and we happened to be nearby to hear about the whole ordeal. We offered to step in and, on short notice, they had no choice but to send us."

My mouth falls open in disbelief.

"You gave me hell for being there uninvited, while you were doing the exact same thing?"

"I had to make it look believable."

"Like you made me believe you care for me?"

His hand comes to my face immediately, his fingers cradling my chin. "That was not part of the plan. Everything I've told you since then is true. My feelings for you, my history, my life. That was all real."

I lean into his hand without realizing. It's comforting, his skin on mine. "How am I supposed to believe that, Pearce? The first thing I ever knew about you was a lie."

His brow lifts. "Weren't you lying about your identity, too, *princess*?"

I redden, having somehow forgotten about that.

"See? We're not as star-crossed as you think. Give me a chance to show you who I am. I might not be some shining knight," he says as his thumb strokes my cheek, "but everything I do is to protect this place. These people."

Trying to process the onslaught of information, I nod slowly and pull my head away to stare into the cave sky. "How is this possible?"

His vision follows mine before explaining. "You know the Range of Unrest," he says. I nod. "Then you know how they were created."

"Terrain manipulators made the mountains after the Great War to put a layer of protection between us and the humans." He almost looks impressed, so I say, "What? Basic knowledge."

He smiles at me before looking back at the city. "Well, a few of those blessed people found themselves needing refuge after the war. They made a major contribution to creating this cavern for us. Really, they did all of it. They're the reason we have the location we do, and they were influential in creating the housing, as well as the keep." He motions behind us to the building we slept in last night.

My brows pinch, overwhelmed, as I try to break this down in my head. "Why did they come underground in the first place? I know that many were displaced from their homes during the war, but that doesn't explain why they would come underground instead of leaving the continent. Or why they've stayed under this long." The words spill out of me before I can give them a second thought, and I hope he doesn't take offense to my abruptness.

He doesn't miss a beat as he answers, "Odin and Freya."

My forehead wrinkles. "Why would the previous rulers of Alunia be the reason an entire population goes underground?"

"Because they were targets of a merciless group of Baetonian soldiers. Their sights were set on the king and queen. If they could take them down, it would fuel their war efforts. But instead of getting ahold of them, they were defended by those who had the means of protection.

It was meant to be temporary, that they would return once it was safe to resurface. But that time stretched and became longer until it would have caused more harm than good to return topside."

"Then why is Kermera still kept a secret?"

His jaw clenches, like he's thought about this a thousand times before. "Because up until recently, the leadership of Kermera thought it was best to not get involved."

"Not get involved with Alunia or Baeton?"

"Both."

A shiver runs down my spine. "They wanted to leave Alunia to the mercy of Baeton?" I clench my jaw. "Why?"

"They didn't think that our safety was worth sacrificing for the greater population. Before I took the position, that was the plan. To wait out the next war and then potentially emerge afterward. I wasn't okay with that. I made it very clear that I wanted our services to be offered to Alunia if needed, and I was shot down every time.

In staying dormant as long as we have, yes, we've been safe. But we also have left thousands of innocent people to fend for themselves against a force that we can offer support to defeat. Once my position was settled, I took the first solid chance I found and went to Alunia. Jaali insisted that he came along to keep an eye on me because he was worried I would appear too aggressive."

"He was right to be worried," I mumble. His head pivots to me, quickly diminishing the smile that was there.

"It's why I made myself necessary on the mission. I needed to get into Baeton and find information that would help us take them down," he says more to himself than to me.

"What do you mean, take them down? The humans?"

He nods while staring at nothing. "They don't deserve to send us into hiding. We should have resurfaced a long time ago, and we will soon." His tone deepens, a shift in the tide.

"What do you plan on doing, Pearce?"

"Nothing they don't deserve. For it to be safe for us to thrive and go topside, we need to remove the threat. The *only* threat that exists on Drennica is Baeton. And they'll be dealt with accordingly."

"I don't think I like what you're implying."

It's his turn to look at me confused. "You don't want these people to return to their homes and friends that haven't been allowed to come here? Not just anyone is permitted into Kermera, ember. Typically, strict guidelines have to be followed to even be considered. I broke countless of my own rules to bring you here." He gets louder the more passionate he becomes.

"I didn't ask you to do that," I say, trying to defend myself from his harsh truth.

He lets out a long sigh and rubs his hand down his face. "You didn't need to. I just...I feel a little overwhelmed."

The tension in his shoulders eases a bit when I place my hands on them. "I understand. Well, maybe not entirely; we have very different views on how to handle the situation. But I understand the feeling."

"I'm going to defend my people how I see fit, princess. I would prefer to have you on my side when I do."

"Even if it means sacrificing my own morals?"

"What about protecting my people goes against your *morals*, Raelenthia? Just because I don't lead the way your parents do doesn't mean I'm in the wrong."

I grind my teeth and consider him for a moment before replying. "Just like many in Kermera didn't choose to be forced underground, not all humans choose to live in Baeton. You cannot blame an entire population for the wrongdoings of their leaders."

He sighs, his head falling into his hands. He rakes his fingers through his hair, neither of us speaking for a while.

"I'm not forgiving them," he whispers. "My people have suffered too much to let their actions go unpunished."

"I know," is all I can say back. This is uncharted territory for me. I can't even begin to comprehend the choices he's already filtered through in his own dark mind and with his council.

"This isn't what I wanted this trip home to be. Can we pin this? Even just for today?"

With a sigh, I plaster on an unsure smile.

Pearce mimics me and takes my hand, walking me into the city.

39

STEAM POURS FROM A chimney on the main street, filling my nose with the smell of fresh bread. I don't even realize I've stopped in the street until the arm I have linked with Pearce is yanked in front of me. Pearce looks back at me and pulls my arm again, intent on continuing forward.

"Do you smell that?" I say as I inhale deeply again.

"Smell what?" He takes a full breath and nods slightly. "Brell."

"What did you call it?"

Pearce chuckles. "It's Brell's bakery. One of the women you, um...*met* this morning."

My eyes cut to him. "The brunette or the older woman?"

His brow furrows. "Odd question."

My face remains deathly still.

"The older woman."

I let a small smile appear. "Let's go in!"

A small bell rings above the door when we push through, followed by a voice. "Just a second!"

Stone walls are broken up by wooden arches. Inside each one are shelves covered with baked goods. Small and large loaves, treats made with apples and figs and almonds. It's an effort not to rip pieces from everything and try it myself. Before I get the chance to, the woman I now know as Brell walks out from a back room.

Her eyes land on me first, filled with questions. "Well, hello."

I offer a sheepish smile and a pathetic wave, and then Pearce's solid warmth meets my back. When Brell notices him, she offers one as well and looks more relaxed.

"I wasn't expecting a royal visit so soon."

He lets loose a breathy exhale and cracks a smile. "I wasn't expecting to see the bakery open. You've kept a full schedule on the council," he explains.

Her brow lifts as her hand juts to her hip. "If I didn't keep this place open, where would your people get the best-tasting desserts?"

The curl he tries to push off his face falls right back over his forehead. "I'm sure Kermera would manage."

Brell's eyes practically jump out of her skull. "With what? Randall's dry blocks of yeast further into town?"

I choke on nothing but the air in my lungs. The laugh still escapes me.

Pearce doesn't stop his, it fills the bakery like the hearth of a fire, warm and welcoming. I don't know if I've ever heard that sound come from him so casually.

Brell eyes me with pursed lips and asks, "You ever made bread before?"

I shake my head.

Her chin juts toward the back room she came from, and then she's gone. Pearce looks over at me with a smirk before following her further into the bakery.

Without looking, Brell starts instructing me to pull out certain things: yeast from the top shelf, bowls from the bottom.

"The grain is already milled, so you missed out on the hard part."

"Oh, pity..." I drawl, earning a chuckle from the older woman.

She looks up at Pearce towering over her. "Make yourself useful and get a fire started in the oven. And you can rake it out when it's hot enough."

Amusement settled in his cheeks, he replies, "Oh, sure. Anything else while I'm at it?"

His sarcasm isn't lost on her.

While he's doing miscellaneous tasks, Brell and I make the dough. Simple enough, yeast, water, flour, and grain until it becomes malleable. Brell relays where to find the long-handed paddle, and we slide the loaf into the oven.

She ushers us out of the back room and we find a seat in the store to sip on surprisingly delicious coffee. Before I get the chance to take a seat, Pearce smacks the side of my thigh. I go to reprimand him when I see a cloud of white dust fly off my leg.

Flour.

And I'm absolutely covered in it.

He revels in swatting me until I'm standing in a cloud of it, and his final smack is to my rear end.

Brell smacks his shoulder before I get the chance. "I saw that."

Mostly cleaned of flour, we sip the hot drink while the bread bakes.

"He was just as irritating when he was younger," Brell says.

"I can imagine," I reply. "How did you two meet, if you've known him since he was young?"

Brell looks to Pearce, checking to make sure she can tell the story. He blinks slowly and nods his reassurance.

"When his parents passed, and he ended up down here with the rest of us he was...lost. In the orphanage, he was troubled. Many children are at that age, but this group even more so because of the state of our world. One evening, when I was closing up for the night, I caught him trying to steal some smaller bits.

Little thing started to run away, but he hadn't yet settled into his Fae instincts so I was much faster—"

"That's what I wanted her to think," Pearce says with a hand to his mouth, as if he could hide his teasing.

"I'm telling this story, you be quiet." She reaches across the table, palm up, and Pearce takes hold of it.

This woman created the soft spot I've discovered in him.

"Anyway...long story short, I told him if he needed food, he could help in my shop. He never left, and now—here we are."

"Can you tell me other stories about him?"

The smell of warm bread cuts the familial bickering in its tracks. Before we leave, she lets us know about a dinner taking place the following evening. Pearce's presence is required, and mine is "more than welcome," she says. Brell hands us our loaf in a cloth for traveling and sends us off with a kiss to his forehead, and one to either of my cheeks.

After a full day of exploring the city, we make it back to the keep around what Pearce says is sunset. When I ask how they tell the time of day if they're underground, he says they have something resembling a sundial. Instead of the actual sun, they use magic like the hairpiece Wilder gifted me to act as the sun to cast shadows. It's not pitch black inside the cave, due to cracks and the light from the charmed tunnel. Those in Kermera can see outside, but those not granted admission can't see inside it from above.

It's a safe haven for the people here.

Although I understand wanting to stay hidden, I see Pearce's point about it being unfair. The people here became stuck and had to retreat from their normal society. Now that he's in control, he wants them to share their intelligence and numbers with the rest of Alunia.

I'm just not sure about his way of doing it. His mention of taking over the humans sounds a lot like what they intended to do to us, which is what caused the Great War in the first place. Given a little more time, I think I can convince him to see that peace is the next logical step. The actions taken by the Baetonian crown are unjust, but committing genocide on innocent civilians would make us no better than them.

Seeming to notice my thoughts have left the current moment, Pearce places his hand on the small of my back. I jolt slightly at the weight of it, still not used to such an intimate action from him. It'll take some getting used to.

Any intimate relationships I've had have been fleeting for the most part. I'm still working on my communication skills. I tend to be overbearing. I want to get everything out in the open and break things down as they happen. Letting situations and feelings fester only leads to miscommunication, and my mind can't handle that. Instead, I tend to pry into the thoughts of those I love so I can fully understand them.

They don't always appreciate my thoroughness.

I suppose most people don't appreciate me prying into their thoughts and making them talk about things before they have time to process them.

Pearce seems to handle it better than others. Maybe not at first, but I think he's learning to understand my need to hash things out in the moment.

The room is comfortable and warm when we get back, a welcome change from the cool underbelly of the earth walls outside. The two of us move around in something close to domesticity, getting ready for sleep. I run a brush through my hair and warm a bath while he insists that he should be allowed to join me. When I laugh at the idea, his eyes darken as he strips, and he gets in the bath anyway.

It's far too small for the two of us but he manages to squeeze in regardless and pours water down my hair, soap running down my back. When we finish bathing, we turn down the bed and slide into it. The two of us lay in silence until I finally find the courage to ask him about this morning.

"Pearce?"

His eyes, which had fallen closed in a light sleep, slowly open. "Yes, ember?"

"Who were the rest of those people in that room today?"

He shifts his head to look at me, and I angle mine to meet his eyes. "You want to get into this now?" I nod against his chest, and he lets out a sigh. "They're my council. Each of them oversees a different part of Kermera, both the city and its people."

"If there's a council, why do they need you?" I ask with a tilted smirk.

"Oh quiet," he says gruffly and tightens me against him like a coiled snake. Not that I'm complaining. "They made sure Kermera stayed in one piece while I was traveling through the kingdom. I wouldn't be able to keep my head on straight without them."

"And the brunette I brought up earlier..." I trail off.

His brow rises. "Yes?" I pull my head down to try and look away, but his hand catches my chin. "What about her, Raelenthia?"

My cheeks heat at the drawl in his voice. "She's beautiful." He doesn't even blink. "Who is she?"

"I believe you're talking about Adira. She helps to oversee the orphanage."

"Oh, wow. That sounds incredibly important."

"It is," he says while his finger strokes my face in a lazy circle. "She's very intelligent, and I'm glad she works with me."

I stiffen in his hold, and the heat in my cheeks vanishes while my entire body runs cold. "I'm sure she's wonderful."

His eyes turn to slits. It's like he's reading my mind. "Are you jealous, little ember?" I don't know why he sounds like he's joking. I feel like I'm going to be sick.

"Of course not, I don't even know her. I'm sure she's very nice. And, apparently, the Gods' gift to Drennica."

He chuckles at my nonsense. "Nothing has ever happened between us."

I look up at him through fanned lashes. "Really?"

He nods softly. "I need someone with more fire, anyway."

The nausea that had taken over starts to fade. "Is that so?" I nuzzle into his chest more, my brain finally quiet enough to rest.

He wraps his arms around me and pulls me closer. "Mhm. Now get some rest, my fire."

40

"What am I supposed to wear?"

Pearce leans against the pillows, laid out on the bed. Without his shirt.

"This isn't some ball, Raelenthia. It's just dinner, you don't need a grand outfit. You'd look incredible in scrap fabric," he tries.

I look at him through slit eyes. "Thank you, but that's not helpful right now." And I sit down on the bed with a huff.

He eyes me for a moment, purses his lips, and gets up from the bed, jostling my perfectly comfortable position. Shirts come flying out of the chest against the wall until he finds what he's looking for and lays it on top of my legs. It's one of his shirts, a deep blue silk one.

"This is very nice, but again, not helpful."

His sultry chuckle fills the warm, cozy bedroom. "I want you to wear it. It hasn't fit me in a long time, and with the pants you brought, you'll look incredible."

I eye him carefully. "You want me to wear your clothes? To a dinner with your council?"

"If they couldn't smell my scent on you before, they will tonight."

Convinced that he won't let this go, I rip the shirt from his hands and piece together the rest of my outfit. In the meantime, he finally gets dressed.

If he had stayed shirtless for any longer, we might not have gone to dinner at all.

After donning his shirt, a brown pair of pants, and a tall pair of boots, I settle in front of the mirror to make my hair look presentable. I've just finished when the reflection shows his body behind mine.

Cool air touches my skin as Pearce pulls my hair to the side, his finger tracing a line down my neck, followed by his lips. An exasperated exhale leaves him. "Remind me to make you wear my clothes more often. That way you feel my touch, even when I am not around."

We barely make it to the dining room on time.

The massive white stone space has a dark brown dining set in the center. The chairs and table are decorated with dark green accents. Long drapes grace the walls in a similar shade, swallowing some of the brightness in the stone box room.

Every member of the council is already inside, including Jaali, who offers me a toothy grin. Jaali tries to pull me from Pearce's side, but he's met with a low growl, causing him to chuckle under his breath.

"My bad, my bad," he says before winking at me. Jaali lands a soft punch on Pearce's shoulder, releasing the tension he'd been holding in a vice grip.

Jaali points to the head of the table, which I assume is where Pearce will be sitting. When I try and take a seat further down the table, Pearce blocks me from pulling out the chair and points further up the table. Everyone else begins to find their seats when I arrive at the one on Pearce's side.

I start to sit down when someone clears their throat behind me.

The brunette woman, Adira, stands behind me in a floor-length, deep violet gown. Simple, but sensual, clinging to every dip.

"I believe that's my spot," she says. Her voice is clear and pretty, like a song.

Pearce's hand rests on the low of my back, pushing me slightly into the chair before me. "I'm sure you can find another open seat for tonight, Adira."

Her hazel eyes flick down my frame, and then she lets out a huff. She tosses a long brown wave over her shoulder and moves further down the table.

Pearce makes brief introductions down the line of people. Brell needs no introduction, neither does Adira. Jaali sits across from me at Pearce's left. Next to him is an older, dark-skinned man with incredibly vibrant brown eyes. Easton is in charge of Kermera's financial matters which, embarrassingly, I hadn't even considered.

The blonde woman that sits next to him, Adrian, looks slightly younger than my mother. Her thin, bright ash hair is pulled to one side, and her ocean-blue eyes meet mine with a soft smile. Adrian is the council's connection to the terrainers. She keeps them in contact with Pearce for security purposes, the eyes of Kermeras walls.

Brell sits at my right, followed by Adira, and lastly, Sylvan. His fire-red hair reminds me of Reynard. Shorter, but just as vibrant. Sylvan is the military advisor.

"I didn't realize Kermera needed a military," I confess.

"We hope to not need it, but we would be foolish to be unprepared." He seems wise, despite looking so young.

When I tell him that, he says he's older than he looks. This prompts a childish discussion about age and who has more say than who because of it.

"If that was the case, I would be leading Kermera," says Brell.

Easton disagrees. "I wouldn't be so sure. How close were *you* to Xylia and Keir?"

Brell glares at him.

A hearty laugh runs through the room. "That's what I thought."

I look between the two of them, my eyes growing tired. "So, how old *are* you?"

At the same time, they look at me and say, "Old." Earning another laugh from the group. At least, most of it. Adira has hardly said a word.

But Pearce would bend me over his knee if I had sat further away. On second thought—

"Welcome home, my lord. While we wish you had been back sooner, it seems that certain—" Brell looks at me, "—delays, can be excused." She raises her glass.

Adrian raises hers and says, "So long as you never do it again." The rest of us raise ours in a laugh.

41

S EVERAL MORE DAYS GO by in a blur, and suddenly I've been away from home for over a week. Somehow, I still don't think I'm ready to leave. I miss my family terribly, but I've come to love Kermera in the little time I've been here. Everything I read has turned out to be true. A utopia with incredible plant life, and the people are some of the kindest, most joyous I've ever met.

I'm sad to go.

Pearce insists that he ride home with me. I ask Jaali if he is going to come as well, but he insists on staying behind to keep things running smoothly in case Pearce decides to stay past his curfew again. He points at his own eyes with two fingers and then motions at Pearce as if to say, "I'm watching you." Fair enough.

The ride takes us a bit longer than it did on the way here, which is most definitely on purpose. I don't want Pearce to leave yet. We haven't addressed what a future between us would look like. Up until seeing

Kermera, I wasn't sure if there *was* a future. But he made it clear that he intends to continue what's growing, even if that means bouts of separation.

It's a small price to pay to spend more time with him.

The castle appears on the horizon too fast. We arrive at the stables, and I'm reminded of our return from Baeton. So much has changed since then, both with Pearce and with me.

I'm sure now that I want to fight for Alunia in whatever is to come. Pearce and I talked more about Baeton and his methods moving forward, and he seems receptive. I won't stand between him and justice. But, I want him to understand the weight of what instigating a war would mean, especially after being dormant for so long.

While tying up the horses, my shoulders fall at the thought of him going away again. Every time things get better between us, it feels like something gets in the way. Usually, it's us, but that's beside the point. He comes behind me and turns me by my hips to face him.

"What's going on in that pretty mind of yours?"

"I don't want you to go. I'm not ready. I finally like you, and we have to separate."

He pulls away a bit to look down at my face. "You like me, huh?"

I swat at his chest. "Don't let it go to your head."

"Too late," he says and places a kiss on my forehead. "It won't be for too long. You can't keep me away, you know."

"Can you at least stay for the night? It's dark now, you can leave at first light." My hands slowly trail up his chest, eyes pleading.

He pretends to consider it for a moment. "I could be convinced," earning an eye-roll from me.

Willow is walking to the kitchen when we enter the hallway, and she spots us. Her eyes land on his hand at my hip, and they go wide.

"Would you look who it is?" she says with a knowing smirk.

I blush and smile at her. She's always looked out for me, and she'll be relieved to know we're no longer ripping into each other.

At least, not in the way we used to be.

I let him go to my room while I stop by all the people I need to see upon returning. My sister is the first, and she welcomes me with a hug before asking about Jaali. Despite her irritation with him, I know she's going to miss having him around so much.

My parents welcome me home without *too* much questioning, saying they'll save it for when I'm rested. They ask what I thought about his city, and I make sure to avoid any distinctive characteristics. It's not my place to tell my parents about Kermera. Pearce will let me know when he's willing to share their existence with the rest of Alunia.

Dessielle, on the other hand, knows something is up right away. She says I look different, happier. I hint at the idea that we're getting along much better now, and she smacks my arm much harder than necessary before demanding I tell her everything that happened. When I inform her that Pearce is waiting for me in my room, her mouth falls open before she places her hand over it.

"You owe me alone time. Lunch tomorrow?"

I nod and smile at her. "I'll see you then," I say before I rush out of the room and down the hall.

Pearce has the fireplace going when I step inside, and a steaming bath running in the other room.

"My goodness, so you *do* know how to be a gentleman," I jest while removing my boots to bathe.

His eyes darken as he watches my hands. "Be careful little ember before I toss you in the bath before it cools."

Pearce strides over to me as I finish undressing. "You'll have to do better than a little hot water. Heat doesn't scare me."

His tongue flicks out to lick his lips. "I can't imagine it would, little ember. You were cast from flames." His hand trails down my now exposed back before he starts to undress, assumingly to join me in the bath, without averting his eyes from mine.

I saunter to the bathing room attached to my bedroom, swaying my hips softly to entertain my audience of one. He follows shortly after, fully nude, and places his hand in the tub. He pulls it away quickly, splashing water onto me and the floor. "Shit," he hisses under his breath. "I'm sorry, it's still too hot."

"Don't be so dramatic, I'm sure it's fine," I say before stepping into the tub. It's a bit warm but feels nice on my aching limbs. Pearce stares at me, dumbfounded, with a crease between his eyebrows.

"That feels alright to you?"

I look down at my body in the water and shrug my shoulders, assuring him I'm fine.

He shakes his head with wide eyes before bringing up a small stool and attempting to sit his large frame on the thing. He manages, but barely. "Suit yourself," he mumbles. He sits there for a few minutes while I run various liquids through my strands and rinse them out into the water. Once I'm finished, he finally joins me in the—again, too small—tub to do the same for himself.

I repeatedly tell him I'm capable of washing my own arms and torso, but he refuses and insists he do it instead.

I would sit in this tub until I became a raisin if it meant he would pour water down my skin. My eyes close without me realizing and I let my back rest on his chest. Soft sounds of water sloshing almost lull me to sleep, and I'm nudged slightly when he tells me it's time to get dressed.

Being the eldest sibling, I've dealt with a lot. The family burdens tend to fall on my ears. Not all of them are bad, but it's not uncommon for me to know everything about everyone, whether I want to or not. My parents already held the crown for a time before I was born, and I was their first child. They didn't know how to assimilate me into royal life while still letting me be a child.

My sister came along and made sure I remained humble. I looked after her a lot. I never minded, despite the mental exhaustion at times. I had to step up at an early age to become a third parent since ours were busy making sure the kingdom was safe and cared for.

I've had to look out for a lot of people in my life. I feel protective over them. The idea that someone else is doing that for me brings tears to my eyes before I can shut them down.

Pearce guides me toward the bed while he gets out clothing for me to wear. As I tie the small bow on my night dress, I look over at him. "I'm proud of you, you know."

His movement stops and he lifts his head toward me slowly. "Why is that, princess?" And he goes back to messing with the pillows on my bed.

"You're a good protector. I could see it in their eyes, your people love you. Your council respects you. You deserve your position, Pearce."

He comes to meet me and cups my face with his calloused hand, the skin scraping against my cheek and awakening my desire for him once more. He doesn't even need to try. It's ridiculous.

"Thank you." He smooths his hands over my hair. "I'll feel better once we have a more solid path to move forward. There are still a lot of unknowns."

"I know." I latch my arms around his waist and breathe him in. "What are we going to do about the slaves in the castle? And the creatures from Alunia?"

He wraps his arms around me too, squeezing softly. "I'm not sure yet, but we'll get them out. We'll make sure they free all Alunians they have in their possession."

I nod into his chest, settled by his words. It may not happen as quickly as I wish, but permanent change doesn't happen overnight. Sustainable things take time and effort without immediate reward.

Something I'm still learning to accept.

We pull back the covers of my lush, cozy bed, and I'm happy to be home again. I have an incredible bed. He's lucky to be in it. I turn over to remind him, but his eyes are already closed, and his chest rises and falls slowly. I wouldn't dare wake him after everything he's dealt with over these last few weeks, so I let him sleep instead of antagonizing him.

The constant buzzing of insects from outside creates the perfect soundscape to fall asleep to. I understand why it took him so quickly. I lean my head on my hand and sit up a bit to look at him. He'll be leaving again tomorrow and, while I know he needs to, I can't ignore the heaviness in my heart.

If I'd been told a few months ago that my heart would be aching because of Pearce leaving, I would have laughed. But now, with it coming to fruition, my body feels cold at the thought of his absence.

He's made me surer of who I am. He taught me not to back down from a fight and gave me the ability to defend myself. Not only that, but he lit the fire under me to make a choice. He trusted me enough to show me Kermera, which is an action I will *never* take lightly.

Kermera is his to defend. When he's ready to make their presence known, he will. I trust that he'll assimilate his citizens into the rest of Alunia with grace. And with me by his side, I have no doubt it will go smoothly.

Does he want that? Me by his side?

I know he feels for me, but I have no idea what that *means*. I won't borrow tomorrow's problems for today. My stomach may be queasy thinking about the future, but I cannot change what I cannot control.

I can control my actions, and that is it. That has to be enough. My finger traces over the harsh lines on his face, trying to ease the tension he holds onto even in sleep.

After trying to fight the urge to close my eyes to enjoy the moment of quiet, I finally succumb while wrapped in his arms, the cicadas singing me to sleep.

42

"**P**EARCE! WAKE UP!" a voice yells from the hall. The sun is barely in the sky, the faintest warm glow coming from behind the curtains.

Loud banging sounds at the door. Pearce and I jolt up in the bed, hair a mess and sleep in our eyes. He holds up a hand for me to stay back. But if he's in danger, so am I.

I step quietly behind him as his shadow. He opens the door to Jaali's terrified expression, hair sticking to his forehead from sweat. It looks like he's been crying. A pit forms in my stomach, scared for my friend.

"Jaali? What are you doing here?"

"Kermera is under siege."

My heart sinks, and my limbs freeze in place.

That's impossible.

Every muscle in Pearce's jaw flexes and his hands turn to fists. "Tell me everything," he growls and storms back into the room, leaving the door open for Jaali to follow. He hurriedly dresses in the clothing he arrived in and pulls on his boots. Jaali doesn't sit, he paces.

"I rode here as fast as I could. The council is working on evacuations as we speak and getting all the citizens to safety."

"Do we have any idea who's attacking?" He moves around the room, throwing his things into a bag. I follow his lead, pulling on trousers and a vest.

"We're not sure yet. At first, it sounded like an earthquake. But the terrainers couldn't sense any internal vibrations; all the rumbling and shaking came from above," he explains. "The ceiling started to crumble, crushing homes."

"Are the people okay?" Pearce clips.

Jaali looks down at the ground, and then at Pearce from under his earth-dusted lashes. He's covered in dust and rubble, even after riding.

"We had a few injuries when I left. But we're working on getting everyone out of the area."

Pearce's balled fist punches into the stone wall behind him. "I should've been there. I should be leading the evacuations and finding the cause myself." His voice booms through the now cold room. "I need to go. Now."

He looks at me, his eyes are filled with something like disappointment. That's when I realize—he's here because of me. He wouldn't be away from Kermera if I hadn't asked him to stay with me tonight. Breathing suddenly becomes difficult, my chest unable to expand fully. The walls around me shift closer.

Grabbing his bag, he heads for the door, Jaali following behind him. With one final look at me, he says, "I'm sorry." The door slams behind him so ferociously, I'm surprised it doesn't splinter.

This is my fault. His people are under attack, and I've kept him away from them. I try and take a few deep breaths, unsuccessfully. My vision starts to blur, and I place a hand on a chair back to regain my balance. He needs to be with them, not with me.

I pace around my room, biting on my nails anxiously. Once I gather my thoughts, I pull my hair away from my face in a pitiful ponytail and put on my boots.

I need to see them. I wanted to be a soldier, and now is the time to show up. There may not be a fight to be had, but I can provide an additional hand around the keep if they'll have me.

One thing after another. I'm starting to wonder if we are truly meant to be in each other's lives. I brush off my shoulders to rid myself of any tedious thoughts spilling from my brain; they won't help me now. Stepping into the hall with a bag in tow, I walk to my mother and father's room. Light shines from under the door, so I push the door open slowly and peek inside.

The two of them are sitting in their matching chairs on the balcony through the open doors. Upon seeing me, they stand with concerned faces.

"Are you alright Rae?" My mother asks. My father moves behind her, his hand on the small of her back.

"I need to leave," I tell them. No use in hiding it this time.

They look at each other, and then back at me. "Stay safe, dear." And then my father rubs his thumb on my cheek.

I look at them, confused. "You aren't going to ask why—or how long?"

My father inclines his head softly. "We know Jaali rode in. We were alerted of his arrival and assumed he was coming back for something involving Pearce. When we saw them head to the stables, we knew it wouldn't be long before we saw you, too."

I chuckle softly and hug them both tightly. "I'll be back as soon as I can," I promise. "They need my help."

They nod curtly and then I move back into the hall. I'm halfway to the stairs when a voice calls out to me.

"You're really following after him?" Reynard's hands are in his pockets, his jaw tight.

I nod. "I have to."

"No, you don't. You can stay here with me and go back to your normal life. Isn't that enough for you?"

My teeth grind in my skull. "I will not apologize for following my heart."

His jaw ticks in anger. "And your heart picks him?"

"Gods, will you leave this alone? I am tired of this argument." I start to turn, buzzing with worry and ready to be back with Pearce.

"And I'm tired of you pretending there's nothing between us!"

I halt all movement, forgetting how to breathe.

Hesitantly, I face him. "There *isn't* anything between us, Reynard."

He stalks toward me. "But there could be. Think about it. I'm a guard now, you're the princess, we go together so well. It would be as easy as breathing for us, Rae." He reaches for my hand, but I tear it away.

"You don't mean that. You're not thinking clearly."

"I'm thinking clearer than I ever have. He's a liar. You deserve better than him. You deserve *me*!"

He tries to close the gap between us, but I shift backward.

"You're right. You don't know me anymore."

Before he can interject again, I turn the corner in a flash. I allow myself a few deep breaths to mourn what our friendship has become and rush to the stables.

Winnie is excited to see me, and I waste no time saddling her and attaching my things. With one last look at the castle, I speed through the fields and under the stone arch I've become so familiar with.

Winnie is pushed to her limits for the entirety of the trip. I don't think I take a full breath until I see the stones I recognize as the cave entrance. I tie Winnie up outside despite not wanting to leave her. The chaos below is no place for her, and I don't know its severity. I pass through the veil without problem, my admittance still granted.

Immediately after stepping through, I have to weave my way through crushed rock and debris from the tunnel ceiling. Step after step drags on until the blue haze from below appears dimly in the distance. It's not as vibrant, and my heart sinks. I arrive at the rock bridge overlooking the city and come to a halt.

It's unrecognizable.

The bridge has large cracks spanning over its entirety, and the homes and buildings that reached the cave sky have crumbled down into the streets. Massive fractures weave through the tiered structures. Dust clouds fill the entire cavern, and I block my face with my arm to avoid it getting into my eyes. They already burn from the invasion on my lashes.

Avoiding the cracks in the path, I move toward the direction of the keep. A few columns have large rifts running down them while others have snapped in the center. The fountain that Pearce and I sat at when we first arrived here is separated in large pieces, barely standing. The water has spilled out onto the ground around it, reflecting the few surviving twinkling stones.

Echoes of despair and terror fill the cavern. Layers of fear and smoke sit heavy on everything inside.

There isn't a single space untouched by chaos. I weave through seas of people, making mental notes of every face I can; all the people whose lives have been changed forever.

While searching the streets, I stumble into a girl screaming for her mother. I try and console her, but she won't look at me.

"Where is she? I can help you get to her!"

The girl wails. "I can't get her out, please!" She yanks me by the forearm in the direction of a crumbling building. Her small knees crack against the hard floor as she howls, taking in the remains of her family home.

She begins to scramble, burrowing through pieces of rock desperately. I pick a spot nearby and begin lifting what I can manage. Nails broken and bloody, I scavenge through the rubble. I go to wipe the mixture of sweat and dust from my forehead, when I see it.

I clench my eyes tightly, willing myself not to break. To remain strong for this young girl.

She sees it then, too.

A hand, reaching up toward the sky, bent at an unnatural angle.

Her piercing cry rattles my bones. I can do nothing but hold her, and weep with her. With heated strength, I lift off the last remaining slabs of destruction. The girl falls before her mother, still and bruised.

Tears flow freely down my face, and I refuse to wipe them. To not let these events affect me the way they should.

"Where's the rest of your family?"

Eyes filled with tears, she tries to look at me. Her response shatters my heart like brittle stone. "She's all I have."

Faintly, I hear a familiar, commanding voice. With the girl in tow, I search vehemently for its source and find a huddle of people, their forms heaving in upset and rage. As I approach, I look around at the grey faces. Rock and dirt are caked into their hair. Many of them have trails of tears down their cheeks, a break in their despair-coated complexion.

I'm able to make out their faces as I get closer. Easton and Brell inspect a younger group of debris-covered citizens while Sylvan assembles bodies in uniforms, shouting orders in every direction.

After placing every other council member, my head swivels through the sea of victims, looking for Jaali and Pearce.

Jaali's head pops up to look for something in the crowd when he notices me. Taken aback, he nudges the large body next to him. Pearce turns around, following his stare.

His eyes fall on me with a flash of relief, followed by concern, as he stalks toward me. "You shouldn't be here. It's not safe."

"I know," I say as I step closer to him. "But if you're in danger, so am I," I expel my earlier thought. "I'm here to help. Just tell me what to do."

He releases a heavy breath. He hesitates for so long that I think he might send me away. Instead, he pulls me in tightly to his chest and wraps his arms around me, plastering me to him. "Thank you," he says into my hair.

We pull our heads apart, arms around each other while we look into a sea of anger and hopelessness. As we stand there, a deep rumbling sound comes from above. We attempt to brace ourselves on one another, grappling aimlessly for support. Pearce towers over me, attempting to cover my body with his.

I look up at his pained amber eyes and offer all I have. "I'm sorry." Our lips connect in a harsh kiss just as large chunks of the ceiling begin falling from the sky, exposing the remnants of Kermera to the world.

Acknowledgements

I wrote the backstory of Calliope and Aidmar back in 2022. I was sitting at the bar in my parents' kitchen with my laptop open, writing down character names and what they all looked like. That OneNote sat on my laptop for an entire year before I got the courage to show it to Mekenzie.

"I need to know what happens next!" And here I am, in 2024, with a finished novel.

My beta readers, you all are troopers. You saw this manuscript when it was unfinished and survived. Veronica, Lu, Jaytee, Michelle, Som, Makayla, thank you.

Marissa, this book wasn't ready until you touched it. Your mind was exactly what Brute needed.

Thank you for letting me live my dream. I'll see you in Winter.

Audrey was born and raised in Florida. A theater kid in every sense of the word, she was born to be dramatic.

She moved away from home after getting married and struggled to put down roots in her new city. Upon finding her bookish community, she blossomed.

When she's not reading until 3 am, she's a gym rat and a cozy gamer. She counts down the days until her local Renaissance fair, as if she needs a reason to dress up like a fairy.